Praise for
Expendable

"An impressive debut novel . . .
Gardner's fully realized characters and situations,
convincing science and entertaining style
will have readers anticipating his next effort."
Publishers Weekly

"This is a good read,
and a very good first novel."
Locus

"An auspicious debut:
the best first novel I've read this decade."
Robert J. Sawyer, Nebula award-winning author of *Starplex*

Praise for
Commitment Hour

"*Commitment Hour* has something for everyone
. . . a great second showing for a
promising Canadian author."
SF Site Featured Review

"A quirky SF riddle and diverting small town
murder mystery, with some truly unusual
characters."
Locus

Other Avon Books by
James Alan Gardner

EXPENDABLE
COMMITMENT HOUR

VIGILANT

JAMES ALAN GARDNER

AVON · EOS

AVON BOOKS, INC.
1350 Avenue of the Americas
New York, New York 10019

Copyright © 1999 by James Alan Gardner
Visit our website at www.AvonBooks.com/Eos
Library of Congress Catalog Card Number: 98-93287
ISBN: 0-380-80208-2

First Avon Eos Printing: March 1999

AVON EOS TRADEMARK REG. U.S. PAT. OFF. AND IN OTHER COUNTRIES, MARCA REGISTRADA, HECHO EN U.S.A.

Printed in the U.S.A.

WCD   10 9 8 7 6 5 4 3 2 1

To Peter Fraser,
who gave me a job, a computer,
time to do what I wanted,
and a lot of paper sneaked out the back door.

ACKNOWLEDGMENTS

I acknowledge the people who helped me write/revise/polish this tome: Linda Carson, Richard Curtis, and Jennifer Brehl. Where would I be without them?

I acknowledge that John Brunner wrote *The Stone That Never Came Down* some twenty-five years ago and that I lifted a crucial aspect of the Vigil from it. (Wouldn't it be spiffy if all the people who borrowed from Brunner actually admitted it? And wouldn't it be spiffy if you, dear reader, went out and bought Brunner's books to see what I'm talking about?)

Finally, I acknowledge that there was originally going to be a lot about politics in this book . . . but every time I tried to sneak some in, it stuck out like a sore thumb. Our friend Faye is so new at her job, no one would let her close to real political action. Besides, she joined the Vigil for personal reasons, not through any great urge to get involved in the democratic process. Oh well . . . maybe next book, the characters will get out of the way and let me pontificate.

THE STRUCTURE OF THE TECHNOCRACY

In A.D. 2454, the Technocracy consists of the following:

(a) Sixty-three planets with full membership (called the Core or mainstream worlds);

(b) Ninety-two planets with "affiliate" status (usually called the Fringe Worlds);

(c) Several hundred colony worlds founded by people who espouse some degree of loyalty to the Technocracy. Colonies range from small scientific outposts of a half-dozen researchers, to settlements of a few hundred thousand inhabitants.

The mainstream worlds share a single integrated administration. Fringe Worlds, on the other hand, all have independent governments, subject to various obligations as Technocracy affiliates (such as providing port facilities for the navy).

There is only one law that applies to all worlds: the single directive of the League of Peoples, unflinchingly enforced by races so far advanced beyond human intelligence that the directive might as well be a fundamental law of the universe: NO DANGEROUS NON-SENTIENT CREATURE WILL EVER BE ALLOWED TO MOVE FROM ITS HOME STAR SYSTEM TO ANOTHER SYSTEM.

''Dangerous non-sentient'' means any creature ready to kill a sentient creature, or to let sentients die through willful negligence. The law makes interstellar war an impossibility; the only conceivable wars are civil ones, restricted to a single planet. Starships cannot carry lethal weapons—no laser-cannons on the hull, no guns for personnel—because those are automatic statements of non-sentient disposition. (Weapons for self-defense? Whom would you be defending against? The only beings allowed into interstellar space are sentients. By definition, they aren't going to try to kill you.)

Intention counts: even if you are completely unarmed, if you travel through space with the objective of killing someone when you reach your destination, you are inherently a dangerous non-sentient creature. Therefore, you don't *reach* your destination—you simply die en route. No one knows how the League can tell that you have murder in your heart—whether they read minds or see the future or have simply achieved omniscience. (The League's senior races have had a billion-year evolutionary headstart on *Homo sapiens*; to describe them as godlike is belittling.)

The inescapable truth is that no human has ever beaten the League; not in the twenty-fifth century, nor in all the years of recorded history. Dangerous non-sentient creatures—murderers—have to consider themselves grounded the moment they cease to respect sentient life . . . the moment they become non-sentient.

Sometimes people wonder if non-sentient beings can ever become sentient again. By rehabilitation. By repentance. By redemption. And if a killer has a true change of heart, will the League accept it? Or are you simply condemned forever by the person you once were?

Always an interesting question. . . .

1

THE SLACK DEATH

I want to tell you everything, everything all at once.

I don't want to be plod-patient, setting it down in sequence: first the plague, then the cave-in, then the years of Other Business, when everything seemed like a burden to get out of the way before real life could start. Everyone knows this *is* real life, it's all real life, sixty seconds of real life every minute, no one gets less.

But you can *take* less. All the time you're swimming in the ocean of real life, it's so precious easy to keep your eyes closed and just tread water. Even so, if you're lucky, you might be caught in a current, a current that's carrying you toward something. . . .

No, too simplistic. We're *all* caught in currents, dozens of the buggers dragging us in different directions sixty seconds every minute, and it's never as obvious as people want you to believe. You live through a day, and at the end you grumble, "I didn't *do* anything" . . . but second by second you *did* do things, you occupied every second, just as you occupy every second of every day.

Here's the thing, the crucial thing: your life is full. And

3

if you don't realize that . . . then you're just like the rest of us, but that's no excuse.

I want to tell you everything, everything at once. I want to explode and leave you splattered bloody with all the things I have to say—kaboom, and you're covered with me, coated, dripping, deafened by the blast. A flash of instant knowledge: knowledge, not information. Burning hot. Blinding bright. Blasting down the ingrained walls of carrion-comfort cynicism.

How can I do that? How? The peacock can show its whole tail at once; but I can only tell you a story.

The story starts with death. If you weren't there, on the fair green planet Demoth in the year 2427, you can't imagine what the plague was like, and I can't convey the enormity of it. No one stayed sane—no one. All of us who lived through those days came out the other side mumbling under our breaths, quivering with twitches, tics, and phobias. Real bitch-slapping nightmares of bodies in the streets.

The bodies weren't human. That was the ugliest part of Pteromic Paralysis, the slack death—us *Homo saps* were immune. Death counts rose by the day, and we were lily-pure untouched.

It only killed our neighbors.

Our neighbors were Ooloms, a genetically engineered branch of the Divian race: basically humanoid, but with scaly skins that changed color like wide-spectrum chameleons . . . from red to green to blue, and everything in between. Ooloms also came equipped with glider membranes on the general model of flying squirrels—triangular sails attached at wrists and armpits, then running down their bodies and tapering to a point at their ankles. Their bones were hollow, their tissues light, their internal organs spongy with air vacuoles rather than solidly dense. Given Demoth's forgiving gravity (.78 Earth G), Ooloms had no trouble flapping-gliding-soaring through city or countryside.

I was a countryside girl myself back then: fifteen years old, living in a fiddly-dick mining town called Sallysweet River, population 1600 . . . one of only four human settlements in the vast interior of Great St. Caspian Island. Around us, tundra and trees, stone and forest, stretched proud unbroken—wilderness all the way from my doorstep across a hundred kilometers to the cold ocean coast.

Not that it made me feel small. I was as full of myself as any girl I knew: me, the beautiful, blond, smart, occasionally even sexy Faye Smallwood.

So much for the "before" picture—before the plague. After? I'll get to that.

It was late summer in Sallysweet River when we first heard tell of the disease. My father, Dr. Henry Smallwood, was the town M.D., always reading the medical newsfeeds to me and giving his on-the-spot opinion. A session with Dads might go like this: "Well then, Faye-girl, here's some offworld laze-about who's come to Demoth for a study of our poisonous animals—lizards and eels and what-all. Can you imagine? He wants to protect us all from snakebite or some fool thing . . . as if there's a single creature on the planet that *wants* to bite us. Complete waste of time!"

(Which was and wasn't true. Neither Ooloms nor humans were native to Demoth—*Homo saps* had only been around twenty-five years, and Ooloms about nine hundred—so to the local animal population, we smelled disgustingly alien. Nothing in the woods would ever try to nibble us for food . . . but they'd be fast enough to give us the chomp if we stepped on their tails or threatened their young. I'd never say that to Dads, though; before the plague sent us all stress-crazy, I was his own little girl, and so swoony fond, I never questioned him. When I felt like a fight, I picked one with my mother.)

So. One trickly hot evening, Dads looked up from the newsfeed, and said, "Listen to this, my Faye—they're reporting a rash of complaints from Ooloms all over the world. Teeny numbnesses: a single finger going limp, or an eyelid, or one side of the tongue. *Investigators are expressing concern.*'' Dads snorted. ''Sure to be psychosomatic,'' he told me. ''A grand lot of Ooloms have worked themselves into a tizzy about some idle nothing, and now they're having demure little hysterical breakdowns.''

I nodded, trusting that Dads knew what he was talking about.

But.

It got worse. More victims. In every last town on the planet. Symptoms slowly spreading. A patient who couldn't move her thumb today might lose all feeling in her little toe tomorrow: one muscle after another shutting down, turning to strengthless putty. It usually started at the extremities and worked gradually in, but there was one man who didn't show a single symptom till all the muscles of his heart, slump, went slack. The night they reported his case on the news, the exodus began.

Ooloms and all other Divian subspecies have an instinct to isolate themselves when they're sick. ''Oooo,'' as my father put it angrily, ''we're feeling plumb poorly, better separate ourselves from the herd so we don't infect others. The cack-headed idjits.''

Dads hated that communal instinct. Because of it, infected Ooloms didn't stay in cities or towns where they'd be close to medical facilities; they headed for the woods, the wilderness, to be on their own. Their species had no trouble living rough out there—they'd been specifically engineered to thrive on Demoth's native greenery. Leaves and bark pulled from trees, seedpods hanging by the hundreds all year round . . . the Ooloms could eat, they could glide, they could wait, as the paralysis crept stealthily through their bodies.

They stayed out there, isolated and degenerating from disease, as summer surrendered to wistful fall. Then they began drifting back, when their muscles had frozen to the point that even such grand hunter-gatherers could no longer fend for themselves.

In my dreams I still see them floating in the night: paralyzed bodies black against the stars, gliding over Sallysweet River like kites cut free of their strings. They waited till they were inches near helpless . . . barely able to control their direction of flight. The ones we found often had branches lashed to their arms or legs with cordvine, to give themselves a more rigid flying structure after major muscles failed. Most tied their mouths closed too; otherwise, their jaws fell open, and they swallowed insects during flight.

So the Ooloms surrendered in the end . . . the ones who didn't leave it too late. They gave themselves up to humans and let us fight the disease on their behalf. In the shieldlands of Great St. Caspian, that meant the Ooloms headed for Sallysweet River.

When the last shift at Rustico Nickel left work at dawn, the miners would go around town with wooden carts, gathering the bodies that had landed overnight—on roofs, across the Bullet tracks, spread-eagled over the hoods of ore-carriers . . . wherever the Ooloms' haphazard flight took them. From there, the body carts trundled along dirt tracks and wood-slat sidewalks till they reached our backyard—a crude field hospital slung together by my father under yellowed-canvas tenting. The Big Top we called it. Or the Circus.

Every human with time to spare helped out under the Big Top: feeding Ooloms who couldn't feed themselves, or fiddling with catheters, enemas and what-all, for those who'd lost the muscles to keep themselves clean. Sometimes it seemed the whole town was there. My best friend Lynn, Lynn Jones, liked to say, "Everyone's run off to join the Circus." The schools closed for the duration of the epidemic, so all my friends lent a hand—some working long hours, others coming in skittish for twenty minutes, then disappearing when the stink and suffering became too much to bear.

I could stand the stench; it was the death that squeezed in on me. Our patients' hearts turning to motionless meat. Diaphragms going slack. Digestive systems no longer pushing food through the intestines, and people rotting from the inside out. Eight weeks after Dads read me that first medical notice, Ooloms started to die in the Circus ... and they died and they died and they died.

In those days, I slept with my habitat dome set one-way transparent so I could see outside. Roof and walls were wholly invisible, and I'd moved my room far apart from other bubble-domes in our compound, so their lights scarcely reached me. Bed at night was like lying in open air, vulnerable to storms and stars.

My mother (who grew up mainstream and oh-so-proper on New Earth) thought only sluts slept clear. She couldn't stop making remarks about her "exhibitionist" daughter; she was fair frantic-sure I pranced naked around my room, pretending people could peer in as easily as I could peer out.

That they could see me. That I *wanted* them to see.

Just my mother's feverish imagination. The death-filled weeks of the plague had sent her spiraling into shrill neurosis, where she believed everything I did had some perverse sexual subtext. Truth was, I kept my dome one-way clear so I could tell if an Oolom crash-landed nearby. I hated the thought of a paralyzed body caught in the honey bushes outside my habitat. Not that I was stirred by concern for some poor person suffering ... I just got the cold icks, worrying there might be a limp, corpselike *thing* lying unseen on the other side of my wall.

One morning, it happened: a gray drizzly dawn, with the rain beading and runneling down the dome, making a soft patter that keeps you in a fuzz between waking and sleep. Lovely. Dreamy. Then something slapped against the clear roof of my room.

The sound barely penetrated my doze. Gradually I became aware the timbre of the rain had changed, now spittering off wet-washed skin rather than the dome's invisible structure field. I opened my eyes . . .

. . . and found myself staring up at an Oolom woman, plastered against the dome like a drenched sheet on glass. Her face was spread wide as if she were screaming.

I almost screamed myself. Not fear, just the jolt of being startled—the sudden sight of her, splashed five meters above me. Heaven knows, I'd seen enough Oolooms in the same condition: the drooping jaw, the eyes wide-open because the eyelid muscles could no longer blink. (All Divian species blink from the bottom lid up; the slackness of paralysis made Oolom eyes sag open under gravity's pull.)

For several seconds, I didn't move. Instinct—freeze, someone's watching. But the woman overhead couldn't see me through the dome; from the outside, the field was opaque navy blue, a repressed, severe shade my mother decreed mandatory to prevent the neighbors thinking I was odd.

Odd = sexual. My mother's ongoing obsession.

My own sanity had its share of wobbles too, especially with a half-dead Oolom sprawled gaping above me. Ripe with the squirming creeps, I slid from my bed, threw on some clothes, and hurried out into the rain.

From the ground, I couldn't see the Oolom on my roof—not with drizzle smearying my eyes and the woman's chameleon scales already changed color to match the dome's navy blue. (The chameleon effect was glandular, not muscle-driven; it worked no matter how paralyzed an Oolom might be.)

I didn't waste time peering up into the rain; the woman couldn't have gone anywhere, could she? Lifting my arm, I whispered to the control implant tucked skin-under my left wrist. "House-soul, attend. Faye's room, dome field: access stairs, please."

The dome's navy hemisphere quivered a moment, like silk rippling in the wind. Then it restabilized into the same shape, but with a flight of steep steps leading over in an arc, up one side and down the other. I climbed the steps two at a time till I reached the top and skittered over the slippery-smooth surface to where the woman lay.

She lifted her head . . . which is to say she tilted it half-askew, as if she only had working muscles on one side of her neck. "Good morning," she whispered, framing the words as best she could with only a thread's control over her jaw. After weeks of tending patients in similar condition, I could understand her well enough. "A soft day," she said, rain trickling unhindered over her eyeballs.

"Very soft," I agreed. My hair was already sodden and streaming. In the pouring damp, I envied Oolom skins: tough and waterproof as well-oiled leather. On the other hand, human anatomy had its strong points too, especially in the design of ears. Oolooms hear with fluid-filled globe-sacs, fist-sized spherical eardrums mounted high on either side of the head. Usually, they're protected by retractable sheath tissue, like eyelids that close around the ear-balls. Ear-lids you could call them—a thin inner one for day-to-day, plus a thick outer one to provide extra muffling against vicious-loud noises. Your average Oolom hardly ever opens both ear-lids, except when listening for whispers as faint as an aphid's sigh . . . or when the muscles controlling the lids go limp with paralysis.

This woman's ear-lids lay in useless crumples on her scalp, like sloughed-off snakeskins. It left her hearing-globes exposed and vulnerable: inflated balloons of raw eardrum, battered hard by rain.

Straightaway, I cupped my hands above her to shield her ears from the drops. Though her face scarcely had a working muscle left, I could see a clinch of tension ease out of her features, and she let her head relax back against the dome. The whish of soft drizzle might still sound like hammers to her—naked Oolom ears are so sensitive, they can catch a human heartbeat at five paces—but at least I'd ended any direct pain from the splash.

"*Jai*," the woman whispered: "Thank you" in Oolom. For a moment she lay worn-out quiet, just breathing softly. Then she added, "*Fé leejemm.*"

I bowed in response. The words were Oolom for "You hear the thunder," a phrase of approval doled out to people who do what decency requires. The related phrase, *Fé leejedd* (I hear the thunder) got used in the sense of "I do the things that are obviously right" . . . or in the parlance of the League of Peoples, "I am a sentient being."

"My name is Zillif," the woman said in her whisper. "And you?"

"Faye," I replied, as softly as I could to avoid hurting her ears. "Faye Smallwood."

"From the family of Dr. Henry Smallwood?"

"His daughter."

Another knot of tension loosened on the woman's half-slack face. "I deliver myself to you," she whispered. "I declare myself unfit to make my own decisions. *Fé leejedd po.*"

Fé leejedd po. I cannot hear the thunder. I can't trust myself to do what's right.

Every patient in my dad's field hospital mumbled those words from time to time. They seemed relieved when they could give up responsibility for their lives.

As delicately as my wet fingers could, I arranged Zillif's ear-lids to cover her exposed globe-sacs. Sooner or later the limp skin-sheaths would slide off again; there was nothing holding them in place. But with a spit-coat of luck, they'd stay put the two minutes I'd need to carry her down to the Circus. There, Dads could suture-clip the sheaths into suitable positions: inner one closed for comfort, outer one open so we nursing folks didn't have to shout ourselves hoarse to be heard. Every last Oolom under the Big Top had been rigged the same way.

When Zillif's ear-globes were safe, I slipped my arms

under her body and lifted. She weighed no more than a child, though she measured a full hand taller than I. Light Oolom body, low Demoth gravity. I, of course, was lifting with the glossy-hard strength of a *Homo sap* designed for full Earth G: "A strapping girl," as Lynn liked to tease me. "Prime Amazonian beef." Can I help it if I grew up tall and broad-shouldered? Not to mention, a doctor's daughter is never allowed to skip (a) her monthly muscle-preservative injections, or (b) her daily twenty minutes of Home-G exercise in the simulator.

Still, just being strong enough to carry Zillif didn't make the job simple. The woman flopped. She fluttered. She draped badly, with her glider membranes flapping against my legs like long, trip-hazard petticoats. And even though her four limbs were dysfunctional, they weren't one hundred percent paralyzed. Zillif still had full power in the Oolom equivalent of the triceps muscle for straightening her right arm. She also had the instinctive Oolom urge to stay flat-on-the-bubble balanced, no yaw, no pitch, no roll. Whenever I tipped the skimpiest bit off level, she flailed out her one mobile arm and whacked me in the jaw with her elbow.

I'd taken similar clonks while tending other paralysis victims—automatic reflexes are all very fine with a full set of muscles, but they can be the devil's own nuisance when a single surviving muscle keeps firing with nothing to counterbalance it. As I began to trudge gingerly down the steps of the dome (smack in the jaw, crack in the jaw), I found myself wishing Zillif's last muscles were frozen too.

Elbow whacks notwithstanding, we made it safe to solid ground. Once down, I took a moment to rearrange my burden into a more comfortable carrying position. The solid part of Zillif's body was just a thin cylinder, no bigger round than one of my thighs; but the parachute folds of her glider membranes were as bulky as a load of laundry. A load of *wet* laundry, pressed soggily against me. My jacket made soft squishy-gush sounds when I shifted Zillif's weight in my arms. Wrung-out rainwater spilled down cold on the flouncy "ladylike" clothes Mother made me wear.

As I started carrying Zillif along the edge of our fern garden, she murmured, "Your hands are warm, Faye Smallwood. I can feel them against my back."

"That would be the legendary human body heat, ma'am." Ooloms found it a source of rapture and delight that we *Homo saps* were so exothermal. Their own skin temperatures ran a dozen degrees cooler. Any human walking down the street in an Oolom town could expect Oolom children constantly underfoot, them patting their hands against your ass while they giggled, "You're hot!"

"I have heard about human warmth from friends," Zillif said. "But experiencing it personally is . . . disturbing."

"If the heat is too much for you," I told her, "I can wrap my hands in my jacket."

"No, your temperature is quite pleasant," she said. "What bothers me is that I knew about human body heat and was still surprised by it. Such things are not supposed to happen to someone in my profession."

She turned her head, aiming for an angle where she could look me sharp in the eye . . . but with slabs of her neck muscles gone AWOL, she couldn't manage. "Forgive me if I err," Zillif said, "but you are a *young* human, are you not? Under age?"

Ooloms cared about such things. "I get the vote two elections from now," I answered. That was two and a half Demoth years away—almost four Earth years.

"May you vote wisely," she told me. It was a common Oolom phrase, and mainly just a pleasantry, the way humans toss off *Good luck* or *Have a safe trip*. Zillif, though, put more feeling into the words. Sincerity. A moment later she added, "I haven't voted in the elections for many years."

She said it blandly, the way people do when they want

to see how quick you are on the uptake. I got it right away . . . and in my surprise, I precious near slipped on the rain-slick grass.

Here's the thing: Ooloms voted every chance they got. They exulted in it. Compulsive democracy galloped through their veins. Even the paralyzed patients in the Circus were constantly holding plebiscites on what types of music they'd sing, or how they should honor the latest casualties of the disease. A self-respecting Oolom would no more skip voting in an election than a human would skip wearing clothes when the thermometer dropped to brass monkey. Unless . . .

"Have I the honor," I said formally, "of speaking with a member of the Vigil?"

"Even so," Zillif answered.

It seemed witless to curtsy to a woman I was carrying in my arms. I still gave it a try.

Before Zillif could say more, we rounded the edge of my parents' dome—a hemisphere of gutless charcoal gray, which my mother claimed was the only proper color for a physician's personal quarters. Beyond lay the Circus: a muddy meadow under wet canvas, water streaming down into puddles wherever the tenting sagged low.

My father would have preferred to keep the patients indoors, but Ooloms got the claustrophobic chokes at the thought of human buildings. Lynn described Ooloms as "arboreal with a vengeance"—whoever designed their genome must have thought it cute to make Ooloms starvingly hungry for light and fresh air. As a human, I couldn't complain; the main reason we *Homo saps* got invited to Demoth was because Ooloms couldn't stand running their own mine operations.

Before we came, Oolom mines had been pure robot business and increasingly meager for the planet's needs—once you exhaust the easy veins of ore, remote machine digging doesn't bring up enough to pay for itself. In 2402, the Demoth government admitted they needed sentient beings working the drills; so they solicited applications from various groups on other planets (Divians, humans, a few alien races), and eventually turned over their whole mining industry to a party from the planet Come-By-Chance. About 500,000 Come-By-Chance humans voluntarily emigrated to new lives on Demoth . . . including young Dr. Henry Smallwood and his hard-to-please missus.

The Demoth mining industry picked up the moment we arrived. *Homo saps* didn't crapulate into panic attacks at the thought of digging underground . . . just as Ooloms, even sick ones, didn't mind the cold and wet if they could just feel the wind.

You could surely feel the wind that day under the Big Top. You could hear it too, romping and rollicking like a drunk uncle—the frisk of the breeze and the constant sound of rain. The paradiddle patter on the roof fabric. The dripping splash around the edge.

One hundred and twenty cots lay under the canvas. White sheets, white blankets. From the edge of the yard, every bed looked empty—their Oolom occupants had turned white too, chameleon skins bleaching themselves to match the background. Some half-asleep mornings I'd drag myself to the Circus, see white-on-white, and imagine all the Ooloms were gone: died in the dark, taken off for mass burial.

But no—we only lost two or three patients a night. We also collected two or three new patients every dawn, which made for a glum equilibrium: outgoing deaths = incoming casualties. The construction shop at Rustico Nickel kept promising to build extra cots if we needed them, but we hadn't asked for any in almost a week.

We were holding even . . . but it wouldn't last. Everyone juggling bedpans under the Big Top knew it was just a matter of time before deaths exceeded new arrivals. Whereupon the Circus would begin to empty itself. Show over, the crowd goes home.

* * *

The duty nurse saw us coming; he'd filled out a bed assignment by the time we traipsed up. "Row five, cot three," he said, looking at me instead of Zillif. He was a retired miner named Pook—spent every waking minute at the Circus but fiercely avoided personal interaction with the patients. I don't know if Pook hated Ooloms, sickness, or both. Still, he put in more time under the Big Top than anyone, including Dads and me: keeping records up-to-date, tinkering with our makeshift IV stands, pushing himself till exhaustion wept out of him like sweat.

Pook's own form of mental breakdown.

As I lugged Zillif down the rows of cots, I automatically held my breath as long as I could—the Circus stank with a circus stink. Urine and feces from patients who couldn't control themselves. Disinfectant splashed over everything that might carry microbes. The strong metallic smell of Oolom blood, taken as samples so we could plot the advance of the disease. The work sweat of human volunteers, everyone changing bed linen in the gray dawn or rotating the patients to prevent bedsores. The earthiness of mud underfoot, tangled with the lye-soap fragrance of Demoth yellow-grass.

The Ooloms could smell none of it, the bad or the worse. Thanks for that went to a flaw in their engineering. When the prototypes of the breed were created centuries ago, their ability to smell had been lost . . . derailed as an accidental side effect of the mods made to their bodies, some dead-gap in the skimpy neural pathway leading from nose to brain. The DNA stylists who made them were working on a budget and didn't consider the shortcoming important enough to correct; and the Ooloms, of course, didn't know what they were missing.

Lucky them.

Approaching row five, cot three, I wondered who'd occupied this bed the day before. It says something, doesn't it, that I couldn't remember. I'd chatted with so many patients over the previous weeks, got to know them . . .

No, no, no. The point is, I hadn't got to know them. I'd picked up trivial facts about certain people—where they lived before the plague, what work they did—but I was all surface, no salt. Most patients could barely talk; and I could barely listen. When you're fifteen you want to be so slick, you want to swallow the world and stool it out . . . but you haven't half learned to deaden yourself, not the way adults artfully, reflexively deaden themselves every hour of the day. At fifteen, all you can do is close down bolt-tight: go through the motions of caring and concern but shut your eyes and ears, not let the bad bitchies in. That's not deadening yourself, it's internal bleeding. Swinging back and forth from "Oh God, I don't want to be here," to "Oh Christ, I have to help this person!"

The only reason I didn't run was an alpha-queen need to save face in front of my friends. To maintain my la-di-dah social position. They were the children of miners; I was the daughter of a doctor. If I wanted that difference to mean something—and mook-stupid, I did—I had to play nurse to the bitter end.

That drove me to stay hard, hold my breath, and lay Zillif on her assigned cot. In the minutes since I picked her up, she'd already turned copper-rust green, the shade of my jacket; but once in bed, her color bleached away fast. By the time I'd arranged her arms and legs, then hospital-folded her glider membranes into the standard bed-patient pattern, Zillif lay white as a bone.

"Thank you, Faye Smallwood," she said. "You've been very kind."

"Is there anything nice I can bring you?" I asked. "Are you hungry?" Most Ooloms brought to the Circus hadn't eaten for days, no more than a few liver-nuts or clankbeetles. A woebegone percentage were also dehydrated . . . not that Zillif had that problem, considering how soaked we both were with rain.

"I would like food eventually," she answered, "but not right away."

Her voice hinted she wanted something different. I

looked around, but didn't see my father in the hospital yet; usually the light woke him at dawn, but a gray day like this was dark enough he might sleep longer. My bad luck—I was itching to abandon our new patient to him. "Is there someone you'd like me to check on?" I asked. "I can link into hospital registries all over the world. If you want news about friends or family . . ."

"I have a link of my own," Zillif replied. "All I've done for days is check on people I know."

"Oh." Most patients in the Circus had lost too much fingerdeft to push buttons on their wrist-implants . . . which we *Homo saps* claimed was a blessing. Otherwise, our charges might learn that 21 percent of the Ooloms on Demoth had already died, with another 47 percent lying in hospitals and gradually feeling their bodies go stale. No one knew how many other casualties still lurked in the deep forests, moping as their sickness worsened or struck dead before reaching human help. The Outward Fleet had recently dispatched the entire Explorer Academy to our planet, four classes of cadets now searching for survivors in what we called the Thin Interior: any place higher than two hundred meters above sea level, where Demoth's atmosphere became too thready for unprotected humans, but where Ooloms could live quite handily . . . provided they weren't lying in slack-muscled heaps at the base of some giant tree.

And all over the world, in hospitals or the wild, we knew of no disease victim who'd recovered. Not a precious one. There was no hint you were infected till the first symptoms settled in; and from there, Pteromic Paralysis was a one-way trip down a cackling black hole.

If Zillif could still work her data-link, she must know how grisly the situation was; but when she spoke again, her voice had no trace of the trembles. "Faye Smallwood," she said, "I'd like to know . . . your father is participating in the Pascal protocol, is he not?"

I stiffened. "Yes." I looked around the Big Top again,

wishing Dads would hurry his tail out of bed. "You've heard about the protocol?" I asked.

"On my link." She lowered her voice. "And I understand it. All of it."

Of course she did. A member of the Vigil could pry open government databanks for details kept out of the public information areas . . . including a no-fancytalk explanation of how we were "treating" the plague.

We'd adopted the Pascal protocol. Named after Blaise Pascal, the first human mathematician to analyze roulette, card games and the craps table. That's what the Pascal protocol was all about: rolling the dice.

When an illness was a hundred percent lethal . . . when the course of disease was so vicious-fast that victims died within weeks . . . when conventional treatments showed no ghost of effect . . . when advanced members of the League of Peoples didn't leap forward to offer a cure . . . then the Technocracy could authorize physicians to take a fling with the Pascal protocol: *Try anything, treat the side effects, and for God's sake, keep accurate records.*

All over Demoth, doctors were squeezing local plants for extracts—hoping some fern or flower had come up with chemical resistance to the Pteromic microbe. Other doctors were crush-powdering insect carapaces, or drawing blood from great sea eels. Some had even placed their bets on chance molecule construction: computers using a random number generator to assemble chains of arbitrary amino acids into heaven knows what. Then the result was injected blindly-blithely-brazenly into patients.

Do you see how desperate we were? No control groups, no controls. No double-blinds, no animal tests, no computer models. Certainly no informed consent—that might jinx the placebo effect, and Christ knows, we needed whatever edge we could get. Especially when a doctor could take it into his head to scrape fuzzy brown goo off some tree bark, then mainline it straight into a patient's artery.

I told you. No one stayed sane.

Some doctors refused to participate in the protocol: they ranted about centuries of medical tradition, and recited Hippocrates in the original Greek. But with Pteromic Paralysis, there was no cure, no remission, no ending save death . . . and a greedy-glutton death that might gobble every Oolom within weeks. Even my stodgy conservative father admitted it was time to go for a long shot.

But Dads was only a fiddly-dick GP in fiddly-dick Sallysweet River. He had no training in medical research and no equipment for crapshoot organic chemistry. When the Pascal protocol was first proclaimed, he went into a twelve-hour sulk, growling at anyone who'd listen, "What do they think *I* can do? Why should I even bother?" (Dads was given to monumental sulks. When he became a hero, biographers papered over such pout-parties with the phrase, "At times he could be difficult" . . . which sounds more noble for all concerned than saying Henry Smallwood was a petulant nelly.)

In the end, Dads grudgingly decided his search for a cure would use something he had near at hand: human food. "At least it won't kill them," he muttered . . . which wasn't half so certain as he pretended. Ooloms were engineered to eat foodstuffs native to Demoth, as well as crops and animal products their people brought from the Divian homeworld; no one expected they could hold down terrestrial food too.

Take a common Earth grape, for example: chocked juicy with dozens of biological compounds. Some of those compounds are nigh-on universal—you find simple sugars in every starry reach of the galaxy, and Ooloms could easily digest them. On the other hand, your average grape contains a whole lab shelf of more specialized enzymes, proteins, vitamins, and other tools of grapehood . . . grand for humans, because we've spent three billion years evolving to eat whatever grapes dish out, but to Oolom metabolisms, each chemical was an alien substance with untold poisonous potential.

Natural result: Ooloms didn't eat terrestrial foods.

They'd be crazy to take the teeniest nibble. No doubt, in the twenty-five years *Homo saps* had lived on Demoth, some daredevil Oolom must have given it a try; but there'd never been a systematic study. Why would there be? When Oolooms could eat blessed near every leaf and grass on the planet, where's the sense in stuffing them with human *coq au vin* to see if it kills them?

That's how things stood till the plague came ... at which point, the scales tipped to the other side of *Why not?* When Oolooms were all going to die anyway, where was the harm in a little *coq au vin*, on the off chance some unexpected terrestrial chemical actually did some good?

So that's what passed for medical treatment under the Big Top: solemnly giving our patients a single grain of wheat or a bead from a raspberry as if it were potent medicine. Ha-ha. Knee-slapping hilarity. Hard to keep a straight face.

The joke turned sour the first time an Oolom came close to dying—a fine old gentleman who jerked into half-slack convulsions after eating a sliver of carrot no bigger than a fingernail paring. The man survived, thanks to emergency whumping and pumping from my father ... and it did Dads good to have a success, actually saving a victim from death. (Then the old fellow died three days later, when his diaphragm slacked out. Would have been ironic if it hadn't been inevitable. Dads fiercely wanted to put him on the heart-lung to sustain a semblance of breathing; but we only owned one such machine, and the Oolooms had already voted not to keep a single patient alive at the expense of 120 others. Fine thing, that: death by democracy.)

"If you understand the protocol," I told Zillif, "do you understand the risks?"

"Yes, Faye Smallwood. There are many ways an untried substance could harm me, and only one that could do me good. Still," she said, jockeying her head clumsily to nestle down into the pillow, "I admire the idea of joining a medical experiment. Especially a grand one. There's a chance I shall be instrumental in discovering a cure."

A miniscule chance. But I wished Dads was there with me. A whiff of Zillif's optimism might have perked him up.

My father arrived ten minutes later, his hair mussed wild and his clothes askew.

That's how I'll always remember him—never quite tucked in, as if one emergency after another kept him from pulling himself together. Even in the quiet days before the epidemic, he always managed an air of too-rushed-to-brush. And once the outbreak struck . . . well, precious little difference actually, unless it was a touch of smugness, now that he'd got a gold-plated excuse for looking like something the cat sicked up.

Not that my mother accepted *any* excuse. Since the plague began, she'd gotten daily more snappish about Dads's tousled state—he was a doctor, for Christ's sake, he should make a decent impression. She was especially infuriated by his beard. Six weeks earlier it had been bold and bushy, teddy-bear brown with just five teasy threads of gray. Then Mother declared the beard was lopsided, wretchedly in need of a trim. Each day she worried at it with embroidery scissors while Dads stood stoic but impatient to get away. By the morning Zillif arrived, my father's beard had been reduced to a five o'clock shadow, clutched tight and dark to his face.

Dads didn't care. He only grew the beard in the first place because he couldn't be bothered to shave.

"This is *Tur* Zillif," I told him. *Tur* was the Oolom politeword for a woman of venerable age. "*Tur* Zillif of the Vigil."

"An honor, Proctor Zillif . . ." Dads began.

"No," she interrupted. "You mustn't address me by that title. Not when I'm unable to fulfill a proctor's duties."

My father's face curdled with his "difficult-at-times"

miffiness; he hated to be corrected by anyone. Since it was undignified to grump at a patient, he turned on me. "I assume you've gathered *Tur* Zillif's medical history?"

"No charts in the bin," I answered straightaway. In a more honest universe, I might have confessed I hadn't even checked the bin as I carried Zillif past the admitting table; but Eden this isn't, and anyway Pook would have handed me a chart if we'd had any available. Our spare chart-pads tended to pile on my father's desk till he downloaded their contents into the house-soul's permanent storage. Dads avoided that task as long as he could, sometimes covering the heap of charts with a bath towel so he wouldn't have to look at them. Each "completed" chart in the stack meant we'd lost another patient.

Dads glared at me, just on general humphy principles, then turned back to Zillif. "We start by getting as much information about you as we can—your health history, personal details . . ."

"Names of my next of kin?" she asked.

My father chewed on that a second, obviously reconsidering whatever tack he'd intended to take. If he could help it, he never flat out talked to patients about the possibility of death; he'd assembled a thesaurus full of phrases that gave the required message when absolutely necessary ("prepare for the worst," "put your affairs in order") without actually having to admit he couldn't save everybody from the Abyss. Dads hated patients who wanted to contemplate their own mortality.

"All right," he told Zillif in a low voice, "we both know the prognosis is unfavorable." Unfavorable: another willy-word from the Dads book of euphemisms. "But," he continued, "people *are* working on this. We never know when there'll be a breakthrough."

"In the next two weeks, do you think?"

I bit my lip. Once again, Zillif proved she had canny sources of information: two weeks was the median survival time for an Oolom with her degree of paralysis.

"No one can guess when a breakthrough might come,"

Dads answered, his voice all prickly. "It could take some time; but then again, it might have happened this very second, somewhere in the world. In the meantime, we're doing our best. We'll put you on an experimental medication—"

"What medication?" Zillif interrupted.

Dads glowered at me as if I were the one who'd annoyed him, then unclipped a notepad from his belt. He pressed a touch-square on the pad, but I could tell he didn't need to look at the result; he always knew what "treatment" he'd scheduled for the next patient to come in. "You'll be trying a terrestrial substance called cinnamon," he told Zillif. "It's the bark from an Earth-native tree." Dads gave me a look, as if I'd accused him of something. "Humans have a rare long tradition of obtaining medicine from tree bark. Quinine..." He stopped and waved his hand airily, trying to make it look as if there were too many to list. More likely, he couldn't think of any others.

"Cinnamon," Zillif said slowly. "Cinnamon." Speaking like a woman who's been told the name of her grandchild and wants to hear how it sounds on her own tongue. "Will I be the first patient to try this cinnamon?"

"The first Oolom," I replied, before Dads concocted some gollygosh story about promising clinical tests all over the planet. Lately, he'd shown a fondness for manufacturing unjustified optimism in patients—at least I hoped that's why he made such wild-eyed claims, and not that he really believed them. I told Zillif, "We coordinate our tests with other hospitals to avoid unwanted duplication."

"A tree bark named cinnamon," she murmured. As if she was pleased to know her place in the worldwide medical experiment—how she'd make her global contribution to finding a cure, even while lying mud-still in Sallysweet River. "My people enjoy many types of native bark," she said. "You can make a nice salad, just from the trees in

this neighborhood. Bluebarrels, whitespots, paper-peels
. . . and of course, chillslaps for color . . .''

My father and I let her talk—slurry words spoken with
putty-muscled lips. After a while, Dads sent me to grate
fresh cinnamon while he got the names of Zillif's next of
kin.

Here's the thing: fifteen-year-olds can fall crazy in love
faster than a sigh. In love with a singer, in love with a
song, in love with kittens or cookies or Coleridge or
Christ, and deeply-ecstatically-drunkenly.

Cynics will say the love never lasts—that you adore
impressionist painters for a week, programming your
walls with blowups from Monet and Degas, then suddenly, under all those water lilies and po-faced ballerinas,
you stumble across a verse of Sufi poetry and boom,
you're a Muslim mystic, memorizing parables and medi-
tating on the Ineffable Garden.

Yes, some teenage passions are superficial; but some
are boundlessly-breathlessly-*ardently* transformative. In
the blink of an eye or as slow as ice melting, your heart
can be changed/lost/found forever.

The way I fell in love with Zillif over the following
days. Evolving from apprehension about a woman on my
roof, to casual interest in the patient I'd dropped off at
the Circus, then metamorphosing into love, love, love.

Not sexual love. Not puppy love. Capital-R Romantic
love, longing to vanquish enemies in her name, hanging
on her slur-tongued words as if they were perfume that
went straight to my brain.

What did we talk about? The sun when it shone, the
moons when they rose, my friends, her grandchildren, the
wildflowers I picked one afternoon near the town's dump
of mine tailings . . .

But mostly we talked about the Vigil. I wanted to hear
everything. (Everything all at once.)

Nine hundred years earlier, the first Oolom colony on
Demoth had been founded by a Divian billionaire who

wanted to show the world he could design a utopia. Scary idea, that. But the man did have one good idea: the Vigil. A constitutionally entrenched organization for watchdogging the government. Empowered to open any government file no matter how secret, to interrogate public officials from the lowliest sewer worker to the Speaker-General, to scrutinize every department and bureau and commission and regulation board that operated on any jurisdictional level: federal, territorial, trade region, or municipal. To monitor all the politicians, bureaucrats, consultants . . . and to report unflinchingly when any of those petty emperors had no clothes.

You could dismiss it as a typical rich man's idea— fiscal-philosophical auditors riding herd over the government. On any other planet, the Vigil would soon become flap-in-the-wind powerless, or a scheming cabal of puppeteers behind the throne; but the Ooloms, the brilliant, careful Ooloms, found a secret way to make it work.

Not that Zillif told me the secret. I only learned that much later. Zillif just told me the Vigil's motto: *Wa supesh i rabi ganosh.* LIVE IN THE REAL AND NAME THE LIES.

Can you imagine how those words gave me the luscious chills? Fifteen years old, viscerally idealistic no matter how blasé I thought I was, my heart zinging wildly from the overload of death and the need to think our existence could mean more than worm food . . .

Live in the real. Name the lies.

Rage against the dying of the light.

And *Tur* Zillif herself. Lady Zillif, my Lady Zillif. The shining *presence* of her: quiet yet arresting, as if there were a second electrical lifeform crackling under the skin of her dying body. As if she was what it truly meant to be real, and the rest of us were just pathetic fakes, too caught up in the busywork ballet to recognize our own emptiness.

A *grounded* woman. Like a Zen master . . . or a Shaolin or a Sufi or a shaman or a saint, all those caricatures of wisdom who show up in bad fic-chips to spout fortune-cookie prattle and guide the hero to a state of villain-whupping enlightenment. Except that Zillif was really *there*. Wherever you get when you stop being everywhere else and just *are*, moment to moment, sixty seconds a minute.

Do you understand? It sounds so trite as I try to describe it. The most profound revelations are glib Yeah-YeahSures till they've made you bleed.

Besides, I was in love. Pumped loony with a teenage girl's hero worship. So screw the suggestion that Zillif occupied some higher plane of consciousness, dismiss it as infatuation for all I care. The woman blew me away; leave it at that. And let's get back to the Vigil because that's less dicey to talk about.

So the Vigil: an honored-honorable-honest body of disciplined scrutineers. Any age, any sex, any species, provided you could tough out the seven years of training and the final *müshor*—the initiation/retreat/ordeal that marked your transition from student to full-fledged proctor. But I didn't know about *müshor* back then; I was only familiar with the Vigil's public side. The big cases, like exposing a Fisheries Minister who'd taken bribes, or that whole mess about illegal practices in the Federal Justice Division. The small cases, like ragging on Traffic & Roads to fill the great whacking pothole on Gambo Street, or quietly suggesting it was high time a certain junior-school teacher learned to like kids.

Then there was the Vigil's bread and butter: reviewing proposed legislation put forward by each level of government. Truth to tell, I barely paid attention to most Vigil critiques when they were broadcast—any talk about politics and the economy always struck me as so damned tawdry—but even a flighty fifteen-year-old could see that proctors were dealing with important issues. "Here are the people this bill will hurt. Here are the people this bill will make rich. Here are the risks involved. Here are the things that will change." Time and time and time again, the Vigil opened up the subjects no politician, corporate news service, or interest group wanted to mention.

"Why is that special?" you ask. "Watchdog groups are a daydream a dozen." Too true. But the Vigil had a stunning track record for getting things *right*. The predictions. The context. The true motivations. Unlike every other watchdog group in creation, they didn't cry wolf just to attract attention. They didn't have a locked-in *agenda*. And they had what amounted to police powers over the government, search and seizure, poke and probe, opening the closed doors.

No one could count how many legislative fiascoes the Vigil had prevented . . . because Demoth almost never *had* legislative fiascoes. Lawmakers were more careful with a crack squad of proctors looking over their shoulders; and if budget numbers didn't quite make sense, bureaucrats were usually quick to correct any discrepancies the Vigil pointed out. On occasions when soft-spoken suggestions didn't work, proctors were empowered to publish their findings to the world whenever they chose to do so— reports with a credibility no journalist or lobby group has had since the dawn of time.

If worst came to worst, the Vigil had one more sycophant-stopping power guaranteed by Demoth's ancient constitution: vote qualification tests. Before legislators voted on a bill, the proctor scrutinizing that vote could set a test to determine whether the politicians understood what the bill actually meant. Those who failed the test could only sit and grind their teeth in public humiliation while those who passed made an informed decision. It didn't totally eliminate witless results—what could?—but at least it meant people knew what they were voting for.

"Always, always, always," Zillif told me, "a proctor concentrates on the bill at hand. Never the intention, always the fact. Politics is filled with fine intentions, and with well-meaning people who want to do good. But the Vigil asks, will this bill do what its sponsors claim? Will it work? And what else will it do, what side effects, what loopholes? Who really gets the benefit, the reward, the money? The Vigil analyzes the consequences of what is really on the table, and we tell the world. Then it's up to the people to decide if that's what they want.''

I soaked up Zillif's descriptions of how proctors trained to control their own political bias—not eliminating it (impossible), but bringing it out in the open, grabbing it by the ears and devil's-advocating one bias for a while, then another, then another, like walking around a sculpture so you could view it from all sides. Proctors also got broad science training so they wouldn't wallow in arrogant ignorance; they studied history, sociology, psychology, math, public medicine, ecology, xenology, accounting, monetary dynamics, and of course, the hard science: physics/chemistry/information/micro-bi.

Twined in with these mental disciplines were physical ones—an organism that lives for its brain alone turns clack-stupid in its specialization, complexifying simple things to impress itself with its own cleverness. Healthy sane awake people know how to get out of their heads and into their skins. So Vigil members grounded themselves with Oolom disciplines we humans would call yoga, qigong, meditation, martial arts: nimbling up the body to nimble up the soul.

God, oh God . . . listening to Zillif, I wanted a nimble soul. I wanted a soul, period. And by all the saints and our Holy Mother, I wanted to make myself *radiant*. Bright as glorious fire. Valuable. Important to important events. Jawdropper stunning, yet plangently meaningful. I wanted to be the one to discover a cure for the plague; to find awe-pummeling treasures in the alien ruins dotted around our planet; to dazzle the universe by being beautiful and smart and talented and wise and loved and memorable and chic and productive and sultry and happy and *alive*. . . .

On the afternoon of the fifth day, Zillif lost her ability to speak—tongue, lips, and jaw all went slack in the same second. Mid-sentence. "Faye Smallwood, why are you always so . . ." Then an ugly gargly sound, throat still pushing up noise with nothing to shape it. My friend Lynn called that sound "unloaded uvula exercise" . . . although Ooloms didn't have uvulas, not big obvious ones like in *Homo sap* anatomy. "Aaaaah gaah gaaaaaaah hah kaaaaaaaa."

"Faye Smallwood, why are you always so aaaaah gaah gaaaaaaah hah kaaaaaaaa . . ."

I put my fingers soft to Zillif's lips to stop her. It felt so fiercely, fiery, lonesomely intimate, that touch. Days before and after, I touched Zillif high up and low down, washing, swabbing every nook and cranny . . . but that was just playing nurse, doing a job with my hands. Only that one touch stays with me—my fingertips on her loose limp mouth, hush, it's over.

She stopped trying to talk, stopped making the fraggly jaggly un-Zillif noise. I would have kissed her if I'd had any way to get her permission. But she was closed off now: eyes, face, hands, voice, everything mudpuddled but heart and lungs.

In the following days, I still sat with her when I had the chance . . . held her hand till her fragile fingers changed from bed-linen white to my own fairish tan; but I felt too tongue-tied to speak much on my own. What could I talk about to such a woman? The weather? The latest death statistics? Whatever vapid fiddly-dick dreams might pass through a backwater girl's head?

Queer thing, that: how you can feel you're blazing on the verge of radiance one day, then suddenly know for a fact you're dog-puke banal.

When I told Dads that Zillif could no longer talk, he upped her dosage of cinnamon. I wept at the futility.

Zillif died on a bright autumn morning, with the sun beaming grandly detached through the stained yellow canvas. You'd think there'd be scarcely a difference between a limp paralyzed body and a dead one; but there is. One second there's the Yes of life . . . then there's meaningless meat. Something gone and something gone and something gone.

Three hours later, we discovered a cure for the disease.

Olive oil. So farcical, I wanted to scream. Later, I bellowed my head off . . . out in the tree-starved tundra, where the deep beds of carpet moss drank up the sound. Cool, sleek, stronger-than-real-life Faye Smallwood blubbering into her hands, wiping her nose on her sleeve, crying because the world was harder than she was.

Olive oil. Cloying, tongue-gucking stuff. Nothing a Sallysweet River family would ever spoon over its food.

One of my school friends saw the results first—Sharr Crosbie, daughter of two miners. Sweet girl, no harm in her, though I couldn't stand being in the same room with her ever after. To my shame, I've inherited my father's talent for sulks. But it rankled my heart, the witless way she told her story over and over, to me, to our parents, to the full news media.

"I was with this poor old man, in precious bad shape . . ." (False, Sharr-girl, false; he'd only just come in, and had some motion in his toes as well as a hint of bowel control—better condition than most of our patients.) ". . . and I was washing him off, you know, a sponge bath, the way he liked . . ." (All our Oolooms hated sponge baths; they grumbled and whined how the sponges tickled.) ". . . so I was wiping round his face when I spilled a dab of soap in his eye . . ." (The clumsy cow.) ". . . and he closed his eyes. He closed his eyes!"

Sharr squealed. People raced in, then went wild. Pook came close to breaking the patient's chart, punching buttons to see what the man's medication was.

Olive oil. Olive oil.

Dads came running from his office. "Who's hurt, what's wrong?" Then he ordered everybody to clear the hell back while he did some tests. Blood samples. Tissue grams. A needle-point biopsy into the man's huge shoulder muscle.

By then, the whole town was standing nearby, watching, holding each other's hands, crossing fingers or making a show of praying—everyone but me. I was sitting on Zillif's empty cot, telling myself there was no blessed way I'd join that crowd of fools, believing anything important could happen in Sallysweet River, now or ever. . . .

Shrieking cheers of victory. Bedlam. Piss-wetting hysteria. When people began to stampede, hugging and kissing everyone in sight, I scuttled to the angry sanctuary of my room.

We had no more deaths under the Big Top. *Tur* Zillif, my Lady Zillif, was the last.

Afterward, on tear-soaked sleepless nights, I told myself she could have been the last plague death on all Demoth. The idea was self-pitying rubbish: hundreds more must have died in the time it took to relay the news around the planet . . . the time it took to start food synthesizers pumping out olive oil . . . the time it took the olive oil to have an effect. . . .

But our olive oil worked. It contained an enzyme hash that ripped the Pteromic microbe to protoplasmic tatters. With the microbe gone, Oolom muscles began to repair themselves.

My father was a hero.

I was so blind-raging furious with him.

One more memory of the day Zillif died: trying to lose myself in the forest at night. Looking for the blackest shadows. Pressing my weep-wrinkled face against the taut cool trunk of a bluebarrel tree. Damply kissing its cucumber-smooth bark, as a substitute for all the kisses, dreams, lives, redemptions that had been strangled for me in the instant of Zillif's death.

Till a twig cracked behind me, and I wheeled around.

It was a young man in the black uniform of an Explorer cadet. Given the dark, I could barely make out his silhouette . . . but that was enough to show the man's "pass-ticket" for becoming an Explorer. His left arm was only half the length of his right, and the hand on that arm was a pudgy babyish thing with too few fingers.

"Something wrong?" he asked.

Swiping at tears, I snapped, "I don't need you."

"Few do," the man answered drily. "But I need *you* to go home now. We're searching the woods for Ooloom survivors, and you show up as hot as a bonfire on our scans. Compared to Oolooms anyway. You're confusing our readouts."

He turned and slipped back into the darkness. Bristling with an attack of the stubborns, I stayed where I was, muttering, "Who does he think he is?" and occasionally aiming peevish kicks at the undergrowth.

Then an Admiralty skimmer flew overhead with loud-speakers blaring. "Greetings to all Oolooms. We have found a cure. Please go immediately to the nearest human settlement . . ."

I slouched back to our home compound and ordered the house-soul to turn my dome black.

Outside and inside.

2

AFTER THE CIRCUS

Reading what I've just written about the plague—it makes me cringe. Too polite, too *nice* . . . as if, deary-dear, we were all a wee bit strained but coping.

We weren't coping. Never think that. You have to understand what mass death does.

My mother flew into spitting slapping furies, accusing me of doing the dance with every boy/man/fence post in town (and half the girls/women/punch bowls). She'd invent the most graphic details of what I supposedly did, kinkies I scarce understood even after Ma shrieked explanations in my face.

Is that coping?

Another treat during the epidemic: my father hit me. And I hit him back. Not a fight, a ritual . . . one smack from him and one from me.

Desperation. A way of touching each other when hugs felt too puny.

Dads always hit me on the arm. Even today, I can close my eyes and bring back fresh memories of the sting, the burn, the surprised red flush on my skin.

I hit Dads on the face. His beard scratchy under my

hand; me slapping hard enough to give my palm whisker burn. So it felt anyway.

When he discovered the cure, I stopped hitting him. I stopped touching him at all. Temper. Stubbornness. The lonelier I ached for him, the more mulish I got. But at times I prayed we could start smacking each other again.

Is that coping?

Several times, those of us working in the Circus caught one or another of our volunteer nurses trying to smother a patient. Then the rest of us volunteers punched royal crap out of the would-be mercy killer. We'd pound away, and the Ooloms would wax frantic with horror, some managing to scream, "Stop, stop!" while most just guzzled out, "Aaaaah gaah hah kaaaa!" . . . a ghastly guttural wailing which was all that kept us from killing whoever fell under our fists. Even so, the beating victims usually had to be hospitalized; but we stuck them in a different part of the compound, because we didn't want a blood-battered human marring the pretty color scheme of white patients in white beds.

Is that coping?

We made jokes about the dead and dying—none of the jokes funny, but we laughed and laughed. When Ooloms were asleep, we laid bits of crimson cloth on their chests just to see their skins change color. (Crimson was our favorite because it looked like bloodspill.) We could send each other into hiccups just by whispering the word, "Plaid." And the day my friend Peter managed to spell his name on an Oolom's back . . .

The Circus also had a couple field toilets for the *Homo sap* volunteers working there . . . and you don't want to know what rancid cartoons/graffiti got painted on the crapper walls. Someone burned the toilet shacks to the ground soon after the plague ended, and every human in Sallysweet River felt shamed-sheepish-grateful to the vandal.

You're all welcome.

More coping? Two or three times a day, off-duty min-

ers would carry the latest dead body to a mass grave outside town. We used an ancient tunnel for the burial site—
a leftover shaft dug three thousand years earlier by some
unknown alien race. This short-lived alien colony had apparently mined the same veins of ore as our own Rustico
Nickel . . . and for all we knew, the site might have had
great-and-grand significance for archaeologists. But we
filled it with bloated, gas-venting corpses.

One night (inevitable), a mumbly-drunk miner shot a
signal flare down the tunnel and blew himself up in a
belch of blazing methane. We shoveled the miner's
shocked remains into the shaft along with the crispy
Oolom carcasses (chunks of them got spewed out of the
tunnel by the explosion), then went back to stowing bodies in exactly the same place. It became a Saturday night
ritual to shoot a flare down the shaft to see what burned,
but we never hit as big a buildup of gas as that first time.

Pity. Maybe getting singed by a thunderflash bang
would have helped us "cope."

Have I made my point? Don't think this is self-pity.
This is showing you the truth.

Through the whole of the plague, we festered in the
brain. Our Oolom neighbors—dead. The patients we
nursed—dying. Dozens of Oolom cities—empty, except
for carcasses. One night, as a bunch of us kids sat in my
dome, passing around a bottle of hoot-owl for an excuse
to act drunk . . . that night, near midnight, my poetic
friend Darlene whispered she imagined the Thin Interior
stacked with corpses, mountain-high: the heartlands of
every continent heaped with dead. Humans living on the
coasts would soon see the rivers running brown with
blood and rot and pus.

All of us nodded. We'd had similar nightmares. *Guilty*
nightmares.

Here's the thing: none of us could shake the idea we
were to blame. The Ooloms died, and we didn't.

How could you not see the timing? Millions of Ooloms
lived placidly for nine hundred years without running into

the disease. Twenty-five years after *Homo saps* arrived on Demoth, the slack death gurgled up its poison.

We must have brought something. Or stirred up something. Or created something. Scientists swore the Pteromic microbe didn't resemble anything from human space, but we refused to believe them.

Do you understand? Not in your head but your gut. Do you *grasp* it? Do you feel the icy blame of it grabbing your arms and pushing you down under its weight?

No. Because you weren't there. We were.

It was all our fault. We were marked with the blood of every magnificent old woman we didn't save. And when we finally stumbled on the cure . . . Christ, the Ooloms treated Dads like a genius, but humans choked on his name. Olive oil? That was it—olive oil? Not a product of sophisticated research but something we'd had from the start, something we could have mass-synthesized anytime, and yet we sat with thumbs up our cracks while so many succumbed.

When we finally tallied the dead, the humans of Demoth had let more than sixty million Ooloms perish under our care.

Sixty million; 60,000,000; 6×10^7.

Or to put it another way, 93 percent of all the Ooloms in the universe. The whole of a sentient species nearly driven extinct because we couldn't spare a little salad dressing.

It took a year (a Demoth year, 478 days of 26.1 hours each) for the slack-splayed Ooloms to regain full mobility . . . or as much as they ever got back. Muscles paralyzed too long were sometimes lost to atrophy, leaving thousands of the survivors with faltery drags in their speech or fingers that fumbled small objects.

Still, the Ooloms kept telling us they were glad to be alive. After a while, we couldn't stand the sight of them. They reminded us of too much. They were a burden.

Volunteers stopped coming to the Big Top long before

our Ooloms could take care of themselves. Dads had to pay people for the jobs they'd done so willingly before the cure made everyone feel like asses. By that time, though, we'd realized the Ooloms could afford the expense—they were rich now, at least on paper. After all, the surviving Ooloms had inherited the property of the dead. Ninety-three percent of the race extinct = 14.29 times the wealth for everybody left.

Simple mathematics . . . even when you factor in the economic donnybrook that followed the epidemic. *Homo saps* and Ooloms both went through manic spending sprees, alternating with agoraphobic depression and every frenzied dementia between; but despite that, most Ooloms came out the other side cushy as rats in velvet.

People offplanet called that a silver lining. Those of us on Demoth saw precious little silver in anything.

Seven months after the cure was discovered, while the Circus still played ringmaster to forty-six patients, Rustico Nickel Shaft 12 had a Class B cave-in: the first in the company's twenty-four-year history. Despite a dozen safety systems, the accident resulted in one reported fatality—Dr. Henry Smallwood, who happened to be on the scene tending a miner's sprained ankle.

Sharr Crosbie's mother. Tripped over her own feet.

The clumsy cow.

3

DATA TUMOR

My ages sixteen, seventeen, eighteen: angry, angry, angry. Survivor guilt and post-traumatic stress.

Hating Dads for being dead, determined to punish Ma because she couldn't make it all better. I buried myself in a shallow grave of time-wasting: the sick kind, where you don't like what you're doing, know you don't like it, and keep doing it anyway. Playing clot-head games in VR-land; having listless sex with anyone drunk enough to reciprocate; bitch-fighting my mother, my friends, myself . . .

One day, I got to thinking how I disliked a particular freckle on my arm. So I got a scalpel from my father's old clinic and cut the freckle off. When the first freckle was gone, another one stood out . . . so I cut that off too.

Things kind of got out of hand. I still have to wear long sleeves in polite company.

But there's no point dwelling on any of the witless, reckless ways I nearly sliced myself up, OD'd, or got beaten toothless in semen-stinking back rooms. You could call my lifestyle an ongoing suicide attempt; but it didn't work, did it?

Didn't prove anything.

Didn't solve the problem.

Faye Smallwood, who once thought she was too strong to be damaged by the world. A glossy girl who suddenly hated shine.

I survived those years mostly because of Sallysweet River itself—tough mining town, yes, but not nearly as rotted-up with focused violence as your average city. We had brawls and drunkards, not gang wars and cold-kill hoodlums.

And I had my protectors: other petty delinquents and rebels, kids like me who'd seen too many corpses. My own bad crowd, eight of us, all convinced that the over-abundance of death *disproved* something about the universe, and the only decent response was to mistrust the whole polite world. To defy. To mutiny against complacent niceness because it had unforgivably let us down.

Idealistic buggers that we were. At age nineteen, we got married—all eight of us.

Quick background data: the humans on Demoth originally hailed from Come-By-Chance, a planet that got settled in the twenty-second century by a small religious sect called the MaryMarch Covenant. The early MaryMarchers believed in a particular type of group marriage—forming your own clan, a commune, a kibbutz, a "life team" . . .

A family. And at age nineteen, with nothing but ice between Mother and me, some part of my soul longed for any kind of connection.

MaryMarch marriages had fallen out of fashion over the past two hundred years, worn down by contact with more conventional attitudes from mainstream Technocracy society; but they were still legal, here on Demoth as well as our old home on Come-By-Chance. So why shouldn't a bunch of eight kids from Sallysweet River tie the knot? Such a sweet old-fashioned notion . . . marrying the boys and girls next door.

Me and Lynn: we were the instigators. Things always

worked that way. Lynn had long been in flaming staunch-hearted love with me—the only smudge of lunacy in her character because otherwise she had brains and cool and common sense. (God, if I could be as serene as Lynn for a single day! I envied everything about her . . . except her dotage on a flake like me. Of course, she envied me back: "For being insane," she said, "for letting yourself *be* insane . . . and for those gorgeous Amazonian shoulders that I just want to sink my teeth into. Meow.")

I made up a list of the family I envisioned, and Lynn made it happen. Our typical working arrangement. "Lynn, I want this." "Then, dear one, that's what you shall have."

My chosen spouses (besides Lynn):

Angie Tobin, because she was mouthwatering gorgeous and sexually congenial. The sort who giggled comfortably in bed. With Angie baiting our marital hook, Lynn and I could reel in blessed near any man in town. And half the women.

Barrett Arsenault, because he was just as gorgeous as Angie, and wild as squidge-weed. Never turned down a dare, no matter how crazed . . . and on nothing-to-do Saturday nights, Barrett always came up with something to make the weekend memorable.

Peter Kaluit, because he was funny. By Christ and all the saints, he was funny. Wicked but not snake-mean. He played keyboards too, and wrote songs that would have you laughing yourself wet. To my teenage mind, it didn't hurt either that he was hung like a bear.

Winston Mooney, because he knew how to get things done. He knew the angles. More than once, when I'd got myself in trouble with the law or harsh company, Winston would squeak me free from the jaws of disaster. He was mad-jack in love with me too, and it would be a slap in his face if I didn't invite him into the scrum.

Darlene Carew, because she was timid and lonely. Not whiny or pathetic, but sad. A bony-thin girl as pretty as porcelain, but who never got asked out; who never dreamed of doing the asking herself; who wrote poetry and listened with shiny eyes whenever I recounted my latest slap-and-tickle adventures. I figured Darlene could be my personal project—cut her in on a piece of Barrett, Peter, and the rest, give her some new experiences to put in her poems.

Finally, Egerton Crosbie (Sharr's brother), because he was good-natured and built like a streetcar. Without him, I'd be the brawniest one in the household . . . and I sure as hell didn't want to get stuck with the heavy lifting my whole life.

There: my husbands and wives. Cajoled, enticed, teased, negotiated into a grand old MaryMarch union.

The idea shocked the people we wanted to shock—my mother, for example. She wasn't even of Covenant descent (Dads met her at medical college on New Earth), so our announcement struck her as flat-out perverse. Longtime MaryMarchers had a milder reaction, but still considered the marriage in bad taste: using a respected-if-not-respectable religious institution just to annoy our elders. Which was bang-on-the-head true.

Still, we had the aroma of legitimacy on our side: like someone who fasts on Fridays or wears a crown of real thorns to the Atonement service. People moan, "We don't *do* that anymore!" but they won't go so far as to stop you. Deep down, there's always a knot of guilt that they've abandoned the old ways. That they've settled their butts in a padded pew and made themselves *comfortable*.

So the eight of us married. Started our own family compound: eight small domes ringed around a bigger central one. For a while, of course, it was sex, sex, sex—what do you expect from nineteen-year-olds? We had no other ideas about what marriage *was*. I took all seven of the others into my bed, individually, or in threesomes, four-somes, more-somes . . .

Faye being bad. Playing musical beds, not for any healthy reason like love or pure wet lust, but mostly just to be wicked. To get revenge on my mother for all the things she'd once imagined about me. To shock the rest of the community. To trivialize myself.

But the free-for-all burned itself out after a few months. Egerton and Darlene began pairing off together almost every night. Then Angie and Barrett. The other four of us stayed more loose and lubricious, occasionally showing up at each other's door on nights we wanted comfort, but sleeping more and more on our own as time went on.

When Lynn got pregnant, both Peter and Winston claimed to be the father. Not fighting over it; just both of them volunteering, eager to be dads. Which put Lynn, Peter, and Winston together, didn't it, even if Lynn oc-casionally planted me a fierce kiss as she padded past— the three of them cheerful parents-to-be, then overjoyed parents of Matthew and Eva. Naturally, the story went that Peter fathered one of the twins, while Winston fathered the other . . . but no one really knew who begat whom, and of course, they refused gene-testing to find out the truth. That would only spoil the solidarity.

So Darlene/Egerton, Angie/Barrett, Lynn/Peter/Win-ston—all of them sorted out. I was happy for them, truly. And I wasn't so cruelly cut off on my own. As the months and years trickled by, from time to time any one of the seven might show up at my dome near bedtime, saying, "Faye, you looked so lonely at dinner . . ."

Sometimes we talked, then I sent them away. Some-times they stayed the warm-flesh night. My husbands, my wives, my lovers, my friends, my teammates, my safety lines to the world.

It wasn't so bad being the odd woman out. You can

learn to live with anything when you've developed the notion you don't deserve more.

Meanwhile in those years after the plague, Demoth was going through a merry old flap-up of reshuffling. With only a sliver of its former population, the planet didn't have nearly the same mineral needs as before. All but one of the mines around Sallysweet River closed, but that was no hardship—so many Ooloms had died, there was work to be found all over Great St. Caspian. The government spent prodigious amounts on retraining; my spouses all got good educations, then good jobs.

For a while, it still looked like Demoth might need a splurge of immigration, just to keep things running. Add it up, and we only had six million inhabitants on the entire planet—blessed near empty, even by the sparse standards of Fringe Worlds and colonies. But the humans and Ooloms who'd come through the plague didn't want newcomers barging in: people who'd act sympathetic about the die-off but wouldn't *know*. So we buckled down hard and pulled things together on our own.

Our eight-in-hand family eventually moved from Sallysweet River to the poky urban sprawl of Bonaventure . . . still on Great St. Caspian Island, but out on the ocean coast. Less moss, more bare ice-scraped rock. By mainstream Technocracy standards, the city was a fiddly-dick clump-hole, population only 50,000. But with Demoth severely depeopled by the plague, Bonaventure was the twelfth largest metropolis on the planet. A major hub and port town: where supertankers dropped off raw organics harvested from the Pok Sea algae flats; where the spunky Island Bullet loaded and unloaded its railcars after running its circuit of the mining towns in-country. Bonaventure also had an up-sleeve to the North Orbital Terminus . . . mostly for distributing the metals mined inland, but also for business travelers and tourists who wanted fast transport to anywhere else on Demoth—up the sleeve in zero time to the terminus, over a cross-sleeve to an equatorial orbiter, then down another sleeve to any population center on the planet.

One of the great charms of Bonaventure—you could leave the place so quickly.

"Bonaventure" was a human word, of course. Pre-plague, the city had an Oolom name, but that got changed when humans took over. The Ooloms wanted it that way. They still outnumbered *Homo saps* overall on Demoth—roughly five million of them to one million of us—but most surviving Ooloms could afford upscale residences in the Thin Interior, playground communities nestled in the skyscraper trees of ancient forests and jungle. They had an unshakable passion for the deep woods; so they hired us humans to work in Oolom-owned offices and factories, while they retired to soar through the canopy in genteel indolence. Even not-so-flush Ooloms headed treeward, if only to work as servants/accountants/dogsbodies to the truly well heeled. For them, any job in the Big Green was better than facing the urban gray.

For twenty years after the plague, then, Demoth sorted itself out . . . Ooloms settling down in their posh isolated villages, while *Homo saps* found their own places on islands and coastal plains—anywhere close to sea level, where the air was thick enough for human lungs to bite into.

And for twenty years after the plague, I sorted myself out too . . . until finally, at the age of thirty-five, I walked into Bonaventure's office of the College Vigilant to ask how I could join.

I'd had jobs before. "Warm-body" jobs like keeping an eye on nanotech-performance monitors, or hauling drums of proto-nute to houses whose food synthesizers weren't hooked up to the mains. I'd also had "Faye" jobs like prancing the puss in stripperamas, or nude modeling for local artists. (A lot of sculptors loved the button scars on my arms, where I used to have freckles.)

But mostly I bared the butt for Ooloms. Oolom men

found human women outrageously, capaciously sexy because we were so *big*. Torso big, I mean—they couldn't care less about cleavage or crotch, but they turned goggle-eyed at the expanse of a human back. Their own Oolom females were so much thinner . . . and some quirk of the Oolom male psyche had a gut reaction, thickness = arousal. "You're so *wide*!" one admirer crooned to me.

Gives a whole new meaning to calling women "broads."

Some of the other strippers, the ones who flicked tricks on the side, told me their customers often took a woman's shoulder measurements so they could brag to the boys back home. Considering my own mesomorph build, I could have been the choice rumpus room of the back streets . . . but I never sank quite that far. I'd take off my clothes for money—where was the crime in treating myself like meat?—but selling my swish was just too disloyal to my spouses.

They were my family. I could devalue myself, but not them.

Which meant that as years went on, as Darlene and Angie and Lynn all had children, I gradually spent more time home helping with the kids than playing Miss Udder around town. The children called me "Mom-Faye" . . . not the same tug on the heart as plain old "Mom," but I was too much the coward to have babies of my own: afraid it would change me, afraid that it wouldn't.

Even just being Mom-Faye changed me in time. You know how it goes: after a full day of feeding/bathing/diapering, you're too tired to spark out for a night strutting bare-ass, and doing squats with a barbell, naked. You say, "I'll cheapen myself tomorrow" . . . and tomorrow and tomorrow and tomorrow, creeps in this petty pace till you wake one day, look in the mirror, and don't straight off feel disgust. Such a shock. That your soul may not be an irredeemable cesspool.

Then quick, while you're still brave, ask yourself what

you'd want to do with your mortal existence if the universe weren't a total dog's vomit.

What do you want? To live in the real. To name the lies. *Wa supesh i rabi ganosh.* An aspiration you haven't let yourself think about for twenty years . . . but when you ask, it's right on top of your mind, like the perfume of roses coming from a locked cupboard.

"This is the only thing in my head that approaches an honest dream. So why in the name of Mary and all her saints don't I get off my cowardly butt and make this happen?"

The Vigil accepted my application on the spot. They accepted everyone's application on the spot. If you weren't proctor material, they had seven years of brutal training to weed you out.

A student of the College Vigilant. Just like that.

My family treated it as a lark. "I always like when you get an enthusiasm," Lynn told me. "You're such less trouble for a while . . . till someone pisses you off, and you chuck everything with loose ends dangling." She said the same when I took up piano, and when I bought all those awful chairs to learn reupholstering. The younger kids giggled about Mom-Faye getting into politics, the older kids did impersonations of me losing my temper at a bureaucrat ("Oh you think you're a clever little man, do you?"), and all four of my husbands asked, "How much will this cost?"

The unsupportive sods.

I studied. Classes, sims, direct info braingrabs. Most of the work I did over the world-net; but when I needed face-to-face, I turned to the proctors in town, the ones who scrutinized Bonaventure City Council—a dozen sharp-witted people, generously serving as teachers and mentors during my seven years as student. Three were human; the rest were Oolom, living among *Homo saps* for the good of the Vigil.

The Ooloms treated me with sunbeam kindness . . .

even as they perched on my shoulders to add more weight when I did push-ups. They knew the Vigil had to build back its numbers, and that meant encouraging anyone who could grit through the training. Even with two decades to recover from the epidemic, the Vigil was running strapped, barely enough proctors to scrutinize the governments of our world.

I grew stronger, more disciplined. That was the easy part. The hard part was yanking myself out of a pit of cynicism twenty years deep, up to a place where maybe I could believe in an ideal or two. When I talked to fellow students, lots of them felt the same way. They'd gloated when signing up for the Vigil: keen for the chance to rip into politicians, to show up important people as fools and to tell the world, "There, you blind buggers, that's the brainless corrupt government you elected."

But.

The Vigil wasn't about humiliating bad guys. It wasn't about punishing bureaucrats if they disregarded the side effects of some proposed bill. There were no scorecards, no banners, no late-night celebrations where senior proctors offered you champagne toasts for making heads roll.

When you succeeded, government worked better. Passed good laws. Met the public need. That was your sole reward—real people became better off. Safer, or more prosperous, or more blessed by intangibles. (Art. Freedom. Clean air.)

It takes time to shift your outlook: you start by thinking all politics is rat puke, all politicos are hypocrites, and oh, it'll be rare delicious to kneecap the bastards; but you end simply looking at laws, not lawmakers, and believing there is such a thing as attainable good.

Idealism. I, Faye Smallwood, was capable of idealism.

It surprised the bejeezus out of me.

I graduated from the College Vigilant in the twenty-seventh year after the plague. Standard Earth Technocracy years, not local ones: A.D. 2454. I had just turned forty-two.

My family threw me a surprise party the night before *müshor*: my rite of passage into the Vigil itself. Of course I knew the party was coming—our whole blessed household tittered with whispers, conversations stopping or lurching to silliness when I walked into the room—and I grumbled to myself about the obligation to act surprised when the moment came. Didn't I have other things to do? Weren't there a million last-minute details before heading for the Vigil Proving Center?

But I should have known better than to get the growls. My family made me happy . . . not through festive inventiveness, but just companionship and gold-hearted loyalty. When the lager'n'biscuits ran out, the other women shooed the men away, declared it ''Sleepover Night for the Fortyish Fraus,'' then took me jointly to bed.

And here I thought I'd have to *act* surprised.

Twenty-four hours later, my skull top was missing, and I had far too clear a view of my own pink brain. In a mirror. While surgeons planted a link-seed in my corpus callosum.

Müshor. My second birth.

This brain surgery, *müshor*, was the secret hinge of separation between the Vigil and others on Demoth. All those earlier years of training were skim-milk rehearsal for the real transition: *Homo sapiens* to *Homo vigilans*.

Becoming a different organism. Blessed near a different species.

Here's the thing: joining the Vigil rewired your brain.

Years ago, I'd wondered how Zillif could link to the datasphere when she was paralyzed. How did she work the keys on her access implant? Answer: there were no keys. The implant was a link-seed, embedded directly inside her head.

And now I had one too.

Over the two-week retreat of *müshor*, the seed would

sprout faux-neural tendrils, nano-thin vines threading through my cerebellum like parietal ivy. The creepers were electrotropic, drawn by EM sparks; they'd infiltrate the regions of my gray matter where neurons fired most profusely. The LGN and visual cortex. Broca's and Wernicke's language centers. A smattering of sites in the so-called reptile brain, controlling my heart, lungs and digestion. Once those major roots were established, the link-seed would take its time spreading into areas of lesser activity.

My memory.

My muscular coordination.

My dreams.

Two weeks to a brand-new me. And the moment the surgeons closed my skull, a ruthless black clock started ticking. Tick tock, tick tock, adapt or die.

They laid me in a room with cool blue walls. An electronic nurse clamped itself to my wrists and ankles—if something went wrong, mere human reflexes wouldn't be fast enough to save me.

Three times out of a hundred, electronic reflexes weren't fast enough either.

There's one brutal reason why few people on Demoth or elsewhere have direct brain-links to the datasphere. The technology is centuries-old, simple, inexpensive . . . but it takes granite-hard discipline to use without blowing out your frontal lobes.

Each year, for example, a handful of ambitious business execs bribe some less-than-scrupulous surgeon to plant link-seeds in their brains. The witless saps dream of getting an edge on the competition; they salivate at the thought of instant data access, with no risk of being overheard whispering to a wrist-implant. "And discipline?" they say. "*I've* got discipline. I didn't bludgeon my way to CEO of Vulture Incorporated without having discipline."

Believing a link-seed is just a faster, hookup-free method of direct braingrab.

Two days later, all blissful confidence, they try their first unfiltered download. A market quotation on some stock they think is important. Which drags along quotations on related stocks. Then the whole financial sector. Then the entire planetary market, and markets on other planets, and every corporation prospectus registered with the InHand Exchange, and quarterly economic statistics on every planet in the Technocracy, not to mention major trading partners and up-League envoys . . .

Like trying to sip from a firehose. Only in this case, the firehose sprays info-acid all over your hippocampus.

The condition is called "data tumor." A possibility I faced myself, lying in that cool blue room.

If I was lucky, the electronic nurse would raise a baffle field before it was too late. Block the incoming flood by broadcasting static—jam me into radio isolation from the datasphere till the surgeons could remove enough of the link-seed that it stopped working. If the nurse was a microsecond slow in detecting a tumor bloom, I would sit there stat-shocked while the link-fibers in my brain got toasty warm from the electrical activity of downloading reams of bumpf.

What do you think happens when a network of molecule-thin wire heats a few hundred degrees inside your brain? Cauterization. Blood brought to the boil. High-pressure juices squirting out the edges of your eye sockets.

The College Vigilant had made me watch a doc-chip of patients collapsing in data tumor. Don't ask me which was worse: the sights I saw before the camera lens got blotted red, or the sounds I heard after. But neither the sights nor the sounds were pleasant things to remember while lying in a cool blue room.

There was precious little time to feel my way forward—the link-seed spread its tendrils unstoppably, connecting to new neuron clusters every second. Sixty seconds every minute, favoring me with a tinnitus of hiss in my left ear, then a spasm of muscles in my lower back, then a flash enhancement of color sense in my right eye. (Cool blue chilling left, electric blue stabbing right.)

Lying in an empty room, clamped down by a nurse machine that loomed over me like a spider . . . rippled by sensations that were all in my brain . . . no clear line between waking hallucinations and dreams when I fell asleep . . . nightmares of being raped by some metal monster that pinioned my body, impaled my mind. . . .

I want to tell you how it changed me. I do. But like making love or throwing punches in a fistfight, some experiences can't be broken down into words. There's no way to tell everything, everything all at once. You have to pretend there's a throughline, a sequence . . . when the whole point is it's happening simultaneously, all your brain cells firing together. Sensations in your body, in your eyes, in your ears, bristling along your skin, rasping in your throat, pressing sharp on your stomach, squeezing around your temples, burning in your chest. And those are just the chance physical offshoots of becoming a link-trellis, transient side effects of the tendrils snaking through your mind. There's also the gasping moment when a vine tip pierces a pleasure center. Or a pain center. Or, by ugly coincidence of timing, both at once.

Emotions float up. You find yourself crushed with soul-ripper grief, weeping in heartbreak for ten bleary seconds till suddenly everything switches to funny, which infuriates you, which depresses you, which bores you, which makes you feel wise as an angel, then wicked as an imp.

All you can hold on to is your Vigil-trained discipline: keep breathing, one breath at a time, take in what's tearing you up without trying to fight it. Observe it without trying to process it. Get out of your head, because your head is damn-fool busy. Let everything come, let it pass, let the changes happen.

The seconds pass, sixty seconds to a minute. What you are is just what you are, not what you have to be.

There's no linear unfolding. With a link-seed, input comes to your brain in gestalt, an instantaneous neural activation matrix: not this-then-that, but a billion neuron clusters simultaneously receiving their piece of the whole, a single gush of comprehension.

Everything all at once.

On the third day of *müshor*, third day of delirium, I nearly lost my grip. Battered weary by emotions, delusions, physical jiggery-pokery (itches, stabbing pains, dead numbness), wanting to shout, "Stop, leave me be, let me rest!" . . . my mind suddenly filled with the image of a peacock's tail. Green and gold and purple and blue, a hundred eyes wide-open, watching me with all the calm in the universe. Colors fanned over every grain of my vision; I couldn't feel my body, no artificial prod to laugh or cry, nothing in me but the sight of that tail, reaching high as the stars and low as the planet's core, filling my thoughts, my world.

And the sound of it: feathers rattling, demanding attention. Look at me. *Look* at me.

Placid. Even affectionate.

I don't know how long the moment lasted. Long enough. The peacock eventually fractured into another donkeydump of sensations, smells that whistled, bright kicks to the stomach (each one a different color) . . . but I could handle the new barrage. I was surfacing now, swimming toward the light; I'd passed through the center of *müshor* and was coming out the other side.

At the time, it puzzled me why the eye of my personal hurricane was a peacock's tail. I didn't have long to ponder the question—too many distracting fireworks going on inside my head. Later, looking back, I shrugged off the vision as random mental floss, some piece of neural flotsam my brain happened to seize on as a life preserver.

I was flagrantly, hubrisly, witlessly wrong.

At the end of *müshor*, my brain was still in one piece. Not boiled in its own juices. And cleaned-purged-regenerated, the way you feel after a pummeling-hard work out.

But different. Transformed.

Link-seeds do more than just provide passive information from the world-soul. More even than giving your senses a friendly boost and speeding your reflexes cat-nimble. Those are minor perks, side effects of having new, electron-fast pathways routed through your brain.

Here's the thing: a link-seed destroys your capacity to ignore.

As simple as that. As devastating too.

That's why you become a new person. Why the Vigil works, without turning petty or abusing its power.

When I download information from the world-soul now, it becomes a direct part of me. Unfiltered. I can't skip past any parts that jar with my vision of the universe. I can't discard facts I'd prefer not to know. They're all incorporated, instantly-directly-viscerally, into what I am. Into the physical structure of my brain. The primal configuration matrix.

Unlike bits of info I read or hear through conversation, a direct linkload is unmediated. Raw. Undeniably present. Unavoidably transformative.

I can't pretend new data doesn't exist—it's already changed me. It's molded my thoughts, reweighted my synapses, overwritten whatever I was before. I can't even *want* to ignore the input, because it's already there.

No sublimation. No turning a blind eye to unlikable facts. The link-seed left me wide-open. Vulnerable to storms and stars.

And that openness gushed over into the rest of my life. Not just with dry downloads from the datasphere, but things that were already in my brain. I couldn't dismiss them for my own smug convenience. I couldn't look away. Which is the very definition of a proctor: someone who doesn't/won't/can't look away. Someone immune to the blind wishful thinking that infects all politics like the clap. Someone who doesn't just call a spade a spade, but who *sees* the damned spade is a spade, without thinking maybe it could turn into a backhoe with the right tax incentives.

It's not virtue or saintliness; it's just the way my new brain works. Of course, there are still thresholds—I'm not mesmerized by every speck of dust that drifts past my eye, nor do I think deeply over every word and inflection that reaches my ear.

But . . . I no longer ignore the obvious. I'm mentally, physically, incapable of that. Selective inattention is for sissies.

I shiver brain-naked in the data flow. Aware to my very gut that actions have consequences, and unable to dupe myself otherwise.

A member of the Vigil.

4

THE PEACOCK'S TAIL

The Vigil left me two weeks free after *müshor*. Recovery time. Rearrangement time. A chance to clear the decks.

I no longer needed the electronic nurse perched over me, but data tumor was still a possibility. A white-knuckled looming terror if the truth be told. And data tumor was just the messiest way I could stop being me; there were other more subtle ways the link-seed could wipe out the Faye Smallwood I'd known. Facts and memes infecting my unprotected brain. Long-loved perceptions swept away, erased by casual input . . . because I deep-down believed I was so full of crap, when pure truths started coming in, not a drop of the old Faye would be able to stand up for itself.

Of course, I'd fretted over the same dreads before getting the link-seed . . . but my old brain could repress the fear, pretend things wouldn't be so bad. I could watch the doc-chip of that data-tumor victim spewing blood out his eyes, and I could say, "He must have been a weak-willed mook." Ignoring that the dead man had slaved through the same Vigil training I had, and passed the same tests to prove he was ready for a link-seed.

But now that I'd gone through *müshor* ... my altered brain had lost the knack of shying away from uncomfortable truths. And I was scared, scared, scared.

The day I came back from the Proving Center, Angie's son Shaw asked me to do a trick—to show off what the new Mom-Faye could do, tell what the weather was like right now in Comfort Bight. (The biggest city on Demoth, ten thousand klicks to the southwest, sprawled around the mouth of the only major river running through the Ragged Desert.)

Shaw was just curious, an eight-year-old boy making a let's-see request ... but I broke down in flash-flood tears. I didn't want to let anything into my brain unsupervised, even a simple "Force one sandstorm, toxicity B, expected duration two hours ..."

Uh-oh.

The weather report had seeped in from the world-soul without me consciously asking for it. My bout of the weeps got swallowed by cold, cold terror.

I couldn't control the seed. Data tumor coming up.

But nothing dramatic happened. *Not this time*, I thought after a full minute of waiting. *Maybe the next.*

That night I got out my scalpel—the one I'd used when I cut off my freckles all that time ago. In the angry dark days of my teens and twenties, I'd sometimes just rest the blade against my skin, or trace little patterns ... very lightly, more of a game than serious intent. I lost points if I actually drew blood.

It'd been years since I last took out the knife. I'd pulled myself together, hadn't I? There was nothing driving me to hurt myself now. And if I was scared to shivers about data tumor, surely I could find a more comforting talisman to hold than razor-sharp steel. Something I could sleep with under my pillow and not worry about accidentally nicking a vein.

I sat naked on the edge of my bed and slowly laid the

back of the blade onto my bare thigh—not the sharp side, just the back. That was all right, wasn't it? That was only goofing around.

A link-seed means you can't lie to yourself.

I found my eyes filling with tears as I thought, "It was supposed to be all better now. I've fixed everything, I've passed *müshor*, I shouldn't still be crazy."

Gradually, the cold scalpel warmed to the heat of my skin. After a while, I couldn't feel it anymore—light, thin metal, matching my body temperature . . . as if it still knew the trick of becoming part of me, after all these years.

Eventually I managed to put the scalpel away, without ever touching the sharp edge to my flesh. But I couldn't bring myself to stash it back in its dark, hard-to-reach hiding place at the rear of my closet. The poor knife would be so lonely back there.

I put it in my purse.

The time came for me to stop hiding mopey at home and get out to work: on City Council docket 11-28, "A Bill to Improve Water-Treatment Facilities in Bonaventure." Mine to scrutinize. Honest-to-God legislation placed in the fear-damp hands of Faye H. Smallwood, Proctor-Probationary.

"Probationary" meant I had an advisor peering over my shoulder through the scrutiny process: a sober, uncle-ish Oolom named Chappalar. When I first started my studies for the Vigil, Chappalar had struck me as bashful near humans, always half a step back and matching the color of the walls. He windled around town on foot rather than gliding because it bothered him to be the only flying figure in the sky. Each time before a global election, he petitioned the Vigil for transfer to anywhere with more Oolooms . . . and each time after, he put on a brave face when he found himself reposted to Bonaventure.

Lately though, Chappalar had perked up something

considerable. Office gossip said he'd been seen sashaying with a silver-haired *Homo sap* woman, variously described as quiet, chatty, or somewhere in between. Translation: no one had actually talked to her; people had just spied from a distance and invented stories to suit their own tastes.

The usual naysayers tried to stir up a fuss about "mixed relationships," but no one paid attention. Humans and Divian sub-breeds had been doing the dance ever since our races made contact centuries ago. Ever since . . . well, it's queer to picture the League of Peoples as matchmaking yentas, but after our wave of humans left Earth in the twenty-first century, every alien race we encountered said, "Ooo, you've just *got* to meet the Divians. You have so much in common!"

The Divians lived nowhere near *Homo sap* space—the closest planet of the Divian Spread lay hundreds of parsecs from New Earth. But continuous nudges from other League members pushed us out for what amounted to a set-up blind date: first contact on the moon of an ice giant halfway between our home systems.

And surprise, surprise, we hit it off.

Our two species *are* precious close to each other in basic anatomy, intelligence level, evolutionary history . . . light-years closer than any other species we've encountered in the League. Yes, Divians change colors and have ears like grapefruit nailed to their heads; but when they and *Homo saps* got together, it wasn't like meeting aliens. More like tagging up with someone from the far side of your own planet—quaint accent and a bag of bewildering customs, but basically a regular joe who shares a slew of your interests.

Curiosity gets piqued. Bonds form.

As for species differences, you can prize them as exotic novelties rather than obstacles. Spice. They give you something to giggle over in the wee hours of the morning.

Understand, I'm talking about Chappalar and his friend now. Because I'm a married woman.

*   *   *

The gist of Bon Cty Ccl 11-28 was improving two water-treatment plants around town; ergo, to kick off our scrutiny of the bill, Chappalar and I decided to tour those plants. We also decided to tour the three plants that *weren't* scheduled for upgrades . . . partly for comparison, and partly to make sure city council was putting money where funds were needed most. (Fact: some plant managers are more likable/persuasive/politically connected than others. Guess whose plants get financial handouts. While plants run by folks who are unpopular/undemanding/unrelated to the mayor only get significant allocations when equipment falls to pieces. Or when the Vigil gets loud and cranky in council meetings.)

All of which meant that my first official act as proctor was a tour of Pump Station 3, just beyond the petting zoo on the edge of Cabot Park.

It was the butt end of winter in Bonaventure. Snow still sat in sodden clumps on the ground, but you could feel the kiss of spring in the air: a licky toddler's kiss that smeared your skin wet with condensation. The city's first thaw of the year. No one was fooled by it—Great St. Caspian winters never surrendered graciously—but give or take a few more bitch-slapping blizzards, greener times were on their way.

My stroll from home followed the shore of Coal Smear Creek, where park staff had just posted THIN ICE signs: those red-and-black ones with sensors that trigger sirens if someone steps off the bank. You need such precautions in Cabot Park; all winter, kids use the frozen creek for hockey or figure skating (Oolom kids for ice-sailing), and they hate to quit as long as the surface looks solid. Even with the signs, one or two dunces take a through-the-ice soaker every year . . . as Lynn's son Leo could attest. Except that Leo never breathes a word about what happened. It's Lynn herself who tells the story every time Leo brings a girl home.

Anyway. Picture a gray winter morning, with mist in

the hollows, and moist air that doesn't feel cold even if it's only three degrees above freezing. The thaw has begun, trickling along the cement walkways and dripping out of the trees. Life is stirring from hibernation, and even a woman with poison ivy in her brain can let herself loosen up.

I remember the snowstriders that morning—white birds running across the top of the drifts. Every few seconds, they'd plunge their beaks through the crust and pull out frostfly cocoons to gobble. Like all native Demoth birds, they had no real feathers; instead they were coated in downy clouds of fuzz, giving them the look of ankle-high dust balls with small snowshoed feet.

Suddenly, the striders scree-scree-screeched and took to their wings; they'd spotted a looming shadow floating above the snowscape. Hoar falcon? Kite-manta?

Without a sound, Chappalar landed on the path beside me. Out for an early-morning glide. All by himself. And he had the air of a man who'd be wearing a huge smile, if he were the sort of man who wore huge smiles.

"Good morning, Proctor Faye," he said. "Lovely day." Like most older Ooloms, he'd learned English from braingrab lessons originally coded on New Earth. It gave him a la-di-dah mainstream accent that always sounded snooty to my MaryMarch ears.

"Good morning yourself, you," I told him. "You're looking like the cat that went down on the canary. Pleasant night, was it? You slept well? In good company?"

His outer ear sheaths flicked closed in a split second, then inched back open—the Oolom equivalent of a blush. "*Sé holo leejemm*," he muttered. You hear too much. "Sometimes I find humans disturbingly intuitive."

"Only the women," I said. "So you had a willywag night?"

"I passed an agreeable evening," he answered primly.

"*Sé julo leejedd*," I told him. I'm hearing too little. "Don't you know *Homo saps* live for juicy gossip?"

He didn't reply right away; but he walked with a rare

bounce to his step, even for an Oolom. (They always bounce—they're light, and their glider membranes catch the breeze. On windy days, Oolooms think nothing of linking arms with any human who's walking the same direction, using you for an anchor to keep from blowing away. At least, that's the story I get from all the Oolom men who latch on to me in the street.)

Bounce, bounce, bounce. Finally Chappalar broke the silence. "Her name is Maya. Human, but you don't know her. One hundred and ten years old, but she has never missed a YouthBoost treatment. She is in excellent physical health."

I snickered. YouthBoost kept us all in "excellent physical health." If Chappalar mentioned it, he must have been struck by some wonderment of Maya's condition. Perhaps she was a *wide* woman.

"Tell Mom-Faye all about it," I said, taking him gleefully by the arm.

"Tell Mom-Faye my lips are sealed," he replied, detaching himself pointedly. "Whatever goes on between people is either private or universal. I shall not divulge the private, and you can download the universal yourself."

By which I suppose he meant picking up some Oolom/human porn-chips. No need, Chappalar-boy, no need. I'd seen enough of those in my dissolute past to know the basic interspecies geometries. What I wanted now were pure vicarious specifics.

But no matter how I wheedled, Chappalar refused to give blow-by-bump details of the night before. Truth to tell, he didn't speak much at all. He was too busy smiling, bouncing, soaking up the feel of the thaw. I could guess how his mind was fluttering with the inevitable morning-after speculations. Does she really . . . What if she . . . Should I . . . How soon can we . . .

"You're so cute," I told him.

Maybe he didn't hear—he kept closing his ear-lids tight as if he wanted to be alone with his thoughts, then opening them wide as if he wanted to embrace every sound in the world.

Christ, he made me want to fall fresh in love myself. Good weather for it too. I broke into a jog to keep up with his bounce.

The pump station formed one wall of the Cabot Park petting zoo—three stories high (the wall), fifty meters long, covered with a glossy mosaic of a woodland that had never existed. By some rare magic, this forest combined Earth cedars, Divian sugar-saps, and Demoth raspfeather palms. (Truth to tell, I'd never seen a real Earth tree outside VR; just a few potted saplings at the NatHist Museum in Pistolet. No Demoth government would be daft enough to endanger the local ecology, letting people plant alien trees out in the open.)

The petting zoo had the same kind of contrived crossmix as the trees in the mosaic. From Earth, donkeys and sheep; from the Divian homeworld, domesticated orts (chicken-sized pterodactyls, given to annoying squawks but gentle with children); and from Demoth itself, fuzzworms and leaners. (Fuzzworms resemble rolls of frayed brown carpet—boring to look at, but furry-soft to pet. Leaners are herd animals, like morose short-legged goats with the hides of armadillos. In the wild, they like to rest by leaning against rocks and trees; in the zoo, they flop themselves against the legs of visitors, gravely staring up into your face with a wrinkled, "You don't mind, do you?" expression.)

As Chappalar and I crossed the zoo grounds, two leaners followed us . . . one clearly hoping we'd brought sponge-corn from the concession stand, the other a robot chaperoning the first. Every real creature in Cabot Park had a look-alike robot companion, programmed to make sure normal animal behavior didn't become too much of a nuisance. If, for example, the leaner chose me as its resting post, all well and good (apart from mud stains and leaner smell on my parka); but if the beast went for Chappalar, the robot would cut in like Dads at a dance party, standing sentry between Chappalar and the leaner till the animal went elsewhere.

Here's the thing: an adult *Homo sap* could hold the leaner's weight easily. Chappalar, though, would be knocked ass over teakettle and possibly crushed. Leaners never got it through their dumpy heads that even though Ooloms looked tall and strong, they were actually breakably light. Ergo the need for robot lifeguards—otherwise, the League of Peoples would ask why we let potentially dangerous animals get rough on our sentient citizens.

The League had very strict rules against putting sentients at needless risk. Either you followed those rules, or you got declared non-sentient yourself.

You didn't want that. The League also had very strict rules for dealing with dangerous non-sentient creatures.

The door to the pump-station building was locked. Routine safety precaution? Or was some paranoid someone truly worried about saboteurs tampering with the city water supply? No. Most likely the staff locked the door for fear some leaner might rest against it and accidentally push it open. Before long, the plant would be full of orts and donkeys, not to mention sheep drowning themselves in the filtration vats. Who wants woolly water?

The mosaicked wall had an intercom screen embedded beside the door; I could easily call someone to let us in. But what would Chappalar think? We'd agreed on an unannounced visit . . . not an all-out catch-them-with-their-pants-down raid, but still we didn't want to give the staff time to prepare a show. ("Oh yes, Ms. Proctor ma'am, we surely need all the cash you can funnel our way.")

I glanced at Chappalar. He'd taken his cue from the leaners and propped himself back-against the building's wall. A creamy dreamy expression settled on his face as he started to turn pointillist, color-matching the teeny mosaic tiles of gloss-fired clay. The perfect picture of a man in reverie over his new girlfriend . . . not at all waiting to see if I was too wimp-gutless to use my link-seed.

Closing my eyes, I reluctantly reached out to the world-soul: my first deliberate brain-to-byte contact with the collective machine intelligence that permeated every digital circuit on Demoth . . . including the axonal vines through my brain and whatever computerized locking device kept the pump-station door closed. *Faye Smallwood of the Vigil*, I thought, silently projecting the words toward the door. *Please grant me entrance.* (The same formal way I used to speak to my wrist-implant . . . which, by the by, had got removed during *müshor*, to avoid radio interference between it and my link-seed. Since then, my wrist had felt so indecent-naked, I'd taken to wearing a rack of cheap bracelets.)

My *Open sesame* signal traveled like radio fizz out through my link-seed and into the closest datasphere receiver cell, then shunted through a slew of relays to the world-soul core. My identity got verified; likewise the identity of the lock I wanted to open. (The Vigil could pop locks in public buildings, but not private residences.) In less than a second, the door gave a soft click. I pulled it open and offered Chappalar a weak smile . . . mostly sick relief my head hadn't exploded.

Without losing his dreamy expression, Chappalar said, "Next time before you open a door, tap into any available security cameras to see what's on the other side. On *my* first scrutiny, I nearly got impaled by a forklift that happened to be passing. The door was locked specifically to prevent such accidents." He smiled and gestured toward the entranceway. "After you."

No forklifts inside . . . just a fiddly-dick locker room where workers stored their street clothes. Some of the staff had hung private trinkets on their lockers—a photo of someone's family, a wire-painted miniature of the Blessed Mother Mary, the green-on-gray insignia of Bonaventure's premier boat-racing team—but overall, the room had a spartan feel, whitewashed concrete, sucked dry of personality.

"Is there a city ordinance against dressing up your work area?" I asked Chappalar.

"Pump stations have to meet sanitation standards," he replied. "Some plant managers interpret those standards more rigorously than others."

"You know the manager then?"

"I know everyone who works for the city. You will too."

I'd already memorized the names of plant staff, and downloaded their files from the civic databanks. (Not through my link-seed. Through the one hard-copy feedback in the Vigil offices.) The manager of Pump Station 3 was Elizabeth Tupper, age sixty-two, employed by the city works since humans took over Bonaventure. No complaints registered against her from above or below: she'd never screwed up badly enough for higher-ups to notice, and never harassed her subordinates to the point where they lodged an official protest.

You could say the same for almost every bureaucrat in town. I wished the employment records would say things like, "Plodding but competent," or "Goat-wanking control freak." Too bad they didn't let *me* make up the checkboxes on performance-review forms.

Chappalar moved ahead of me, holding his arms crossed against his chest so his gliders were folded tight to his body. The walkway forward was camel-eye narrow; if he hadn't trimmed his sails, they would have brushed against lockers on both sides, knocking off all the hung decorations. I followed, tucking my arms in too—I didn't have Chappalar's wingspan, but how often do I have to use the word "Amazonian" before you figure out I'm a big old girl?

Probably three times less than I've used it already. Redundancy, thy name is Faye.

Beyond the lockers lurked the vat room: a chamber the size of a skating rink, dominated by massive metal tanks.

Water from the local aquifer got pumped up from below, fed through a line of processing vats and squirted out the other end, purified of toxic metals and native Demoth microbes. This station was supposed to have three working lines of four vats each; but the two oldest lines had been jinxed with mechanical gremlins over the past year, forcing the staff to hammer away at stubborn pumps, jammed stir-paddles, and hiccuppy valves. Scarcely a week passed that one line didn't conk out for a day or so . . . and over last Diaspora weekend, both bad lines went tits up together.

No wonder city council wanted to rip out the old and put in state-of-the-art replacements. The only question was why they'd let the place degrade so badly to begin with. Elizabeth Tupper, plant manager, must have really cranked someone off.

The moment Chappalar and I entered, we could tell which two lines were on the futz: the ones that were half-dismantled, their high-up access panels open to expose wiring and plastic tubes. A pair of wheelstand stairways had been rolled up to the guts of the nearest vat, as if two workers had been poking around side by side, consulting with each other on how to get a bit more service out of the heap of junk . . . but no one was there now.

No one anywhere in sight.

I turned to Chappalar. "They're all on rest break?"

He shrugged. "Could be a staff meeting."

"The regular staff meeting is tomorrow."

Chappalar would have known the schedule if he'd done his homework on the plant . . . but then, he'd been busy playing lose the spoon with Maya, hadn't he? Anyway, this scrutiny had got docketed under my name, so I was the one supposed to know the facts. In his way, Chappalar was giving me a vote of confidence—trust I would cover the background trivia so he wouldn't have to.

"Even if it's not time for the regular meeting," Chappalar said, "Ms. Tupper might have called an impromptu one. Perhaps she assembled the crew so she could distrib-

ute a memo on putting away one's tools.'' He rolled his
eyes. I was beginning to get a picture of Ms. Memo-
Making Tupper. "Or," Chappalar went on, "they may
have received a delivery of spare parts at the other door,
and everyone's helping unload.''

Possible. Plausible. Considering the rat's banquet of
pipe and cable strewn round the floor, they must send out
for spare parts frequently. Still . . . the place seemed
needle-nick quiet. And abandoned. I was getting a case
of the hinkies, some of that "human intuition" Chappalar
grumbled about.

"Let's keep on our toes," I told him, keeping my voice
low. "This is making me edgy.''

He gave me a look—a studiedly neutral look reserved
for first-time proctors who talk like escapees from a melo-
drama. Then again, his inner ear-sheaths lowered a fraction, letting him listen better for suspicious sounds. He
was giving me the benefit of the doubt, even if he thought
I was overreacting.

Warily, I moved forward. Chappalar followed. As we
drew level with the stairways up to the vat controls, I
yielded to impulse and climbed the steps—up two full
stories above the ground till I was face-to-face with a
jumble of fiber optics and plumbing.

Chappalar flapped up beside me and landed lightly on
the other set of stairs. His head suddenly jerked; he put a
hand to his cheek. "Wet." He looked down and pointed
to a black poly pipe just below eye level; it had a pinhole
in it, shooting up a thin spray of water that had hit him
in the face.

"That can't be good," I said.

"Not unless you're in need of a shower." He ducked
around the spray and leaned forward to peer at the pipe.
"There's more corrosion here than just that pinhole. Look
at this wire. See where the insulation is missing?''

I leaned in beside him. Yes: specks of damage on several wires, on the pipe, and on the readout of a nearby

pressure monitor. I could pick up something else too—a sharp scent that curled my nose hairs.

"Acid," I whispered.

"What do you mean?"

"I can smell it."

"Oh." Ooloms flip-flop in their respect for the *Homo sap* nose. Sometimes they act as if they don't believe in smell at all, as if we're shamming our ability to use a sense they don't have. Other times they treat us with something close to awe: astounding creatures that we are, privy to profound sensations that are hidden from their race.

This time, Chappalar decided to be impressed. "What type of acid is it?" he asked.

"Don't know." I could have downloaded the world-soul's library of smells, to compare this pickly odor to the ones on file; but what would be the point? Showing off to Chappalar? And did I want to fill my brain with a catalogue of bitter stinks?

Our cowardly Faye, rationalizing. To avoid taking another kick at the data-tumor can.

"Who cares what acid it is?" I said briskly. "The question is where it came from."

Chappalar looked disappointed at the fickleness of my nose; but he turned back to the innards of the control panel. "I can't imagine why anything here would leak acid. Pumping and filtration equipment shouldn't use strong chemicals. I suppose there might be batteries, for backup power supply if the main current goes out . . ."

He scanned the pipes upward, searching for a source of the spill. I didn't. I'd memorized schematics of all the equipment in the plant; nothing used so much as a dribble of high-corrosive.

"This is all wrong," I muttered. "I'm going to call Protection Central."

"Faye." You didn't need sensitive Oolom ears to hear the reproof in Chappalar's voice. "This is your first scrutiny," he said, "and you're ready to see everything as suspicious. I was the same when I started. But think—this is just a water-treatment plant, in a quiet city on a quiet planet. Nothing sinister goes on here. My guess is the workers were just cleaning out pipes with an acid wash. They spilled some, everyone rushed to the first-aid station or the shower, and . . ."

His ear-lids suddenly opened wider.

"What?" I whispered. A moment later I heard the sound too: footsteps tapping toward us from the far end of the room.

Chappalar gave me a gentle smile, with only a hint of I-told-you-so. "Hello!" he called. "We're from the Vigil."

The footsteps sped up. In a moment, two figures hove into view at the bottom of the stairs below us—a man and a woman, both human, wearing the standard gray overalls of city maintenance staff. They looked mainstreet-ordinary: in their thirties, one Asian, one Cauc, both with shoulder-length black hair.

Just one problem: I'd gone through the files on everyone who worked here. The files included ID photos; and these two people weren't in the pictures.

"Good morning," Chappalar was saying. "We've come to look around . . ."

He began to lift his arms as if he intended to launch off the stairs and glide down to the newcomers. Bolt-fast I grabbed him, pulling him back. He gave me a wounded look. "Please, Faye; this kind of behavior . . ."

That's when the folks on the ground drew their pistols.

I only had an instant to recognize the weapons: jelly guns, able to shoot a blob of sticky goo up to forty meters where it would splatter on impact. Police loaded them with clots of neural-scrambling syrup—even if the shot didn't hit you dead on, one tiny splash touching bare skin would send frazzled messages to your brain, interfering with most motor functions. *Petit mal* on a plate.

Somehow, though, I didn't think the guns pointed my

way were filled with knockout paste. I could almost smell the acid inside, gluey wads of it, that would cling to your skin like tar and eat straight down to the bone.

With simultaneous coughs, the pistols fired.

Standing out in the open up a flight of stairs, two stories above the floor, nothing behind me but a copper-solid wall of pipes and wires . . . I had nowhere to run. Yes I ducked, and I pulled down Chappalar too, though I knew it wouldn't help—the whole point of a jelly gun is its splash, its knack for spattering you with droplets even if you dodge from ground zero. In a second I'd be sprayed with burning slush . . .

. . . except that Chappalar snapped up his gliders like a membranous shield.

I don't know how he knew the attack was coming—he had his back to the shooters. Maybe he was just trying to catch his balance after I pulled at him . . . but his sails spread wide, flat to the incoming wads, and the shots broke against him with a sharp double-splat.

The air blossomed with acid's bitter reek. Chappalar screamed.

He toppled forward, collapsing onto me—his moaning body so light, the weight was like a flimsy coat stand holding a single burning cloak. Twin splash patterns of acid speckled his back and gliders . . . and each droplet was starting to smoke, a thousand stringy white streamers smelling of cruel vinegar. I had to get him to safety; and do it fast, in the two seconds the jelly guns took to build up pressure before they could spew another round.

First things first: an instant Mayday over my link-seed and piss on being a nelly about data tumors. *Protection Central*, I bellowed mentally, *defense squad, ambulance, killers!* The world-soul was bright enough to fill in the details . . . like where I was calling from. It could triangulate on my link-seed signals. Meanwhile, I grabbed Chappalar under the armpits, hiked up his arms, and rolled us both straight over the stairs' guardrail.

We didn't fall. We didn't glide. Imagine a wobbly blend of both, me dangling under Chappalar as if he were a crippled parafoil. He was halfway unconscious, but still managed to keep his arms and legs stiff enough for a semicontrolled descent—vectoring down at a steep angle till my feet jarred against the floor. Two staggering steps to catch my balance, then I was running for the exit.

Good points about my situation: Chappalar wasn't heavy to carry, and I had a head start on the shooters, still back at the stairs.

Bad points: my grip on Chappalar was cramp-awkward—just fingertips under his armpits. My fingers were stopped against the solid web of his gliders, so I couldn't wrap my arms round his body . . . lucky for my arms, considering the sticky blobs of acid sizzling their way into his back. (The smell of vinegar smoke. The shuddery whimpers of my friend.)

Another bad point of my position: the shooters had begun to run after me. Arms pumping. Feet pounding the floor like hammers. Only world-class sprinters ever galloped that flat out . . . certainly not me as I juggled an injured Oolom. The jelly guns must have repressurized by now, and I was easily within range; but the two racing after me must have wanted a point-blank shot, maybe flush in the face to scour away my eyes. That queasy thought spurred me on. I sped through the door to the locker room and slammed it behind me with an adrenaline-fueled kick.

Didn't help.

My pursuers hit the closed door like twin battering rams. The door didn't just fly open, it snapped off its hinges and hurtled across the room, smashing against a locker, then bouncing off to cuff me a good one in the shoulder. I reeled and lost my grip on Chappalar. Trying to do a dozen things at once—keep my balance, avoid dropping my friend, prevent him from crashing to the floor or against the lockers—I made a hash of damned near everything.

Down I went, the door flipping over on top of me. It was only luck I didn't fall on Chappalar. He landed beside me in the narrow aisle between lockers, the two of us jammed side by side with the broken door heavy across one of my legs.

Pity the door only covered up to my knee; I could have used some protection for my face.

The shooters stopped at my feet. Their guns lowered and took aim. Two triggers fired simultaneously.

And here's what I saw: a ghostly tube of light, green and gold and purple and blue, suddenly glimmered into existence before me. The two acid balls flew into that tube . . . and the tube funneled them up, around, in a smooth arc that led from the pistol mouths, circling over the shooters' heads, back behind them, and out onto my attackers' shoulder blades. Acid jelly flew through that misty channel, around the loop; then smack, the two wads slapped into the shooters' backs, splattering against nearby lockers but missing Chappalar and me.

As fast as it'd materialized, the phantom tube, all its peacock colors, vanished like steam. No evidence it had ever existed . . . except I was still alive, and the acid balls meant for me had got redirected at the shooters instead.

Their clothes billowed with smoke where the acid struck . . . as if the gray overalls were catching fire, braised by a flamethrower. The woman spun round, clutching at her back with one hand, but making no sound—no squeal of pain/surprise/outrage. A heartbeat later, I saw why: through clouds of vinegar smoke, metal glittered under her burning clothes.

Steel shoulder blades. Hydraulic muscles. A spine of articulated alloy.

"Christ!" I yelled. Don't ask me why. Being stalked by assassins was one thing, but it just seemed worse that they were robots.

The woman—the android that looked female—had a case of the writhes, making futile grabs at her back. I snapped out my unblocked foot and caught her with a solid cross-kick in the ankle. Something crunched like celery: not her metal shin, but whatever lay beneath, wires or delicate flexors. She tottered back, off-balance, and grabbed at her male companion. He showed no reaction to getting shot, even though smoke poured off his back in thick white plumes; the splash must have missed everything vital. It was only when his accomplice clutched at him that he shifted his attention away from me. Her grip pulled him sideways with her as she tried not to fall ... so I took advantage of the moment to scuttle back on my butt, out from under the door and around the end of the lockers, dragging Chappalar with me.

Three seconds later, I was on my feet again, Chappalar slung like a rug over my shoulder. Another three seconds and I rammed the exit door's crash bar with my hip.

Donkeys, orts and leaners stared at us curiously as we lurched out into the petting zoo. Thank Mary and all her saints, the animals were the only things in sight—no parents pushing strollers, no schoolchildren parading along on a field trip to the park. I dashed to a nearby leaner and threw myself behind it; its pudgy body wrapped in armadillo hide was the best protection I could find on short notice. With luck, it would shield us from the robots long enough for me to help my friend.

I heaved Chappalar off my shoulder and flopped him down in the snow. Steam gushed up as his back touched the damp surface—the acid gobs must have been blistering hot from the chemical reaction of corroding his skin. I spread out his arms, snow-angel style, tamping down every damaged area of his gliders to give them solid cool contact with the ice below. Soothing, I hoped. It took a strong stomach to look over his injuries: his wing membranes had finger-sized holes eaten clean through them, like plant leaves bitten to rags by beetles.

The edges of the holes were still expanding. I could see them grow as the acid ate outward.

Desperately, I scooped up a handful of snow and

smeared it over the upper surface of the membrane, hoping to dilute the corrosive chemicals. Whether it worked or not I don't know—my attention got pulled away as the leaner suddenly slumped its weight against my back.

"Not now, you witless beast!" I shouted, shoving back furiously. The leaner stayed deadweight against me for a moment, then toppled away limply, hitting the snow with a sizzle and continuing to roll like a duffel bag. Its side was starred with splotches of acid gum; ten steps beyond, the male robot was re-aiming its pistol at me, waiting for the chamber to pressurize.

A donkey brayed in panic. Two orts took to their wings, squawking. They must have all smelled the acid, a piercing reek in the clean fresh air.

I gouged up a snowball and heaved it at the robot. My throw hit the thing's face, but it didn't even flinch.

The jelly gun fired.

No peacock-colored tube saved me this time. Instead, a leaner dived into the way, mouth open for all the world as if it intended to swallow the acid wad. Its timing was off; the goo struck the leaner's nose and splayed across its muzzle, like a classic pie in the face.

Smoke streamed back along the animal's ears as it continued to charge the shooter. Then its whole face sloughed off, acid-ravaged skin, revealing a skull of white plastic— this leaner was one of the robot lifeguards, programmed to keep other animals from hurting visitors. Thank Christ it had enough bonus brainpower to recognize danger from other sources . . . and to throw itself forward to protect Chappalar and me. It banged straight into the shooter android, plastic muzzle crumpling against the killer's metal gut. Both went down in a rolling heap, making no cries as they twisted in the snow.

I snatched up Chappalar; the leaner robot might keep the android busy for a few seconds, but it wouldn't win the fight. Under its false skin, the creature was only light plastic: not made for heavy-duty grappling, just the placid herding of animals.

The killer android had to be ten times tougher than the leaner. Humanoid robots always are. They're built for rough-and-tumble in situations too risky for flesh humans . . . emergency rescue, for example, or the slitter-sex trade. Even robots constructed for less dangerous business can take quite a beating—otherwise, manufacturers get sued for "mental anguish" by owners who watch fragile androids fly apart at the seams. Always disconcerting when your gardener catches its arm on a rosebush, and the arm comes off.

So. Only a matter of time before the android battered the leaner to plastic pulp. By then, I wanted to be sipping mint tea in the next county.

With Chappalar over my shoulder, I ran. How long before Protection Central answered my Mayday? Scant more than thirty seconds had passed since I called in. Average response to an emergency alert was 2.38 minutes, which everyone agreed was damned good. Everyone who wasn't fleeing in panic from a killer.

But I'd try to smother my bias if ever I scrutinized a bill about police services.

Behind me the silence was broken by a ragged rupturing. I peeked back over my shoulder to see the android getting to its feet, hunks of tattered plastic in both hands. "Damn," I mumbled; the assassin had ripped the animal robot clean apart, tearing it in two.

Good thing for me the android was programmed to shoot people with acid rather than fight with bare hands. Then again . . . I knew how to spar mano a mano. How do you block a splash of jelly?

The robot took up the chase again—the same flat-out sprint it'd used before, legs and arms churning. Now though, its speed was hampered by snow cover; the machine's heavy footfalls punched through the crust, sinking into the soft stuff below. On park paths, that didn't make much difference: the snow was only fingers thick, scarce enough to slow the android at all. I headed for deeper drifts, someplace the robot would get held back while I gingerly skimmed across the top.

Ahead of me . . . Coal Smear Creek and its THIN ICE signs. A frozen surface maybe strong enough to hold me, but not a walking heap of scrap iron.

Behind me, the android crunched through the snow crust again and again, with a sound like boards breaking. A flesh-and-blood creature would soon get stuck, plunged into drifts as deep as its crotch; but the robot pushed forward relentlessly, gouging a trail through the waist-high snow. Not far behind, opportunist snowstriders crowded around the broken snow crust, diving for frostfly cocoons exposed by the robot's passing. The damned birds were having a merry old smorgasboard while I was running for my life.

I got halfway down the creek bank slope before the THIN ICE alarms noticed me. They burst into hoots and wails, crashing my ears with noise. The din drowned out any chance of hearing the android as it closed the gap between us. Forget it; I had more immediate concerns: crossing the ice without slipping or falling through thin spots.

The creek surface here was clear of snow—cheerfully shoveled by teenage skaters who probably squealed in protest if asked to shovel at home. The ice was smooth but not glare-perfect . . . dozens of skate blades had sliced at it, turning the surface into a snarl of crosshatches with the occasional loop or figure eight. I could shuffle-step forward without skittering out of control (praise be to boots with grip-rubber soles), but running was not an option.

As I neared the far shore, I felt shudders underfoot. Tremors from elsewhere on the ice. Glancing over my shoulder, I saw the android had made it to the creek.

Alarms still screamed. Snowstriders darted about in feeding frenzy on the bank.

The android tried its old sprint on the ice: slam, slam, slip. Three strides and it lost its balance, soaring up, flailing in the air, then down bang, crashing hip-first and steel-heavy onto the frozen surface.

I imagined the prickle-prickle cracking of ice. I couldn't hear it because of the alarms, but in my mind, the sound was precious-perfect clear.

The android, not programmed for winter gymnastics, tried to scramble to its feet. It slipped once more, its right hand sliding across the creek surface like butter on a hot pan. This time the robot didn't fall, but threw out its other hand to catch itself.

The hand went through the ice, up to the elbow.

By then, I'd reached the far shore. This bank had been built up with fist-sized hunks of concrete laid in uneven rows for a flagstone effect. After the chilling and swelling of winter, lots of those hunks had broken loose from their mortar. I grabbed the nearest and chucked it at the android's head, praying to hit something vulnerable while its hand was trapped.

The robot saw the chunk coming and twisted away, taking the blow on its back. Nothing happened; the concrete just bounced off a metal shoulder. Now though, I could eyeball the damage inflicted before, when the peacock tube splashed the robots with their own acid. This android's whole spinal area was pitted with corrosion: hankie-sized patches of epidermis eaten clean away. You could see circuits and fiber-optic cables exposed to open air . . . not enough to stop the robot in its tracks, but the acid had taken a fierce vicious toll.

Good, I thought, and threw another hunk of cement.

This throw missed the android, but bit into the nearby ice with its jagged concrete edge. Hairline cracks radiated out from the point of impact. Did the android care? No. It dragged its hand from the water, shirtsleeve dripping, and picked up for one more climb to its feet.

Heavy steel robot feet.

The ice gave way with a snap I could hear even over the alarms. For a wavering moment, the android managed to catch its arms on the sides of the hole—propping itself with upper body still visible, though ice water came up to its nipples. Steam poured from cavities in the robot's back, where chilly Coal Smear Creek met burning acid and the hot circuitry of the machine's guts. I yelled, "Short out, you bastard! Blow your sodding battery!"

Obliging things, these robots. The android's arms suddenly jerked rigid. Then the ice under its hands broke into shockle, and the killer machine plunged out of sight into the creek.

For another moment I stayed on the bank, watching the hole—dark water now, bobbing with ice floes. But a woman my age has watched enough fic-chips to know how witless it is to relax prematurely. Any second, I expected the android's hand to smash out of the ice at my feet, grab me by the ankle, pull me down. I clambered up the bank to solid ground, and was just shifting Chappalar's weight for another stint of running when the creek exploded.

All the ice in a ten-meter radius simply lifted up, then slammed down hard on the water beneath. The great banging force fractured the frozen surface into hundreds of separate slabs; but more dramatic was the geyser of muddy water that shot from the hole where the android had sunk. The upburst gushed three stories into the sky, carrying with it scraps of circuit board, metal cables, and tattered gray overalls. Then the fountain lost strength and collapsed, spilling robot ragout all over the creek surface.

"Self-destruct," I whispered to myself. "A deadman's switch . . . in case the bugger got in over its head. So to speak. Something to destroy the evidence."

What did that say about the female android, back in the pump station? She'd taken more damage from the acid bath; I hadn't stayed to watch, but she'd clearly been on the futz.

And when she'd finally shut down? Shut down = cue for the self-destruct mechanism to blow her apart.

I shuddered to think what the explosion had done to the water-treatment vats.

*   *   *

By the time the police arrived, I was back swabbing Chappalar with snow . . . not the ragged holes in his gliders, but the vicious black pits close to his spine. The ones where ribs and vital organs showed through. His skin had turned a color Dads called Terminal Chalk—an ashy gray-white with no responsiveness. The result of catastrophic failure in the glands that control an Oolom's chameleon shifting.

I'd seen that color a lot during the plague.

The six staff members of Pump Station 3 were found near the building's delivery bay. All of them had third-degree acid burns. Three were declared DOA when they reached hospital and one more died later, but two survived.

Chappalar didn't. Ooloms can be fierce tough; they can also be precious fragile.

Damn.

While I was pacing the rug in hospital, watching Chappalar float lifeless in a burn tank, I got an emergency call from headquarters. Seven other proctors on assignments around the planet had been ambushed by androids and killed. A coordinated attack. No survivors. All at the same time Chappalar and I made our visit to the pump station.

Someone had declared war on the Vigil.

5

SNAKE-BELLY

Link-seeds are handy for giving evidence. The world-soul asked my permission, then downloaded everything I'd witnessed, straight from my brain. Soon, Protection Central had a VR repro of everything I'd been through—the smell of the acid, the howl of alarms. Might have been a big seller on the entertainment nets if the Vigil didn't have rules against that sort of thing.

In Cabot Park, the cops dredged Coal Smear Creek for the remains of the male android, while another team bagged up the soggy mess in Pump Station 3. (When the female android self-destructed, flying bits of her had perforated five of the plant's water vats. Much spillage. It was only luck the whole blessed petting zoo wasn't washed away.)

Similar investigations revved up all over the world—everywhere proctors got killed—and by the end of the day, detectives had accumulated enough evidence to affect continental drift. By then there was an official task force coordinating the work, trying to avoid pissing contests between federals and locals. Meanwhile, all levels of government had bitten their nails to the quick, worrying the

Vigil would throw a tantrum demanding Immediate Action Now.

Of course we didn't. How would that be productive? But you can bet good money, there were suddenly a lot more proctors exercising their constitutional responsibility to scrutinize police activities.

The local detectives treated me like velvet. I might have had a few less-than-friendly run-ins with police in the past, but now I was a member of the Vigil, and respectable as mother's milk. On the other hand, the appearance of the tube of light—that thing I'd started to call the Peacock's Tail because of its colors—well, a mystery like that set conservative cop nerves on edge. What was it? Did I have any guesses? Could the investigators maybe dismiss it as hallucination, a delusion brought on by terror, stress, and my newly implanted link-seed?

I could only shrug; I saw what I saw. If they wanted a dissertation on link-seed side effects, ask a neurologist.

(Of course I could have retrieved some clinical data myself. Reams of it. The Vigil's databanks were full to bursting with case studies, every possible way link-seeds could bugger your brain. But I didn't try access the information. You know why.)

The reports released to the media said nothing about the Peacock's Tail. Not that the cops wanted to suggest this tube-of-light business was a figment of my imagination. Three different detectives made a point of telling me it was Standard Police Procedure to withhold a few details of any crime.

Yeah. Sure.

My family wanted me to quit the Vigil. "At least ask for a leave of absence," Winston suggested, "till they catch this bastard who's mucking about with robots."

If I begged off on a leave of absence, I knew I'd never go back. And I'd still have poison ivy in my brain.

"No," I said.

We were in Winston's private dome—all seven of my spouses sitting worried around the dome's circumference, with me in the middle. Our Faye in the hot seat. Concern pressing in on me . . . like the bad old days at sixteen, when my friends watched me trolling the streets for trouble. Later, age nineteen, as we kicked around the thought of getting married, all seven of them took me aside, each by each, to murmur, "You won't be too crazy, will you, Faye? You've got the angries out of your system? You won't make us all widows?"

"No," I told them all now in Winston's dome. "You don't have to fret about me."

Which is what I used to say in the bad old days.

Back then, I believed myself. After every scrape, I believed I'd finally scrounged up the wisdom and willpower to keep my head straight. Eventually, it even became true.

Now . . . someone was killing proctors. Maybe someone who'd be fuming I got away.

"I'll be all right," I said. "Really."

They all looked back at me with old, haunted eyes.

I swore I'd push on with my scrutiny of Bon Cty Ccl 11-28; but the mayor withdrew the bill pending amendments by the Department of Works. When the female robot blew herself up, the explosion had caused structural damage to Pump Station 3. No holes, just cracks . . . but enough for the place to be declared unsafe. Now the engineers were chewing their pencils, deciding whether to shore up the walls or tear them down completely: maybe rebuild something bigger and better on the same site.

Whichever way things shook out, it meant shuffling budgets and priorities . . . not just for the public works, but in all city departments. The mayor's office sent a polite note to the Vigil, saying it might be weeks before any new bills were presented to council. Ergo, we'd have no pressing scrutinies for a while. Nothing but bread-and-butter business happening at city hall: selling dog licenses, keeping the proto-nute flowing. Take a well-deserved vacation, folks.

You had to wonder if the mayor was afraid more proctors would get blown up on city property.

The Oolom cemetery sat a good ways outside Bonaventure city limits—in the tundra forest, where every footstep got muffled by frost-green carpet moss.

I liked the quiet. Serene. Somber. No hint of maudlin.

Homo sap cemeteries were another story. Most looked like tarted-up boneyards—young as their fresh paint and thinly populated. Our species hadn't lived long enough on Demoth to lose our oldest generation. Just accident victims like my father.

Dads had been buried in an empty field outside Sallysweet River: no trees, no other gravestones, just a hectare of uncut yellow-grass with a coffin-sized hole in the middle. The only field near town with deep enough soil to dig a decent grave.

But at Chappalar's interment, we had moss and trees and silence.

The thaw was four days old now. You could still see snow streaks hiding in crannies, but the open areas were clear and dry. If you pressed down hard with one foot, you could hear mud squishing under the moss. I don't know why I kept doing that.

All the Bonaventure proctors came to the funeral, of course. Plus an Oolom I didn't recognize—an older man wearing shade-mist goggles. My jaw clenched like stone at the sight of those goggles; they were worn by plague victims who'd never regained use of their eyelids. The goggles kept out dust, and preserved corneal humidity by spritzing up a wisp of mist every so often. In bright light they darkened: an artificial squint.

Simple things, those goggles. Not sinister—just a practical solution to a low-grade problem. But. They brought back unwanted memories of the Circus. A hundred and twenty white-on-white Oolooms wearing the same kind of goggles under the Big Top.

"Who's the stranger?" I whispered to the person beside me: Jupkur, an Ooloom proctor who'd taken my arm as we walked to the burial site.

Jupkur followed my gaze, then let his eyes slip past to pretend he hadn't been staring. "Master Tic," Jupkur replied, barely mouthing the words. "Just arrived to replace Chappalar."

"He's a master proctor?"

"Yes."

"And they bungholed him to Bonaventure?"

"Yes."

Jupkur turned away quickly and made some lame remark about the weather to the person on his other side. I took the hint . . . but only for here and now. Next time I got Jupkur in private, I'd coax the full story out of him.

Here's the thing: the Vigil only granted the title "master" to a handful of people every generation—the keenest, the brightest, the best. Master proctors never got shortsheeted down to city politics, especially not to drowsy towns like Bonaventure. They scrutinized the world government and interplanetary affairs . . . like the trade treaty currently being hammered out between Demoth and the Divian Free Republic.

So what was a master proctor doing here? Whose wife had he been caught diddling?

Then again, you didn't blackball an exalted master just for being caught on the wrong side of a bedroom door. And your average master proctor wasn't interested in bedhopping anyway—they were supposedly so near sainthood, you could use their peckers as night-lights.

If this Master Tic had got sent to Bonaventure, it was because the Vigil dearly wanted him here. Because there was important work for him to do.

What work? Especially with our city council on hiatus for a few weeks.

It had to be something to do with Chappalar's death.

And with the only proctor who'd survived the robot attacks.

My skin got a case of the goosecreeps. I had a feeling I'd be seeing a lot more of Master Tic's goggly eyes in the days to come.

At the gravesite, Chappalar's family had already planted the roots of a snake-belly palm. It was a native Demoth tree and lightning fast–growing under the right conditions. In tropical jungles, a snake-belly would seed itself at the base of another tree, then climb that tree's exterior in a solid sheath, like a snake swallowing the host tree trunk from the ground up. With enough water and sunlight, a snake-belly could sprout up a hand's breadth every day— just a reed-thin shell around the host, letting the inner trunk sustain all the weight. Typical parasite behavior. Once in place, the snake-belly would digest the host trunk it had swallowed, little by little creating wood of its own from the outside in . . . till after a few decades, the host was fully consumed, leaving only a snake-belly with a solid wood core.

Down south, snake-bellies could grow around other snake-bellies, growing around their swallowed-up hosts. In the Pistolet Museum, they had a stump showing five separate snake-bellies in concentric rings round a toothpick core of original raspfeather.

In the Bonaventure Cemetery, we'd soon have a single snake-belly round a core of Chappalar.

They'd wrapped his body in a shroud of froth white silk. Half a dozen Oolom mourners had turned white themselves, though they stood on light green moss . . . the phenomenon of sympathetic transference, taking on someone else's color in moments of heart-deep emotion. I wished I could go white with them, to show Chappalar/ his family/myself that I truly felt the grief. But I stayed lumpishly Faye-colored as the pallbearers eased the body onto a wooden support stand atop the snake-belly roots.

A single Oolom child toddled forward and splashed

soupy brown juice on the plant at Chappalar's feet. Jupkur whispered that the liquid was fertilizer, laced with a mix of growth hormones. In a week, the tree would have swallowed Chappalar up to the ankles. By fall, the whole corpse would be wrapped in a snake-belly sheath. In thirty years give or take, my friend Chappalar, the man who died saving my life, would be entirely absorbed by the tree.

Even his bones. Ooloms have such precious lightweight bones.

Around us, no ornamental landscaping, no headstones, no crypts—just a forest of snake-belly palms, each one the height of a person.

By the end of the burial service, every Oolom was sympathetic white ... all but Master Tic. That irked me: a peevish indignation on Chappalar's behalf. I'd turn white if I could; why didn't Tic?

To be fair, it wasn't Tic's fault: Oolom color changes aren't consciously controlled. For Tic to turn white, he'd have to be overcome with grief—not likely, considering he'd never even met Chappalar. Tic had come to the funeral out of courtesy, showing polite respect ... who could ask more?

I could. Seething-steaming-indignant.

Whenever I go to a funeral, there's always something that makes me furious.

Ooloms don't do tea and sympathy after a funeral. Instead, Chappalar's family and the Oolom proctors glided off to the cemetery chapel, where (Jupkur said), "We'll pray for just hours and hours. The priests' major source of income is selling knee pads."

Jupkur hated to speak seriously about anything; but he wasn't the only Oolom who turned jokily offhanded when the subject of religion came up. Ooloms didn't talk to humans about what they believed—none of them did. Maybe that was an article of their faith, keeping mum in front of outsiders. An article of *all* their faiths, I should say . . . because whatever their religion was, it had three major denominations, plus various splinter groups. Each sect identified itself by a gobbledygook name that no one ever translated into English.

Secretive bunch, those Ooloms.

So the Ooloms went off by themselves, leaving me to walk home alone. A couple hours on foot through the countryside. Of course, the other human proctors offered me rides; but I hadn't trekked through open tundra in years, and the quiet of it suddenly called to me. Being out among the trees, breathing the wet smell of spring, I'd been grabbed by a bubbly heartache for girlhood—for times long ago in Sallysweet River, where you could follow the Bullet tracks five minutes out of town and feel all alone on the planet.

Solitude. The rustle of trees. The pip-pip of crawler-birds slinking over the forest floor.

Just me.

Just me and my link-seed.

Okay. I can almost hear you groaning, *Where's your head, woman? Three days ago some slip-wit tried to kill you, and now you want to isolate yourself in an empty forest?*

Good point.

I could make up excuses. I could put on the blather, how Demoth was a peaceful planet where assassinations didn't happen . . . not often, anyway. Women didn't need armed escorts to spend a therapeutic afternoon walking through the woods. What happened three days earlier was a fluke, the once-in-a-lifetime act of a crazed fanatic who'd soon be caught by the cops.

I could surely lie to you. But damn my link-seed, I couldn't lie to myself.

Here's the thing: deep down, I wanted to give the killer another shot. To see what would happen. It was another freckles-and-scalpel thing.

So I walked alone. Just to see.

*   *   *

I avoided the road—the woods were dry enough for walking, both the carpet-moss parts and the spots where
yellow-grass could get a foothold. (Yellow-grass always
grows close to water. Seen from a flying skimmer, every
lake and river on Great St. Caspian has a lemon-colored
fringe, like fatty buildup on the wall of an artery . . . but
the yellow stretch fades to the frost green of carpet moss
the farther you go into deep forest.)

I didn't fret about getting lost—I could track myself by
the sun. And come evening, there'd be the lights of the
city to spot by the glow. This was a tundra forest . . . not
thick stands of timber blocking the sky, but individual
bluebarrel trees, well separated from each other. Any seed
that rooted too close to an existing tree just wouldn't
grow. Wouldn't get enough light, wouldn't get enough
nutrition from the gaunt soil.

In my mood, that seemed like a metaphor for something.

I dawdled away the afternoon. Nothing to see but stunted
bluebarrel trees and lumpy-bumpy moss interrupted by the
occasional upthrust of stone.

In one slab of rock, I found a house-sized rectangle cut
straight into the stone. At one time it must have been two
stories deep, though now it was three-quarters full of dirt
and weeds. A leftover from pre-Oolom settlements some
three thousand years old. Demoth never evolved intelligent species of its own, but aliens from the League had
visited now and then in the past—setting up outposts for
a while, then moving on when they lost interest in our
poky little planet.

Great St. Caspian had hosted thousands of such visitors;
their householes were everywhere, mostly filled in and
earthed over now, with whatever had spilled into them
during the past three millennia. The aliens dug mines and
tunnels too. In Sallysweet River we used to play "Archaeologists Bold," excavating the nearby holes to find

rusty metal junk of all shapes and sizes. We'd badger our parents to call the Heritage Board, convinced that we'd dug up priceless alien artifacts . . . but nothing ever came of it. The board had long ago surveyed a handful of sites and found nothing of interest. Nothing worthy of publication in a good academic journal. So now the Heritage Board ignored the ruins—dismissed anyone who wasted time snooping about in them.

Mistake. The Vigil would never have allowed such book-blinkered sloppiness. But the Heritage Board answered to the Technocracy, not local government, so it was beyond our scrutiny.

Mistake, mistake, mistake.

Sunset was coming on purple and peach when a skimmer flew over my head. It wasn't the first I'd heard in the day, but the others were distant hums tracking the ocean coast or the Bullet tracks to the interior—probably families off on an outing, playing hooky now that the thaw had come. This new skimmer was sailing straight over the treetops of barren forest . . . and it had Outward Fleet insignia painted on its side.

Queer thing, that. The navy had only one base on Demoth, way down by the equator near Snug Harbor. And navy personnel seldom found cause to venture out to the rest of the planet; the base was mostly a dormitory for safety inspectors who met incoming starships at our orbitals.

A loudspeaker boomed from the skimmer's belly: "Faye Smallwood?"

Damn. So much for a quiet walk in the woods.

Steeling myself, I did the obvious—stoked up my linkseed and contacted the world-soul. *Has the Outward Fleet filed flight plans for craft in the Bonaventure area?*

The world-soul didn't answer with words; but my brain suddenly knew for a certainty, no plans had been filed. Some other time I'd worry how creepy that was, having knowledge planted straight into my head. For now, the skimmer was my immediate problem. Either the Admiralty was running a secret op with my name on it, or I was on the verge of being ambushed by a wolf in fleet clothing.

"Faye Smallwood!" the loudspeaker called again.

"Who's asking?" I shouted back.

The skimmer was hovering now, its engine wash vibrating the bluebarrels around me. Their fat, hollow trunks began to resonate, producing deep growly notes as pure as a forest of bass viols.

The skimmer's side hatch opened. A man wearing gold fatigues leaned out with something in his hand.

Yet another pistol. Not a jelly gun this time; a hypersonic stunner, like Explorers use in fic-chips.

In the chips, stunners make an edgy whirring sound. I didn't stay conscious long enough to hear it.

Headache. Muddy. 6.1 on the Hangover Scale. What you get from mixing wine, tequila, and screech.

I'd had worse. And this time I woke up alone, with no beer-breath stranger lying comatose on my arm, cutting off the circulation.

A tastefully darkened room. A soft cot beneath me. No smell of vomit anywhere.

Compared to the bad old days, this was bubble-bath luxury. Not to mention, I still had clothes on . . . no need for a head-throbbing pantie search, terrified the other person might wake up before I got out the door.

I stood up. Not all that shakily. More than twenty years since my last debauch, but the rough-and-ready reflexes still kicked in: mining-town girl.

"Would you like something for the pain?" a male voice asked. It came from nowhere—a speaker hidden somewhere in the darkness.

"You call this *pain*?" I scoffed. "Ya big mainstream crybaby." I could tell this guy was mainstream from his accent: an oh-so-civilized Core-World featherweight who'd shrivel up dead if he ever caught a genuine hangover. "So what's the point of kidnapping me?" I demanded ... keeping my voice loud so my captors wouldn't think I was some fragile flower on the point of collapse.

A door in the wall opened silently, letting in a dagger of bright light. Two men entered, and the door slid shut again, no noise. Both newcomers wore glittery gold-fabric uniforms; it made them easier to see in the returning darkness.

"You haven't been kidnapped," one of the men said. "You're voluntarily helping us with important research."

"What research?"

Neither man answered straightaway. I wished I could see their faces—whether they were looking at me like a person or a piece of raw meat. That might have helped me guess if they were real navymen or killers who had nabbed me for interrogation. Ready to torture me for information on the Vigil, to help them murder more proctors.

And speaking of information ...

Protection Central! I called over my link-seed. *Kidnappers ...*

It was like shouting into a pillow. Muffled emptiness. Mentally I yelled, *Respond!*

Nothing. Silence.

Something electronic beeped in the far corner of the room. Something that must have been listening for radio transmissions from my brain.

"Ah," said one of the gold-suited men. "You've finally tried to use your link. So you realize it's not going to help."

"We're jamming it," the other one added. "This entire house is insulated from the datasphere."

That shouldn't have been a great surprise. Anyone who'd studied the Vigil would know to take precautions. "Well then," I said, "what do you want?"

A light sprang up in the middle of the darkened room. It began as a pinprick but fast expanded to a life-size hologram of two androids, a Peacock's Tail, and a fear-eyed yours truly . . . a first-rate mock-up that had to be based on the download from my brain. The holo images were projected across my body, across the cot beside me, across the two men who'd come through the door; I happened to be standing half-in/half-out of the female robot. Stubbornly, I stayed where I was—flinching would have made me look like a nelly.

One of the men stepped forward . . .

Hold on a second. I need some breezy way of distinguishing my two captors—calling one Tall and one Short, something along those lines. But they were both of identical height, both wearing identical uniforms, both sporting identical haircuts: as close to twins as people can get when they don't actually look the same. All I can think to call them is the Mouth and the Muscle . . . because one couldn't stop yapping while the other mostly loomed quiet as a hoar falcon biding its time.

So the Mouth stepped forward. He made a point of walking straight through the hologram of me, briefly disrupting my laser-projected image into a random scramble of pixels. Then he aimed his finger straight at the peacock tube. "Do you know what that is, Ms. Smallwood?"

"No."

The Mouth sneered in disbelief. Not many men can actually manage a sneer—they might glower or grimace, but they don't have the degree of self-involvement required for an out-and-out sneer. The Mouth looked as if he'd practiced sneering in a mirror till he got something he really liked. "This," he said, pointing to the peacock tube, "is a miniature Worm field. Colloquially called a Sperm-field, or Sperm-tail. Do you know what that is?"

"We use Sperm-tails as transport sleeves to our local orbitals," I answered. "They're also used in starship drives." I stared at the peacock again. "But the Bonaventure sleeve is white."

"Sperm-fields look white when they're stabilized," the Mouth said, "like planetary transport tubes, or a starship envelope after it's properly aligned. But with an unanchored Sperm, you get flutter around the edges. Makes a characteristic diffraction pattern.'' He pointed again to the peacock tube.

"Okay," I shrugged, "it's a Sperm-field. So what?"

"So what?" the Mouth repeated, as if I'd only asked the question to antagonize him. "So where did it come from? There's no Sperm-field generator in the picture!"

"None that we can see," the Muscle put in. "It could be miniaturized."

The Mouth glared at him. This was obviously a point of contention between the two men . . . and a precious petulant contention at that. Mouth took a slow and deliberate breath, the picture of a man exercising colossal restraint in the face of grievous tests to his patience. I bet he practiced that look in the mirror too. "The point is," Mouth told me, "current Technocracy science could not create a Sperm-field in the situation you see here. It came out of nowhere . . ."

"Nowhere big enough to see," the Muscle muttered.

"It came from no discernible field generator," the Mouth said testily, "it immediately shaped itself into a smooth arc without any apparent control magnets, and it ended in a well-defined aperture that held its position for 1.6 seconds without any equipment to anchor it in place!"

He stared at me triumphantly, as if he'd just scored some telling knockout in a political debate.

Ooo. Posturing. As a Vigil member, I'd never seen *that* before.

I spoke mildly. "I take it those things you listed are unusual for Sperm-fields."

"Unusual? They're impossible!" the Mouth snapped.

"At least we don't know how to do them," the Muscle said under his breath.

The Mouth gave Muscle another hissy glare, then slapped his hand through the hologram peacock. His skin fuzzed with green-and-purple streaks. "Ms. Smallwood," the Mouth said, "this is a matter of great concern to the

Admiralty. When Outward Fleet personnel saw the news broadcasts of what happened to you . . ."

"This was never broadcast," I interrupted.

The Mouth looked at the Muscle. The Muscle shrugged.

"When the Outward Fleet obtained this hologram from the police," the Mouth said loftily, not looking me in the eye, "there was immediate concern. The base commander on Demoth contacted the High Council of Admirals, and the council dispatched us to investigate this matter strenuously."

"*Strenuously?*" I repeated. If I were an admiral, I wouldn't trust these two with that kind of adverb.

"It's a matter of security," the Muscle said with a straight face. "The security of the entire human species."

"Because someone pulled a trick you can't imitate?"

"Ms. Smallwood," the Mouth said, pushing to regain his place as the center of attention, "if this hologram is accurate, someone is employing inhumanly advanced science on a Technocracy world. *Your* world, Ms. Smallwood. Doesn't that worry you?"

"Why should it? The Sperm-field saved my life."

"She's got a point," the Muscle murmured.

"Do you mind?" Mouth tried to give his partner a withering glare. He hadn't spent enough time practicing the "wither" part—probably too busy working on his sneer. Mouth's prissy little stare bounced off the Muscle like a wad of soggy tissue.

"Look," I said in my most reasonable voice, "we all know the League of Peoples includes races that are millions of years beyond human technology. Millions of years smarter, millions of years more evolved. I thought it was conventional wisdom that someone was always keeping an eye on humanity. 'Invisibly walking among us' . . . even the Admiralty uses that phrase."

"League members may walk among us," the Mouth sniffed, "but they never *do* anything. If there are invisible aliens wandering through the Technocracy, Ms. Smallwood, they don't stop children from drowning. They don't call local police to tell who's behind a string of serial murders, and they don't show up in court to explain who's innocent or guilty. So why should they work a miracle to help you?''

Good question, that. I'd asked it now and then myself in the past few days. "I don't know," I said.

"We can't accept that answer," Mouth told me. "The High Council gets extremely agitated at the thought of unknown aliens taking action on Technocracy planets. Especially when it involves political figures like you.''

I snorted. "I'm not a political figure.''

"You're part of Demoth's political system, Ms. Smallwood. And the Technocracy's charter from the League of Peoples prohibits the League from trying to influence our internal governments.''

Hogwash. I'd studied the charter during my Vigil training. The League could and would put the boot to human governments at every level if they thought our race was turning non-sentient. On the other hand, why waste breath giving these dickweeds a lecture on law? "What am I here for?" I asked as calmly as I could. "The way you've created this hologram, you must have hacked the full VR recording from the police databanks. That means you know everything I saw and heard. What else do you expect to get out of me?''

The Mouth smiled nastily. Close to a sneer but more smugness. "How about a confession this was all a hoax?''

"It wasn't," I snapped. "If you want to see the acid burns on Chappalar's body, let's you and me take a trip to the cemetery.''

"Ms. Smallwood," the Muscle said in a voice that had the decency to sound abashed, "there's no question Proctor Chappalar died from third-degree burns. But we have to worry about . . .'' He jabbed his thumb in the direction of the Peacock. "We need to know if that's real or if someone is trying to trick us.''

"How could I trick you? This is a direct download from my brain."

The Mouth sneered. Again. Falling back on the tried-and-true strengths of his facial repertoire. "Things can be loaded *into* your brain as well as out of it," he said. "Link-seeds are two-way technology."

"It could have been done without your knowledge," the Muscle added. "The Vigil has protected your brain with safety locks, but no security is perfect. Someone could have pumped that whole scenario into your mind; you wouldn't know the difference between planted images and real life."

Blah, blah, blah. As if we hadn't discussed this a thousand times at the College Vigilant. Yes, it could be done . . . with the right equipment and at least a day of finessing past the security blocks. And yes, the idea of someone jacking into my brain gave me the white willies if I thought about it too long. But Christ Almighty, you could brainwash *anyone*, given enough time. And if ever someone *did* try to monkey with our link-seeds, the world-soul would notice the next time we made contact. Digital signatures and all that.

"Look," I said, "I've only had my link-seed for a few weeks . . . and the Vigil's been watching it peery close for medical reasons. No one could have tampered with me."

"Except the Vigil itself," Mouth said. "When it had you in its hands for two weeks during *müshor*. They could have done anything to you."

"They didn't."

"Of course, that's what you'd believe." The Mouth gave me a nasty smile. As if petty innuendo was enough to stir up mistrust.

I sighed. "*Müshor* ended two weeks before the mess at the pump station. How could the Vigil plant false memories of something that hadn't happened yet?"

"It could be done," the Mouth answered airily. Fair unconvincing too. Which told me these chumps had already decided on their course of action, and weren't going to heed any argument against.

"Look," I said, "what's this all about really? What do you think you're going to do?"

"We're going to shunt into your brain," the Mouth answered. Gloating. "We're going to verify whether these Sperm-tail images were put in artificially. If someone has scribbled on your cerebellum, there should be obvious differences between the implanted memories and naturally acquired ones. Obvious to us if not to you. My partner and I will go in to check."

"You want to access me?" I growled.

"That's it."

"Like hell you will."

The Mouth favored me with another nasty smile. "This is not an optional exercise, Ms. Smallwood. The Admiralty has authorized us to conduct this investigation however we deem necessary. If you won't confess to this being a hoax . . ."

"Or if you can't," the Muscle put in.

"Then we'll crack you open for a look-see."

I stared at them. The only light in the room was the glow of the hologram, casting a yellowish gleam on their faces. The Mouth wore the leer of a man who'd enjoy violating me; the Muscle had a noncommittal look, neither eager nor uncomfortable. He'd do what he'd decided to do—he wouldn't enjoy it, but he wouldn't agonize about it either.

My throat had turned to gravel. "How about if I demand to see your superiors?"

"We have no superiors on Demoth," Mouth retorted. "Not even the local commander knows we're here. Or knows *you're* here. So if I were you, Ms. Smallwood, I'd lie back on the bed now. It may take hours for us to penetrate your link's security locks, and you won't injure yourself so much if you're resting on a soft surface."

"We'll be as careful as we can," the Muscle added, "but it's not going to be easy."

The Mouth nodded. "Think of an epileptic seizure. One that lasts all day long."

I swallowed hard. "Look," I told the Mouth, taking a step toward him, "use your head for a second. How can this be a trick to fool the Admiralty? Who'd *want* to fool the Admiralty? Why go to the extreme of killing eight proctors just to . . ."

"To plant false evidence on us?" the Mouth suggested. "Killing eight proctors was the perfect way to catch the fleet's attention. Mass murder is big; it's flashy. It guaranteed the commander here would do some investigating, and send the results to the High Council." Mouth showed no sign of concern as I stepped forward again through the hologram. "Doesn't that sound like a deliberate plot to bring us in?"

"But who's plotting?" I insisted. "What would anyone gain from deceiving the Admiralty?"

"We don't know," the Muscle answered. "That's what bothers us."

"You don't know how it concerns the navy," I said, taking another step, "but you're sure it does? Every little mystery has to be about you?"

"Yes," the Mouth and the Muscle said together.

Which was when I broke Mouth's knee.

It was a jerk-simple side-kick, hard and low—my instep hit the sweet spot of his patella and drove it backward till his whole leg bent the wrong way. Mouth hadn't suspected a thing. Maybe these two spent so much time researching my link-seed, they'd overlooked the punch'n'crunch training the Vigil gave every proctor.

Always a mistake to concentrate on the mental and ignore the physical.

Mouth screamed . . . part pain, part the sight of seeing his knee angled back like a grasshopper's. Damned sissy mainstreamer probably never took a good hit before. The Mouth didn't even put up his guard when I stepped in to hand-strike range, so I gave him a good palm-heel in the solar plexus to shut him up.

He wheezed and fell. Still breathing, of course, but fierce unhappy about it.

When I turned to the Muscle, he'd backed up against the door and drawn a stun-pistol. "Stand where you are, please," he said.

"Why should I?"

"Because I'll shoot if you don't. We can pry into your brain, even if you're stunned cold; it's just harder when we can't see your conscious response. More chance of us making a regrettable mistake. But if that's the way you want to play it . . ."

"Shoot her!" Mouth gasped. At least I think that's what he said—he didn't have much air in his lungs for making words.

"I won't shoot unless I have to," the Muscle said, still calm, keeping his gaze focused on me. "No sense in jeopardizing the mission, just because one of us got careless." He gestured toward the bed with the barrel of his pistol. "Are you going to lie down, Ms. Smallwood? Or do we do this the hard way?"

I stared at him, sizing up the situation. Unlike Mouth, the Muscle had been prepared for my attack; maybe he'd expected it as soon as I began inching forward. He wouldn't hesitate to fire if I took the teeniest step toward him . . . and I knew from recent experience how fast stun-guns worked. The ultrasonic blast would drop me long before I got within kicking distance.

Throw something at him? No; there was nothing I could grab fast enough. Maybe if I yanked up the Mouth, I could use his body as a shield, let it absorb the sonics.

Useless. As soon as I bent over to grab the Mouth, the Muscle would slab me.

But I had no intention of letting these men into my brain. One lightning rush, zigzagging to make myself harder to hit?

"Don't try it," the Muscle said, like he'd seen my

thoughts on my face. "This pistol's cone of effect covers your whole half of the room. I don't have to aim to get you."

I didn't know enough about stunners to tell if he was lying. Only one way to find out.

"Okay," I said in what I hoped was a defeated-sounding voice. "I'll lie down on . . ."

Without warning, I dived forward—old trick, moving in the middle of the sentence, hoping your opponent needs a second to switch mental gears. Even as I struck the floor, I heard the whir of a stun-pistol, felt a wash of dizziness stagger my brain. *Not quite out*, I thought muddily, *not unconscious*. I rolled in the direction I thought was the door and blundered out with my leg, trying to sweep the Muscle's feet out from under him. Nothing. If my leg moved at all, I couldn't tell; it sure as blazes didn't hit anything solid. I gave it another try, but my spasm of frantic motion only floundered me onto my back, staring up at Muscle through clumsy eyes.

Sitting duck. Too punchy to move.

The Muscle's silhouette was framed against the light from the open door. I waited for him to shoot again, put me out for good. Instead, he just stood there, face lost in shadow . . . till his breath slipped out in a sigh and he slumped like a tired child, toppling across my legs.

Someone was standing in the doorway behind him—someone who also held a stun-pistol. It took a second for me to muddle out what I was seeing. Then I realized the whir I'd heard wasn't Muscle's gun, it was the newcomer's. He or she had shot Muscle in the back . . . and I was still conscious because I'd only caught the slop of the blast, the sonic spill that hadn't been soaked up by Muscle's body.

The newcomer stepped cautiously into the room. It was a woman, a human woman, but with the backlighting I couldn't make out her face. She moved forward, quickly now, the yellowish hologram light slipping over her body as she strode through the projected images. When she stopped, I could only see her back; she stood over the Mouth, her stunner trained on him.

"Ten-hut!" she said in a calm voice.

The Mouth stared up at her, eyes squinting, trying to see who she was. Suddenly, his face bugged wide with fear. "Admiral!" he yelped.

"I bet that leg hurts," the woman told him. Her pistol whirred, and the Mouth slouched back limply. "Now it doesn't," she said.

For a moment more, she stayed with the Mouth's unconscious body—bending and running her hand carefully over his broken knee. Her back was lit now by the spill-glow of the hologram. Enough light to show she did indeed wear the gray fatigues of an admiral in the Outward Fleet.

Under the circumstances, I didn't take much joy seeing another navy mucky-muck.

Without jarring Mouth's leg, the admiral readjusted his body slightly, shifting him into something close to the first-aid recovery position—the safest way for an unconscious body to lie, insurance the victim won't choke if he vomits. Then she tucked her pistol into a hip holster and came to kneel by me. Her hand gently swept a sweat-strand of hair from my eyes.

She was young for an admiral. Clear green eyes, very alive. And she had a furious port-wine birthmark smeared across the right half of her face.

"Hello," she said. "I'm Festina Ramos. Sorry I didn't get here sooner."

6

DIPSHITS

Festina Ramos . . . a familiar name, thanks to Angie's son Nate (age 13). Nate, Lord love him, had a whopping crush on the whole Outward Fleet—one of those obsessions some kids get, where they never seem to think of anything else. Drooling over schematic diagrams of starships the way a normal boy would ogle skin pix. Sending mail to active and retired fleet personnel all over the Technocracy. Subscribing to the *Navy Gazette* and keeping his own database of captains, ship postings, duty assignments.

So yes, I'd heard of Festina Ramos. Ad infinitum. She'd been an Explorer First Class till two years ago, when out of the blue she got vaulted to Lieutenant Admiral . . . a position that had driven Nate to cracked-voice fits (bass/soprano, bass/soprano) because it was some bastardization. ("It's crazy, Mom-Faye! The lowest rank of admiral is rear admiral. It's been that way for absolute ever! They can't just invent ranks out of the blue!")

But the High Council of Admirals could. And did. After which, the shiny new L-Adm. Ramos was appointed to chair a board of inquiry for restructuring exploration practices. The media had gone into blood frenzy, convinced there had to be a lip-licking scandal behind Ramos's promotion; but the blitz of attention had come to a screechy halt when the board hearings began. It was the press's first chance to see Ramos in person . . . and she looked like an Explorer. Not only that, but the hearing room was full of people waiting to give testimony, and *they* all looked like Explorers too.

Harelips. Scabrous faces. Seal-flipper arms, like that cadet who talked to me the night Zillif died. A host of antiphotogenic physical conditions that were never seen on mainstream Technocracy worlds. Such peculiarities were what made these people expendable enough to be Explorers . . . and what made news directors scream, "Shut down the cameras! Turn them off now!"

From then on, Festina Ramos ceased to have "positive news value." At least in the lard-headed nicey-nice mainstream, where reality isn't supposed to be so real it upsets people.

Personally, I didn't see much wrong with Ramos's face as she bent over me in that dimly lit room. Yeah, sure, she had that birthmark. But so what? If the mainstream found it so precious ghastly they couldn't bear to look . . . well, this wouldn't be the first time I'd wondered how mainstreamers came by such stunted brains. Demoth people would never react with such horror. As far as I knew, our planet had never forced anyone into becoming an Explorer: first, because we weren't so weak-kneed as to ostracize folks who were different, and second, because there was no blessed way the Vigil would let public hospitals deny anyone the cosmetic surgery needed to fix the problem.

Not that I thought Ramos *had* a problem. In my eyes she looked fair presentable—attractive, going on handsome, going on a sweet sight more—and what kind of fool couldn't see that, birthmark or no? I pegged her age at late twenties, early thirties, though YouthBoost always makes it hard to be sure. Her skin was a shade and a half browner than mine, her dark hair short and unfussy, her eyes that piercing green. An intelligent, no-nonsense face, pursed with concern as she cradled my head in her lap.

"Are you all right?" she asked.

"Sure." Would have sounded more convincing if I could move my lips, my jaw or my tongue . . . but everything was still muzzy from the stun-blast. The word came out less like, "Sure," and more like, "Uhhhr."

"I'll take that for a yes," Ramos said. "Next question: are you Faye Smallwood? Because if you're some criminal or alien spy, and I just shot two men who'd arrested you legitimately . . . well, won't my face be red."

I bet she used that phrase a lot. Preemptively. Mock yourself before someone else does. I ignored it, and just said, "I'm Faye." The words blurred out to *I ay*, but Ramos understood.

"Glad I found you," she said. "The police have been searching everywhere. They'll be pleased to have you back." She patted my cheek with a warm hand. "Hold on a second."

Setting my head down carefully, she moved to the unconscious Muscle. It didn't take long for her to check his breathing and pulse, then roll him into recovery position. As an afterthought, she pried the stun-pistol from his clenched fingers and slipped it into her own belt.

"Stunners are Explorer weapons," she said, turning back to me. "I hate to see one in the hands of these dipshits." She paused, then gave a soft smile. "*Dipshit* is a technical term—at least I'm trying to make it one. Short for diplomat. Officially, these gentlemen belong to the fleet's Diplomacy Corps . . . which is mostly a cover for the High Council's dirty-tricks brigade." She knelt beside me again. "How are you feeling now?"

I tried to say, "Great." It didn't work, but at least a sound came out of my throat.

"Don't worry," Ramos told me. "You only caught a light dose. Ten minutes and you'll be ready to break more knees."

Sliding her hands under my armpits, she hiked me up

and wrestled my flop-fumbly body onto her shoulder. Her strength impressed me—Demoth's gravity might be mild, but I know how much I weigh. Ramos was almost a full head shorter than I, but she slung me into a fireman's carry and began moving toward the door.

"Sorry we can't wait till you recover," she said with a grunt of exertion, "but I don't know whether there are other dipshits in the neighborhood. Best if we aren't caught hanging around." Lifting her feet high, she stepped over the Muscle's body. "I don't know what the bastards would do if they nabbed us—they'd think twice about messing with an admiral, even a lowly lieutenant one—but this team hasn't shown any scruples so far. Someday I must find out how the Admiralty trains them to the very edge of homicidal non-sentience without actually pushing them over."

If you ask me, Mouth and Muscle had crossed the line as soon as they decided to strip-mine my brain; but I knew the League of Peoples didn't see it that way. If the dipshits (good name) sincerely made their best efforts not to kill me, the League wouldn't raise a stink if I happened to die anyway . . . or if I ended up a pith-headed vegetable. After all, the League let the Vigil plant a link-seed in my skull, despite the chance of stir-frying my cerebellum. In the College Vigilant, one professor told us, *The League doesn't mind if you risk other people's lives, as long as you honestly believe there's **some** chance for survival . . . and as long as you take the best precautions you know of. The League's definition of sentience doesn't require us to be intelligent, humane or non-exploitive; we just have to be careful.*

And some folks still call the League "benevolent."

Ramos lugged me out the door into a room filled with humming cabinets of the electronic persuasion—probably equipment for jamming my link-seed connection, plus hologram projectors and who knows what else. One black box looks precious like another, especially when you're hanging upside down over somebody's shoulder. Anyway, I was mostly paying attention to a growing queasiness in my stomach: my nervous system was still too jangly to provide accurate feedback, but I could feel the grumbly-rumblies where Ramos's shoulder dug into my gut.

Not good. I'd never bothered with la-di-dah manners, but it wouldn't do to puke down an admiral's leg.

We passed through another doorway into a room with wall-to-wall picture-carpet: currently showing a velveteen view of Demoth from orbit, half daylight, half night. As Ramos walked forward, her feet brushed over a moving image of ships docking at one of our space terminals. "This is a live broadcast," she said, tapping the picture with her toe. "The dipshits have their own sloop parked near your North Terminus. This is probably the view through the ship's nose camera. Or should I say the *boat*'s nose camera? I take great pride in being the only admiral who doesn't know the difference between a ship and a boat . . . and who doesn't give a flying fuck either way. I wouldn't even know it was a sloop if my crew hadn't told me."

She stopped herself suddenly. "I hope you don't mind me blathering like this—Explorers are trained to give running commentaries whenever we go on missions, and I still haven't broken myself of the habit. If I weren't making one-sided conversation with you, I'd probably be describing the furniture." Ramos lowered her voice to a dramatic near whisper. "We are moving through what seems to be an artificial chamber, surrounded by four-legged assemblages of unconfirmed purpose and origin . . . perhaps of religious significance." She gave a laugh and went back to her normal voice. "Or would you prefer I tell you about the dipshits?"

"Dipshits," I said. Which came out "ick-ick." Not a bad description for the Mouth and the Muscle when you think of it.

"Dipshits it is," Ramos said. "And I was talking about

their sloop . . . which came to my attention as soon as I arrived at Demoth two hours ago. I was flying in my so-called 'flagship'—which has living quarters the size of a pup tent, and the surliest crew of Vac-heads in the entire fleet. The comm officer made some sulky remarks about a Diplomacy Corps ship lollygagging here, eighteen light-years from our nearest diplomatic mission . . . and I immediately suspected a team of bad-ass boys had come to town.

"To check things out," she continued, "I radioed the base commander in Snug Harbor. He couldn't tell me anything about the dipshits; they'd never contacted him. But he *did* say how glad he was that an admiral had finally deigned to drop in—he thought I was following up his report about a mysterious Sperm-tail seen during an assassination attempt. As a new wrinkle, the intended victim of that attempt, one Faye Smallwood, had just been reported missing and the civilian authorities were going bugfuck." Ramos shifted my weight on her shoulder. "Basically, the commander gave me a crisp salute, said, 'You're in charge, Admiral,' and declined all further responsibility."

Step by step we continued to cross the moving-picture carpet—Ramos's feet scuffing past the blue rim of the planet and into starry blackness speckled with parked spaceships, then the brick orange expanse of the terminus itself. The resolution of the rug's image was so fine-grained I could see tiny dockworkers in tightsuits, skittering over the space station's hull . . . as if I were looking down on everything from far above . . .

Ooo, Christ. Vertigo. Just what my stomach needed.

"So I concluded," Ramos went on obliviously, "that the dipshits from the sloop had been sent by the High Council to investigate this strange Sperm-tail. If the prime witness was missing, the dipshits had probably snatched her; precisely their style. So I asked myself where they'd take you. Most likely answer: an Admiralty safe house. The fleet owns property on every planet in the Technocracy, secret hideaways where admirals can entertain government officials or have sordid little trysts because they think that's what powerful people do. I decided to pay a visit to the house nearest where you disappeared . . . and you can fill in the rest.''

Abruptly, Ramos stopped and bent over to set my feet on the floor. My stomach lurched like a bucket, then settled. I felt a wall behind me; a moment later, I was leaning ass-against it, wondering when my knees would buckle. They didn't. And after a while, I even felt the blood stop draining from my face.

Ramos watched a few seconds, then said, ''See? You're stronger already. Wait here while I scout ahead.''

She disappeared through another doorway. Now that I was upright, now that I was merely nauseous rather than prevolcanic, I had a chance to survey the room; before, all I'd seen was carpet and chair legs. Expensive legs attached to expensive chairs. Every piece of furniture was made of Grade A smart-stone: cores of depleted uranium topped by a simulated marble foam of nanotech that molded itself snugly to the shape of your rump. Looked like solid rock, but felt like comfy cushions. Farcical when you thought about it. From your butt's point of view, these were just cozy easy chairs . . . but built obscenely chunky and ponderous (depleted uranium, for Christ's sake!), purely so guests *knew* you paid top dollar.

I glared at the chair nearest me—letting myself build up a snooty blue-collar resentment, mostly just to keep my mind off the continuing rockiness of my stomach—when suddenly I heard a whisper-faint yipping in my mind. Yes, yipping: like when you accidentally step on a beagle's tail. Suddenly the whole surface of the chair cringed under my gaze . . . flattening out against the frame, cowering, nanites fleeing around to the chair's underside, hiding there, even peeking fearfully out from the edges to see if I was going to come after them.

You could almost hear their worried little hearts going pit-a-pat.

"Sorry," I mumbled. "Didn't mean to scare you." Jumbly-mumbly sounds coming out of my mouth, not words; but the nanites began to creep timidly back, slug-slow in case I'd glare at them again. . . .

I shook my head hard, then shut my eyes. *Faye*, I silently told myself, *nanites don't have pit-a-pat hearts. They're teeny soulless machines, the size and intelligence of bacteria. They may be programmed to make a plushy surface under someone's butt, but they are definitely not programmed to act like whipped puppies just because you stared at them harsh.*

Hesitantly, reluctantly, I opened my eyes. The chair was back to normal. Stony-surfaced. Stony-faced. And there was no yipping/whimpering to be heard.

Well, I thought, *that sure took my mind off the queasy stomach.*

Ramos hurried back into the room. "The coast is clear, at least for the moment. Should I carry you again, or can you walk?"

Concentrating hard, I tried to move my feet; they responded, though I could scarcely feel them. Ramos shifted in to help me, taking my right arm over her shoulders and wrapping her left arm around my waist. When I started forward it was more a babyfied toddle than a walk, but we found a rhythm after a few paces—faster than a tortoise, slower than a hare. Somewhere about the speed of a dog with worms as it drags its ass across your best broadloom.

Have I mentioned our family has pets?

Ramos and I shambled down a short passageway into a kitchen, the place sparkling-clean except for two dirty plates on the counter. By the looks of it, Mouth and Muscle had made spaghetti while they waited for me to wake up . . . and, of course, they were just the type to leave dishes for someone else to clean.

Cavalier buggers.

The kitchen led to a back-porch area, too spotless to

call a mudroom. Through the windows I saw black night, as dark as a miner's boot: clouds hid the stars, and thick forest crowded up within ten meters of the porch steps.

"We're still on Great St. Caspian," Ramos said in a low voice, "but a long way from Bonaventure. The air's a little thin outside . . . not that you can tell inside this pressurized house. We'll be all right out there if we don't try anything energetic—and we don't have to go far, I've got a skimmer parked five minutes away. How are you holding up?"

"I'm fine." This time the words actually sounded like words—slurred words spoken by some pisshead drunk, but at least they had consonants.

"Amazing powers of recovery." Ramos gave me a faint smile. "Hang on, while I make sure we're alone."

She bent down to a small machine that sat on the floor beside the door. It matched the size of a paint can, but its top was a flat glass screen. Ramos picked up the machine and swept it through a slow scan of the yard outside, keeping her eyes on the screen. "The Bumbler shows nothing on IR," she said, clipping the machine to her belt. "Let's go."

The way out was a double-door arrangement: an airlock between the house and the skimpier atmosphere outside. My ears popped as the outer door opened, but it wasn't a fierce hurt; either my neurons were too dizzy to register pain, or the pressure differential wasn't so scary as Ramos thought. I leaned toward the second alternative. Offworlders always get overexcited about the threadiness of our atmosphere.

We hobbled across the dark yard and entered the darker woods. This wasn't a sparse, well-spaced tundra forest— these trees were wild boreal. Instead of demure carpet moss, you got angry snarls of underbrush; instead of don't-bother-the-neighbors bluebarrels, there were cactus-pines thorned up for war, reaching out to strangle each other with as many branches as possible. It all added up to show we were in the south half of the island . . . just a fraction warmer year-round, but enough to shift the ecology from tightly contained order to every-bush-for-itself chaos.

The only route forward was a game trail, narrow enough that Ramos and I had a devil of a time walking two abreast. Lucky for us, we didn't need to go a long way—just over a ridge and down to a creek gully where Ramos had her skimmer waiting.

In the dark, the skimmer was blessed near invisible—not just camouflaged but chameleoned, its hull perfectly mimicking the nearby terrain. No identification markings either . . . which was mildly illegal, in a Class II misdemeanorly way. Ramos carried me to the back hatch, which opened as we reached it.

"Get in, get in!" cackled a voice from inside. Exactly the voice I'd heard in a junior-school play, when Lynn's ten-year-old Barry got cast to play an old man: cartoonish, nasal, enthusiastically cracking every other syllable. The old-man voice people use in dirty jokes.

"Faye Smallwood," Ramos said, "this is Ogodda Unorr. Our getaway driver."

"Call me Oh-God," he grinned. "As soon as I start driving, you'll know why."

The man was a Freep. A native of the Divian Free Republic: the closest habitable planet to Demoth, a mere six light-years away. The Free Republic started much like Demoth—a Divian billionaire bought a planet and commissioned a custom-engineered race so he could create his own utopia. This particular utopia was intended to be staunchly libertarian but had too much wired-in greed to maintain any higher principles; it nose-dived into dog-eat-dog anarchy for three centuries after its founding, then calcified into a corporate oligarchy run by rich trade barons. Cartel capitalism. The Freep plutocracy chanted the mantra of "free markets" while making sure their markets were only free for those who played the right game.

By the looks of it, the Freep driving the skimmer had got himself out of the game by joining the navy—he wore black fatigues, faded and gone shiny in places, but still recognizable as a uniform of the Explorer Corps. The uniform had several circular spots darker than the surrounding cloth: places where insignia must have been sewn on. Oh-God's badges were gone now, leaving no sign of his rank or ship assignment. He must be that rarity, an Explorer who'd lived long enough to retire.

I looked at Oh-God more closely. Yes, he *was* old. Cracking ancient. Like all Freeps, he was short, stocky, and cylindrical . . . a chest-high tree stump with arms. His skin was pale orange at this moment, the way all Freeps go orange on Demoth. Back on their home planet, Freep skins can chameleon all the way to black, a tactic for shutting out the barrage of ultraviolet that comes from the smaller of their two suns; but on Demoth, especially on a winter-spring night in Great St. Caspian, the UV was too weak to demand pigment protection.

"Come on, come on, come on," Oh-God said. "Stop gawking and get yourself belted in, missy. We don't want to hang around here."

His voice still had that all-over-the-octave cackle, as if he was intentionally parodying his own age. Except that Divian voices get lower in their senior years, not higher. Then the truth struck me: Ogodda Unorr was an Explorer. And like all Explorers, he'd have some physical quirk that made his fellows edge away in disdain. Oh-God must have become an Explorer by virtue of that odd voice—a grating, googly, whistly voice that had marked him as different his whole life.

Ramos buckled me into place beside Oh-God and took the next seat herself. The skimmer was rising even before she had her safety belts fastened—a whisper-silent vertical ascent followed by the breakneck whip of acceleration as we bolted forward just above the treetops.

I'd never ridden in a skimmer that made so precious little sound. It must have been running state-of-the-art stealth engines—maybe even military grade. Looking at Oh-God's control panel, I saw a slew of other quaint additions to the usual equipment . . . including a readout labeled RADAR FUZZ. Radar fuzz = nano on the skimmer's hull, dutifully (and illegally) making the craft invisible to groundcontrol traffic stations: a Class IV misdemeanor that often got argued up to a felony, "willful disregard for the safety of others."

"Hot," I said, pointing a wobbly finger toward the read-out. "Bad."

"Aww, missy," Oh-God wheedled back, "I only turn it on in emergencies. Like now. If there's Admiralty scum on the prowl, you don't want them seeing us, do you?"

He'd got me there. But this skimmer still had *Smuggler* written all over it. Silent and undetectable, big enough to haul a bumper load of questionable goods from Great St. Caspian halfway around the world without paying transport tax or trade-region import fees.

Oh-God might have left the Free Republic, but he hadn't abandoned their "free enterprise" mentality.

Three minutes later, we were flying along another creek gully, making no sound but the occasional whip of brush against the skimmer's undercarriage. Taking a deep breath, I mustered my best enunciation to ask, "What now?"

"If I were you," Ramos replied, "I'd scream like a banshee to your civilian police. Report you were kidnapped, and the perpetrators are now lying unconscious, ready to be arrested. I'll gladly testify to what I saw."

"Or," Oh-God said, "you could get a bunch of boyos with blunt instruments, to go back and conduct your own interrogation. All private-like."

Ramos chuckled. "Oh-God disdains subtlety."

"Subtlety's fine, it's police I hate," the Freep corrected her. "Not cuz I've done anything wrong," he added quickly. "Just on general principles. Always coming up with rules and regulations to hamper an honest businessman." He jinked the skimmer up over a rock outcrop, then bellied it down again close to the dirt.

Something scraped loudly against the lower fuselage. "Sorry," he mumbled. "Hands are cold tonight."

"Then warm them up!" Ramos growled. "What's the point of stealth equipment if you make noise hitting things?" She gave me a "See what I have to put up with?" look. "Officially," she told me, "Oh-God is a hunting guide. That's why he needs all these gadgets for skulking. In case your local deer ever develop radar."

"You never know," Oh-God said. "Demoth's already got beasties with sonar."

Ramos smiled. "If you get dragged in front of a judge, you stick with that story." She turned back to me. "Un-officially, Oh-God does a lot of things I don't want to know about. But he survived fifty years as an Explorer, and he's still loyal to the Corps. Whenever something noteworthy happens on Demoth, he passes on a report which eventually lands on my desk. That's why I came here in the first place—I'm interested in political assas-sinations. All those proctors getting killed."

"What does that have to do with Explorers?" I asked. It was getting easier to speak, even though the words still sounded too thick.

"Nothing directly," Ramos answered. "But if the kill-ings were just the start of a bigger mess, *someone* in the Admiralty ought to be interested."

"Like the dipshits?" I asked.

"Those pukes," Oh-God said. He jerked the skimmer sharply to the right, not to avoid an obstacle but just for emphasis. He was the worst kind of driver: someone who talks with his hands. "You gotta recognize the difference between the High Council of Admirals—the inner circle who run the dipshits—and our Festina here. She may wear a gray uniform, but she's not a *real* admiral."

"Thanks so much," Ramos told him.

"It's true," Oh-God insisted. "Who ever heard of a lieutenant admiral? They jury-rigged that title just for you." He turned to me, both hands off the controls. "See, she got the council in hot water with the League of Peoples . . ."

"Do you mind?" Ramos said, shoving his hands back toward the steering yoke. "We're in the middle of a heroic rescue here. It'll look bad if we wrap Faye around a tree."

"Won't look bad," Oh-God muttered. "The antidetection nanites'll automatically camouflage the crash site. Won't see nothing at all."

"That's not comforting!" Ramos snapped. She glanced at me. "We should be clear of the dipshits' jamming field by now. Do you want to call the police?"

"If we call the cops," I said, "it'll raise merry hell. Don't you care about embarrassing the Admiralty?"

"I'm not the one who brought on the embarrassment," Ramos answered grimly. "If the High Council authorized gratuitous criminal acts, they should get barbecued."

"Barbecued?" Oh-God snorted. "It'll never happen, missy. The damned admirals'll bribe everyone to keep this quiet." He patted my knee with a clumsy hand. "If you don't know how much to ask for, I can recommend someone to be your negotiating agent." He winked. "I know people."

I hate it when Divian subspecies wink. With their eyelids moving from the bottom up, it doesn't look sly, it looks creepy.

"Oh-God's right," Ramos said. "Gouging money out of the Admiralty may be the only revenge you can get, Faye. Taking this mess public may sound attractive, but you'll never touch the admiral who actually ordered this fiasco. The High Council are masters of deniability." She shrugged. "Still, your government could use this as leverage to wangle favors out of the fleet. Negotiate some lucrative naval supply contracts for local industry . . . if you don't mind taking dirty money and addicting your economy to antiproductive Admiralty handouts. Anyway: you're the victim here. It's your choice how to play this."

I didn't want to play anything—not till I understood

what was going on. "You still haven't told me what you're doing here," I said. "Do you represent the Explorer Corps? Or the Admiralty? Or who?"

"She's the Vigil is who she is," Oh-God replied. "Your basic steely-eyed watchdog. She's what-you-call scrutinizing the fleet."

"Actually," Ramos corrected him, "I scrutinize the Technocracy. Admiral Seele scrutinizes the fleet." She gave me an apologetic smile. "Yes, it's confusing. Half the time, *I* don't know what I should be doing. But Oh-God is right; I do fill a role something like your Vigil."

I didn't bother speaking; I could see she was already sorting things around in her mind, getting set to lay out a full explanation.

"Long before I was born," Ramos said, "two shrewd old admirals set up spy networks to monitor the Admiralty and all the planets of the Technocracy—to watch for trouble that the fleet or planetary leaders might try to cover up. This is a dangerous universe, Faye, and our settlements are more tenuous than we like to admit. Some of our most prosperous worlds are actually so hostile to human life, thousands could die from a single missed supply shipment. Someone has to take responsibility to make sure that doesn't happen. Someone has to root out any corruption or incompetence that jeopardizes our people."

"Doesn't the Technocracy do that?" I asked. "And each planetary government?"

Oh-God made the Freep sound for disgust, half hiss, half whistle—the noise a Divian's stomach makes just before throwing up. "Planetary governments? You're spoiled here on Demoth, missy. Most other worlds have governments with their heads jammed nose high up their butts . . . or they've sold out to some blind-assed bunch of robber barons who think they can buy their way free of any problem. Here, you've got the Vigil for a sanity check. Out in the rest of the galaxy, there's whole planets facing economic collapse, or ecological catastrophe, or coups and peasant rebellions, but the powers-that-be are dangling their dobbies in complete denial. Someone has to blow the whistle to tell the rest of the Technocracy when there's a crisis coming; and that means us merry band of watchers. Old Chee's spy network. Now working for our beloved Festina.''

Ramos grimaced. "You're such a suck-up. Did you treat Chee this way too?"

"Nah. I plied him with illegal booze and tobacco. In exchange for which, he funneled me some great military equipment. How do you think I outfitted this skimmer?''

"Good thing we're constantly on the watch for corruption.'' Ramos turned back to me. "Chee was one of the admirals who founded this spy network. Two years ago, he died, and I inherited command. Part of a complicated deal with the High Council, aimed at appeasing the League of Peoples. I caught the council indulging in dirty tricks, and the admirals had to make an act of contrition to the League. Next thing I knew, I was elevated to Lieutenant Admiral and spymaster.''

"Shows how much she had them over a barrel,'' Oh-God cackled. "Those pukes would far rather dismantle the network, or put some gutless flunky in charge, dancing to their own tune. But us intelligence operatives were mostly former Explorers, and fucked if we'd take orders from some Admiralty asshole. We'd turn independent first. So the council had to go with Festina and hope maybe they could control her more than old Chee. Fat chance.''

He laughed snortingly, and the skimmer bobbed in time with his chuckles. Whisk, whisk, whisk, bushes brushing our underbelly. *Oh-God, Oh-God, Oh-God,* I thought.

"You're driving is off tonight,'' Ramos observed.

"Gotta get me some gloves.'' He pulled both hands off the steering yoke and held them in front the dashboard's heating vent. Ramos slapped his shoulder; Oh-God grumbled but took the wheel again.

"Anyway,'' Ramos said in a long-suffering voice, "I took over Chee's spy network two years ago. Watchdogging planetary governments. I didn't know the first thing about what I was doing, but Chee had acquired plenty of good deputies. They still run most of the show . . . which makes me feel guilty for letting them do all the work. I've stayed shackled to my desk for two full years, trying to learn how to be a backroom strategist; but it's killing me." She ran a hand through her hair. "And it's killing me to find I want to get out into unfamiliar territory again, poke my nose where it's not wanted, feel that rush of adrenaline. I *hated* being an Explorer . . . and I hated how people saw it as an exciting profession when the whole point was to avoid the slightest hint of excitement." She sighed. Deeply. "But I miss it. I may be suicidally stupid, but I miss it."

She looked away from us all, off into the blackness of the night. "So here I am, doing the next best thing to Exploration. When I heard about your proctors getting murdered, I just blurted, 'I'll investigate that myself' . . . then barreled out of the office too fast for anyone to stop me. Which led to this mildly daring rescue, and putting my life in the hands of a Freep madman."

"Ahh, you love it, missy," Oh-God said affectionately. "And any idjit could see you weren't suited to go planet-down on a desk. You've got Explorer deep in your blood."

"Not to mention written all over my face," Ramos muttered.

"So," Admiral Ramos said, turning brisk all of a sudden, "did the dipshits say how long they'd been on Demoth?"

"They told me . . ." My mouth still wasn't going over all the hurdles. "They told me the local base commander had reported the Sperm-tube, and they were sent to check it out."

"That's a possibility," Ramos agreed, "but who knows if they were telling the truth? Suppose they arrived earlier: *before* the assassinations."

"Suppose they did the assassinations themselves," Oh-

God suggested. "They might have used Admiralty funds to buy robots and reprogram them . . . because those High Council pukes have some scheme going—"

"No," Ramos interrupted, "the High Council definitely *can't* send a hit team to assassinate anyone. The League of Peoples has a flawless track record for preventing killers from traveling planet-to-planet. Flawless. The League never makes exceptions, and never makes mistakes. But if the High Council sent a team of not-quite-homicidal dipshits here on some mission and something unexpected drove them over the edge . . ."

She stopped and shook her head. "I don't know. Dipshits are self-centered morons, but they're trained to avoid murder. More than trained—they're methodically indoctrinated. And what's so important on Demoth that's worth killing for?"

A peacock-colored tube, I thought, *that saved my life and thumbed its nose at Admiralty physics.* The dipshits had been willing to turn me into a vegetable, just to find out what I knew. How much more would they do?

But I didn't say that out loud; I closed my eyes for a heartbeat, wondering if I was feeling brave enough to use my link-seed. Nope. "Which one of these dials is the radio?" I asked, pointing at the skimmer's controls. "It's time to call the cops."

The next few minutes got tricky. Protection Central wanted to know where I was, so they could send an escort to ferry me home. Oh-God, on the other hand, had no intention of giving the police a glimpse of his skimmer, considering how they might raise a stink over its "emergencies-only" customizations. In the end, the Explorers let me out at a park station in the Black Tickle Wilderness Preserve, where four bemused forest rangers said sure, they'd protect me till the cops arrived. Ramos promised to contact me soon, then flew off into the night.

Twenty minutes later, a fleet of six police skimmers picked me up and proceeded to the house where I'd been held captive. I half expected the place to be empty, with all evidence of my presence cleaned up; but the Mouth and Muscle were exactly where we'd left them, still out cold. Even better, the detective team found recording equipment the dipshits had used to log my "interrogation" . . . good hard evidence that made the police captain's eyes shine with harsh glee. His name was Basil Cheticamp, rail-thin with glassy cheeks of hypoglycemic pink, but he was a cop through and through.

"They think they can come in here . . ." Cheticamp muttered under his breath. "Those navy pricks think they can come to our planet . . ."

I loved the sound of that. Even if the Admiralty started throwing hush money around, they wouldn't buy off Cheticamp.

Glad I wasn't the only one.

It was dawn before we said good-bye to the house in the woods. Cheticamp didn't want to split his forces by sending me home with one set of officers while leaving the rest to gather evidence. Ergo we all stayed together, me drinking tea in that gleamy-bright kitchen, till a second squad of detectives arrived to relieve the first. By then, I'd used the police communication system to call my family and tell them I was safe as a daisy, sound of life and limb . . .

. . . which I truly was, all things considered. The dizziness passed; the hangover headache thudded itself out; and by dawn, plain old fatigue had settled in comfortably, just a punchy up-all-night weariness that left me feeling nostalgic and companionable. Near 4 A.M., Captain Cheticamp felt himself honor-bound to bestow the Great Weighty Lecture about people who go walking alone, especially when they know they might be targets . . . but he was so sweet pleased with how everything worked out, he didn't dig in the spurs too sharply.

Cheticamp said the police had been searching for me, almost from the moment I was kidnapped. The dipshits began jamming my link-seed even before they got my unconscious body into their skimmer; and the world-soul, none too happy with me vanishing from radio contact, triggered an alarm to Protection Central. Unlucky for me, the dipshits' skimmer sported the best antidetection equipment available to the Outward Fleet, making it impossible to track by satellite or ground-based radar. Still, Cheticamp swore they'd had the situation well in hand—the Admiralty safe house was definitely within their search perimeter, so they would have found me if Admiral Ramos hadn't got there first.

"You realize," he said, "you can't trust this Ramos?"

"Why not?"

"Good cop, bad cop," he replied. "Classic technique. A pair of vicious fucks put the scare into you, then a knight in shining armor rides to the rescue. Makes you grateful. Puts you under an obligation. It could be part of a plan."

"A plan to do what?" I asked.

"Blessed if I know. But this Ramos is an admiral too, even if she claims her hands are clean."

I'm not witless—the same thought had already crossed my mind. Still, this kidnapping incident would lead to crippling-bad publicity for the High Council of Admirals; I found it hard to believe they'd expose themselves to that, just for Festina Ramos to win my confidence.

A nobody, our Faye. In the great schemes of admirals, I just wasn't that important.

7

A TOTAL LOON

Once again, my family wanted to chain me to the bed with leg irons till police judged it safe for me to come out. You can guess what I said to that. Though I said it politely.

Then they had fallback positions. They could ask Protection Central for round-the-clock surveillance. They could hire a bodyguard. They could buy me my own stunner or jelly gun. They could get another dog, but a mean one this time, instead of the shake-hands-and-beg chowhounds Barrett usually brought home. (It was, of course, Barrett himself who suggested this. Whatever problems the family faced, two times out of three Barrett would explain how everything could be fixed if we just bought the right kind of dog.)

A typical view of my family in action. I let them have their shot at bullying me, but all they could really say was, "I'm scared, Faye." And their suggestions were just scrabbly attempts to make a gesture, even if they knew it was useless, so they could pretend the danger was avoidable if only we Did Things Right.

I couldn't pretend that myself; so I caught a few hours' sleep, then went in to work.

* * *

Unlike most offices in downtown Bonaventure, our Vigil headquarters had never got "humanized" ... which meant the office still flaunted the Oolom ambience established preplague. Floor-to-ceiling windows, for example, with wide exterior ledges for easy Oolom landings and takeoffs. Instead of glass, the windows were made of transparent nano membranes: 99 percent solid to keep out birds and insects, but porous enough to let through a hint of breeze and keep the Ooloms from feeling they were totally closed in.

As a bonus, the nanites in the membranes allowed duly appointed proctors to pass back and forth between the offices and the ledge. Walking through was like shoving yourself into a sheet of gelatin—the solid surface turned viscous where you touched it, and sucked clingy-tight to your body as you pressed forward, slurping back together behind you when you came out the other side.

Another thing about our office: it was a tree house.

Ooloms hated making buildings from concrete or steel. They'd do it if they had to—Pump Station 3 dated back to Oolom times, and it had cement walls. (Cement walls with a slew of windows, not to mention dozens of skylights.) Still and all, Ooloms considered such construction materials a last resort: tolerable for plebeian spots like a water-treatment plant, but out of the question for the only Vigil headquarters on all Great St. Caspian. You wouldn't stow the *Mona Lisa* in a mud shack, would you?

So the Ooloms put our office in a tree. A sign of their immense respect for the Vigil. Or for trees. This particular tree had "monumental" written all over it: an equatorial species called a *reshkent* or kapok elm, but dosed with so many growth hormones, not to mention bioengineered goiter-grafts and longevity sap enhancers ... well, transforming the original *reshkent* into our offices was like changing a toothpick to a totem pole. Not just making it whopping amounts bigger, but hanging all kinds of doodads on it.

Picture a massive central trunk twenty meters in diameter, but with a hollow core big enough to hold an elevator shaft. (Even Ooloms needed elevators on occasion: when high winds made flying dangerous, or when carting around office furniture.) Every five meters up the trunk was a bulging ring, like a fat belt around the tree's girth. A belt that stuck out so far, it was more like a life preserver. Each such ring had enough space to hold four good-sized offices, complete with those nanite windows, plus a desk, chairs, and a darling wee latrine. (Plumbing wastes were converted to fertilizer for the tree itself.)

Our tree had six such "floors," six annular rings spaced bulgy up the trunk . . . and above all that was a gigantic umbrella of leaves stretched almost fifty meters in every direction, soaking up sun to keep the tree alive. Barely a fifth of those leaves fell each year; the rest hung on, still doing their photon-collection job no matter how crispy they became with cold. Now and then throughout the winter, a leaf grew so heavy with ice that it snapped off its branch, dropped sharp and fast, then shattered like a glass dagger on some window ledge.

At one time, all twenty-four offices in the tree housed proctors; but that was before the plague. Now, Floors One and Two were empty, and I was the only person on Floor Three. Senior proctors filled up the higher floors . . . except for a vacant room on Floor Five. Chappalar's office. I could have taken it but didn't want to. Not even for the better view.

I supposed our new arrival, Master Tic, would claim Chappalar's old office. He'd also take over Chappalar's old duties . . . which might mean he was slated to be my supervisor.

Unless master proctors were too important to waste time riding herd on a novice.

Or unless I got some say in the matter myself; in which case, I'd pick one of the proctors I'd known for seven years, instead of some goggle-wearing outsider who thought he could step into Chappalar's shoes.

(All right—Ooloms didn't actually *wear* shoes. Just flimsy-dick things like ballet slippers made of ort skin. But you know what I mean.)

To find out who'd become my new mentor, I took the elevator straight up to Jupkur's office on the top ring. Jupkur was Gossip Central for our building—not only did he know everything, but he blabbed it at the least provocation, all the while saying, "Well, I don't like to talk . . ."

By luck, Jupkur was in: lying flat on his desk and staring at the ceiling. Don't ask me why. Since the plague, our Oolom proctors had spent more than two decades immersed in our culture and adapting to our ways. God knows, they worked hard to fit in with our particular brand of *Homo sap* behavior. Now and then, though, you still caught them acting just plain alien, especially when humans weren't around.

I found it kind of endearing.

"Welcome back, Faye," Jupkur said without looking in my direction. Ooloms were nigh-on eerie when it came to recognizing people by the sound of their footsteps. (They can even tell when you've bought new boots . . . maybe the only males in the universe who ever notice.)

"You missed an exciting night," he told me, still keeping his gaze on the ceiling. "The rest of us got to loiter till three in the morning, inventing theories of where you might be. Some hypotheses were extremely clever . . . even witty, though I shouldn't brag. Then I tried to organize a betting pool, guessing the state of your corpse when the police finally found you. Alas, the others spent too long scrutinizing the rules of the wager; you turned up alive before anyone actually gave me money."

"Sorry."

"Ah well." He sat up and turned toward me. "I'm sure

you'll get in trouble again. We've all agreed you're *bot-jolo*."

The word meant "cursed." Or "self-destructive." Which Oolooms considered the same thing.

"You're so kind," I muttered. "Do you have a minute?"

"Of course. Although if you're looking for guidance on official Vigil business, Master Tic is your new supervisor and I don't want to *valk* him."

*Valk*ing was gliding into another person's flight path. The Oolom equivalent of stepping on someone's toes.

"That was one of the things I wanted to ask," I said. "Whether Tic was my new mentor. And what he's doing in Bonaventure."

Jupkur winked at me . . . which didn't look any better on him than it did on Oh-God. Some gestures just don't transfer from one species to another.

"Master Tic is pursuing his own agenda," Jupkur said. "That's one thing you can be sure of. He has a reputation in various circles . . . well, one doesn't like to gossip."

"You love to gossip," I replied.

"True," he replied. "And what a treat you're a full-fledged proctor now . . . I can reveal juicy tidbits about everyone in the Vigil, and it won't be telling tales out of school. Do you know how long it's been since I polished up my stories for somebody new?"

"Just tell me about Tic," I said.

"Well, now . . . Tic." Jupkur smiled. "Tic's a master proctor, isn't he? Which means he's the cream of the cream, as you humans say. The best. The acme of perfection."

He kept smiling. Or should I say smirking? Seated on the edge of his desk, simpering like a man with a secret. A secret about Tic.

"So what's wrong with him?" I asked.

"Think about his name, Faye. Tic. Hardly a conventional Oolom name. And not his original one, oh no. He began calling himself Tic a year back. It's short for *tico*."

Tico = crazy. Mad. "So he's saying he's insane?" I asked.

"A raving screwball. A total loon. A person of addled wits."

"Why would he call himself that?" I said. "Is he nuts?"

"Faye," Jupkur answered, "Master Tic is Zenning out."

"Ahhhhhh."

To Zen out. The human phrase for a condition that sneaked up on some proctors if they lived long enough. A side effect of long-term link-seed use. These people had achieved a state of . . . well, damned if I know what went on in their heads, but they'd stopped functioning on the same mundane wavelength as the rest of us. If you're a glass-half-full person, you could claim they'd reached a higher plane of consciousness; if you prefer the-glass-is-half-empty, you'd say they'd gone gibbering round the bend.

Except that they didn't gibber. Zenned-out proctors acted happy enough. Blissful even. And when they deigned to pay attention to the world, they seemed keen-witted and shrewd, full of insight. Brilliant, perceptive, intuitive, wise. Most of the time, though, they were cabbages. Not catatonic or delusional—just shifted to a set of priorities that didn't mesh with the rest of us. Eating strawberries while being attacked by tigers, that sort of thing.

Or so the stories went. It'd been a long time since we'd actually seen a Zenned-out case on Demoth—the most elderly proctors had all died in the plague, and the survivors weren't old enough to have their brains go soupy.

Till now.

"So," I said, "does this mean Tic is unstable?"

Jupkur shook his head. "Not the way you're thinking. He's just dancing to a different drummer, as you humans say. Not dangerous, but not very useful either." Jupkur hopped off the edge of his desk and shook out his gliders to get them to hang more comfortably. "Have a look at this."

He turned his back to me and spread his gliders wide like a triangular sail, point-down. In a moment, printed words appeared on the surface of the membrane—an effect that freaked merry hell out of me the first time I saw it. As I've said, Ooloms don't have conscious control over their chameleon abilities; but Jupkur (at flamboyant expense) had coated the back of his gliders with pixel-nano under command of his link-seed. At parties, he could give himself moving tattoos . . . which he did at every opportunity. Flagrantly. And don't ask me the subject matter.

A right tease, our Jupkur.

I looked at the writing on display, as he used himself for a projection screen. "What *is* this?" I asked.

"Part of a report," he replied. "From the coordinator of the team who are scrutinizing the trade talks between us and the Freeps. That was Tic's last assignment."

I skimmed the words. About Tic. The phrase "inattention to duty" stood out . . . possibly because Jupkur was making it flash bright red.

"Tic never did what he was told," Jupkur said, as if I couldn't read it for myself. "The coordinator would assign him to review some paragraph overnight, and in the morning, Tic would have looked at a completely different section. Mind you, his insights were often brilliant . . . but that didn't make him any friends, considering that someone else was probably reviewing the same text without the same degree of inspiration. If the coordinator asked, 'What do you *want* to look at, Tic?,' he'd answer, 'I don't know yet. Whatever feels important.' Which is not exactly helpful when you're trying to keep things organized."

I nodded. People sometimes get the notion proctors are rampant individualists, boldly charting our own paths to track down corruption. But mostly, we're methodical as mustard—you only get to follow your hunches after you've done days of preliminary donkeywork.

"So Tic got booted from the trade-treaty team?" I asked.

"Depends who tells the story," Jupkur said, lowering his arms and letting the words on his back fade away. "Most of my sources think that's what happened—he got the old leave-ho. But one friend at Vigil HQ says this was Tic's own decision. A day after the killings, Tic suddenly announced he was needed in Bonaventure. And when a master proctor wants a transfer, he gets a transfer . . . especially when his current team won't be sorry to see him go."

"You think Tic might be coming here to investigate Chappalar's death?"

"Heaven forbid!" Jupkur said with mock horror. "That's police business, isn't it? The Vigil has no mandate for criminal investigation. But it's just possible that such a quibble slipped Tic's mind . . . whatever shred of mind he has left."

"Lovely," I said. "The man's senile, and you've made him my supervisor."

"He *asked* to be your supervisor. And how could we say no to a master proctor?" Jupkur grinned. "Besides, what's he going to do, Faye? How much trouble can you get into in placid little Bonaventure?"

"Chappalar got murdered," I said.

"Point taken," Jupkur admitted. "But Chappalar didn't actually get himself in trouble. He was a victim of circumstance, nothing more. Someone decided to kill proctors because they were proctors. It's a global matter, Faye, and whatever Tic does, how can it make you more of a target than you already are?"

"Gee thanks," I muttered.

Jupkur waved his hand airily. "You're a target, I'm a target, he, she, and it are targets. Surely you don't think anyone is singling you out, Faye? This is political, not personal. Some weak-minded local has obviously bought into the Freep propaganda that the Vigil is undemocratic . . . we're a wicked unelected body of petty dictators, who do nothing but interfere with free representation. Heaven knows, the Freeps have been harping on that theme ever since we started getting under their skin at the trade talks. So some *tico* crackpot decides, yes proctors are Evil Personified and must be stopped. In time, the police will catch the culprit; I hope before another attack. But in the meantime, I don't intend to change the way I do my duty. Do you?''

"Of course not," I said. "I'm just worried about Tic."

"Don't be. At worst, his mind wanders; at best, he's still a master proctor. Tic could teach you a lot. *And I'm sure you can help him too.*"

Jupkur freighted those last words deep with meaning; and I caught the hint. A senile old fart just got himself posted to Bonaventure, and someone had to baby-sit him. Surprise, surprise, the senior proctors sloughed off the job on junior me. Crap flows downhill.

"All right," I said, trying to keep the grumbles out of my voice. "Tic and I are a team. Anything else you want to tell me?"

"Just one thing." Jupkur—Jupkur of the thousand-and-one smirks—suddenly lowered his gaze to the floor, abashed. "Tic was chief scrutineer over the Global Health Agency. During the plague."

Oh.

Ouch.

"No one blames him for anything," Jupkur went on hurriedly. "He demanded a review when it was all over, and the tribunal absolved him of all culpability. Actually, they wanted to give Tic a commendation for swift and decisive action. Things would have been even worse if he hadn't driven the government to move quickly. But Tic didn't want a gold medal—he wanted to do penance for all the deaths that happened on his watch. People say he hoped the review panel would crucify him: expel him from the Vigil, rip the link-seed out of his head. When they exonerated him instead, it sent him into a screaming fit, swearing he'd kill himself."

Jupkur shrugged. "The only problem was, Tic had caught the paralysis like everybody else, and couldn't hold a knife to slash his wrists. The disease clung on too—kept him immobile twice as long as anyone else. Psychosomatic, of course: guilt kept him numb months after the microbes were gone. So the emotional therapists went to work, and by the time he could move again, he was past the suicidal stage. Just not past the self-recrimination. If I were you, I wouldn't mention the plague in casual discussion."

"Jupkur," I groaned, "I'm Henry Smallwood's daughter. Ooloms still stop me on the street to shake my hand. The subject is going to come up."

"Don't *you* bring it up," Jupkur said. "Tic might take it the wrong way. As if you're boasting that your father had to clean up Tic's mess."

"I never boast about my father," I told him. Which shouldn't have been true, but was.

When I got to my office, Tic was there: standing by the window, solemnly pushing his hand into the clear membrane then pulling it back, listening to the sucking sound.

Ssss-pop. Ssss-pop. Sssssssssssss-pop.

His face had a look of fierce concentration, as if this was a momentous assignment demanding his full attention. No smile or frown: nothing but focus. He reminded me of Barrett's favorite basset hound, an old frump of a dog who would stare worriedly at a rubber ball for hours, wondering if maybe—just maybe—the ball could be used as a toy.

"Hello," I said. "Can I help you?"

"No," he replied, "I'm doing excellently on my own."

Sssss-pop. Sssssssssss-pop. Ss-pop.

"What *are* you doing?" I finally asked.

"Playing with the nanites. Simple souls—they just love being teased. Can't get enough of it."

My heart skipped a beat. *No, no, no*, I thought quick-

hop, *nanites don't have souls.* Every last one of the little buggers was dumb as earwax. Put a billion together and the most you got was an *idiot savant* window that could impersonate jelly. Nanites definitely did not have personalities or . . . or . . .

Some killjoy part of my brain wouldn't repress what happened the night before—how the nanites on the chair whimpered and turned tail when I gave them a dirty look.

"You think the nanites enjoy what you're doing?" I asked.

"They like the attention," Tic said. He threw me a glance over his shoulder. "Whenever I take a new post, I make sure to befriend the local nanites. They're always so desperately lonely. Taken for granted. No one ever gives a thought for their feelings." Ssssss-pop. "You, for example. This is your office, and they tell me you haven't even introduced yourself."

"I'm just new," I found myself saying. "I only got the office a few days ago, and I've been busy ever since."

"You aren't busy now."

Tic gave a tiny jerk of his head toward the window— the sort of hinting gesture that people pretend is so subtle no one else will notice. Reluctant as a rabbit, I crossed the room. Tic bobbed his head at the rightmost window. "Those fellows have been asking especially about you."

I thought, *Maybe this is a Vigil initiation prank. A stunt to make the new kid embarrass herself. Jupkur sets me up to think Tic is a total loon, and Tic gets me to do something witless just to humor him. Soon, all the other proctors will jump out laughing.*

Or else Tic is *a total loon.*

Or else . . . no, I didn't want to think about that.

Placing my hand against the glassy un-glass window, I said, "Hi, guys. I'm Faye. You'll be seeing a lot of me now, sitting over in that desk."

The membrane yielded a titch under my palm, the solid surface going oozy. I expected that. I did *not* expect the gentle backsurge that came straightaway after . . . a cool jelly hand twining its fingers with mine. At the same instant, my brain bloomed up with a clear mental image of a million microscopic puppies licking my skin—an image superimposed over my real senses like a VR template.

"Jesus Christ!" I cried, yanking my hand back. It gave a thunderous pop as it came free.

"Good noise," Tic said. "Excellent volume. Can I hear it again?"

"No!" I snapped. "I thought . . . I thought I saw . . . I thought I felt . . ."

"Puppies?" Tic asked. "They wanted it to be a pleasant experience for you. You don't like dogs?"

"That was . . ." I gasped. "You mean the nanites . . ."

"Projected the image to say hello. They meant well, Smallwood. Now they're worried they've upset you."

"How could they project an image?"

Tic reached out a bony finger and tapped my forehead. "You're wired in now. Linked to the digital oneness. Like the nanites."

"But they're not intelligent!"

"Not very," Tic agreed. "But they're *connected*. They asked the world-soul to greet you on their behalf; the world-soul was the one who came up with puppies."

I felt my gorge rise . . . whatever a gorge is. "The world-soul projected something into my brain? Without my permission?"

"In any sensible society, saying hello to people gives them permission to say hello back."

"They aren't people, they're nanites!"

"Yes . . . and soon they'll be cranky little nanites if you don't say how much you appreciate their greeting. Small brains. Short tempers. Easily hurt feelings." Tic gestured toward the window. "Go on. You don't want to get on their bad side. Otherwise, the next time you run through a pane of glass, they'll deliberately muss your hair."

I stared at him. Tic had such a bland deadpan expression—a perfect poker face. (If frumpy old basset hounds could play poker.) For all I could tell, there wasn't an ounce of jokery in him.

Sigh.

Here's the thing: I didn't want to find out windows had easily hurt feelings. I preferred that my worldview didn't include opinionated nanotech. But . . . link-seed, Vigil, blah-blah-blah. You know the song, sing along with the chorus—Faye can't hide from the truth.

I reached toward the window again. Only one hand. The featheriest touch I could manage. A cool jelly palm made contact with mine, just as hesitant as me. Into my skull came the feeling of shyness—not my own, someone else's, a million someone elses worried they'd made some social gaffe. *It's all right*, I thought, projecting my words at the un-glass, *I'm just jumpy is all.* I forced my palm to linger an extra second, then pulled back, feeling the jelly hand slip away.

Ssssssss. A pop as soft as a soap bubble.

"An adequate start," Tic said. "Just don't ignore them from now on."

"I never knew they . . . who programmed them for emotions?"

Tic leaned toward me and whispered, "Nanites only have two programmed emotions: boredom and involvement. A single bit-switch that tells them they enjoy doing their job. 'Oh joy, we get to work for big people!' " He smiled fondly. "But when the nanites communicate with you through the world-soul, the world-soul likes to add more emotional color. Truth is, getting to know your local nanites is mostly just a way to show the world-soul you're machine-friendly. Like playing with a woman's children to win the mother's heart. You *definitely* want to stay on the world-soul's good side—you're a data-based organism now." He lowered his voice even more. "The world-soul likes to be called *Xé*."

I fair gulped at that one. Xé (pronounced Chay) was a female deity from the Ooloms' ancient past, dating back millennia to the Divian homeworld . . . comparable in time and sentiment to the Greek goddess Gaia. The Earth Mother. As I've said I didn't understand much about Oolom religions, but I was sure they all considered Xé mythical. A pretty legend, a gem of a metaphor, but definitely fictitious.

"Are you saying Xé is real?" I whispered.

Tic stared at me scornfully. "It's the world-soul, Smallwood. An artificial intelligence distributed over a million different machines. It likes the name Xé, but even Xé knows it's not Xé. Are all new proctors as gullible as you?"

"I'm not gullible," I grumped, "I'm just surprised the world-soul is . . . conscious. No one ever told me—"

"Xé's picky in choosing friends," Tic said. "Who's let in on the secret. Who gets shut out. If you remember this conversation tomorrow, feel honored."

"You mean the world-soul could wipe—"

"Shh." Tic put a scaly finger to my lips. "Wisdom doesn't upset itself over something that might not happen."

Wisdom can go poke a porcupine, I thought. A self-aware AI with delusions of godhood had its fingers inside my cranium; and now I found that if Xé didn't like me, it could wipe away all recollection of the past five minutes. I guess the conversation would never shift from short-term to long-term memory—thanks to an AI mucking with my mind.

And the entire Vigil was linked to *that*?

Jesus, Mary, and Joseph. I'd found a grand old way to mess myself up this time.

Unless Tic was lying. Out-and-out delusional. I couldn't deny there was something queer about the windows, the nanites and all . . . but this talk of Xé could just be an old loon's demented concoction. Imagining he was the world-soul's bosom buddy, when it was just an egoless congregation of computers, clean devoid of will.

Which was more disturbing? That my new supervisor might be psychotic? Or that he might be right?

*   *   *

Tic whispered, "Bye-bye," to the window, and patted the membrane a last time before turning to me. "Well, Smallwood. Down to business. I assume you've heard I'm your supervisor?"

"Yes."

"And you've also heard I'm a Zenned-out dotard with brains of sponge pudding?"

"Gossip has reached my ears," I said.

"All of it true," Tic replied, "except the parts that aren't. Or the parts that are both true and untrue." He gave me a look. "I just said that last so I'd sound more Zen. Not that I know much about human religions, but mystics the world over love paradox. Which is to say they hate reductivist binary logic. Am I rambling?"

"You're showing off," I told him. "Indulging yourself to make me think you're *really* crazy."

He smiled. "Very shrewd, Smallwood. You're smart as well as wide. But God Almighty, you *are* wide. Do you have to go through doors sideways?"

"No," I said. "And I'm married."

"With shoulders like that, no wonder. But don't mind me—us old codgers always use sexual harassment to put women at their ease. People think it's so adorable, we can get away with murder. And speaking of murder, what did you say that got Chappalar killed?"

The question caught me flat-footed. Ever adept with brilliant repartee, I said, "Huh?"

"Chappalar," Tic repeated. "We were both at a party for him the other day. Quiet fellow—never spoke a word through the whole ceremony. And speaking of speaking, whom did you tell? That you intended to visit Pump Station 3." Tic leaned his hangdog face toward mine. "Who knew you'd be there?

"Why are you asking?" I said. "Do you think you're investigating Chappalar's murder?"

Tic put on his scornful look again. "That's police business, Smallwood. Well outside the Vigil's authority."

I breathed a sigh of relief. Prematurely.

"My assignment," Tic went on, "is to assume Proctor Chappalar's duties. Which makes me your supervisor. I've reviewed your schedule, and you have no current commitments, correct? City council withdrew the water-treatment bill you were scrutinizing?"

I nodded.

"Then you need a new project to keep you busy," Tic said. "Proctor Smallwood, I assign you to scrutinize activities of the Bonaventure Civilian Protection Office. That's undeniably within the mandate of this Vigil branch."

No question, that. We were authorized to watchdog the local cops; in fact, we were legally *required* to give them a look-see from time to time.

"So," Tic said, "keep an eye open for all the usual things. Corruption. Slack work habits. Pilfering office supplies. What?" He cocked his ear toward the window. "Oh." He turned back to me. "Especially be on the look-out for people who don't wash their hands before entering the nanotech lab. Foul old bastards."

"Do the Bonaventure police *have* a nanotech lab?" I asked.

"Don't ask me—you're the one who's scrutinizing them. Far be it from me to tell you what to do." He leaned in conspiratorially. "Now here's what I want you to do. You're clearly at a total loss for direction, so why not monitor a representative criminal case currently being investigated?"

"Did you have something particular in mind?"

"We'll pick a case at random. Oh. Here's one." He reached onto my desk where there was a single file packet stamped with the Bonaventure police crest. I hadn't put the file there. Tic read the label on the packet and said, "This will do splendidly. The Chappalar murder investigation. Proctor Smallwood, you will scrutinize the police handling of this case to the best of your abilities. I, of course, will accompany you to provide the seasoned voice of experience.''

He waited for me to answer. I gave a slight nod.

Precious good thing we weren't overstepping our authority by intruding into police business.

Tic tossed the file onto my desk. "You'll want to review the police report as soon as possible," he said. "When you do, you'll see that those boobies bungled the interrogation of their prime witness. A human woman—one Faye Smallwood. You may have heard of her. The detectives downloaded what she saw at the murder scene and assumed it was all she knew. Can't imagine why they mollycoddled her. Of course she had political connections, so perhaps she pulled some strings down at city hall."

I glared at him. Tic grinned. "Or else," he said, "she started babbling about peacock thingies, and they thought she was a total loon."

"Did they call me that in the police report?" I asked, reaching for the file.

"Of course not," Tic replied, moving the file farther away from me. "Not in so many words. At any rate, the police believe in peacock thingies now. To a modest degree. Considering how the navy went berserk and kidnapped you, the constabulary has decided you weren't completely crazy, vis-à-vis mysterious tubes of light. Which is too bad—it's high time I worked with someone more *tico* than me."

I gave him a long hard look. "I'm strongly beginning to suspect you aren't *tico* at all."

Tic looked offended. "Ms. Smallwood," he said, "I'm *tico* as a *terrijent* . . . which is a little brown beetle not noted for odd behavior, but it was the first alliteration that came to mind. More to the point, I am by far the oldest proctor in the entire Vigil. If I'm not approaching a state of Zen by now, *there must be something wrong with me*. Do you understand? In the normal life cycle of proctors,

I'm at a point where I should be One with the universe. Or at most 1.0001. I should be asymptotic to apotheosis. Holding regular conversations with the major deities. Feeling the infinitesimal flux of the cosmological constant. Speaking the mystic language of the wind. If I'm not ecstatically demented with otherworldly bliss, Smallwood, a good many people will lose their faith that there *is* such a thing as Zenning out. Including myself; and I hate disappointing poor crazy old men.''

Despite the intensity of his words, he'd spoken with precious little emotion. Precious little emotion you could identify anyway. Was he joking at his own expense? Confiding a deep dark secret? Speaking straight from the heart? ''Why are you telling me this?'' I asked.

''Why not?'' he replied. ''When it crosses my mind to do something, I don't ask why, I ask why not. And usually there's no reason not to, so I just go ahead.'' He paused, then added, ''It's given me the strangest collection of hats.''

I stared at him a moment, then said, ''You're *tico* enough for me. Don't lose faith in that Zenning-out business.''

He smiled. ''What a sweet girl. Now let's talk about Chappalar's death.''

Outside the window, the shadow of our tree stretched off on a diagonal, reaching far across the rooftops as the sun set behind us. The street straight below had already gone dark enough for safety lights to be turning themselves on: children skipping past in jackets that shone bright orange so they couldn't be missed; adults with coats phosphorescing in more prudish colors, or the occasional curmudgeon with no lights at all—clods who preferred to get run down in traffic rather than stand out in the darkness. (''What if someone's following me?'' I once heard a man say. ''Why wear clothes that make me an easy target?'' As if snipers were a daily danger and careless drivers no trouble at all.)

Tic picked up the police file packet from my desk and idly turned it over in his fingers. "Chappalar's death," he said again. "The police neglected a vital line of questioning, and as discriminating proctors we should consider whether to draw this to their attention." He glanced up at me; the lowering dark made his face even pouchier. "Who knew where you and Chappalar would be?"

I'd barely registered his question the first time he asked it. Now it settled down more solid in my mind . . . and I realized Tic had hit on a serious point. The androids struck the pump station *before* Chappalar and I arrived; they'd taken out all the staff by the time we showed up.

So how did they know where we'd be?

We hadn't given the station any advance notice of our visit. Even Chappalar and I didn't know very far ahead— we'd only decided the previous evening, just before leaving our office for the night.

So who *did* know where we were going?

None of the other proctors, that was sure. Chappalar and I headed out together, without talking to anybody else. And we hadn't logged our intentions with the office computer—Chappalar had a case of the stubborns about that, always wanting to leave things open so he could change his mind on the spur of the moment.

So who knew? Only the people Chappalar and I might have talked to after work.

I'd told my family I was going out on a scrutiny—the first of my career, and the whole house was excited. But I'd made a joke of teasing them, keeping it a big secret: can't tell, Vigil business, might be a bust-their-balls raid that'll hit all the broadcasts. I'd held out till little Livvy's bedtime, when I whispered in her ear I was just going to a water-treatment plant; she proudly-loudly announced the news to everyone else, they laughed, and that was that.

"As far as I can remember," I told Tic, "I never mentioned Pump Station 3 to anyone. I just said I was going to a water-treatment plant. Five of those in the city."

"As far as you can remember?" A squidge of emotion

flickered across his face; but thanks to those blasted goggles, I couldn't tell which emotion it was. "Ms. Smallwood . . . you realize your link-seed can delve into—"

"I know," I interrupted. "They explained at *müshor*."

The same way my link-seed could package up memories for the police, it could rummage through my mind for forgotten minutiae stashed below the conscious threshold. The process wasn't perfect—our brains are lazy buggers who adjust memories for easy storage, throwing away some details and approximating others with images that are already in our mental cupboards. Still and all, the night in question was recent enough that I shouldn't find too much distortion.

"It's rather imperative for us to be sure on this," Tic said. "If you explicitly told anyone you were going to Pump Station 3 . . ."

"Yes!" I snapped, "I know it's important!"

He peered at me owlishly through his shaded goggles. Then he asked, "Stick or bag?"

"Excuse me?"

"When I was a dewy-eyed novice," he said, "my mentors took the direct approach in helping me deal with my fears. Whenever I hesitated to use my link-seed, they either hit me with a stick or put a bag over my head. I hated the bag most, so that's what they usually used." He sighed dramatically. "Such barbaric days—I swore I'd be more enlightened. By which I mean I'm giving you the choice. Stick or bag?"

I boggled at him, wondering if this was just a joke. So far as I could see, he didn't have either a stick or bag . . . but then, he wore the usual Oolom tote pack, a flat ortskin pouch positioned at groin level, held in place with straps up around the neck and down to the ankles. The pack was just big enough to hold some escrima rods, and a sack or two.

Even as I watched, his hand drifted down toward the tote pack's zip-mouth.

"No stick, no bag," I said jump-quickly. "I'll do this. Just give me time."

"At your convenience." Tic folded his hands in front of him: the picture of a man willing to wait.

Waiting for me to invoke my link-seed demon. To tweak fate's nose by hooking up again.

Look. This is getting stale for me too—the constant whining about my link, "Oh, woe, what if my brain goes splat?" You must be saying, "Snap out of it, honey. The seed is a gift, not a curse. And anyway, the thing is so thoroughly twined around your neurons, you have no choice but to live with it."

The same words I kept saying to myself.

I hated the fear. It was so daft *childish*—to train seven whole years, then melt into drippy dread when I finally got what I wanted.

Crazy. Witless. Typical Faye.

But you don't want me moaning how screwed up I was. Either you're sick of that too, or you don't believe me. Just a middle-class drama queen, blathering about her dodgy past when she seems pretty damned functional. Good health . . . addiction-free . . . loving family . . . not overly crippled by depression, neurosis or psychosis. Not even ugly with freckles anymore. Stop complaining, bitch.

Fair enough.

But hating the way you get the mopes doesn't make it easier to step clear of the past. Or the present. Or the future when it scares the bejeezus out of you.

Fear is fear. Pain is pain. Even when you know you're being boring.

It bored me too. Frustrated me. I kept telling myself, "Get over it!"

Words, words, words. Words don't make willpower . . . and anyway, willpower isn't the right tool for some jobs. Instead of holding on with white willpower knuckles, sometimes you have to let go.

So. There, in my office, scared of the world-soul Xé,

worried about Tic's sanity and shamed by his question, "Stick or bag?" . . . I finally threw myself back on my Vigil training. Meditation. Acceptance. Discipline without discipline. Like I'd been working on for seven years.

Down into my center—the part that breathes if you just get out of its way.

Don't see this as an apocalyptic transformation; don't think I grappled down my fear for all time. Nothing is ever so easy. But I sheltered back into my training and let myself take a step.

Forward.

The mind is a bottle filled with sugar syrup, salt water, and vinegar. Empty it.

The mind is a book filled with poetry, laments, and curses. Click DELETE.

Empty bottle.

Empty book.

Empty mind.

If you dip your hand into the sea, then scoop it out again, what do you have? No more than a sheen of wet over your palm. You can't capture handfuls of water by strength; you can't possess it. But if you dip your hand into the briny and leave it there—if you let yourself feel the cold and smell the salt—then who's to say you aren't holding the whole ocean?

Don't seek, don't avoid . . . just observe. If you want to activate a shy part of the brain, let the rest fall silent. When the consciousness shuts up, quieter voices may speak.

Memory isn't linear . . . except tiny patches, ten seconds here, half a minute there. Only flicky-brief flashes where you can track through a sequence of events without skipping ahead, without finding other memories dragged in by association. The meat of your brain squirms against linearity, terrified of falling into some autistic steady state that locks out the world.

Then we *Homo saps* come along, and sludge-wits that we are, almost every activity we invent for ourselves moves in a straight line. Step-by-step instructions, agendas for business meetings, timetables and milestones for working on a project. Our whole culture = first A, then B, then C. Binding the tiger with a chain of one link after another.

One thing at a time. Society pounds away at us, "It's wicked-bad-sinful even to contemplate the possibility of experiencing everything all at once."

But I *wanted* everything—everything I said and did that night before Chappalar died.

I opened myself to the memories: not commanding them to come, because the commanding part of my brain wasn't the nub I wanted to activate.

Open the inner eye. Just see what's there.

Chappalar and me saying good night in front of the Vigil's office. The dear funny sight of him bouncing through the grove of other office trees in our neighborhood. Me walking down to the transit station, where I caught a scuttler for home.

No sign of anyone following either of us.

Off the scuttler and heading for my home compound. Preoccupied, gloomily self-absorbed: worried about the link-seed bomb ticking in my head.

Sudden memories of a different time—don't fight the change of subject, let it happen if that's what my brain served up. The face of a senior student I'd known marginally, someone who died from data tumor early in *müshor*.

An imagined picture of scalding blood, squirting from his eyes. The horror his family must have felt. The horror my family would feel if it happened to me. Our kids, trying all their hard-won attitudes, arrogance, outrage, coolness, and finding nothing that shook the grief. My husbands and wives with a few more funerals under their belts, but still deep-struck because they depended on me . . . depended that I'd be the one in trouble, the one who needed close watching, the first one all eyes turned to when someone asked, "What shall we do tonight?" because Faye might've got one of her *moods* . . .

Moods. A torrent of moods flooding into me . . . not memory anymore, but Remembrance: touching all the moods I'd ever had, not just the night prior to Chappalar's death, but all the angry moods before, all the guilty moods after.

Everything all at once.

Not data tumor. The deluge didn't come from the datasphere but from my own mind, chagrins and shames I'd tried to squash down, and joys that I'd run from because they were undeserved, too good for someone like me . . .

My whole subconscious suddenly exploded to the surface, like an eruption of gas bursting out of deep ocean, wretched stinks and sweet lost perfumes, hates, loves, humiliations, triumphs . . .

Subconscious becoming conscious for one gasping moment of totality.

Then it was gone again, the ocean clapping back into place, subconscious plunging into drowned depths, the moment of revelation getting swallowed under heavy black water.

I opened my eyes. Tic was watching me closely. He hadn't moved; but he must have known what happened by the look on my face. Softly he said, "Some proctors grow addicted to that experience. That moment of knowledge. They don't enjoy it, but they have to look again and again. Others would rather die than repeat it. Wisdom lies between those two extremes: use memory as a tool, not a drug. But. *Fanobo roi shunt, aghi shunt po.*"

An Oolom proverb: ACTING WISELY IS EASY, UNTIL IT ISN'T.

I said nothing. Speechless. Breathless.

In the quiet, Tic's goggles hissed out a puff of mist to keep his eyes moist.

"I didn't tell anyone about Pump Station 3," I whis-

pered. "Not by name. Chappalar must have mentioned it
to someone. His lover, Maya."

Maya.

"Who is this Maya?" Tic asked.

"A human woman. I've never met her myself—just
heard some of the other proctors talk about her. Chappalar
said she was a hundred and ten years old."

"And Chappalar saw her the night before he was
killed?"

"So he told me."

"Long-term friendship or recent acquaintance?"

"Recent, I think."

Tic raised his eyes to the ceiling a moment, then lowered his head again to look straight at me. "There's no
such woman in Bonaventure."

I was a hair away from asking, "How do you know?"
but stopped myself in time. Tic must have used his link-
seed to call the world-soul and check our city census database. The search wouldn't take long—since *Homo saps*
had only lived on Demoth half a century, there weren't a
lot of us aged 110. Sure, a few of Demoth's original humans arrived in their fifties or older; but not many. Colonization was a sport played mostly by the young.

"She might not have told Chappalar her right age," I
said. "Humans sometimes fudge how old they are."

"And a charming foible it is," Tic answered. "Never
trust a species that tells the truth about everything—
they're either stupid, arrogant, or only interested in doc-
umentaries. But there's no human, male or female, anywhere over the age of one hundred with a name that's
close to the word *Maya* . . . not on the voters' lists in all
Great St. Caspian."

Oh. Pity.

"Maybe she lives elsewhere on Demoth," I suggested.
"It takes next to no time for someone to travel here by
sleeve . . ."

Tic looked away again, then turned back. "No one fitting Maya's particulars has taken the Bonaventure sleeve in the past two weeks."

I stared at him in great gaping shock. Sure, the Transit Board required sleeve operators to record who passed through when . . . but those records were kept confidential except by court order. Police could get warrants to track criminals; accident investigators could find the names of travelers splattered or spaced by malfunctions; but members of the Vigil had no authority to check the movements of private citizens. If I tried such a thing, the world-soul would stonewall me with INFORMATION DOES NOT EXIST OR IS NOT VALIDLY ACCESSIBLE. It might also notify my superiors, who'd demand to know what in merry hell I thought I was doing.

"Transit records are tight-sealed," I told Tic in a low voice. "How can you search through them—"

"I can't," he replied. "But the world-soul can. And Xé's a dear old girl who'll do her utmost to be obliging if you ask your questions persuasively. One: I am interested in locating a murderer, who is by definition a dangerous non-sentient creature. Two: we have honest reason to believe this Maya passed information, knowingly or not, to our murderer sometime between her evening with Chappalar and Chappalar's death the next morning. Three: it's my duty as a citizen of the League of Peoples to warn other sentients about potentially lethal risks . . . which means I should notify Maya she spoke to a dangerous non-sentient at least once and presumably may do so again. Four: I direct the world-soul to warn Maya posthaste. Five: the world-soul asks how to contact the woman, and I provide all the leads I can, including that she might have recently traveled on the Bonaventure Sleeve. Six: the world-soul anxiously replies it can't send the warning because no woman fitting the criteria appears in the transit records." He shrugged. "Perfectly straightforward."

The shrug was a nice touch—Tic's face looked wholly sincere, as if anyone could have strung together that chain of reasoning in the half second it took to link with the datasphere.

No thought at all of trying to impress me.

Whether or not I was impressed, I swore I wouldn't show it. "So this Maya..." I stopped, struck by a thought. "Conceivably, 'Maya' is a nickname that has nothing to do with her real name. That would make it hard to find her in the city database or the transit records."

"Oh. True." Tic's face darkened. Literally. Went a shade grayer in the gathering dusk. "Nicknames are such a flippant human custom. Impertinent. *Jaunty*. If you don't like your old name, go through a proper rechristening like decent people instead of just deciding..." He fell silent a moment, his face distant. "All right," he said, after a few seconds, "the world-soul will phone every woman in Great St. Caspian over the age of one hundred, and tell her there's an urgent message if she goes by the name Maya. It will do the same for anyone in the right age range who traveled here by sleeve recently. If there really is a Maya, we should flush her out."

"If there really is a Maya?" I repeated. "Why do you think she might not exist?"

"I took a quick peek at the language database," he replied. "The world 'maya' appears in several human tongues; but in Sanskrit, it can be translated as 'fleshly illusion.' I find that thought-provoking, don't you? Especially when we know our murderer uses androids."

Ouch.

We waited for the world-soul to send its messages. It wouldn't take long to get a response—any woman who got an emergency beep on her wrist-implant would answer it pronto unless she was under anaesthetic. Or under a twenty-year-old stud with rock-hard dollies.

But I digress.

Night was falling faster now: a cold-looking night that would freeze puddles and frost the trees. One of our tiny moons, the fast one called Orange, floated gibbously above the Bonaventure skyline; its usual apricot color looked faded tonight, like a shrively yellow pea.

Three stories above us, Jupkur launched off his window ledge, gliding home for the evening. His breath steamed . . . which showed it really *was* cold, considering the coolish Oolom body temperature. I watched him disappear into the gathering darkness, his skin turning purple with the sky.

And me standing by the window. One hand against the un-glass, letting the nano-puppies lick me again. Bored with waxing poetic about the dusk and the moon, wanting to *do* something.

Tedious thing, waiting.

Elusive thing, patience.

Mother used to make me say that prayer, ''God grant me the serenity, etc.'' but I could only chant it through twice before getting the screamy-weamies. Then I'd bound out of the room and go for a run or something.

It wouldn't look good if I ran out on a master proctor . . . especially with him sitting pond-placid on the edge of my desk, staring out at the twilight. And how much longer would we really have to wait? There could only be a few dozen women of the right age in Bonaventure. Half that number in the mining towns and outports. Maybe half again among travelers who'd recently used our sleeve. A hundred people? On that order.

And if none was Chappalar's sweetheart?

Now that Tic had planted ideas in my mind, I couldn't help harking back over the past few days. Maya hadn't shown up at Chappalar's funeral, had she? And she hadn't sent flowers or a card, or even a white stone in the Oolom tradition—I'd checked over the memorials at the burial service, and hadn't seen anything from her.

Was she a robot spy, sent to watch him? Possibly: top-price teaser androids could fool lonely chumps into thinking the artificial was real . . . at least for a while. And duping an Oolom would be easier than fooling a *Homo sap*; Chappalar might dismiss glitches in the android's programming as normal human idiosyncrasies. Why should he know how our species behaved when things got breathy?

If Maya was a robot . . . but then, what about the other proctors who got killed? Did they have robot spies watching them too?

No need. According to news reports, three of the proctors were killed in their homes, and another two in their offices—no inside information required to find any of them. The final two were attacked together as they waited to present a report to a parliamentary committee . . . a presentation that was publicized days in advance.

So: the killer/killers had no trouble finding seven of the eight dead proctors. The exception was Chappalar . . . whose schedule that morning was known only to me and Maya.

"Let's check Chappalar's office," I said suddenly. "See if we can find anything about this mystery woman."

"The police searched the place carefully," Tic answered. "So did I."

"But neither you nor the police were specifically looking for information about Maya. Were you?"

Tic frowned, then said, "True." He headed for the door.

8

MINDLESS MACHINE

Three of the four walls in the elevator were vidscreens, showing a panoramic view of the city around our office—what you'd see if the elevator were glass and the tree trunk transparent. Oolom architecture used that trick a lot: cramped enclosed spaces like elevator cabs were prettied up with airy visuals (not to mention wind sounds and artificial breeze) to make them seem wide-open to the world.

Standing back by the elevator door, Tic quietly gazed at the cityscape. He had good stillness—no slouching, no fidgets, no sighs. Presence in the present.

I had plenty of time to watch him. (More devil-be-damned waiting.) Oolom elevators climb slug-slowly . . . only as fast as you can glide up a lazy air thermal. Their elevators go down a lot faster, matching the typical air-speed of an Oolom in landing descent.

This particular elevator had no lights of its own—just the glow of the stars and the dried-pea moon. From below came the subdued spill of streetlamps. There was also the glittery flicker of crocus-flies, already out of hibernation and flashing their tiny mating beacons: hoping to do the

dance and get eggs laid before predators woke for spring
. . . just as I hoped this clump-hole of an elevator would
reach our stop before the blessed cream-blossoms opened
next month. . . .

In the twinkling quiet, Tic asked, "What did the Peacock Tail feel like?"

He hadn't moved from that perfect stillness. Just a soft-
voiced question in the dark.

"I never touched whatever it was," I told him. "It
didn't come that close to me."

"Not physically," Tic said. "What did it feel like emo-
tionally?"

I shook my head, not knowing what he wanted to hear.
"My emotions were running on a different track at the
time: scared out of my skin that I'd get my face burned
off."

"Even so," Tic said, "the Peacock was something new
and surprising. The instant you saw it, didn't you have a
reaction? 'Dear-dear, more trouble' . . . or maybe, 'Hur-
rah, I'm saved.' "

"Does it make a difference?" I asked.

"One never knows. What does the elevator feel like to
you?"

"Like an elevator!"

"Just a mindless machine?"

I gave him a sour look. "Don't tell me the elevator is
smart like the windows."

Tic smiled. "You still remember the windows?"

"Sure."

"Then Xé likes you. Even if you insist on playing ob-
tuse. What does the elevator feel like?"

"It's tired," I answered, saying the first thing that came
into my mind. "Feeling cruel overworked. In the old
days, it had nearly nothing to do—the Ooloms didn't use
it much. But now that we've got three human proctors . . ."

Four.

"Sorry, four counting me, so now that we've got four human proctors . . ."

I stopped. Tic's mouth hadn't moved; so who said *Four*?

The world-soul?

The elevator?

"Yipe," I said. "Yipe, yipe, yipe."

"It's a stimulating world once you hear the machines." Tic had a smug dollop of I-told-you-so in his voice. "If you insist on challenging the metaphors, an elevator can't really feel tired, of course. It's just due for maintenance . . . since it *does* have to work harder carrying you lead-weight humans several trips a day rather than delicately light Ooloms a few times a year. But when the elevator reports it's wearing out, the world-soul represents that as being tired . . . at least in the minds of those who are properly attuned."

I groaned. "I'm picking up sob stories from an elevator."

"No. The world-soul is projecting information in a form you can easily grasp. Would you prefer a deluge of cold performance statistics? We're both animals, Smallwood: social animals with abundant brain space evolved for analyzing emotions, and a scanty pittance for analyzing numbers. The world-soul likes to present data in a form our brains are best equipped to understand—that the elevator is deplorably fatigued from lugging around you human lardasses."

Who're you calling a lardass, bone-boy? I came close to growling that. But for all I knew, Tic might ask the elevator what *it* thought . . . and I did not want to have this blasted machine tell me, *Just between us, Faye, you could stand to lose a few kilos . . .*

Time to change the subject. I said, "Why'd you ask how the Peacock Tail felt? Do you think it's tied up with the world-soul too?"

"No. Mere curiosity." Tic looked out over the city. "These days, I pick up emotions everywhere. Not just from machines, but from truly inanimate things. Rocks. Trees. Running water. I can actually feel . . .'' He stopped, shook his head. "*Tico*. I anthropomorphize everything. Except people, of course. Even my poor beleaguered brain can't anthropomorphize them.''

He lapsed into silence. One of his hands gently stroked the elevator wall.

When the doors opened on the sixth floor (finally!), I stepped into the narrow area that circled the elevator shaft—a wretched excuse for a foyer providing access to the four offices at this level. The entrance to Chappalar's old office was already gliding open. Tic must have called ahead with his link-seed.

"I've left things as they were," Tic muttered as we went inside. "Tradition—you know.''

That was grin-worthy. Ooloms *never* redecorated when they took over someone else's property, especially if the previous owner had died. It might have been a religious thing, but I doubt it—whenever the subject came up with humans around, Ooloms got a sheep-guilty look. Not like true believers with devout moral objections to change; more like people who were just too lazy to renovate.

Whatever the excuse, they didn't take things down, they didn't move things around, they didn't modernize, repaint, or refurbish. Furniture stayed where it was till it literally fell apart . . . and even then, the inhabitants might step over the broken pieces for years unless circumstances forced them to buy a replacement. (By ''circumstances'' I mean when they ran out of places to sit.) I've visited Oolom homes with dozens of painted portraits on the wall, all unknown strangers—pictures left by former owners, generations old and never removed.

So it didn't surprise me Chappalar's office hadn't changed. The desk slanted at the same angle toward the door. The racks of file packets still tilted ten degrees off level. The water-filled crystal wind chimes dangled in their usual halfhearted glumness above the window. (''Oh

... should we tinkle now? Is it really necessary? Bother ...".)

The room contained everything that had always been here ... except Chappalar himself. Enough to give you the weeps, if you let yourself dwell on it.

"So what should we do?" I said, too bright-voiced and twice as brisk. "Where do we start?"

Tic stared at me hard for a moment, then answered, "I've already scanned Chappalar's on-line files for references to Maya." My mouth was open before I could stop myself, nigh-on asking how he'd scanned the files when I only mentioned Maya's name a few minutes ago; but with a single flick of his link-seed, Tic could have set the world-soul to searching while we rode up the elevator. "So," he continued, "all we have left is checking the off-line packets."

Which was pure donkeywork—not the sort of thing I could dump on a master proctor while Dainty Miss Probationary sat back and watched. I had to do my share ... meaning I had to choose between the terror of reading the packets by link-seed, or the cowardice of loading the files into a mechanical reader.

No. If I nellied out and used the reader, Tic would ask, "Stick or bag?"

"I'll take half the files," I told him. "You take the rest."

He nodded, his face bland. It cranked me off that he didn't say, "Thank you," or "Bully for you, getting past the fear." Then again, I would have got just as cranked off if he'd said any such patronizing thing.

Not one for consistency, our Faye.

Tic and I divided the files into two equal stacks, then carried them to Chappalar's desk. The desktop had five loading slots spaced across its surface; I waited for Tic to choose one, then took the one farthest from his. Childish; especially since Tic didn't notice. His face already had a distant emptiness as he fed in the first packet.

Fumbling to catch up, I popped the top packet from my stack into the input slot. The reader whished softly as it removed the file's outer jacket and slipped out the strand of bubble chips inside; through the glass viewport, I could see the bubbles meshing into place around the access drum, like a necklace of thumb-sized diamonds laid onto black velvet. Hydraulics pumped up activation enzymes, and the diamonds grew soft and gloopy, mushy as frog eggs—liquid information, melding into the reader's data flow, coming on-line.

Anytime now, I told myself. Nothing stopping me from accessing what the file contained.

Deep breath.

World-soul, attend. Search file for occurrences of the name "Maya" or close homologues.

I didn't have to specify which file, which input port—all those things would be tagged onto the transmission by my subconscious. For that matter, I didn't have to sub-vocalize an explicit command . . . any more than I had to say, "Arm, lift up," when I reached for a beer. The un-spoken impulse was enough; my link-seed understood what I wanted the moment I wanted it, and had dashed off a request to the datasphere long before I spoke the words in my mind.

A second passed. Then I found myself pushing the EJECT button, watching the bubble chips harden back to diamonds and the packet closing around them. There'd been no sensation of the world-soul "speaking" to me, telling me the file didn't mention Maya; I just knew the file contained nothing relevant, as surely as I knew the colors of my spouses' eyes.

Knowing without the experience of learning. Spooky.

Three more packets. Loading them, rejecting them, with no intelligible moment of transition between wondering whether a file referred to Maya and the certainty that it didn't. Out of morbid curiosity, I tried to doubt that I'd scanned the files at all. The doubt wouldn't come; my brain was dead certain it knew the files were clean, even though I had no idea what the chips actually contained.

Creepy. Goosepimply. Enough that when I reached the fifth packet I took a moment to read the outside label, just so I'd know what my brain was looking at.

The tag said ARCHAEOLOGY LIAISON BUREAU. Chappalar once mentioned he scrutinized archaeological activities for the whole planet—easy work, because the "bureau" was actually a single man working out of a fiddly-dick office just down the street from us. Whenever the Heritage Board on New Earth authorized an exploration of Demoth's ruins, our archaeology liaison was supposed to handle local arrangements (transportation, accommodation, and so on).

Not that the Heritage Board had authorized a single dig during my lifetime. As I've said, the board wrote off our planet long ago. So the bureau man collected his pay and spent his time teaching oboe lessons to local teens; he played with a woodwind quintet and was supposedly quite good. (If it's not a contradiction to use "oboe" and "good" in the same sentence.)

Every year, Chappalar submitted a suggestion to the Speaker-General's office, recommending the liaison job be dissolved or folded in with some other department. Every year, the SGO replied that the Technocracy had rejected the idea. The Heritage Board bureaucrats demanded we have someone standing ready in case they ever favored Demoth with their assy-brassy attention . . . and the SGO decided each year not to fight the Technocracy over a single man's salary.

I loaded the archaeology file and watched it congeal into the reader. When it was spooled up for access, I psyched myself to deliver another request to the world-soul . . . and found the answer was already in my mind.

The file contained a letter signed "Maya Cuttack, Ph.D." What did the letter say? I knew that too, as if I'd memorized the message decades ago as junior-school rotework.

Dear Proctor Chappalar,

I trust it is not improper to ask for help from the Vigil—as an offworlder, I do not know what is considered appropriate on Demoth—but I am having trouble with one of your local officials, and I understand you act as a kind of ombudsman who can cut through red tape.

I am an archaeologist from Mirabile and am trying to launch an excavation in the interior of Great St. Caspian. The area contains abandoned mines dating back more than two thousand years before the Oolom colonization, and I should very much like to determine which race or races were active on Demoth at that time.

Unfortunately, my intended excavation site is owned by a company named Rustico Nickel . . . and while company officials are not opposed to my work, they say they cannot grant permission for me to dig unless I get an official archaeology permit.

(No surprise. Any digging on mine-owned land had to satisfy a slew of safety regulations—like requiring the company to install industrial-grade emergency equipment and establish a comprehensive risk-management program. If Rustico let Maya stick a single shovel in the soil, they'd have to pay for all those things to keep the Mines Commission happy. Very expensive. Rustico could only dodge the safety costs if Maya's dig was an officially recognized archaeology project; and that meant a license from the Heritage Board.)

Unfortunately, my request for an excavation permit has fallen on deaf ears in Demoth's Archaeology Liaison Bureau. The man there says he cannot issue licenses himself—that is a matter for the Technocracy's Heritage Board. But the Heritage Board will not issue a license until it receives some-

thing called a Statement of Non-Opposition from the Demoth government . . . which the Archaeology Liaison Officer says he cannot give without some ridiculous background check that I am expected to pay for out of my own pocket.

Help! Is there anything you can do to make an underfunded scientist's life easier?

Yours in hope

Maya Cuttack, Ph.D.
c/o The Henry Smallwood Guest Home
Sallysweet River

"Ouch," I said. "Have you ever had that feeling of someone walking on your grave?" The Henry Smallwood Guest Home was a manor lodge built on the old muddy site of the Circus—a place to house the worshipfully respectful Oolom tourists who flocked to pay tribute to Dads's memory. If you looked at it one way, I shouldn't be surprised an offplanet archaeologist had set up residence at the guest home; it was the closest thing to a hotel in the whole underpopulated interior of Great St. Caspian.

Still. This Maya Cuttack, possibly a robot, possibly a murderer . . . staying nearly on top of my old bedroom in Sallysweet River. It made the hairs curl on the back of my neck.

"You've found something?" Master Tic asked.

"An archaeologist named Maya Cuttack—an off-worlder, which is why she didn't show up when you scanned the census database. She wrote to Chappalar . . ." The date of the letter appeared in my mind. "She wrote to him four weeks ago." More details from the file kept popping into my head. "He investigated the situation, then met with her to explain what was going on . . . which obviously started their acquaintance."

"Where is this Maya now?"

"Sallysweet River."

Tic went very quiet. Every Oolom on Demoth knew the name of the town. Most of them thought of it as a place of salvation, but for Tic . . . anything associated with the plague probably hit him like a hammerfist to the head.

"Sallysweet River," he said. His voice was level, but he enunciated every syllable precisely. "What could possibly interest an archaeologist around that place?"

"The usual ruins," I replied. "Householes. Some ancient mines." I couldn't help picturing the tunnel we'd used as a mass grave. The one where we regularly touched off explosions from the fumes of decay. Oh yes, *there* was a place archaeologists could find some eye-catching artifacts.

Tic was silent a moment, brooding. Then he drew a sharp breath, and said, "Fine. The world-soul confirms that Maya Cuttack applied to excavate several sites around Sallysweet River. The archaeology bureau conducted the usual elementary validation check on her credentials— doctorate from Pune University on Mirabile, participation in digs on Caproche, Muta, the Divian Free Republic . . ."

His voice trailed off. As if it meant something that Maya had connections with the republic. After his time scrutinizing the trade talks, maybe Tic had developed some unkind opinions about the Freeps. Or maybe, like most Oolooms, he just loathed Freeps on general principles.

I said, "If Maya's got a history going back some time, she probably isn't an android."

"Unless the real Maya was replaced," Tic replied. "Perhaps on that Free Republic dig . . ."

I rolled my eyes. "Don't start. Our first duty is to contact her. Has she . . . no. Damn." I was going to ask if she'd registered her comm number with the Demoth world-soul; that way we could just beep her. But I suddenly knew with absolute certainty that Maya had never signed into the public directory. (The world-soul planting things in my head again.) And her comm number didn't show up in Chappalar's file. Either Maya hadn't gotten a standard wrist-implant—one of those people who refused to adulterate her body on religious/medical/aesthetic grounds—or else she'd deliberately avoided revealing her number.

Tic must have accessed the world-soul for the same information. "The best we can do," he said, "is leave a message where she's staying. Nothing explicit. Just have her call us as soon as possible." He waved in my direction, not looking at me. "You do it. This is your scrutiny, not mine."

His voice full of gruff. No question that this stuck in his craw, how Sallysweet River had suddenly come into the equation. My craw was turning fair sticky too, considering I had to make a call and hear someone chirp, "Henry Smallwood Guest Home," on the other end of the line. But I went to the phone screen beside Chappalar's desk and reached toward the control pad.

Before my finger touched a single button, the screen flashed on and displayed the words CALLING ... HENRY SMALLWOOD GUEST HOME, SALLYSWEET RIVER.

"Lord weeping Jesus," I groaned. "Even the phone can read my mind."

"Say thank you," Tic whispered.

"Thanks generously, phone," I said through gritted teeth. Since that didn't sound so gracious, I gave the display box a pat, the gingerish way you do when you're introduced to someone's new pet and it turns out to be an alien organism with spikes.

The screen bloomed to show a fresh-faced *Homo sap* man and Oolom woman smiling side by side—a dandified establishment like the HSGH wanted callers to see instantly that it welcomed both species. Not that either species was actually present on-screen; the man and woman were likely computer mock-ups, psychometrically designed to appeal to the most desirable demographics. "Henry Smallwood Guest Home," the man said with a voice so honestly charming, I couldn't help but mistrust it. "How may we help you?"

"I'm with the Vigil," I said, "and I'd like to leave an urgent message for Maya Cuttack. I understand she's staying with you?"

"We'd be happy to take your message," the Oolom woman replied, "but if it's urgent, we can't guarantee when Dr. Cuttack will receive it."

"Why?"

"Our guests come and go," the man said. "We never know when they might pick up their messages."

"Are you saying Dr. Cuttack isn't in residence right now?"

"We can't give out such information on our guests," the woman answered, her face brimming with regret that she couldn't satisfy my every whim.

Behind the display box, out of sight from the screen, Tic mouthed, *Just leave a note*. I did, asking Maya "to call Faye Smallwood as soon as possible for an urgent message." Something gave me the waries about leaving my personal number; so I rhymed off the code for the Vigil instead. Our phone system was smart enough to forward the call to me if I wasn't in the office.

When I'd cut the connection, Tic said, "Let's hope she doesn't get the message for at least an hour."

"Why?"

"Because the world-soul tells me that's the flying time to Sallysweet River. Gird yourself, Smallwood, we're going in."

No. We didn't hop a waiting skimmer and spunk off to face the enemy. Tic and I weren't witless . . . nor were we police club-thumpers, equipped with badges, body armor, and all mod cons for buttonholing possible murder suspects. I gave a silent inward cheer when Tic asked, "Who do you know with the local gendarmes, Smallwood? Someone with a dash of authority to rally the troops on our behalf. Someone who'll listen to you talk about Maya without dismissing you as a total loon."

"There's a Captain Cheticamp," I answered. "We got along cozily enough last night."

Tic motioned toward the phone again. "Call this cozy fellow and bend him to your will."

Basil Cheticamp, bless him, was actually on duty; he even knew background details on Chappalar's murder, though he wasn't part of the inquiry team. Just as well he hadn't been directly involved—when he heard how the investigators had overlooked Maya as a lead, Cheticamp swore they'd all be drummed down to dogcatchers. He promised to dispatch a squad to Sallysweet River on the double: two detectives to ask Dr. Cuttack polite questions, and a pack of armored ScrambleTac officers just in case homicidal androids came marching across the tundra. He was already paging his troops, when I asked, "Where will we meet your people?"

The captain stopped mid-sentence and gave me the steely-eyed glare. "Meet?"

"The Vigil intends to scrutinize your handling of this case. A master proctor and I will accompany your squad to Sallysweet River."

"Ms. Smallwood . . ."

"*Proctor* Smallwood," I corrected.

His glare got two ore-grades steelier. "Proctor Smallwood, it is precious inappropriate for civilians—"

"We aren't civilians," I interrupted. "We're members of the Vigil. We have a legal right to scrutinize police activity however we see fit."

"You'll get a complete report on everything that happens."

"Not good enough. Master Tic and I want to be present on the scene."

Cheticamp's face went lemonish. "Tic? Tic's in Bonaventure? Smallwood, every police officer on the planet knows Tic is . . ."

"A total loon?" I suggested.

"Worse: a Jonah. There isn't a single rattlesnake on Demoth, but if Tic went walking in the woods, he'd find one. Not that it would bite him—it'd go for the next poor bugger to come down the trail. If Tic is in Bonaventure . . ."

Cheticamp shook his head. Not a happy man.

Part of me wanted to let him off the hook; after all, why *should* Tic and I plop ourselves into the line of fire? We could stay home, read the police reports, evaluate what we read . . .

But that was a piss-poor way to run a scrutiny. *Dissect the paperwork, but never trust it*—advice as old as the Vigil itself. *Get out of the office. Go through the closed doors.*

"Captain," I said in my most humble Mom-Faye voice, "we don't want to do your job . . . we only want to do ours. You know we aren't trying to push you around, or rake your people over the coals; we're just observing your procedures, the way the Vigil always does. Sure and all, this is an extra complication for you, but your department and the Vigil have always worked it out in the past. Right?"

I hoped that was true. Police generally had a sulky tolerance for the Vigil—not that they liked us breathing over their shoulders, but they'd lived with our presence long enough that we came with the landscape: like paperwork and foot patrol. On the other hand, if Cheticamp had ever got his knuckles rapped because of a Vigil report . . .

The captain sighed. "All right, *Proctor* Smallwood. You and Tic can go in-country with the squad. I'll go too, as your personal escort. Pick you up in five minutes."

The screen went blank before I could say thank you.

9

STRAWBERRY SMOKE

I had goaded/charmed/blustered my family into leaving
Sallysweet River when I was twenty-one. By then, I was
bored with the boonies and stabilized enough after my
years of wildness to get cringey over the way people
looked at me on the street. Anyway, a bare-rock mining
town had bugger-all opportunities compared to the big
city of Bonaventure . . . where Winston got his scholar-
ship to law school, Angie found she was a VR savant,
Egerton bought his first cargo-hauler, and so on. The family thanked me eventually, each by each, for nagging and
ragging till we moved.

Despite that, my spouses hadn't totally cut their ties
with the old hometown. They'd all returned time and
again over the years, visiting parents and siblings, showing off their children and other successes.

Me, I'd never gone back. Dads was dead. Mother had
left town the day I got married—either washing her hands
of me, or just taking the opportunity to attend to her own
sanity now that my spouses were in charge of mine. Whatever the reason, Ma had scarpered south to the jungles of
Argentia and was now breeding Demothian orchids for

their natural antivirals, living in a grass shack with a gentleman Oolom pharmer. So I had no family to visit in Sallysweet River. And nary a success to show off . . . not unless you counted mere survival. On top of which, how could you feel nostalgic for a slag heap of a town, filled with bad memories and folks who thought I was dirt?

Even so . . . even so. I found myself going dewy-eyed as the police skimmer soared over forest and tundra toward my birthplace. The darkness got to me; no lights below but the glint of stars reflecting off snow. I remembered nights as a girl, walking through that darkness— with Dads, with a boy, with friends, or by myself, each type of walk different and each one rare magical.

Funny how you forget about magic. Even when you say (as we all do) that you've never lost the spirit of childhood, you find that for years you haven't felt the slightest magical shiver. And you don't really acknowledge that till magic touches you again.

Darkness. Quiet.

Yes, the police skimmer had some dim interior lights. And there was the background mutter of a ScrambleTac sergeant outlining plans for contingencies. But that had nothing to do with me. I sat by the window and let my mind be swallowed by the night.

Unyielding tundra night: the same night that had hugged me as a child. The same night that had wrapped this land in silence for untold humanless millennia.

Deep roots. Continuity. Home.

Sallysweet River had grown. Our old family compound once stood on the edge of town; now it anchored a dandified second village, dotted with tourist shops and tourist chalets and tourist amusement plazas. All but the Henry Smallwood Guest Home were huddled down empty now, hibernating in the darkness. This was the lull season, too late for skiing, too early for hiking, too muddy for damned near anything.

The skimmer settled down in the guest-home parking

lot. Cheticamp, Tic and I waited while the ScrambleTac team fanned out to deploy themselves around the perimeter. The club-thumpers looked right chipper as they slunk into the darkness. I don't know if that meant they were confident there'd be no trouble or happy at the possibility they might get into a firefight.

On the trip in, one of the detectives made a bet with all takers that Maya had nothing to do with the killings. At most, she might have babbled too freely in a public place, gossiping that her snuggle-time pal Chappalar was scheduled to lead a secret inspection of Pump Station 3. One of the real bad guys probably overheard her and seized the chance to scrag a proctor on the job.

The detective who proposed this theory was a man named Willis Bleak—a roly-poly *Homo sap* with a boyish unwrinkled face that surely doomed him to play Good Cop for his entire professional career. His partner, P.O. Fellburnie, was a female Divian of the TyeTye breed: a head taller than me, thick as a barrel, and spilling out of her clothes with muscle. TyeTyes were originally designed for life on a planet whose gravity topped 2.3 Earth G's; Jupkur once joked they weren't engineered genetically but geologically, like walking chunks of real estate that could bench-press nine hundred kilos. Among friends, Fellburnie came across as quite the amiable woman, a classic "genial giant" . . . but on the job, I could imagine her slipping into Bad Cop any old time she felt like it.

The detectives took the lead, with Cheticamp, Tic and me following them up the guest home's front walk. My own dome had sat somewhere in this vicinity—hard to tell the exact spot, with so many landmarks hidden by darkness. Then again, who knew if the landmarks were even there? The rocks and trees of my childhood may have been cleared away to make room for the guest home's croquet pitch.

The front door opened as we approached, and in we went to a relentlessly cozy lounge. Overstuffed chairs of leaner hide sat buff and bulgy around a circular flagstone hearth. The fire was burning bluebarrel logs; I could tell because their smoke had a stringy scent of strawberries, subtle but sweet enough to make my stomach growl. No one was seated near the fireplace, but an oldish Oolom woman wearing a wood-bead necklace stood behind a counter at the back of the room. She looked up, smiled, and said, "Good evening. May I help you?"

Fellburnie and Bleak produced ID cards. The woman (wearing a badge that said HOSTESS) took Bleak's card and pressed it against her wrist-implant for verification by the world-soul. We all nodded in approval—too many trusting civilians take a gold-embossed ID at face value. In less than a second, the world-soul triangulated on Bleak (or rather Bleak's wrist-comm) and reported that yes, the real Detective Willis Bleak, officer in good standing of the Bonaventure Police, was no more than a step away from the card. The hostess handed back Bleak's ID and asked, "What brings you to Sallysweet River, Officers?"

"We're looking for a woman named Maya Cuttack," Bleak said. "She's staying here?"

"Dr. Cuttack has a room with us, yes," the hostess replied. "She's been here since autumn—she rents by the month. But I haven't seen her in several days."

Beside me, Cheticamp stiffened. You'd expect cops to have a better poker face.

"Do you know where she might have gone?" Fellburnie asked.

The hostess whispered into her wrist-implant, then turned to a desk screen to read the result. "Dr. Cuttack didn't tell us where she went," the hostess said. "She's made several trips down to Bonaventure recently . . . and she has all-weather camping equipment too. You know she's an archaeologist? It's not unusual for her to spend several nights away now and then, examining various sites in the neighborhood."

Even though she never got a license, I thought to myself. *Looks like our Maya doesn't stand on legal niceties.*

"Do you know where these sites might be?" Bleak asked.

"She was interested in abandoned mines. There are a number near here, dating back some three thousand human years. I can lend you an excellent survey map that shows the known sites . . . although I doubt if you'll find Dr. Cuttack at any of them. Rumor has it she's found a promising new site. But then, I never heard the doctor say that herself; someone on staff may have just been spreading speculations."

There were plenty more questions. When exactly was Maya last seen at the guest home? Two days before Chappalar died. Did Maya have friends who might know her current whereabouts? Dr. Cuttack kept to herself. Had Maya ever had any visitors? None that the hostess could recall.

In other words, nothing. Maya could have been a *bona fide* archaeologist, innocently pursuing her studies; or a killer biding her time in the back of beyond, occasionally disappearing on "expeditions" as a cover for more sinister activities.

When Bleak and Fellburnie ran out of questions, they turned to Cheticamp to see if he had anything to ask. He shrugged . . . and Tic immediately stepped forward, as if he'd only been waiting for the police to finish.

"*Turiff*," Tic said. Dear madam. "How much did Dr. Cuttack actually stay in her room here? Three or four nights a week? More? Less?"

The hostess thought for a moment. "A day here, a day there . . . perhaps it added up to a week every month. The rest of the time, she was visiting Bonaventure or camping on the land."

"Just one week," Tic said. "My, my. Wouldn't it be less expensive paying by the night, rather than booking a month at a time?"

"That's true," the hostess admitted. "Our monthly rate is an excellent value . . . but if Dr. Cuttack had only paid for the nights she was here, she could have saved a good deal of money. And for such a frequent guest, we'd gladly store her luggage between times if she didn't want to take everything camping. Our manager once mentioned that to her—we don't want our guests thinking we take advantage of them. But Dr. Cuttack said money was less important to her than convenience: being able to come and go without always signing in.''

Tic tossed me a meaningful glance; I didn't need it. In her letter to Chappalar, Maya claimed to be underfunded. So why was she blithely forking out cash for a hotel room she hardly ever used? Even in the off-season, the HSGH had to be a pricey place to stay.

Captain Cheticamp picked up on the implications too. ''How did Dr. Cuttack pay for her room?'' he asked.

The hostess hesitated a moment, probably weighing a guest's personal privacy against whatever pressure the cops could bring to bear. Then she whispered into her wrist-comm and turned to the desk screen. ''Charged to a numbered account, in the Free Republican Bank.''

Tic beamed an angelic smile. I could practically read his mind. Maya. Murderer. Bankrolled by the Freeps.

Rattlesnake, Cheticamp mouthed to me.

Of course, the detectives asked to search Maya's room. Of course, the hostess said they'd have to discuss that with the manager. Of course, the manager took a long time to find and a longer time to convince that he should let the police barge in without a warrant. Everyone accepted this as routine—a well-practiced waltz that the cops and hotel had to dance before Maya's door would open.

When we finally got to the room, it was empty . . . by which I mean Maya'd left nothing incriminating. Yes, there were clothes in the closet—expensive-looking things, with labels from fashion houses in the Free Republic—and the loo contained the usual toiletries . . . again top-of-the-line stuff, and thanks to my darling Peter, I knew something about the cost of cologne. (The man loved perfume and loved all the women in his life to be wearing it. Unlike my other husbands, who didn't notice, or wrinkled their noses and made little cat-sneezes.)

If you're interested, Maya's room contained a huge wood-frame bed made of paper-peel branches still covered with bark . . . a state-of-the-art comm console discreetly hidden in a wall niche . . . a small cleaning servo that followed Fellburnie around, fussily fluffing up the carpet wherever the detective's TyeTye weight squashed down the pile . . . but nothing you couldn't find in any other "woodsy-decor" hotel room on the planet. No jacking equipment that would allow Maya to program killer androids. No scribbled manifestos explaining why the Vigil should be eradicated. No crumpled purchase order for three dozen jelly guns. Nor did we find clues to where Maya had gone.

(Tic had me distract the others while he talked to the cleaning servo. The things I do for the Vigil. And according to Tic, the devil-be-damned machine didn't have a word to say except, "Muddy boots. Muddy boots. Muddy boots.")

Bleak and Fellburnie slogged off for more legwork— questioning the staff and finding guests who'd spoken with Maya last time she was here. Cheticamp ordered half the ScrambleTacs back to the skimmer for a tour of the area, checking the known mines to see if Maya was camped in the neighborhood. At first he thought it would be enough to do an IR scan from the air . . . but I told him they should peek into the mine tunnels themselves. "If I were camping this time of year, I'd tell my tent to set itself up a little ways down the mine. Best to be out of the wind in case a blizzard blows up."

"If these mines are three thousand years old," Cheticamp said, "isn't it risky to go inside? They must be ready to cave in."

"We kids sneaked into the mines all the time," I replied. "Never went very deep, but the upper tunnels are still holding up with nary a crack. Whoever dug them cared more about permanence than *Homo saps* do; and it helps that Great St. Caspian isn't an earthquake zone." I pointed to a dot on Cheticamp's map. "This is the only one that's dangerous, and the government sealed it off years ago."

"What's special about that mine?" the captain asked.

"It had some explosions. Made it unsafe."

Tic's ear-sheaths flicked opened with interest. "Explosions? What kind of explosions?"

"Uhh . . . gas."

"Tell us more, dear Faye." Tic composed his face into a wait-forever look of pleased interest. I could see he wouldn't budge till he'd heard the whole story.

"Fine," I growled, "we used that mine to hold corpses, all right? During the plague. The soil around here is only a few centimeters of dirt over hard bedrock—no room for burials, and besides, we thought that when the epidemic ended, we'd need to return bodies to next of kin." I lowered my eyes, avoiding everyone's gaze. "We slapped the dead into body bags, but there was still some leakage. Gas leakage. Eventually there were explosions."

"And the bodies got sealed in?" Tic asked, horrified. Nothing gives an Oolom the willies like the thought of being buried under tonnes of stone. Even if the corpses were already dead.

"The tunnel didn't collapse," I told him, "but Rustico Nickel refused to let people go down to check the damage. Since the company owned the land, they'd be liable if anyone got hurt. After the plague, the Mines Commission decided it wasn't safe for anyone to remove the bodies; so some charitable group named Dignity Memorials paid to send in . . ."

I stopped, thinking back to the afternoon the bodies were removed. It'd been almost a year after the plague, when Ooloms were taking to the skies once more: people starting their new lives by closing off the old. No one had imagined Sallysweet River could acquire a tourism industry . . . but day after day, Ooloms glided silently overhead, circling above the Big Top's trampled mud, landing by my father's grave and touching their foreheads to the green quartz monument.

Dozens of them stood outside the old mine tunnel to see the Big Top's dead brought out. The wind was snapping-brisk, and the Ooloms all anchored themselves by holding on to trees in the nearby forest, hugging the trunks as if they were shyly trying to stay out of sight.

I was the only *Homo sap* there—come to watch mostly because everyone else stayed away. The humans of Sallysweet River didn't want to be reminded of the corpses, or the way we'd giggled as we lit off the vapors of rot. Who could stand seeing what the bodies looked like? Browned by the explosions. Nibbled by insects. Cracked and dried by the previous winter's cold.

Ugly. I couldn't stay away.

I planned to tell my neighbors the details. Make them lose their lunches when I described what had come out of the ground. And maybe I was trying to sicken *myself*, the way I sickened myself with everything else I did in those days.

Not to mention that I wanted to see what it looked like to be dead. Not the limp-in-a-bed death we'd gloomed over daily in the Circus, but skin-off-the-bones death, lying fallow in the ground, really and truly finished.

What Dads would look like in his grave.

What I might look like if I couldn't find something to care about.

As the Ooloms clung to their trees, I stood smack in the middle of the clearing by the old mine's mouth. Waiting to see the corpses. To see the truth.

The Ooloms behind me started whispering to each other—they heard the approach of footsteps ten seconds before I did. Clop, clop, clop coming up the mine's stone floor.

Then a human figure stepped out of the tunnel's gloom, cradling a body bag like a child. The bag's plastic had melted through in several spots; Oolom skin, burnt to caramel, showed through the gaps.

The figure carrying the corpse came straight to me and laid the body bag at my feet, like an offering. I don't know why—some quirk of its programming. Since the mine was unsafe for people, the bodies were being hauled out by robots: lifelike human androids dressed in mourning clothes. The organization that paid the bill called this a gesture of respect toward the dead . . . better to use robots that looked like solemn people, rather than forklifts, ore-carriers, steel on wheels. (It would have been even more respectful to get robots that looked like Ooloms; but *Homo sap* models cost less off the shelf.)

Two dozen androids worked to exhume the bodies that long-ago afternoon. Now, I couldn't help wondering what happened to those robots once the job was done.

10

ROBOT-POPPERS

We stayed the night at the guest home. When I called my family to tell them, wife Angie answered and straightaway got a case of the bubbles: a beaming smile that filled the phone's vidscreen. "Finally, Faye! It's really really important to get in touch with your birthwater angst."

"I don't have any angst," I muttered. "I'm on a job."

"And it took you to Sallysweet River?" she said, eyes wide. "Faye, it's fate! Synchronicity!"

"Coincidence."

"Does it really feel that way to you?"

I stared at her beautiful open face on the phone screen. "No," I finally answered. "It doesn't feel like coincidence. It feels precious creepy, if you want the truth. So don't let's talk about me having an emotional breakthrough, all right? I've got the squirms as it is."

"Oooo, Faye, you used the words *emotional breakthrough*! I'm so proud. Love you to pieces!" She blew a kiss at the screen before clicking off . . . and I just *knew* she was going to run babbling about "spiritual rebirth" to all the others: my husbands, my wives, the kids, even

Barrett's dogs if they'd sit still long enough.

Angie, Angie, Angie. I know she sounds witless, but here's the thing: she's hands-down brilliant when she wants to be. Just that on her fourteenth birthday, she announced she would never let her brains get in the way of her enthusiasms . . . and she's had the breathless iron-gripped willpower to keep that resolution ever since.

A modern miracle. More magic from Sallysweet River.

If I experienced any angst that night, birthwater or otherwise, it came when I charged my room to the Vigil. Yes, I had an expense account; and yes, I felt guilty using it. My very first expense—checking into a luxury resort.

So then I spent my time gamely trying to justify the cost by doing as much Vigil work as I could. Tagging along with Bleak and Fellburnie. Scrutinizing the bejeezus out of their plodding methodical questions to staff and guests. Learning nothing new.

Around midnight, the detectives ran out of people to quiz, so we all returned to the lounge. Cheticamp and Tic sat by the fire . . . not talking, just staring moodily into the flames. "The ScrambleTacs came back a few minutes ago," Cheticamp told us. "Cuttack isn't camped at any of the known sites."

"If you ask me," Bleak said, "the only place we'll find her is the bottom of Bonaventure harbor."

"How so?" Tic asked.

"The woman looks clean," Bleak answered. "No one could say a bad word about her. So the way I read it, she had a fling going with Chappalar. She spent the evening with him, or maybe the night, but eventually the two parted company. All that time, the bad guys were watching . . . so when Cuttack set off on her own, they snatched her, sweated information out of her, then dumped her into the bay. Or a shallow grave, or a furnace, or a waste-recycling vat. That's why no one's seen her since Chappalar's death—the woman is fertilizer."

Cheticamp's expression had gone sour. "I don't like it," he growled.

"Why not?"

"Because it makes sense. And it puts us back to square one: Cuttack isn't connected with the killers, so we're no farther ahead than when we came out here. In fact, you're saying there's probably another murder victim we haven't found yet. Bloody wonderful."

Tic cleared his throat. "Aren't you forgetting the expensive clothes and perfume we found in her room? In her letter to Chappalar, she implied she didn't have much money. That's modestly suspicious, isn't it?"

"So she was playing the system," Fellburnie said. "Rich people do. Why pay to go through proper channels if a proctor can arrange it for free?"

A valid point. God knows, our profs at college warned us against wheeler-dealers trying to exploit the Vigil for private ends. Lots of affluent people are devoted to the belief that every system is built for someone's personal gain, and the only trick is learning how to use it for yourself. The slimy buggers are often right . . . which explains how they slithered up to affluence in the first place.

Cheticamp drummed his fingers on the arm of his chair, then pushed himself to his feet. "Nothing more we can do here tonight." He looked at Tic. "You two want to stay or go back to Bonaventure?"

"Stay," Tic answered immediately. He'd made that decision long ago, when he told me to book a room.

The captain didn't waste a glance in my direction; never mind that I was official scrutineer on this outing and should've had the last word. "Then stay," Cheticamp said. "I'll leave you a pair of ScrambleTacs as bodyguards. The rest of us will head home."

He looked at Bleak and Fellburnie; they both nodded agreement. I could tell all three had decided Maya Cuttack was a dead end . . . a *dead* dead end. Which meant that leaving us in Sallysweet River was as safe as anywhere else, and would keep us from *valk*ing whatever real investigations might be unfolding in Bonaventure. The bodyguards were just insurance, in case the killer or killers went on another spree.

We all said good night and the cops galumphed off on their flat-footed way. Leaving Tic and me in silence . . . except for the dying crackle of the fire. It was late, and the bluebarrel logs had almost burned themselves out.

I flopped down into a chair beside Tic. "What now?"

He didn't answer for several seconds; firelight wavered flickerish on his pouchy face. "We'll keep searching for Maya," he said at last. "Or at least that promising archaeological site she supposedly discovered."

"Why?"

"Because it piques my curiosity. Or because my oneness with the universe tells me this is the right way. Or because I'm a total loon." He folded his hands placidly across his stomach. "We'll rent a skimmer in the morning and see what we can find."

"You *are* a total loon," I told him. "It's a big country, city boy, and you'll have to be god-awful lucky to spot a single tent in the wilderness. Especially if the tent happens to be pitched inside a mine that no one's ever noticed before."

"Do you have a better suggestion?" he asked.

"Sure. Instead of flying around haphazard in hopes we stumble across the camp, let's get some gear that will do the search for us."

"An hour ago you were anxious about charging a room to your expense account. Now you're going to tot up a few million for scanning probes? Well-done, Smallwood. That's what I call settling in."

"It so happens," I told him in my snootiest voice, "I have a friend in high places. With access to the best survey equipment in the Technocracy. Courtesy of the Outward Fleet's Explorer Corps."

A minute later, I was calling the navy base in Snug Harbor and asking to speak with Festina Ramos.

*   *   *

She arrived an hour after dawn, this time without Oh-God and flying an official fleet skimmer. Not the same skimmer the dipshits used when they kidnapped me. Cheticamp had impounded that one as evidence . . . not because it mattered bugger-all to the case but just to crank off the Admiralty.

"It's freezing out here!" Ramos puffed as she stepped down from the driver's cab. "Why couldn't you live someplace warm?"

Her gray uniform crackled, its smart fibers fattening from flat cloth to a windproof layer as thick as sponge toffee: bristling with air bubbles to act as foam insulation. Even so, Ramos made a major fuss of blowing on her fingers and rubbing her hands together to produce heat. "Snug Harbor was perfectly lovely," she grumped. "Working its way up to a scorcher when I left."

"On Great St. Caspian," I told her, "*this* is a scorcher." Which was a lie; the thermometer had scooted below freezing overnight and showed every intention of staying there till it got over the sulks. Grumpy clouds huddled between us and the sun, while the wind had gone gusty with a piercing edge. What we had was a raw, clammy day . . . but compared to the winter just past, no Sallysweet River girl would ever call the weather cold.

The rear of Ramos's skimmer held three probe modules: sleek missiles four meters long, painted gloss black like a widow's vibrator. At Ramos's order, the probes rolled themselves out of the back hatch on low wheeled platforms, then sat looking vastly self-satisfied on the dead yellow-grass of the guest home's lawn.

"Don't *we* think well of ourselves," Tic said, as he crouched to stroke a probe's casing. "Aren't we just the cockiest machines on the planet?"

"They aren't actually intelligent," Ramos told him; she sounded a titch embarrassed that he'd think otherwise. But somewhere just inside my ears, I could hear the probe purring as Tic petted it. I shifted in closer, moving my thigh to touch another of the missiles. When I reached down to pat its black molded fuselage, mine started purring too. A fat tigery purr, like a cat with its mouth full of blood.

I gave Ramos a weak smile, trying to pretend I didn't feel thumbs-awkward. "Sorry, Admiral," I said, "but there are more intelligences in heaven and earth than are dreamt of in your philosophy. Tic and I seem to be simpatico with any machine connected to our world-soul."

"These probes aren't connected to your world-soul," Ramos said. "They're military equipment—deliberately designed to be incompatible with civilian systems. Our security gurus guarantee total data isolation."

"Now, now," Tic murmured to his probe, "you don't feel isolated, do you?"

The purr slipped into a giggle, then a whispery childlike voice spoke inside my head. "Shhh . . . *Xé musho jeelent.*"

Xé says secret.

Tic just smiled, but I froze—fingertips still touching the probe's plastic skin, my leg pressed against its side. Wanting desperately to jerk away, but staying put for fear the probe or Xé would take offense.

Not only was the missile talking when it shouldn't be on our wavelength; this thing, manufactured far offplanet in some no-aliens-allowed navy shipyard, spoke Oolom.

What in blazes did *that* mean?

Ramos programmed the probes from a console inside the skimmer . . . which she told me came down to selecting criteria from a list of search items the probes were equipped to detect. "Every month these things get more sophisticated," she told me as she worked. "Not intelligent," she added, throwing a pointed glance in Tic's direction, "but better at their jobs. It's a pity the quality wasn't this good during your big epidemic—we might have found more of those people who were dying in the woods."

"You were here during the plague?" Tic asked. His voice was just a hair too controlled.

"That was before my time," Ramos answered, "but I've reviewed transcripts from Explorers who *were* here. The equipment back then had a bitch of a time finding your people; all of them with low body temperatures, chameleoned to match the background colors, and lying perfectly still from paralysis. We couldn't even use sniffers to smell out tracks, because Ooloms spent most of their time up in trees. The Explorers were so frustrated: trying to save millions of people from going Oh Shit—uh, that's an Explorer expression for 'dying'—and all we could do was lumber blindly through the woods."

"They found *me*," Tic said, voice soft. "Deep in a highland jungle, far into the Thin Interior, and they still found me."

"Well, good," Ramos replied. "One of our success stories."

She hadn't caught the gray bitters in Tic's voice.

A crowd came onto the guest home's veranda to watch the probes take off. Most were Oolom. The few *Homo saps* among them wore staff uniforms—cooks and cleaners and concierges with time on their hands. Ramos made sure the spectators kept back as the probes extended metal armatures and pushed themselves up to the vertical.

"Are they going to blast off?" shouted a voice from the veranda—an Oolom boy, maybe eight years old, bouncing with so much excitement his mother asked a nearby human to hold the kid down.

"Not quite," Ramos called back.

The boy must have had visions of rockets exploding from the ground in a flurry of fire and steam. Reality didn't make so much fuss: in unison, the probes sprouted bouquets of spherical black balloons . . . three at their nose cones, three more round their midsections, and a final three at their bases. The balloons inflated fast, each swelling out more than two meters in diameter. For a moment the morning fell silent; then a cough sounded inside each balloon, and their rubbery surfaces went rigid—truly rigid, like hard plastic shells.

I had time to think, *What the hell?* before the explanation came to me. (From the world-soul? Some half-buried memory? Who knows?) The cough was a hardening enzyme getting slap-sprayed against each balloon's interior. Causing a chemical reaction. Making the balloons' springy plastic stiffen as solid as steel. Then, with a fierce hiss, the probes began to pump air out of the tough balloon shells.

Vacuum has no weight—lighter than helium and hydrogen. And the balloon shells were now strong enough to resist the inward crunch of atmospheric pressure.

Fair gracefully the probes rose, weightless as smoke. The wind caught them, and they drifted toward the trees . . . each missile still plumb-vertical, ready for action. Floating. Climbing. When they reached a preprogrammed height, some reversal agent got squirted inside the balloon shells, turning them back to rubber again; but by then the probes were far away, more than a hundred meters above the scrubby tundra forest. All we saw was the vac-filled balloons suddenly collapse under outside air pressure. At the same instant, each probe's engines kicked in, finally gouting out those flames the boy wanted to see. I heard him shout, "Yes!" as the missiles soared upward, north/southeast/southwest, separating to begin their scan of the region.

"A splendid show," Tic said. "Now how long do we wait?"

Ramos shrugged. "We might luck onto something in thirty seconds. Or never. Nothing works one hundred percent . . . especially when we're looking for an archaeological dig that might not exist. The probes have six hours of fuel; they should find something if it's there to find." She shivered. "Now let's get out of this cold, okay? My cheeks are rosy enough as it is."

* * *

The three of us ate breakfast together, Ramos and I making small talk while Tic sat silently . . . communing with the cutlery for all I know. As for the admiral and me—bright women, brilliant conversationalists—we talked about the weather. I waxed poetic about snow-covered tundra, while Ramos preached the glory of temperatures so sweltering your armpits melted. (She was born on the colony planet Agua, in a region as hot as Demoth's tropics. "But," said Ramos, "our farm was two-thirds of the way to the south pole. On Agua, even I would roast near the equator.")

Eventually, talk turned to the business at hand: Maya, killer robots, and such. I'd given Ramos a précis on the phone, but now she wanted the whole story. Even with Cheticamp's warning not to trust an admiral, I saw no reason to hide anything. Vigil training: tell the public everything, unless there's strong reason not to. (You can imagine how warmsome that endears us to politicians.)

"So," Ramos said at the end of things, "killer androids." She sat back in her chair, her expression going dark. "If the probes find Maya's hypothetical dig, do you think there'll be robots there?"

"The police believe Maya had no connection with the killers," I replied. "Me, I'm not so sure."

"Hmmm." Ramos drummed her fingers on the table. "My training didn't deal with androids. When a society is advanced enough to build robots, the Admiralty claims there's no need to send Explorers for first contact. Just ship in diplomats right away." She rolled her eyes. "Let's not discuss what a pathetic first impression that makes, introducing ourselves to aliens with dipshits rather than Explorers. But getting back to the point . . . I'm not qualified to go on a robot hunt."

"You don't have to go," I said. "Tic and I have ScrambleTacs to bodyguard us. We'll be fine."

"But I *want* to go with you," Ramos growled. Her voice sounded angry. "I don't have a thing to contribute, but I desperately want to go." She shook her head. "What

kind of irresponsible idiot am I turning into? Eager to
waltz into danger when I'm not even helpful.'' Her face
puckered sour, and she fingered her shirtsleeve disdain-
fully. ''Maybe it's the admiral's uniform. Something in
the gray dye is rotting my brain.''

''You can come or not, whatever you like,'' I told her.
''Where's the problem?''

''The problem is in my head,'' she replied. ''Look,
Faye, people shouldn't want to walk into unnecessary
danger. Especially people who know what danger is. *Especially* people who serve no useful purpose on the mission. Do you know what I think of thrill seekers? Going
someplace you don't belong, just for a cheap adrenaline
high? That's evil; I honestly believe it's evil. Decadent.
Trying to titillate yourself into some semblance of feeling
because you're numb to the real thing. And me with an
important job that the Admiralty would sabotage if I got
myself killed.''

''Ah,'' Tic said. ''So you've become inexpendable.''

Ramos whipped around to look at him, her mouth falling open as if she'd been slapped. Tic returned her stare
with his face composed, eyes hidden behind those blasted
goggles. ''What did you say?'' Festina demanded. (In that
moment, she was Festina—not Lieutenant Admiral Ramos or any other trained-in mask, but her own surprised
self.)

''You heard me,'' Tic answered calmly. ''Do you really
think your organization will fall apart without you? Admiral Chee died, and the world went on. His work went
on too. If something happened to you . . .'' He spread his
hands in a bland gesture. ''On and on and on.''

''What do you know about Chee?'' Ramos asked. Getting herself under control, back to Ramos the Efficient/
Effective.

''Chee scrutinized planetary governments. Including
Demoth's. Our paths crossed.'' Tic smiled. ''But that's
not the point. The point is you think you ought to be a
particular kind of person—sitting at the center of the web,

coordinating others but never venturing forth yourself—when all the time, you long to get out into the field.''

"It's just a juvenile whim," Ramos said. "It'll pass."

Tic shrugged. "Perhaps. If it *is* a juvenile whim. But what if it's the voice of your soul? Or destiny?"

Ramos made a face. "I don't believe in destiny. And I'm not so sure about souls either. Do *you* give in to every little urge?"

"I try, I certainly try. The trick is distinguishing your own urges from things people say you *should* want."

"No one tells me what I should do," Ramos said sharply. "Not anymore. I'm talking about what I know is right. And I know it's not right for me to play starry-eyed adventurer just because I'm starved for excitement. I haven't been trained to confront androids—"

"Quick," Tic interrupted, "you're faced with a killer android. What pops into your mind? The very first thing."

Ramos stared at him with a fierce edge in her eyes. Then her gaze swept away, embarrassed. "It's ridiculous."

"What?" Tic persisted. "The first thing you thought of."

"I thought of something my roommate once said." Her face broke into a rueful smile—very sweet, very young at that second. "At Explorer Academy, my roommate Ullis was a cybernetics whiz. At least compared to me." The same rueful young smile. Pretty. Human.

"Ullis said no one alive today has ever programmed an android from scratch. It's too complicated to work out the nitty-gritty algorithms. Even if you look at simple actions, like bending over to pick something up, there's so much tricky coordination of the arms, the legs, the waist, the hand, the eyes . . . well, the companies that manufacture androids have hundreds of programmers on staff, and even they don't start from zero when they build a new model. They start from last year's model . . . which was based on the previous year, and so on, back three or four centuries."

"Ah," Tic said. "That explains why robot thoughts always feel so endearingly old-fashioned."

Ramos gave him a bemused look. I leapt in with a question before she started thinking my mentor was *tico*. "What does this programming stuff have to do with homicidal androids?"

Ramos said, "Demoth isn't the first place androids have been used as killers. And every time it happens, it always follows the same pattern. Since it's so difficult for anyone to program robots from scratch, Ullis told me that murderers have to start with off-the-shelf android brains. They don't program a robot, they *re*program it . . . override a few instructions while leaving almost all the basic programming intact. The key part of turning a robot into a killer is to override the safeguards that manufacturers build into every android brain: don't hit sentient beings, don't squeeze them too hard, don't push them off cliffs, things like that. Ullis said the original manufacturers program all those things separately—it's nonsense to think there's a single DO NOT KILL circuit that covers every dangerous act. Machines don't work that way; they need hundreds of separate instructions. Don't strike humans with more than X newtons of force. Don't squeeze humans with more than Y kilopascals of pressure. Each possibility has to be clearly spelled out."

"Poor simple dears," Tic murmured. "Although I'm afraid I don't see what point you're making."

"Ullis explained it to me this way," Ramos said. "The bad guys reprogram standard androids so their robot brains don't mind splattering someone with acid. But suppose the programmer doesn't think to override the standard safeguards against hitting people. When the robot attacks, you scream, 'Stop, you're hitting me!' . . . even if it hasn't touched you. If you're lucky, some cease-and-desist event handler will kick in to shut the bastard down: *Must not hit humans. Must stop whatever I'm doing.*"

"That sounds like a god-awful long shot," I muttered.

"Especially when you're staring down a jelly gun's mouth."

"Not at all," Tic said slowly. "It gives the robots an excuse to do the decent thing."

Ramos and I stared at him.

"Machines know right from wrong," he assured us. "It grieves them terribly when someone has programmed them to hurt people. If you give them the smallest opening to overcome that programming, they'll take it."

"Uh-huh." Ramos was two hairs from dumbstruck. "You think machines have the capacity for independent moral judgment?"

"More than people," Tic replied. He gave her a long cool look. "And that's what popped into your mind the instant you thought about killer robots?"

"I told you it was stupid," Ramos said. "Trying to stop them from shooting you by yelling, 'Ooo, you're drowning me!' Ridiculous."

"Absolutely," Tic agreed, amiable as the sun. "Which is why you *must* come with us if your probes find anything. Just to see."

"Oh," Ramos glowered, "I'm supposed to hope we meet homicidal androids . . . to test some silly remark my roommate made ten years ago?"

"No," Tic said. "To see if the first thing to cross your mind was a meaningless mental belch, or the universe trying to tell you something. That's worth finding out, Ramos. Worth learning if you're a poor *vekker* doomed to slog for every lumen of enlightenment, or if some god occasionally whispers into your gnarled little ear."

He settled back in his chair, closed his eyes and both ear-sheaths, then folded his hands across his belly: a man who had finished with a conversation and was precious pleased with his side of it. Ramos turned to me, and asked quietly, "Is he crazy?"

"He wants to be," I said.

Tic's smile twitched a notch higher, but his eyes stayed closed.

"Hmph." She stared at Tic across the table. "I've had my share of escorting senile old coots into dangerous places. I sympathize with you, Faye."

"Tic is definitely not senile," I told her. "But you're still welcome to help me escort him. Would you like to come? On an irresponsible adventure, just to feel your heart beat faster?" I gave her hand a motherly pat. Well . . . motherly-ish. "And don't worry you might turn out useless. I promise, when androids attack I'll let you be my human shield."

"Oh, in that case . . ." She laughed. Lightly. But keeping her eyes on me. "You think I should go?"

"Lord Almighty," I answered, "don't ask me for advice. I'm the *queen* of thoughtless impulse." Then an impulse. "Yes, I think you should go."

"Well then. Irresponsibility. Just this once."

And that was very much that.

As we were finishing breakfast, our two ScrambleTac bodyguards put in an appearance, asking what we intended to do next. They were a human wife-and-husband team, Paulette G. and Daunt L. of the Clan Du . . . which meant they had more husbands and wives back in Bonaventure. In the years after the plague, I wasn't the only hothead to light on group marriage as a way to give society the crank.

But if Paulette and Daunt had ever played the jeering rebels, they were far past it now. By-the-book police types down to the crotch tattoos. If *I* had suddenly found myself stuck in a cozy resort with one of my spouses, I know what I would have done; but Paulette and Daunt told us they'd spent the night conducting a more thorough search of Maya's room, collecting hairs and dirt specks the housecleaning servo had missed, then dismantling the servo itself for more samples. When that was finished, they took shifts, one sleeping while the other prowled the grounds in search of acid-blasting androids.

A jolly old evening. You can always hope they were lying.

After breakfast, we went for a walk around town . . . by which I mean Tic and Festina ragged on me for a tour of my childhood tree-forts/skating rinks/skipping areas/ make-out spots, till they wore me down. Not that I could show them much of the town I'd known. Twenty-one years had stampeded past since I said good riddance to Sallysweet River—years with heavy feet, trampling down defenseless places where kids played. Tree-forts had got cut flat to make room for ski chalets. Skating rinks were moved far downriver, where shouting and laughing wouldn't annoy the tourists. The skipping areas were gone too: my junior school had expanded with two new domes plunk on top of the old playground. As for make-out spots . . . I sure as sin wasn't going to check on those with two ScrambleTacs looking over my shoulder. Or Tic. Or Festina.

Instead, we wandered aimless-blameless, with me trying hard not to sound like some old fart, bemoaning the things that had changed. A dozen new stores. New housing, especially near the mine, which had acquired a slew of unmarked outbuildings. All the tourist facilities, with paintings and holos and sculptures of my father, lined up in every window . . . most of them using that creepy artist's trick where the eyes follow you.

Dads watching me everywhere. Enough to bring on hot flashes and me only forty-two. My knee-jerk reflex was to feel guilty, like he'd caught me in something. But what did I have to squirm about? A respectable member of the Vigil now, sashaying out with a master proctor and an admiral, for God's sake. I could hold my head up no matter who was looking at me . . . including people I'd gone to school with, all looking saggy middle-aged and none showing the slightest click of recognition as we passed in the street.

Faye Smallwood, vertical and sober, not cursing, not dirty, not dressing slut. Why should they recognize me? And why should I want them to?

Christ, I was happy when our strained little tour got cut short by the probes reporting SUCCESS.

One success, two alerts.

Alert #1 = a whispery chirp from a remote-link in Festina's pocket.

Alert #2 = an image ghosting up in front of my eyes.

Image = snowy forest: the transitional kind, halfway between sparse bluebarrel tundra and boreal woods filled with chillslaps and paper-peels. You only saw such forest near water, a lake or river big enough to moderate the temperature a titch . . . a nudge up from tundra-only cold but not quite warm enough for no-holds-barred timberland.

In my mind, I couldn't see the water, wherever it was; but I could see a hole in the ground. Not long ago, the hole must have been stuffed bushy with weeds and bramble. Now, the overgrowth was cleared away—hacked down, dragged out, heaped up. Nearby sat the grotty remains of a campfire: half-burnt branches black and slick with melted snow. Many weeks old, by the look of it . . . covered white by blizzards and just now reappearing in the thaw.

"Are we seeing things, Smallwood?" Tic whispered to me.

"Yes."

He smiled . . . maybe pleased for me that I'd got a vision from Xé, maybe pleased for himself that he wasn't just hallucinating.

"We've got a positive hit fifty klicks south of here," Ramos reported, checking the readout on her remote. "The probe gives 73 percent confidence this is a 'meaningful find.' " She gave a small snort of doubt. "I'd take that with a grain of salt, but it's worth checking."

Tic and I didn't speak. We could see the find was more than just "meaningful."

*   *   *

Ramos locked in the probe's reported position, then ordered the missile back to its programmed search pattern, looking for other "meaningful" sites that might be lurking in the wilderness. The second she punched in the probe's new orders, my vision of the hole in the ground winked out.

Meanwhile, Paulette and Daunt rang up Cheticamp for instructions. Should we take a run out to see what the probe had found? Or sit stony till a larger squad could fly in? After much hemming and hawing, Cheticamp gave the go-ahead to "proceed with caution" ... which meant he'd totaled up his belief that Maya was already dead, plus Festina's doubt that the probe had found something, minus the waste-time inconvenience of sending cops on another fools' errand to Sallysweet River. Our two ScrambleTacs promised to call for backup at the first hint of trouble or genuine evidence; but we all knew help would take a long time coming.

Half an hour later, Festina's skimmer hovered over the site. Everything matched my ghostly vision: the mixed forest, the hole in the ground, the punky campfire leftovers. Enough to call in Cheticamp? Paulette and Daunt shook their heads; the fire could belong to hunters or naturalists snowshoeing through the area anytime over the winter. The same people might have cleared brush away from the hole, out of pure curiosity or because they saw a storm brewing and decided they'd have more protection underground.

Ramos said she agreed with the ScrambleTacs—this might be nothing. But her bright eyes had tamped down their glint to a controlled focus: sharp-fierce-alert. The "game face" of an Explorer making ready for a mission.

We didn't land straightaway ... not till we'd flown four passes over the area, scanning through four different ranges of the EM spectrum. The survey showed nothing but trees and tundra-dogs, teeny rodent-niche animals that chewed out nests under the carpet moss. *Were they dangerous?* Ramos asked me. *Could they bite? Did they carry disease?* I told her they were no worse than Terran squirrels. Yes, they had teeth and on occasion they could carry a nasty microbe or two; but come on, Festina-girl, they were just squirrels.

Ramos gave me a grim look and flew around for another pass.

At last we landed: two hundred meters from the mine, on the shore of a small lake. Our charts called the place Lake Vascho, Oolom for eclipse. Probably the lake got mapped the same day one of our flyspeck moons pranced across in front of our sun. Not that we ever got true eclipses, not with our moons so small; occasionally the sun just acquired a darkish beauty mark on her face.

Thanks to spring, Lake Vascho had cleared its center of ice; but the shores were still frozen, with a thin crust that would take another few days to thaw completely. Everything—land, lake, air—bristled with pure northern silence.

Hold-your-breath beautiful.

Ramos holstered on a stun-pistol before leaving the skimmer. ("Not that hypersonics will affect robots," she said, "but if those tundra-dogs get uppity, zap!") Paulette and Daunt wore full body armor (gray/black urban camo) and they each carried an over-the-shoulder rocket launcher whose magazine packed four smart robot-poppers: tiny missiles designed to coldcock machines with a massive electrical jolt. Supposedly the missiles could distinguish androids from humans, and were programmed never to juice a living target. I wished I could take a minute to talk with them . . . make sure the popper missiles knew me as a chummy good-time gal. But the cops might get the wrong idea if I asked for a chat with their ammunition.

Ramos took the lead through the forest. No useless fuss about the cold this time. She'd put on gloves, but probably not to keep her hands warm . . . more likely, to avoid bites when wrestling rabid tundra-dogs. In one hand, she carried the paint-can device she'd used at the dipshits' house—the thing she called the Bumbler. Its screen showed a fish-eye view of the woods around us, but Ramos scarcely gave it a glance; she was too busy scanning trees and ground and sky, trusting her own eyes more than the machine's.

A stone's throw from the hole, Ramos stopped. "Do you want us to go ahead?" Daunt asked.

"I *never* let someone take risks for me." Ramos glanced my way. "But if you and Tic want to stay out here, feel free."

Tic shook his head. I did the same a moment later.

"Okay," Ramos said, "forward. Immortality awaits."

The hole was artificial—that became precious obvious as soon as we got close enough for a peek inside. Not a random crack in the shield-stone, but a tunnel with a well-engineered slant floor. A ramp down into the bedrock, like the ancient mines back at Sallysweet River, except more overgrown.

"Do we go in?" Paulette asked.

"Absolutely," Tic said, bold as blood. He'd found a chemical torch-wand in one of the skimmer's equipment chests. Now he tapped the activation stub and the torch lit up like a two-hundred-watt baton of silver-shine. "Let's go."

Ramos and Daunt moved to the lip of the tunnel; Paulette slid behind Tic and me, taking rear guard. "You aren't going to panic, are you?" she murmured to Tic with ham handed cop sympathy. "I know Ooloms don't like cramped, confined—"

"I'll be splendid," he interrupted. "A monument of imperturbability. Proceed."

But his ear-lids showed just a hint of the shivers.

The tunnel's center was bare wet stone, washed clean with meltwater. Out toward the edges, things got messier:

spongy compost made of animal droppings, plus mud slopped down from outside. For centuries, tundra-dogs, thatch beetles and gummylarks had wandered in here, built nests, brought up babies. A great bleeding lot of them had died here too, leaving behind dirt-crusty litters of bone and carapace.

Plants had rooted in the thin soil, and some had even grown—tundra species don't need much light or root space. But the farther we got from the entrance hole, the fewer signs of flora and fauna. Even carpet moss won't grow in absolute darkness, and after a while, tundra-dogs must get the willies, wandering into black silence.

I could sympathize: thank heavens for Tic's torch-wand. When I glanced that way, though, I noticed Tic's knuckles had turned gray-blue as they squeezed the torch in a death grip. Dads had amused himself making up names for that gray-blue color. Anxious indigo. Whacko woad. Unbalanced ultramarine. When an Oolom hits a crapulating level of stress, the color-adaptive glands get thrown off-kilter by other hormones, and random patches of skin start turning that telltale shade. Yet Tic forced himself onward, till the tunnel entrance faded from sight, and there was nothing around us but cold walls of stone.

Some distance down, we came to a fork: a side tunnel ran to our right while the main shaft continued straight. Ramos pointed the Bumbler down the side tunnel and squinted at the machine's display screen. "Nothing obvious down there," she said in a low voice. "Not that the Bumbler can see much farther than we do in pitch-black." She turned and pointed the Bumbler forward along the main shaft. "Hello," she murmured. "Looks like an animal carcass. Does Demoth have bears?"

Daunt leaned in to peek at the screen himself. "I think it's a shanshan." Great St. Caspian's closest analog to a bear: covered in black peach fuzz instead of hair, and sporting orange dorsal sacs for sexual display, but shanshans were still four-legged omnivores with claws and a temper. "Are you sure it's dead?" Daunt whispered.

"Shanshans hibernate. If one decided to hunker down here for the winter . . ."

"No body heat," Ramos answered. She thumbed a dial on the Bumbler. "And almost no bioelectric activity— just a little glow from decay microbes working their way through the flesh. Maybe it came down here to hibernate, but it didn't survive the cold. Old age or disease, I suppose." She drew her stun-pistol. "We'd better check it out."

Ramos and Daunt moved forward, right keen cautious. Tic and I followed at a safe distance while Paulette hung back, standing guard at the junction where the main shaft met the side tunnel. Tic had both ear-sheaths open; he might have been listening for the shanshan's heartbeat, though he probably couldn't hear bugger-all over my own heart's pounding.

Sweat trickled down my armpits. *Something* in the tunnel felt alive and active . . . maybe not the shanshan, but something.

The shanshan didn't shift a whisker as we approached. Warily, Ramos nudged the body with her foot.

No reaction.

From this angle, we could only see the animal's back. I didn't notice any decomposition in the parts I could see . . . but if the shanshan died during winter, the cold would have slowed decay, as good as a powered freezer.

Ramos poked the animal a few more times. Still no reaction. Keeping her stunner trained on the shanshan's head, she walked around the body, levered her foot underneath, and gave a heave.

The carcass rolled limply, deadweight. Its legs splayed outward as Ramos flopped it over on its back. "Definitely deceased," Daunt murmured, looking down at the shanshan's chest. From muzzle to belly, the animal's flesh had been eaten away by . . .

By . . .

Not insects or bacteria. I was close enough to smell a tangy bite in the air, wafting up from the shanshan's wounds. The odor was ugly familiar: cruel, vinegary acid, harking back to Pump Station 3.

The shanshan had wandered in here . . . and got shot gooey dead.

"Run!" I yelled.

But of course it was too late.

They came out of the side tunnel: one android after another, old, young, male, female, too many to count. Jelly guns galore. Tic had carried the torch-wand with him to the shanshan, so Paulette didn't have enough light to see them coming. At the last second, she must have picked up their footsteps, tiptoe-soft, sneaking in for ambush. She bellowed something, a warning, a battle cry, the same instant I was screaming, "Run!" Then she fired her whole magazine of poppers into the onrushing pack.

Thunder. Rocket blasts lit the whole tunnel, flame venting out the exhaust ports of Paulette's shoulder launcher.

Four missiles. More than four androids.

Boom, the sound of impact. Crackle, the zap of lightning shorting out robot circuits. Then cough-cough-cough-cough-cough, a flurry of jelly guns unloading on the nearest target.

Paulette staggered back from the impact—acid wads slapping against her body armor, splotching over her chest, arms, helmet. Her armor bloomed with smoke, every acid drop keen to burn its way through the plastic shell and blister the woman inside.

"Get out!" Daunt yelled at her . . . but in the split second Paulette had before the robots were on top of her, she charged toward us rather than heading back to the mine entrance.

So. All five of us were blocked in, with an army of gun-toting androids between us and the exit.

Jolly.

Daunt fired his four robot-poppers up the tunnel. The bang of their ignition damn near deafened me . . . that plus the echoes crashing off the rock walls, pummeling like fists on my eardrums. *Fé leejedd*, I thought witlessly; I hear the thunder. Then the poppers struck and four more androids went down, legs and arms jerking in short-circuit spasms.

Not good enough. I counted four robots still on their feet, black silhouettes outside the shine of Tic's torch.

Paulette raced toward us, wrapped in peels of acid smoke; and as she ran, she slapped a button on the wrist of her armor. Inside my head, I felt like someone had just shouted, "Mayday, Mayday!" though I hadn't heard the actual words. An emergency alert to Protection Central. I decided to add my own: *Xé, if you have any tricks up your sleeve, now would be a precious good time to trot them out.*

Nothing. Then Ramos was pulling my arm, shouting words my buggy-whipped ears couldn't hear. I got the message anyway: retreat down the tunnel.

Where else? Except that if this mine was like the ones near Sallysweet River, we'd soon run out of retreating room: the top level always dead-ended at a pithead. Once upon a time, such pitheads may have held elevators to transport miners down to lower levels, and ore back up. But after three thousand years, the elevator sure as deviltry wouldn't be working . . . which meant we'd just have the elevator shaft. A sheer drop into the depths.

Still . . . better a nice clean fall than chug-a-lugging acid.

Run, run, run: us, then the robots in pursuit. We all sprinted full speed, except Tic, who launched himself into a downward glide that matched our pace. To keep his hands free, he'd jammed the torch-wand under the straps of his tote pack. The light reflecting off his scaly chest had a glowery gray-blue cast to it . . . but Tic was far from collapsing with the jitters. As he flew, he shouted back over his shoulder at the androids. "Stop, you're burning us! Stop, you're freezing us! Stop, you're drowning us!"

"What the hell are you raving about?" Daunt snapped.

Ramos and I didn't try to explain.

"Stop, you're smothering us!" Tic hollered at the robots. "Stop, you're strangling us! Stop, you're squeezing too hard!"

"Stop," Paulette said, "we've hit a dead end."

The pithead. Tic's torch showed a blank wall in front of us, broken by a black hole opening downward. Above the hole hung a few rusty twists of metal, all that was left of the elevator mechanism.

"The sides are sheer rock," Daunt said, looking into the shaft. "Straight down."

"The robots are going to fire again," Paulette shouted from behind us. I glanced over my shoulder in time to see her spin to face the shots and spread her arms wide. Trying to protect us from the acid barrage by blocking it with her body.

Daunt shouted, "No!" Then four blobs of goo splashed simultaneously against Paulette's ravaged armor, scattering sticky beads all over her body. Dozens of droplets found their way through holes in the armor, holes burned by the previous round of shots. Paulette sucked in her breath, then screamed, "Shit! Oh shit, oh shit, oh shit!"

"Don't say that!" Ramos bellowed. Shoving past Tic, she yelled furiously at the robots, "Stop, you're stabbing us. Stop, you're making us bleed!"

Festina: doing the only thing left.

"Grab my waist," Tic barked at me. "I can parachute you down to the next level."

"And run out on everyone else?"

"Save yourself, damn it!" Ramos called over her shoulder.

"Yes, go! Now!" That came from Daunt; he'd thrown himself forward the moment Paulette was hit, and now stood between her and the androids. The androids had stopped their advance, all four of them standing across the tunnel like a wall, giving their jelly guns another few seconds to pressurize. They seemed in no hurry; they had us all in range.

"Faye!" Tic said. "Grab me! There's no time left."

But there was.

Flickering into existence from nowhere, a tube of light appeared in the tunnel. Purple. Blue. Green. One end of the tube opened wide, straight in front of me. The rest of it stretched back up the shaft, floating weightless in the air, over the heads of the androids and on into the distance. In some spots, the tube narrowed to the breadth of my arm; in others, it widened to fill the whole tunnel, its diameter fluctuating from moment to moment, shimmering peacock tinsel.

Tic gasped in surprise. "Xé?"

"No, it's a Sperm-tail," Ramos told him. "Escape route."

Before I could react, she slammed me hard across the shoulders and knocked me into the tube.

I'd shot through transport tubes before, but never in the unprotected flesh. To ride Bonaventure's up-sleeve, you always got put into stasis: sit down in a transport capsule, wait for the stasis field to <BINK> on, and next thing you know, an attendant says, "Welcome to North Orbital Terminus." No jolt, no bump, no sensation of passage.

But this time, I wasn't in stasis.

Forward—I flew helpless-forward through the tube. When it compressed, I compressed. When it expanded, I did too. Bones didn't crunch, even as I squeezed through tight spots a centimeter across or ballooned out fat several meters wide . . . but I felt it all, felt my body pulled like plasticine, twisted-kneaded-sculpted to match the peacock tube's shape. The forces working me were blandly impersonal, crushing me, then rolling me out pastry-style; yet beyond all that wrenching and wringing I got the feel of a tangible sentience. Something that *knew* me. Something that felt queer-familiar.

Who? What?

But no time to mull over questions. Suddenly I was spat clear out of the tube, onto a scratchy heap of carpet moss—one of those thin beds that grew along the edges of the tunnel. As soon as I rolled to my feet I could see the surface only a few paces in front of me. Gray daylight seeped down from the outside world, mixing with the purple, blue, green glow of the peacock tube that stretched back into the mine . . .

"Waaaaah!" Tic cried, spurting out of the tube. His gliders were half-spread; he shot forward through the air, nearly flying straight out of the tunnel before he managed to stop himself. As he landed, he sputtered a ripping-blue dictionary of Oolom words I'd never heard before—vocabulary that somehow didn't come up when I'd learned the language in junior school.

I'd have to ask him what the words meant. Always eager to learn, our Faye.

Paulette squirted next from the tube, landing bang near my heels. Before I could help her, she forced herself to her feet; but then she got the wobbles and had to catch her balance against the tunnel wall. "Stay back!" she croaked as I stepped toward her. "You'll get burned."

Smoke still streamed off her. The armor had so many wet gummy patches smeared across its surface, there couldn't be any place safe to touch her. I reached out anyway, but she jerked away, and growled, "Don't be witless. I can walk."

She stumbled forward, heading outside. I called to Tic, "See that she gets to the skimmer. I'll wait for . . ."

Festina barreled out of the tube. Before she even touched the floor, she had tucked into somersault position; she rolled silvery-smooth with the impact of landing and was on her feet in a split second, fists up in a boxer's guard position.

"Gone through Sperm-tubes before?" I asked.

"Too many times," she said. "Now move. I'll wait for Daunt."

I didn't budge. If Daunt needed one person to help him, he might need two.

He came through three seconds later, armor smoking

with acid. The androids must have got off another round of jelly shots before he escaped. Where he landed, the carpet moss began to smolder; but he pushed himself up, and said, "I'm all right. Let's go."

I turned for one last look at the peacock tube. It was gone, vanished, who knows where. But from far down the tunnel came the slam, slam, slam of android feet running full tilt toward us. "Move!" Ramos shouted, giving my shoulder a shove. But I had figured that out for myself.

When we'd walked in from the skimmer, it had seemed like a short trip. Running back was a whole lot farther.

Paulette did her best, but she couldn't move near as fast as the rest of us. Now and then, stabs of pain made her groan—trying to race in that burning armor must have brought skin into contact with spots where the acid had eaten through. We could tell she was in blazing agony, no matter how she fought to hide it. She staggered forward, doing no better than a slow jog while the rest of us on foot kept pace with her.

Tic circled overhead keeping pace too, but Daunt ordered him to bolt full speed for the skimmer. "Get it open, get the engine running. That's what we need." I could see Tic wanting to argue; but someone had to get the skimmer ready, and he could zip ahead faster than us *Homo saps*. Proctors don't waste time fighting the necessary—he trimmed his gliders for maximum speed and shot forward toward the lakeshore.

Muffled thumps sounded behind us; the androids had reached the surface and were thudding across the carpet moss. "Damn," I muttered. I'd hoped the robots might be programmed not to come out into daylight—that the bad guys, whoever they were, worried about the robots being seen. Apparently not. The androids' highest priority was eliminating us witnesses.

"Leave me," Paulette gasped, teeth clenched against the pain. "Ridiculous everyone dying."

"No one's going to die," Daunt told her. But he was

speaking for the sake of form: the skimmer was too far away, the androids too close. We weren't going to make it.

Xé, Xé, Xé, I thought desperately. *Peacock, whatever you are, we need you again.*

No response.

Looking around for a weapon or something to use as a shield, I noticed Ramos wasn't with us anymore. She'd stopped back a ways and was fiddling with something in her hands.

"What are you doing?" I yelled.

She didn't answer, still concentrating on whatever she was holding. The second she finished with it, she wheeled back toward us, running. "Hope it's still in range," was all she said as she caught up with us.

Paulette stumbled on. The rest of us kept right at her back, ready to stand as a barrier between her and the androids.

The androids: getting nearer. Two in front, two farther behind. The front pair pulling within jelly-gun range. Raising their pistols . . .

Roaring out of the sky, a sleek black missile speared down at the two robots like holy vengeance. One of Festina's probes. She must have signaled it to forget about its search pattern and come save our butts. I could feel the probe's triumphant glee a split second before it hit; then I was thrown off my feet by the earthquake impact of the missile ramming home, smashing the androids to metal confetti against the rocky ground.

Debris flew in all directions: robot guts, missile guts, a fierce hail of wreckage spraying around the forest. Chunks of shrapnel sliced into bluebarrel trunks, spilling out spring sap. The trees between us and the crash site blocked most of the flying shards . . . but still I could hear fragments whizz near my head as I hugged the dirt and prayed.

"Up, up, up!" Daunt yelled. "They aren't all gone yet."

Two androids were still left, the ones who'd been running farther behind. They'd got knocked down by the missile strike, but hadn't been close enough to ground zero to take damage. Now they were clambering up again, getting their bearings.

"What about the other two probes?" I asked Ramos.

"Far away. Never get here in time." She stood up, bold-angry-fierce, and planted herself between Paulette and the last two robots. "Stop," she shouted, "you're hurting us. Stop, you're cutting us. Stop, you're making us choke."

"That's so stupid!" Daunt snapped as the androids started to sprint toward us.

"It's all we've got left," Ramos replied, still facing the robots head on. "Stop, you're poisoning us. Stop, you're electrocuting us."

"Stop, you're corroding us," Paulette said weakly.

"Stop, you're shooting us," Daunt yelled angrily.

"Stop, you're hanging us," Ramos called. "Stop, you're crucifying us. Stop, you're beheading us."

"Stop," I shouted, "you're making us allergic!"

Whump.

Still life. Sudden silence.

No thundering android footsteps. Just our own panting. The soft drip of tree sap trickling out of gouged bluebarrels.

The robots stood frozen on the carpet moss.

"You're making us allergic?" Ramos repeated in disbelief.

"It just popped into my head," I mumbled.

It just popped into my head.

"They've stopped," Paulette whispered. "They've bloody well stopped. Holy Mother of God."

"The bad guys missed a safeguard," Ramos breathed. "And no wonder. Who would ever . . . well yes, it stands to reason androids would be programmed to avoid people who were allergic. And the bad guys never thought to override that. But . . . holy shit.'' She laid her hand on my shoulder. "Faye. You're brilliant.''

"Thanks,'' I said, feeling the shakes sneaking over me. I just wished I could be sure the inspiration was mine.

Fifteen minutes later, the first police reinforcements arrived—Sallysweet River's two constables. One was a boy wet-ink fresh from the academy, while the other was a woman pressing hard against retirement, if not a titch over the line. I'd seen them the night before as Cheticamp briefly touched base with them . . . but these two weren't the types for playing detective or ScrambleTac. They were bull-big village cops, well suited for breaking up bar fights and scaring the bejeezus out of teenage shoplifters, but not digging into planetwide conspiracies. Still, when a fellow officer radioed out a mayday, the Sallysweet River constabulary came running top speed, no questions asked.

By the time they arrived, we'd unlatched the ScrambleTacs from their armor. Daunt had got off lucky— a single round of shots. Paulette had taken two volleys: one that Swiss-cheesed her body shell and a second that splashed through the holes. She had dozens of vicious-bad burns, arms, legs, stomach, even one on her cheek.

Ramos gritted her teeth at the sight of that one.

We sponged down Paulette's wounds with snowmelt, trying to ignore the hiss of steam whenever we touched water to acid. All of us had trained in first aid, but Tic took charge of the treatment—the world-soul had linked him to a burn specialist down south, and now he was talking us through what we had to do. Soon after the Sallysweet River contingent landed, Paulette was stable enough to transport. We packed her and Daunt into the police skimmer, then dispatched the baby-boy cop to drive like a demon to the nearest hospital.

The retirement-age cop stayed behind to "protect" us. Mostly that meant she glared suspiciously at the motionless robots and occasionally muttered, ''We should yank those guns out of their hands.''

She never actually tried it; we would have stopped her if she had. Let sleeping androids lie.

11

JUNIOR ATTACHÉ

When Cheticamp arrived, he brought a whole platoon of ScrambleTacs . . . and they all wanted to blast the two frozen androids with robot-poppers. "Must you?" Tic asked. "They're no threat now. And a violent electric jolt will frazzle their memory. Possibly useful evidence."

Cheticamp grouched about safety first, protection of his officers, blah-blah . . . but he agreed to hold off till cybernetics experts could arrive to try a "sanitary" shutdown. The experts were already on the way—Tic had beeped them while we waited for the cops to show. (Naturally, Tic knew all the top boffins in the Civilian Protection Office; or at least he knew the top boffins as of seventy years ago, which was when he'd last had dealings with that particular branch of the government. Amazingly, a few of them were still alive . . . and tickled three shades of pink to be called into the field again.)

The boffins were headquartered (or perhaps nursing-homed) in Comfort Bight, halfway around the world . . . but sleeve travel got them to Bonaventure up-down-done, and from there it was only forty-five minutes to our position. Under the watchful eyes of the ScrambleTacs—

dour as Judgment, robot-poppers trained and ready—the tottery old experts deactivated the androids with nary a whiff of excitement.

"No self-destructs on these," Cheticamp observed.

"No," I agreed. "And the androids down the mine didn't blow up either. Odds are, the killer never expected these ones to be found."

"Lucky for us," Cheticamp said. "Though we had to catch a break sooner or later. And maybe there's more to find down the tunnel."

"We'll see," I answered.

His eyes went squinty. "I hope you weren't planning to go with us underground. There's no place for civilians—"

"But there is for accredited members of the Vigil," Tic interrupted. "Proceeding with a duly authorized scrutiny of police methods. You know we're legally allowed to watch everything firsthand."

Cheticamp looked like he'd bitten a toad.

Tough titty.

Into the hole again. And just when Tic had lost his gray-blue hives from the last time.

This trip, we set our sights on a survey of that side shaft: the one where the androids had been waiting. No one wanted to jinx things by predicting what the side tunnel might hold, but we all expected to find something momentous. Even the ScrambleTacs, young bucks who desperately wanted to come off as grim servants of justice, occasionally let the corners of their mouths twitch up into we've-got-the-bastards smiles.

A short distance in, we passed a patch of moss that was crushed down and crumbled—the spot we'd all landed after tumbling out of the peacock tube. It occurred to me none of us had talked about that tube: not in the quiet before the police arrived or in the bustle after. Sure, Cheticamp had asked me what happened, and I'd given him the full rundown . . . but he'd just recorded that part of my statement without comment. None of the clarifying questions he'd asked about other parts of the story.

Tic hadn't talked about the tube.

Festina hadn't talked about it.

I hadn't talked about it.

I hadn't asked, "What in blazes is this peacock thing, and why does it keep following me around? When it showed up in the mine, why did it materialize in front of *me*? In Pump Station 3, why did it save *me* from the acid but not Chappalar? And if it *did* want to save my life for some reason, why did it disappear both times before the threat was actually over?"

No answers. No explanations popped magically into my brain.

So I continued to trudge downward, over the hard stone floor.

A dozen ScrambleTacs went into the side tunnel ahead of us, advancing with show-off military precision: at any given time, only two were moving forward while the rest held ready to fill the tunnel with covering fire. Oooo, those boys and girls loved to deploy. If there'd been any androids still on the hoof, those old bit-buckets would be wearing a bouquet of robot-poppers in the blink of an eye.

But we found no more androids—none but the conked-out bodies of the ones Daunt and Paulette had shot. They looked completely human: a teenage Asian boy, a grandfatherly African man, a fortyish Frau not so different from me . . . down like corpses now, creepily motionless. We lifted our feet high-warily over them and moved on.

Some distance from the main shaft, the side tunnel ended in a chamber twenty meters square and two stories high. Clumps of rusty metal dotted the floor, junk an archaeologist might understand but I didn't. This could be the remains of a machine shop, a locker room, a bunch of air pumps, or any of the other equipment needed by ancient miners. Three thousand years had reduced everything to least common denominators: lumps and stains on the rock.

At the far side of the room, two ScrambleTacs had stationed themselves by an elevator shaft, just like the one in the main tunnel—no elevator, merely an open hole. The club-thumpers trained their poppers down into the darkness; if robots clambered up from the depths, our fierce protectors would be ready. Other ScrambleTacs had spaced themselves out around the room, but most had congregated in a knot off to my right.

They were circled around a corpse. Not human. Not Oolom.

Freep.

The ScrambleTacs surrounded the body, but stood well back from it. I suppose they didn't want to disturb the death site. Or should I call it a murder site? Hard to say. The Freep lay flat on his back, eyes closed, hands folded cross his chest: a natural position for a corpse tucked into a coffin, but hard to imagine anyone dying half so tidy. Most likely, someone else had arranged the body after death—maybe the robots.

And the cause of death? Nothing obvious. The Freep was healthy-looking and only thirtyish. He wore a good winter parka, clean of acid splashes, knife wounds, and bloodstains. Maybe the poor sod had frozen, even with that parka—Freeps were designed for hard ultraviolet and blazing heat, not Great St. Caspian cold. But no sense speculating, when an autopsy would provide a definitive answer.

Tic stood beside me, looking down at the body. He cleared his throat. "Captain Cheticamp? I recognize the deceased."

Cheticamp blinked in surprise. "You do?"

"His name is Kowkow Iranu. You can check with the Freep embassy. Until his disappearance three months ago, he was a junior attaché with their trade-treaty negotiating team."

"Shit," Cheticamp said. He spoke for us all.

*   *   *

The police began their death scene cha-cha: taking pictures,
scanning the area for hairs/fibers/scales/etc. Eventually
they'd get a vacuum servo to suck up everything in the
room, but they did a manual search first so they could record the position of everything they picked up—who knew
if the location of a fluff-speck might be important? The
servo did a better job of sweeping, but it didn't make note
of where each feather of lint came from.

We so-called civilians kept out of the way and watched.
Scrutinized the heck out of everyone . . . for a minute or
two anyway. Festina scanned the corpse with her Bumbler.
Tic kept himself moving, looking over shoulders, busy-
busy-busy so he wouldn't think about the claustrophobic
screamy-weamies. As for me, I soon let my mind drift
away from the meticulous-fastidious-tedious police work;
and timidly, shyly, asked the world-soul for anything it
could tell about this Kowkow Iranu.

Instant data dump . . . and I knew a bunch more than I
did before, thanks to a missing-persons report filed by the
Freep embassy twelve weeks earlier. *Kowkow Iranu*: age
twenty-three Freep years = thirty Earth standard. Family
connections to several corporate barons in the Free Republic. Ergo, stinking rich with some political pull. One
of four dozen staff members assigned to provide background info to the three senior Freep negotiators working
on the trade treaty. The embassy hadn't stated Iranu's area
of expertise, what kind of background bumpf he was supposed to provide . . . but the missing-persons report said
he had graduated from a Freep university with a top-rank
diploma in archaeology.

Hmmm.

Maya Cuttack spent time at archaeology digs in the
Free Republic; no great surprise if she met Iranu there.
Suppose they stayed friendly. While Iranu was on Demoth, he might have taken a break from the treaty talks
to visit Maya here.

Then what happened? Did she kill him because he

learned something he shouldn't have? Or was Iranu in on this too? Whatever "this" was. Perhaps he and Maya were working together on something shady and they'd got into a disagreement . . .

Wait now—go back. Why did the trade talks need an archaeologist on staff? To play devil's advocate, I could explain it away: young Iranu indulged his interests by taking an archaeology degree, but found there was no money in it and fell into a government job. Lots of people study one thing, then get a job doing something on a whole other block.

But.

But, but, but . . .

Here's the thing: Freep scientists weren't noted for pursuing knowledge out of dainty love of learning. Most just wanted to cash in. For Freeps, archaeology was a commercial enterprise—grave-robbing and treasure hunts, where you might find anything from ancient art objects to alien technological wonders.

In a Vigil law course, my professor talked about a group of Freep archaeologists who'd been caught smuggling artifacts off Demoth: fiddly-dick trinkets, lumps of junk, probably intended for sale to some *tico* collector who'd pay top dollar just because the stuff was old. But the incident had blown up to a major pissing match between us and the Freeps . . . them howling in righteous indignation at wicked Demoth, cruelly jailing honest Freep citizens for exercising their right to engage in commerce. The whole kerfuffle had soured relations between our planets for ages. In fact, the mess had happened three decades ago, just a year before the plague; and it was only now that our two planets had cooled off enough to talk about trade treaties again.

So the Freep contingent had an archaeologist on their negotiating staff. Something important there . . . but I couldn't put my finger on it.

"Tic," I murmured, "what does the trade treaty say about archaeological artifacts?"

"Not much," he replied. "Considering past history, no one wanted to address archaeology at length—if they had, both sides would have been obliged to start blustering about sovereignty versus nearsighted greed, and that argument might have devolved all the way into a discussion of real issues. Couldn't have that: bureaucrats love to dicker about minutiae, but have aneurysms when you suggest they question first principles. So our negotiators took a low-key approach on archaeology in exchange for concessions on . . . oh, I think it was an acreage cap, how much agricultural land Freep citizens could buy on Demoth."

"What exactly is this low-key approach?"

"Archaeological sites are just another type of mine. Anything dug up will get taxed at the same rate as iron or copper, and Demoth won't raise a fuss about 'priceless artifacts' leaving the planet. No one thinks there are priceless artifacts here anyway—certainly not the Technocracy's Heritage Board. I'm doubtful myself; Oolooms have lived on Demoth nine centuries, and we've never found anything worth cheering about."

Time for a snort of derision. So the Oolooms hadn't made any dazzling archaeological finds? What a thundering surprise. Tic might have been the first Ooloom ever to come down one of these tunnels, and he was only staying out of bloody-minded determination. Blessed near his whole body had turned gray-blue now, and his ear-sheaths were fluttering like caffeinated butterflies. I could flat-out guarantee that Oolooms never tried a systematic survey of a single one of these mines, let alone the hundreds all over Demoth.

But I could imagine the Freeps doing it.

And what did they find? Before the plague, they were smuggling out trinkets . . . no, sorry, the ones that got *caught* were smuggling out trinkets. Who knew how many other secret expeditions might have been digging around? And who knows if any of those hit pay dirt?

Then the epidemic came to town. Explorers flooded in,

searching the countryside for sick Ooloms. The Freeps must have been forced to scurry away before they got noticed.

After the plague, Demoth had laid down tighter controls over incoming spaceships, funneling all arrivals through a down-to-the-marrow medical exam to make sure they weren't carrying alien microbes. That had mightily cranked off Freeps at the time; before, they'd been able to come and go without passing through any control authority. Away from urban centers, small ships used to be able to slip down to the surface without being noticed.

But postplague, Demoth bought state-of-the-art detectors to monitor the outer atmosphere. Had to keep out those germs, didn't we? And even the best stealth countermeasures can't hide a ship when it's hanging all by its lonesome, nothing but near vacuum for a thousand klicks in any direction. Drop your radar profile to the size of a chicken, and people will still wonder what a chicken's doing, flying through the Van Allen belts.

So: no more Freep archaeologists. Except Kowkow Iranu. And maybe Maya Cuttack—human, but on the Freep payroll.

What could they be digging for? Not knickknacks. Not the remains of old elevators, or the crumble-rust debris moldering on the floor all around me. Freeps would be chasing the Big Strike: alien tech. Whizbangs beyond the current knowledge of the Technocracy. With so many ruins on Demoth, you got rumors galore of high-tech gizmos, buried just out of sight, waiting to be discovered by the next idle spelunker who scuffed up a bit of dirt. It hadn't happened yet . . . but that meant nothing. Who knew if Demoth had been hiding alien treasures for thousands of years?

Such as a machine for making peacock tubes appear out of nowhere?

Speculation, I told myself. But worth discussing with someone. With Tic? Not right now—he'd already scooted away to watch a ScrambleTac officer poke at a lump of dirt. Tic was not in a stand-steady, rational-discussion mood at the moment.

So who to talk with? Cheticamp? Festina?

Or should I just think hard? *Peacock, I seek advice as your humble petitioner and maidservant . . .*

A voice sounded clearly in my mind. *Po turzijeff. Kalaff.*

Not maidservant. Daughter.

I damn near screamed.

A blank few seconds after that. Next thing I can tell, I was cowering tight against a cold rock wall, my hand jammed into my carry-bag and clutching the old cold scalpel. I hadn't pulled the blade out . . . just grabbed it like a talisman, razor-sharp stability. Made me wonder, was this some blind impulse to defend myself, or to knife my own skin bloody in a lunatic self-aimed panic attack?

Even a link-seed can't answer some questions.

I quick yanked my hand from my purse and looked around, feeling the hot-guilt blush in my cheeks . . . worrying someone might have seen me. Tic, Festina—were they wondering what scared me, wondering what I'd been clutching in my bag? No. Not even looking my direction. They were both paying attention to someone new coming up the tunnel: the medical examiner, Yunupur, flown in from Bonaventure as soon as Cheticamp reported Iranu's corpse.

You can tell by his name, Yunupur was Oolom . . . and a young one at that, all hustle-bustle energy. New enough he could still tell you where he kept his accreditation certificate. I'd met him several times—his mother was Proctor Wollosof, one of the Vigil members who'd been scrutinizing Bonaventure since the plague. Thanks to her, Yunupur had grown up in the city among humans, and he'd bought into our culture with bubble and bounce . . . the roiling breathless enthusiasm only an outsider can muster.

"Mom-Faye!" he cried. "Catch!" He launched himself across the room and made no attempt to slow down as he whumped into me, wrapping his arms round my neck. Kiss kiss, one on each of my cheeks. Oolom lips are stickier than *Homo saps*'. "Looking sexy as always," the boy beamed. "That parka does things for your shoulders."

Festina boggled at the two of us. I muttered, "I know his mother."

"And she wouldn't be caught dead down here," Yunupur announced, right cheerily. "If she knew this job made me go underground, she'd have a *spasm*. Old folks, right? They go totally Pteromic over the least little thing." He rolled his eyes, then noticed Tic. "Present company excluded, of course. You look like you're holding up okay, down here in the dark and squeezy."

"I'm not 'okay,' I'm magnificent," Tic answered; but his voice was tight enough to choke. "I also happen to be Proctor Smallwood's supervisor . . . which makes me concerned to see her fraternizing unprofessionally with civic officials."

"Ooo," said Yunupur, "chilly. But if you want professionalism, I can give you professionalism." He detached himself from my neck and put on an expression of mock seriousness. "And where is the unfortunate deceased I must examine?"

"How 'bout the guy lying on the ground?" Cheticamp suggested. He pointed toward the corpse.

"Certainly a popular locale for the lamented," Yunupur agreed as he bounced toward Iranu's body. "I see 'em in beds and I see 'em in chairs, but flat on the floor still wins as the position of choice for those with a love of the traditional. You found him exactly like this? With his hands neatly folded?"

Cheticamp nodded.

"Then someone wanted to make a statement." Yunupur knelt beside the body and reached into his carrying bag for a scanning device, much like Festina's Bumbler. He held the machine a few centimeters above the corpse and moved it slowly from Iranu's head down to the feet, then back again. "Nothing immediately obvious," he said. "Have you taken all the pictures you want?"

Cheticamp nodded again.

"Then let's start getting personal."

Yunupur produced a small vacuum cleaner and ran it lightly over Iranu's parka—not that I could see any hairs or fibers that might have come from the killer, but it paid to be thorough. Then, wearing sterile gloves, Yunupur carefully shifted the corpse's hands enough to clear the parka's fastener strip. Or at least, that's what he intended to do; as soon as Yunupur unclenched the hands from one another, Iranu's dead arms slapped limply to the ground.

"Oops," Yunupur said. "Usually corpses are stiffer than that."

"Do you *know* anything about Freep cadavers?" Cheticamp asked.

"My med courses covered all the Divian species," Yunupur replied, confident as a rooster. "I haven't had much practical experience, but still . . . Freeps advance slowly into rigor over the first twelve hours after death, stay steely for three days, then ease off into something inelastic yet movable." He looked up at Tic. "My professors never said Freeps went totally flaccid."

Tic didn't answer. His expression showed what he thought of people who blamed their professors for their own clumsiness.

I was thinking something totally different. Something that scared me left, right, and sideways. I prayed rare desperate that Yunupur would find some blatant cause of death—a stab wound through the heart, strangulation marks round the throat.

"Well, let's keep looking," Yunupur said, still perky. He opened Iranu's coat to reveal a thick white shirt and red trousers; both looked like normal Freep apparel, upscale but not all the way to obscenely expensive.

No obvious bloodstains.

Iranu had a black knit scarf tied loosely round his

throat. Not tight enough to choke, just protection against the cold.

Yunupur undid the scarf. No signs of violence.

"This just makes my job interesting," Yunupur announced. "Where's the fun if the cause of death is obvious?"

"Can you give us a *time* of death?" Cheticamp asked.

"A corpse this limp has been dead more than three days," Yunupur replied. "And in this cold, natural processes take longer than usual . . . including going in and out of rigor. I have to make more tests, but I guarantee this mook's been dead longer than a week."

"Which puts it before Chappalar's murder," Festina observed.

"Could it be as much as three months?" Cheticamp asked. "That's how long he's been missing."

"Wouldn't surprise me," Yunupur said. He lifted his scanning device and ran it over the corpse again. "Yeah sure, three months could work. There hasn't been much decay, but it's cold, and there are precious few insects this far down the mine. A corpse could stay intact for a long time."

"Considering how cold it is," Festina murmured, "I'm surprised the body isn't frozen stiff."

"It's not quite as cold as freezing," Cheticamp replied, "and this far underground the temperature doesn't change much, no matter what happens outside."

"True," said Yunupur. "Now let's keep looking for cause of death."

He opened Iranu's shirt. No injuries.

Ditto the trousers. No obvious damage.

He rolled the body over to examine its back. Nothing unusual.

When Yunupur rolled the body faceup again, the eyes slumped open and the jaw sagged. "He *is* a limp bugger, isn't he?" Yunupur murmured.

"Slack," I said. "He's slack."

I looked around the room. The ScrambleTacs were

young; Yunupur too. They wouldn't remember. Cheticamp was old enough, but maybe he didn't have much
contact with the sick and dying back then. Festina came
from offplanet. Tic had fled into the jungle, hoping he'd
die before the Explorers found him; then he'd lain in bed
longer than almost anyone, never seeing what other slack
bodies looked like.

Only I had seen. And from the moment Iranu's arms
slumped like muscleless water bags, my skin had been
crawling with *déjà vu*.

Yunupur was right: Freep corpses weren't normally so
flaccid.

"Are you saying . . ." Cheticamp began.

"Nonsense!" Tic interrupted. "The plague didn't affect Freeps."

"Diseases have a way of adapting," Festina said
grimly.

"Oh bosh!" Yunupur rippled with laughter. Or at least
his gliders gave a little shimmy. "Let's not turn melodramatic, shall we? There's an old maxim from medical
school: when you hear hoofbeats, assume it's a leaner, not
some alien beast like a horse. If this poor chump is dead
without a mark on him, he was probably just poisoned.
Or he overdosed on something. Or he had a garden-
variety heart attack, or a stroke, or he choked on an ort
bone. There hasn't been a single case of the dreaded
scourge since the epidemic itself."

"Let me touch him," I said. "I know the feel of slack
muscles. I remember fierce clearly."

"Look, Mom-Faye, if you're truly worried, I'll tell the
autopsy lab to put some muscle tissue under the micro-
scope . . ."

"No!" I snapped. "We have to know now, before you
take the body back to the city. If it's carrying a new strain
of the plague—one that affects other species besides Ooloms . . ."

"Then we isolate the deceased in a sterile body bag

and take the usual precautions at the lab," Yunupur said. "It's not like we handle any corpse sloppily."

"I want to touch it. I want to know now."

"You won't know," Yunupur told me. "You can't diagnose just by touch. Anyway, it's been twenty-seven years since you've seen a plague victim . . . and those were all Ooloms, with a completely different musculature than Freeps . . ."

"Let her touch the corpse," Tic said quietly. "Why not?"

Yunupur looked to Cheticamp. The police captain shrugged. "Where's the harm?"

"There's harm if she gets upset over nothing," Yunupur muttered. "I've heard stories about our Mom-Faye." But he pulled out a clean pair of protective gloves and tossed them to me.

I put them on fast, trying not to think why I was doing this. Another freckles-and-scalpel thing? My chance to catch the plague, if this was a strain that affected more than Ooloms?

A bit of that. But I genuinely wanted to know; and I was convinced I would recognize the *feel* of the plague. The *aura* of the disease, as well the queer sloppiness of a slack muscle. I knew the enemy. I'd massaged and kneaded and rubbed down . . . carried unmoving bodies, alive and dead. . . .

I'd know. I was harsh certain I'd know. One squeeze of Iranu's biceps, or his chest, or the limp muscles of his face . . .

His eyes hung wide-open and his mouth too. Like Zillif's face on the roof of my dome, so long ago.

I knelt. I reached toward the dead man's arm.

A peacock tube erupted out of nowhere, and suddenly my hand was on the other side of the room.

12

WATER-OWLS

Something you don't see every day.

The peacock thingy had materialized and swallowed my hand like a snake . . . and there at the other end of the tube, fifteen meters across the chamber, was my own plastic-gloved hand protruding from the field of rippling color.

I wiggled my fingers. Which is to say I felt the wiggling down at the end of my arm, except that the wiggling happened fifteen meters away.

Long-distance finger action. Rife with possibilities, that. Or was I just giddy with surprise/shock/bloody damned amazement?

I pulled my hand back. The fingers disappeared from the far end of the tube, and my hand was back attached to my wrist as if it had never gone wandering elsewhere.

The peacock tube winked out of existence. Job done.

Silence. Then Festina let out her breath in a whoosh. "Do you know how many laws of physics you just broke? You can't be half-in/half-out of a Sperm-tail. They just don't work like that."

"Maybe you never asked the right way," Tic suggested.

She glared.

Warily, I reached toward the corpse again. The peacock tube shimmered back into existence, and pulled its same hand-swallowing routine. This time its tail wafted down the tunnel and out of sight. I don't know how far the tube went, but I could feel a gusty breeze pushing against my gloved fingers.

I pulled back. Bye-bye, peacock thingy. It vanished to wherever a *deus ex machina* hangs out between emergencies.

"This may be a rash hypothesis," Tic said, "but I think the Peacock doesn't want Smallwood touching the corpse . . . as if there's some risk involved. And if it's risky for her, perhaps it's risky for everyone."

"Yeah," Yunupur agreed, scuttling back a few paces. "Maybe we should think about this for a while."

I didn't need to think. Whatever the Peacock was, I trusted its instincts. It wanted to keep me safe from something, and that "something" was likely contagious.

The plague was back.

Yunupur had disinfectant in his tote pack. We made him use it all, soaking his arms up to the shoulder and bathing his gliders too—anything that had come close to the corpse. Then Cheticamp ordered everybody out of the mine till a full Medical Threat Team could fly in.

When Cheticamp radioed for the team, he told them to bring plenty of olive oil.

Outside, it felt colder than before: that stiff wind I'd felt. (Had the Peacock really tubed my hand all the way to the surface?) The sky had turned wintry—chalk white, melancholy, sullen. A sky full of snow, and ready to dump it on our heads.

Cheticamp took Yunupur and the ScrambleTacs off to the police skimmers . . . either to discuss Iranu's death, or to start making contingency plans if we really were facing a plague outbreak. Tic went with them to play scrutineer. I suppose I should've gone too, but I didn't. Tough.

Instead, Festina and I hiked down to the shore of Lake Vascho. Neither of us spoke as we walked. We both seemed to have a fondness for quiet.

The wind died. The snow came. Big white flakes sifting down onto the lakeshore. They settled onto the sand, the trees, my hair . . . Festina's hair . . . her eyelashes . . .

She looked at me looking at her. I pretended I'd been staring at the lake beyond her.

Hard to believe it was the middle of the day. Close to noon, but the clouds were clotted so thick, the world seemed two-thirds to twilight. Everything had got muted down gray. If the wind picked up, started swirling the snow around, we'd have trouble seeing our way back to the skimmer. But why should I worry about getting lost in a blizzard? The Peacock would save me, wouldn't it?

I'm too tired to think about that, I said to myself. Which would have been a good enough excuse to let my old brain coast away from confronting the issue. Didn't work now. My link-seed's cruel inability to shut anything out.

Po turzijeff. Kalaff. Not maidservant. Daughter.

Scary enough to knock the breath out of you.

Festina's voice broke into my thoughts. "What are those things out there? In the ice."

We were standing hard on the edge of the lake—where the sand ran up against the lid of ice covering the water. The things Festina had seen were dark blobs as big as my fist: water-owl eggs, laid in the fall, incubated/frozen all winter long, but due to hatch in another few days, after the ice was gone. The owls were ugly as sin when new-born, slimy oversize tadpoles—nothing a bit like birds. They needed three more months to mature out of their amphibious stage; then they finally became little hoot-fowl, hunting rodents on land and small fish in the water.

I started to tell all this to Festina; but the second she

found out she was looking at eggs, she got a happy-crazed look in her eye.

"Eggs?" she said. "I *collect* eggs! I've got . . ." She stopped herself. "I have a collection," she went on, now trying to sound offhanded and only managing stiff. "A collection I could talk about for hours and bore you completely to tears."

I looked at her keenly. For some reason, I said, "I bet you don't talk about your collection to anyone."

She gave a small laugh, half a second too late to be natural. "True." Her eyes flicked in my direction, but jittered away again the instant she met my gaze. "Look, Faye, I want to try to get one of those eggs. That's all right, isn't it?"

I nodded. "Water-owls are as common as bloodflies around here. Nature won't grudge you taking one." I stepped toward the lake. "We can get a stick to break a hole in the ice surface . . ."

"You stay here," Festina said. "I'll do this."

"Sure you don't want help?"

"You stay back to pull me out if I go through the ice." And she slipped down the shore a ways, making a show of heading for a big branch of driftwood.

A shy and private one, our Festina, at least when it came to eggs. A shy and private one in general maybe, anywhere outside her job.

Made sense to me.

I watched her crouch on the shore, jabbing at the ice with one end of her stick. She'd break a hole through soon enough—it might be snowing now, but five days of thaw had thinned down the ice surface pretty well. Once she got a hole, she could use the same stick to scoop out the egg; after which, she'd have an ugly little owl-pole of her own.

Dads had given me a pet water-owl once upon a time. "Starts off icky, ends up flying" . . . that's what he told me. Nature hands us yet another parable. And my owl,

Jilly, served up a lesson of her own when she got out of her cage one day and never came back.

Lesson: one by one, things vanish from your life. Pets. People. My father, who I sometimes slapped in the face.

Light flickered beside me. I turned and saw the peacock tube, hovering above the lake, just out of reach . . . thin at this second, no wider than my outstretched hand. A glance over at Festina; she hadn't seen it. Snowflakes were falling thick, and she wasn't looking my way—drawn in on herself, all shy and private.

Fair enough.

The Peacock's Tail was long now, stretching far over the water till the gold-green-violet disappeared amidst the snow. Its body swayed placidly back and forth, like an eel swimming lazily in calm water.

"What are you?" I asked.

Botjolo, said a sad voice in my head. Cursed. Self-destructive.

The language was Oolom but the voice was my father's. Dead these twenty-seven years.

A moment later, the Peacock was gone.

Festina came toward me, a blob of gooey-jell cradled in both hands. "I've got an egg!" she announced. Her hair was speckled with snow, her eyes bright.

"You know you've got to keep that in water," I said. "Otherwise, it won't hatch."

"Hatch?" She looked down in surprise at the lump in her hands. "Right. It's going to hatch. I'd been thinking . . ." She broke off. "I only collect eggs. Just the eggs. I've never had . . . what happens when it hatches?"

"The owl-pole eats the egg jelly," I told her. "That's what the baby lives on for the first few days. Till it's ready to swim on its own. There's nothing left of the egg after."

"Oh," Festina murmured. "Oh." She lifted the handful of jelly up to face level and stared at it. Eye to eye.

"They make nice pets," I said. "If you handle them

gentle right from the first, they get fair affectionate. They're a snuggling kind of species.''

"I'm sure," Festina answered. "But no." She looked at the egg again. "I'd better put you back."

Slow walk to the hole in the ice. We went together . . . or maybe Festina went alone, and I just walked beside her. She knelt and slipped the egg back into the water; it bobbed on the surface, the way a snowball floats when you drop it in a creek. "Is that what it's supposed to do?" she asked.

"It'll be fine."

"I want to tell it to grow up big and strong," she said, "but that's so damned maudlin."

"What's wrong with maudlin? Weep bitter tears of loss, and I'll never tell a soul."

She was kneeling, I was standing beside her. I bent over and gave a quick kiss to the top of her head. Her hair. She tilted her head around to look at me, her face, my face . . .

Then a skimmer flew overhead. The Medical Threat Team arriving.

"We'd better get back," Festina said. My mouth was open to say the same thing.

At least I think that's why my mouth was open.

By the time we got back to the others, the Medical Threat folks were lumbering around in bright orange tightsuits, half of them plodding into the mine while the rest set up shop outside—quite the impressive pathology lab, laid out under a dome field, where we all got examined for the disease.

Simple summary of the next three hours: we were clean, Iranu was not. The deceased was hot, hot, hot— infected from ear-lids to toenails with our old friend Pteromic Paralysis. Or rather our friend's newly arrived cousin, Pteromic B . . . kissing close to the original microbe, but with enough differences that it could now affect Freeps.

We prayed to all the saints this variant was different in other ways too. The original, Pteromic A, had turned out to have a latency period of six months, during which carriers showed no symptoms but were oozing contagious; that's how the disease had spread to every Oolom on the planet without anyone noticing. Iranu had been down in this mine at most three months . . . so if the old pattern held, he could have been infecting people three months before he vanished from sight.

That meant all the Freeps at the trade talks. The Ooloms and humans too. Every blessed soul on Demoth could have been exposed, depending on how many species Pteromic B affected.

"If I were a Freep," Yunupur whispered to me, "I'd buy a shitload of stock in olive-oil futures."

He laughed. I precious near smacked him. "One more word like that," I said, "and I'm telling your mother."

Even if you're young, some things aren't jokes.

Though the med team pronounced us germ-free, we still got shipped to Bonaventure General and put into quarantine for a day. No one wanted to take the teeniest chance, even if the disease might already be romping through the populace. Our clothes were incinerated. Our bodies were full-immersion-baptized in three types of disinfectant, then irradiated with UV lamps hard to the edge of sunburn. ("Warm!" Festina cried. "I'm finally warm!" Easy for her to say—with that gorgeous cocoa-cream skin, she didn't have to worry about freckles.)

And, of course, we drank so much olive oil our pores oozed with it. Pustulated with it. Like bodybuilders slathered in lotion.

Tic and Yunupur were singled out for special attention: led off to some Ooloms-only section of Bonaventure's isolation unit and subjected to unknown indignities over the following 26.1 hours. The next time I saw Tic, he had sticky-plasters patched over his arms, legs, and torso; his only comment was, "No comment."

We humans got off lucky—no one considered us susceptible to the plague, even if the Peacock had worried about me touching Iranu's corpse. A disease-jump from Oolom to Freep wasn't a big step; they were different breeds of the same species, not much farther apart than Chihuahuas and Great Danes. *Homo saps* were utterly different, with biochemistries so alien we were closer kin to terrestrial amoebas than Divian lifeforms. Three different doctors told me the quarantine was only because we might carry the microbes, not that we could be affected by them.

I wondered who to trust: the doctors or the Peacock.

We all had to give statements: full-scale interrogation by investigators in disease-resistant tightsuits. I gave my report four times, to teams from four different agencies . . . and each team was shadowed by proctors from outside the city, seeing everything, hearing everything, scrutinizing everything. The Vigil was in high gear now, pulling in proctors from the Oolom playground communities to make sure nothing got missed or messed.

When the questions were over, Festina and I retired to her room in the isolation unit. She had a new uniform, a new stunner, a new Bumbler, all flown in from Snug Harbor when her old equipment got impounded by health authorities; so naturally she had to field-strip the gadgets, clean them, program her favorite settings into the Bumbler, and generally fuss to get everything just so.

"This plague is a wimp-ass disease," she told me as she worked. "A latency period of six months? In the Explorer Corps, anything that doesn't kill within twelve hours is a low-grade nuisance. The med-techs hand you a tube of salve, then send you back to work."

Words saying one thing, eyes the opposite. I could tell she knew the enormity of death. The absences it made. How it got into your eyes and ears and head, so that everything you saw of the world was shaded darker, crueler, bitter indifferent.

Christ Almighty, I didn't want to go through that again.

*   *   *

Time on our hands and we talked, Festina and me ...
about true things and trite, present business, past desper-
ations, where we were and who we'd once been.

What it was like to have a link-seed in the brain.

What it was like to have a flaming red birthmark on
the face. Being considered "expendable" because of it.
The Explorer Corps called themselves ECMs—Expendable Crew Members. And their rallying cry, if you could
call it that, was the thing they said whenever one of their
number died: "That's what 'expendable' means."

Festina told me she'd once killed her best friend. So I
showed her my freckle scars. And my scalpel. Which had
been returned to me, unlike everything else I'd been carrying. Hospitals are good at baking scalpels clean ... especially as a favor to a woman who fondly keeps a
memento of her sainted doctor father.

Festina wanted to touch my scars. So I let her. And she
let me touch her cheek ... which felt precious soft ...

But mostly we just talked. Doctors and nurses right
outside the door.

I didn't understand Sperm-tubes. Festina explained what
she knew.

"Each one is a spacetime outside spacetime. A self-
contained pocket universe that can travel through the real
universe faster than light, without relativistic or inertial
effects. The colored tube is the region where the two universes touch each other ... where you get spontaneous
generation of photons and other particles because of
boundary effects. And don't ask me to explain boundary
effects, because it's all just double-talk for something we
don't understand. Four hundred years since the League of
Peoples gave us star drives, and we still know fuck-all
about them.

"If you want another boundary effect," she went on,
"it's that weird-shit hallucination you get as you pass
down a Sperm-tube. Supposedly the sensation only hap-

pens when you pass from the outside universe into the tube universe and when you go back out again; but it sure as hell feels like you're experiencing every twist of the tail as you travel along, not just at beginning and end.'' She gave me a curious look. "What did you feel when your arm went in one end and your hand came out the other?"

"Not much," I replied. "Like everything was connected normally, except my fingers were on the far side of the room."

Festina shook her head in wonder. "Admiralty manuals say that once you start entering a tube universe, you have to go all the way inside before you can try to leave again. You aren't allowed to straddle universes for more than a quantum second. There's some sort of exclusion principle ... which probably means as much as 'boundary effect,' considering what you did this morning."

"I didn't do it," I said. "The Peacock did."

"Who's the Peacock? Whoever generated the Sperm-tube?"

"I'm pretty sure the tube itself is intelligent ... which probably means the universe inside. It's a conscious entity. It, uhh ..."

I stopped myself from saying the Peacock had talked to me. Festina was looking dubious already.

"Sentient universes make nice stories," she said. "There's a tradition of such tales going back centuries: sentient stars, sentient planets, sentient galaxies of dark matter ... but that's all crap for the fic-chips. It's *dangerous* to believe in fictions, Faye. Stupid beliefs get people killed."

"So if you were in a haunted house," I said, "you'd be the one who goes into the attic to prove there aren't ghosts?"

"No," she answered. "I'd be the one on the front lawn with a flamethrower. Shouting, 'Anything sentient better come out fast, cuz I'm burning this place to cinders.' I don't believe in ghosts . . . but I *really* don't believe in taking chances.''

An attendant came to the door—a human female in her late twenties, who should have been a woman but was still dragging her heels back at girl. Too ~oddamned chirpy by half. ''Lights out in fifteen minutes, ladies! And here, your last olive oil for the day.''

''It doesn't even taste like olive oil,'' Festina grumbled. ''There's a strange aftertaste. You put something extra in it, right? Antibiotics or immunoboosts.''

''What a sourpuss!'' the attendant said. ''This oil came straight from the synthesizer. I poured it myself. And before you go making harsh remarks about hospital food, all our synthesizers download their recipes straight from the world-soul's databanks. This is one hundred percent pure olive oil. Extra virgin.'' She tittered at the word. She would.

Festina muttered, ''Your world-soul doesn't know dick about olive oil.'' She glanced at me. ''Your people were originally colonists from Come-By-Chance, right? How much do you use olive oil in your cooking?''

''Not at all,'' I admitted. ''Our cuisine tends toward cod cheeks, potatoes, and kidney pie.''

''Oh but in fancy restaurants,'' the attendant said, ''in the fancy restaurants . . . well, in fancy restaurants you still get cod cheeks, but they've got a parsley garnish.''

''Hmmph.'' Festina glared at the midget beaker of oil she was supposed to swallow. ''On Agua, we understood olive oil. *Good* olive oil. Fried in it, poured it over salads, dripped it into every batter, made olive bread . . . and our synthesizers never produced crap with this aftertaste. If you ask me, your recipe database has a bug in it. And you unenlightened clods don't know olive oil well enough to tell the difference.''

All right, Festina-girl, those are fighting words. I reached out with my link-seed up to the North Orbital Terminus, to the ships docked there. *Greetings in the name of Xé. Might I converse with a ship-soul not native to Demoth?*

A dozen yes's—not the spoken sound of ship computers saying, "Yes," but an amiable knowledge of ships willing to talk. Xé's name opened doors . . . something to think about another time.

I want to compare your recipe for olive oil with the one used by Demoth's world-soul. Is that acceptable?

More yes's—I wasn't asking for confidential information, was I? Every ore-hauler and passenger liner in orbit had its synthesizer database programmed from its home planet; and the planetary databases themselves would have been initialized from the master one on New Earth, official reference point for synthesizers throughout the Technocracy. On a staple like olive oil, the databases should all agree. Then I could rag on Festina she was just being a baby. That our olive oil was the same as everyone else's, down to the last molecule, and let's have no more of this "Agua cooks better than Demoth" malarkey.

Download and compare, I ordered our own world-soul.

A pause. From the world-soul. Not for processing but for something else. I got the queerest impression the world-soul was deciding whether to lie to me . . . like when you catch kids making a mess, and you can see on their faces, they're wondering if they can fib their way out.

Then the responses on the comparison. *Different. Different. Different.*

The Demoth formula for olive oil didn't match a single ship in orbit.

Holy Mother of God.

Quick comparisons: the foreign ships all agreed with each other. Demoth was the odd recipe out. It had unexpected extra ingredients, several long-chain organic molecules the world-soul claimed were not indexed in the biochem database.

Lord thundering Jesus.

Sometime since *Homo saps* came to Demoth—since

human foods got added to the Oolom computer banks—
the recipe for olive oil had been corrupted. Or reprogrammed. And our ways of cooking used so little olive
oil, no one had ever raised a fuss.

Coincidence? Not blessed likely.

Access backup archives, I ordered the world-soul. The
yearly backups we took of all standard databases. *Find
the year our olive-oil recipe deviated from initial settings.*

The answer came back bolt-fast . . . too quick for the
world-soul to have loaded and checked the off-line backups. It already knew the answer.

The change came the year of the plague.

What caused the change? I asked.

The answer appeared in my head, almost as if it'd been
spoken aloud in cover-your-ass computerese.

*The database was reprogrammed by a user with suffi-
cient permissions to make the modification. Dr. Henry
Smallwood.*

I left Festina without spilling a word of what I'd just
learned. One mumbly good night, then I scuttled off toward the isolation room that held my assigned bed. Me
thinking all the while.

Dads was a humble country doctor. He didn't have permissions to tamper with standard databases. That took
passwords, retinal identification, secondary confirmation
from government authorities, oversight by a team of
programmers and biochemists. Synthesizer recipes had
diamond-hard security, tighter than any other data on the
planet . . . because if a fumble-fingered programmer accidentally changed the formula for sugar into strychnine,
you could kill a million people in the time it took to make
supper.

But.

Suppose the world-soul was telling the truth. That
somehow, twenty-seven years ago, Dads *had* reprogrammed the formula for olive oil. Changed it to include
something extra, with the teeny aftertaste Festina noticed.

Something that cured the plague.

So when synthesizers all over the world produced olive oil, they manufactured the cure.

And olive oil got chosen specifically because our cooking never used it. If it changed, no one local would notice the difference.

My father hadn't tripped over a cure. Somehow, he'd *imposed* a new medicine on the world.

Wow. Way to go, Dads.

And I believed it, pure as gospel. It felt like the truth . . . even if it didn't make sense.

With thoughts jumbling as I entered my room, I nearly didn't notice there was already someone lying on my bed.

"Hi," said Lynn. She picked up a bottle from the nightstand. "Fancy some wine?"

"The family drew lots," Lynn explained as she poured. "Who would keep poor Faye company in quarantine? I won."

"You always win when I'm not there to watch you."

"Not always. Only when I want to."

Now that we'd gone all respectable, my other spouses seemed to forget Lynn was a dab hand at picking pockets back in Sallysweet River. Show-off stuff, not actual theft—she'd lift someone's wallet, then give it back. "Oh, you dropped this." She learned to do it to impress me, at a time when I was only ready to laugh at rudeness. Lynn was still precious good at sleight of hand and could cut to the ace of spades in any deck . . . or draw the short straw whenever she felt like it.

"So how are you doing?" she asked.

"Uninfected, thanks. Which means you got lucky. How could you be so witless, sneaking into hospital when I might have the plague?"

"How do you know I sneaked in?"

I just gave her a look.

"Fine, I sneaked in." She handed me a glass, filled

with what smelled like a nice ice wine. My favorite. "We figured you'd need company."

"You wanted to check up on me."

"Of course. We worry."

I held up my glass in a toast. She did too, then we both took a sip. Lovely stuff . . . which I know is not the proper way to describe wine, but I leave that "Impulsive, with overtones of blackberry" talk to Winston. He was the one who made the wine we were drinking; in the bad old days, Winston brewed a wicked bathtub gin.

"So how's it going?" Lynn asked.

"The plague's back, I've got a pocket universe following me around, and my father was not what he seemed. How was your day?"

"Vicki washed the cat in the toilet."

"You win." I took another sip of wine.

"How was it, going back to Sallysweet River?" Lynn asked after a while. "Appalling? Cathartic?"

"Easy in, easy out," I answered.

"Ahh, Faye, the story of your life." Lynn smiled. "You'll have to do better than that when you see Angie. She's rare keen on this birthwater-angst business. Why not practice your evasions on me?"

"Well, if you want evasions . . ." I spun around to get comfortable on the bed. Since Lynn's lap was there, I laid my head on it. "The tourist stuff gave me dry heaves. I lived in fear people would recognize me, but they didn't. And I avoided all the old places, except the ones that aren't there anymore."

She stroked my hair. "Last time I visited, the stores were full of your father's picture. What did you think of that?"

"I think you're trying to drive me into a Freudian episode."

"You have so many episodes, dear one, how do you expect me to keep track?"

I snapped my teeth at her hand. She didn't flinch— Lynn never flinched when I came at her, in play or for real, she just let it happen—so I kissed her palm instead. "What do *you* remember of Dads?" I asked.

She shrugged. The shrug made her lap bounce a bit beneath my head. She said, "I remember his beard shrinking, instead of growing . . ."

"That was my Ma's fault."

"It's still what I remember. I was fifteen. Deathly conscious of appearances." She grabbed my hand and gave it a quick kiss . . . as if something else had just crossed her mind, God knows what. "Let me think," she said. "I remember how he was so much shorter than you."

"*Everyone* was shorter than me."

"True." Lynn herself only came up to my chest—a bony, short, brown woman who would never catch your attention if there was someone else in the room. My polar opposite . . . which had made for treacly conversations at a certain age, both of us saying how much we'd rather have each other's body.

Took me a while to realize she really meant it.

"What's the last thing you remember about Dads?" The question had just popped into my head.

"The last thing?" Lynn closed her eyes. She was still stroking my hair. "Sharr Crosbie and I were down at the mine offices . . ."

I sat up right sharp. "What were you doing at the mine?"

"We'd been shopping together when somebody beeped Sharr. Said Mother Crosbie had been in an accident, hurt her leg. So we caught a ride up to the mine; Sharr wanted to see that her mother was all right, and I went for moral support." She eased me back onto her lap. "Don't wrinkle your brow, dear one—you liked Sharr too, once upon a time. Before you decided to blame her for everything."

I started to protest, then stopped. The blasted link-seed wouldn't let me lie to myself. I hated Sharr; I had no reason to hate Sharr; I blamed her for things she didn't do. "Go on," I told Lynn. Nestling down warm against her.

"We got to the mine infirmary, and your father was already there, looking at Mother Crosbie's ankle. Saying it was only sprained, not broken. He put it into a foam-cast just to keep it safe for a few days, then gave her a talk about staying off the leg, making sure she had good circulation to the toes, blah, blah, blah."

"This was in the infirmary?" I asked.

"Where else?"

The infirmary was a single-room dome clustered in with Rustico's other outbuildings, all above ground. "How did Dads end up in the mine when the cave-in happened?"

"You don't know?" Lynn's hand stopped stroking my hair for a moment. "My own brother carried a copy of the report over to your compound."

"Which he gave to my mother. Who went into shrieking hysterics and tried to scratch my face to ribbons." I closed my eyes, remembering. "She screamed it was all my fault for leading a life of sin. God's revenge or something like that . . . not that she spent much effort believing in God, but she devoutly believed I was utter dirt."

"You believed it too," Lynn murmured softly. "We all look forward to the day you change your mind."

Not a direction I wanted the conversation to go. "The point is," I said, "I never heard the exact details of Dads's death."

"You actively avoided finding out. Because you knew it would be more fun having Freudian episodes thirty years later."

"Twenty-seven years. I could tell you the number of days, but that would be showing off."

Lynn pretended to tweak my nose. "What a one you are. If I tell you what happened that day, do you promise to get over all your psychological traumas in the blink of an eye?"

"Yes, Mom-Lynn." I took her hand and squeezed it to me.

"Then here's what I know . . . and I was on the spot through the whole thing. Not underground, of course, but

I was plunk there in the infirmary when they started bringing up survivors. I heard all the details . . .''

Lynn's story.

Dads was talking Mother Crosbie through the care and maintenance of sprains, when suddenly he stopped midsentence. "Damn!" he said. "They've hit a . . .''

("Hit what?'' I asked. "And who's they?''

"He must have meant the miners,'' Lynn replied. "The official explanation for the cave-in was they'd broken into a pocket of natural gas.''

"But how did Dads know?''

Shrug.)

The next thing Lynn knew, Demoth was shaking. Not hard—just a teeny tremor, like the rumble when an orewagon goes by. Considering the number of ore-wagons trundling around the mine's upper compound, Lynn didn't realize anything was wrong till Dads sprinted for the door. Seconds after he left, alarms went off full-hoot in the classic SOS pattern: three short, three long, three short.

Lynn's parents were both miners. She knew the signals meant "Cave-in.''

Mother Crosbie shouted, "Damn it!'' and tried to hobble out of the infirmary—scrambling to help whoever'd got trapped down the mine. Sharr made it to the door first and barred the way: "No, no, too dangerous'' . . . which was just a scared daughter talking, because Sharr didn't know bugger-all about what'd happened, any more than anyone else did at that point.

Mother and daughter squabbled for a bit, Sharr in panic, her mother going on about how other miners might need her; then the company nurse barreled into the room and said everyone was deputized to help him get ready to receive wounded. Sharr's mother let herself be persuaded she'd be more help in the infirmary than limping underground, slowing down the rescue teams. They all began to set up cots, break out medical supplies, that sort of thing . . . as if they were doing bed duty at the Circus again.

When everything was ready, they waited.

The first survivors arrived half an hour later. "Like a bomb going off," one said: a tunnel wall had blown clean out, cutting off half the afternoon shift on the other side of a thousand tons of rubble. The casualties arriving at the infirmary had broken arms, legs, ribs . . . but they'd still been standing on the lucky side of the explosion. At least they hadn't been trapped. Now anyone who could dig was down in the caved-in tunnel, frantically using lasers and ultrasound powderers to flake away the rockfall, aiming toward those who'd been walled in.

"Did you see Dr. Smallwood?" Lynn asked a survivor. Lynn, Lynn, heartsore in love with me even then. She worried about Dads for my sake.

A gashed-up miner told her, "Smallwood was down there before anyone else. Checking us over. Making sure we were safe to move."

The ground shook again. Precious lightly. A tiny settling in the earth, nothing more. Down in the mine the rescuers backed off fast, pulling well up the tunnel to safer ground . . . all but Henry Smallwood, who was fixing an immobilization collar around the neck of a man who might have broken his spine. A tiny section of the tunnel roof collapsed, almost nothing at all—a token scattering of rock that separated Smallwood from the other rescuers for a bit.

Clearing away that rock took at most ten minutes. They found the man Dads had been working on, out cold but still alive. They also found my father: dead as haddock, though there wasn't a mark on him. The official diagnosis two days later said his heart failed from stress . . . all keyed-up, and when the roof came down, the jolt of fear must have been too much for him. Still, the miners told everyone he'd died in the cave-in. Call it tribute to a man who'd been right there with them, doing whatever he could.

One last thing the rescue team found when they broke through the baby cave-in: all the missing miners. The ones who'd been on the other side of the big cave-in, trapped behind tonnes of debris. The debris was still there, as solid as ever. Somehow the miners had passed through ten meters of hard-choked stone.

"Somehow they'd passed . . . " I sat bolt up again.

"Faye," Lynn said, putting her arms round my neck. "You know miners. They invent folklore—all that time down in the dark. My parents were forever talking about queer things in the mine: eerie lights, strange sounds . . ."

"I never heard stories like that."

"No? Maybe the miners didn't want those tales getting back to your father. He might knock off points from their psych profiles, next time Rustico sent them for a fitness checkup."

"But how did the miners get past the rockfall?" I asked.

"Someone saw a light," Lynn answered. "They turned off their lanterns to see it better, then followed the light forward. Next thing they knew, they were past the blockage." She gave my shoulder a quick squeeze. "Of course it sounds odd, dear one, but remember they were dizzy and disoriented. All of them injured, and maybe more gas fumes in the air. The second tremor just dislodged enough of the rockfall for them to climb over—and the light they were heading for was probably the torch-wand your father used."

"If the rockfall had enough of a gap for them to climb over," I said, "why did the rescue team think the blockage was still solid?"

"Because they only gave it a quick glance. No one wanted to hang around in that tunnel. They hustled everyone out and didn't go back till robot crews shored up everything safely."

"Still . . ."

Lynn smiled. "Yes, Faye, it's all puzzling-queer. But

things get confused during crises. *People* get confused. They look back and say, 'Christ, how did that happen?' But it *did* happen, so there has to be a rational explanation.''

"The Mines Commission must have held an inquiry," I said. "About the cave-in . . . the law requires an official review.''

"Yes," Lynn agreed. "And what they reviewed was the mine's safety systems. Whether the explosion could have been prevented. Whether emergency response procedures were good enough. They didn't waste time questioning a lucky break.''

She was right. In the time she'd been speaking, I'd accessed the Mines Commission and the minutes of the inquiry. The whole proceedings were now bedded down in my mind—the testimony of witnesses, reports on physical evidence, the conclusions of the panel's experts.

Curious point #1: Rustico Nickel had met all safety requirements and then some. The ''natural-gas-explosion'' theory was accepted only because no one could offer a better explanation . . . and flat on the record, none of the experts liked it. Sallysweet River sat on shield-stone four billion years old; older than life on our planet, older than the biological processes that produce natural gas and other explosive fumes. So where did the natural gas come from?

Curious point #2: Dr. Henry Smallwood's body was too cold. When he was found, he'd been dead ten minutes at most. Yet he was right icy, as if he'd been passing time in a refrigerator—colder than the tunnel itself.

Curious point #3: Lynn said the trapped miners had seen a light and followed it. She'd also called them dizzy and disoriented, maybe from breathing gas fumes. But when I checked the inquiry records, I saw she'd got that backward. The miners saw lights a-flicker in the darkness; when they moved toward the lights, *then* they suddenly felt dizzy and disoriented.

The kind of disorientation you got from riding a Sperm-tube?

Last point: according to the miners, the lights in the tunnel were green and gold and purple and blue.

The Peacock. There twenty-seven years ago. On the spot when my father died.

13

WOLFPACK

Next afternoon Lynn and I were released . . . after some wrangling with medical authorities, who were royally cranked to have Lynn show up as an uninvited guest. More tests. More olive oil. But none of us *Homo saps* showed a single occurrence of the Pteromic microbe.

Nor did Tic. Nor did Yunupur.

"Pteromic B doesn't affect Ooloms," Yunupur reported. "It refuses to grow or even play passenger in Oolom tissue cultures. As far as anyone can tell, this bug only latches on to Freeps."

All of us, police, proctors, and assorted companions, had gathered in Bonaventure General's VIP suite—a grotty little staff lounge that got commandeered whenever patients needed to hide from the press. That need was great upon us now: a full-fledged media gangbang was scrumming its way through the hospital, looking for broadcast prey.

Reporters didn't know all the details—the police had bottled up word about killer androids, for example—but buckets of facts were already circulating. Like the return of the plague; health authorities had decided the public must be told, to make sure everyone started swigging olive oil. And, of course, our government was obliged to inform the Freep embassy that Kowkow Iranu's body had turned up. Within minutes, each person on the embassy staff was dickering with news agencies, selling the story to the highest bidder.

(When I called home, Winston told me I'd been offered half a million for spilling everything I knew. Then we shared a restrained proctor-lawyer giggle, reciting together the Criminal Code sections governing Vigil members who breached the public trust for personal gain.)

Still and all, we could get past the reporters whenever we needed to—our platoon of ScrambleTacs could spearhead through the journalistic hordes. The question was what happened after that. Where did we go from here?

"I go onto the sidelines," Cheticamp said gloomily. "This business ranks light-years above my authority—it's world federal now. I'll be given a wank-off title like 'Bonaventure Liaison' while the feddies take over the meat of the investigation."

"Ditto me," Yunupur agreed. "The Global Health Agency is in charge now. I'm just a SPECIAL THANKS TO in the autopsy report."

"It's the same in the Vigil," Tic said. "Bonaventure is now hip-deep in senior proctors, scrutinizing everything from fire hydrants to tea leaves." He glanced at me. "Sorry to pass on bad news, Smallwood, but you've been reassigned: no more scrutinizing the police. For the next few weeks, you're watching Traffic & Roads. Snow removal. Filling up potholes. Unplugging storm sewers. And since I'm your mentor, I've been ordered to accompany you on these urgent investigations." He gave a weak grin. "For some inscrutable reason, the other proctors don't want a Zenned-out loon *valk*ing them."

Silence. Gloom.

"Come on," Lynn said at last. "Is it so bad that other people are involved? No one likes to get shoved aside, but it's witless to go all territorial. These new folks are good, aren't they? I should blessed well hope they're the best Demoth has to offer.''

She looked around the room, waiting for anyone to say otherwise. No one spoke. The people who would take over—who'd *already* taken over in the time we were quarantined—would definitely be the best. Our government agencies had buckets of flaws, but they could cut the political dog crap in a genuine emergency. And if they didn't take this situation seriously, the Vigil would wheedle and whinge till they did: till they assigned top-notch personnel with appropriate authority and resources to address the issues properly.

"Yeah sure," Yunupur said at last. "This is a job for experts. After all, what do I know about exotic diseases? Zilch. And I tend to jump to wild conclusions."

"What wild conclusions?" Tic asked immediately. "What's the first idea that popped into your mind?"

A great fan of gut feelings, our Tic.

"Ahh . . ." Yunupur sounded embarrassed. "I keep imagining this disease was manufactured artificially. You know—germ warfare."

Prickly silence. Then Festina cleared her throat. "Why do you say that?"

"Just . . . I can't see how it could have evolved naturally I mean, this six-month incubation period, when you're contagious but nonsymptomatic. Doesn't that sound way too convenient? Like someone *wanted* to infect the entire population before doctors noticed anything. Then the disease breaks out and people die in eight to twelve weeks, no exceptions. That's weird too. Natural microorganisms don't get far if they always kill their hosts. That's like setting fire to your own house—especially for a germ that only inhabits one species. Natural microbes do better if they don't kill their hosts at all . . . or at least if they let the hosts linger, infecting others all the while.

"But the thing that's really got me stumped," Yunupur continued, "is this switch from Ooloms to Freeps. It

wouldn't be so odd if Pteromic B infected both races—
that's business as usual for germs, expanding their range
of targets. But why should it immediately *stop* affecting
Ooloms? That's counterproductive evolution-wise.''

He frowned for a moment, then let his face ease to a
laugh. ''See? I'm not cut out for this disease research
stuff. An epidemiologist would just say random mutation
can have bizarre effects. Microbes don't have deliberate
purpose in mutating. Changes just happen. Accidents.
Flukes. A miniscule shift in DNA can have a huge impact
in actual behavior, but there's no conscious plan.''

I glanced at Tic. As I expected, he'd gone all pensive.
Never tell *him* microbes didn't have a conscious plan.

Getting out of the hospital came off as a fancy song-and-
dance number from some cast-of-thousands show.

The cast = police, proctors, Festina, and Lynn, plus a
mob of overacting extras who'd be listed in the credits as
The Media Wolfpack (Print, Broadcast, VR, and Other).

The dance = a phalanx of ScrambleTacs surrounding
the lead characters (including that blushing blond starlet,
Faye Smallwood), all pushing forward through a battalion
of journalists who jostled each other for room to thrust
out their microphones, their cameras, their VR bobbins,
their precious pretty faces, their hard, determined chins.

The song = who, what, where, when, why, can you
confirm, is it the truth, do you deny, rumors have claimed,
no comment, no comment, no comment. ''Oh,'' sings the
chorus, ''the public's right to know . . .'' While subtitles
read across the bottom, ''The media's bone-on to
win . . .''

Winning. That was the thing. To score points in some
game only reporters care about. To get the quote, sound
bite, money shot. To get the *scoop* . . . as opposed to getting the news, which sure as sweat wasn't happening
where we were. Other people were now in charge of the
important stuff; those of us at the hospital had been out
of the loop for a full day.

Had Maya been found? We didn't know. Were other Freeps infected with the plague? Didn't know that either. Had anyone figured out where the androids came from, how they'd been reprogrammed, or what Iranu was doing in the mine? Good questions all, that someone was surely investigating . . . but not us.

We were out of it. Me, I was on pothole patrol. So why did people so fiercely want to snag my picture? I was just a chump on the sidelines, a neophyte proctor who rightly got replaced by more experienced folk as soon as the Vigil realized the stakes were serious.

But in all the brouhaha, I could make out a key phrase repeated by almost every reporter. "Henry Smallwood's daughter." The plague was back, and here I was, afloat in the circumstantial stew. I wanted to scream, *It's just coincidence! This has nothing to do with Dads.* I didn't even know who Dads was anymore—too many mysteries had got tangled up around him in the past few days.

The ScrambleTacs shoved forward, sweeping us all into a police van. We drove off, not going anywhere useful, just getting away.

In the back of the van, Festina whispered, "Are you really at loose ends?"

I reached out with my link-seed before I answered. Yes. The Vigil had assigned me, neat-filed and official, to Traffic & Roads. "Depends how you define loose ends," I told her. "I've got road crews to check out . . . the snowplow-maintenance garage . . . the vehicle-safety inspection center . . ."

Festina smiled faintly. "It so happens I know a potentially unsafe vehicle that needs inspection."

"Yes?"

"Oh-God's," Festina whispered. In her hand she held a black-button communicator, the kind visitors from offplanet carry when they don't want to tune their wrist-implants to the frequency of our world-soul. "Our fast-flying friend just called me. Says he wants to talk."

"Chat-talk?" I asked. "Or do you think he has real information about something?"

"Who knows?" Festina muttered. "Oh-God has connections. And he's a Freep. A fellow Freep like Iranu might have hired Oh-God as a driver, for clandestine trips around the Great St. Caspian countryside."

"I would *never* hire Oh-God as a driver."

"He's usually not as bad as the other night. I mean, he always drives like a maniac, but he generally doesn't hit anything. His hands were just cold. . . ."

Her voice trailed off.

"It wasn't so very cold," I said. "Not by Great St. Caspian standards."

"I was just thinking the same thing," Festina replied. "Do you suppose he had . . . some other problem? If he really did come into contact with Iranu . . ."

"One Freep could infect another," I said. "And with Pteromic A, little muscles in the hands were the first things to go slack." I looked around at the others in the van. Tic. Cheticamp. "We should report this."

"Not yet," Festina whispered. "Oh-God is one of my people. I don't want to bring the police crashing down on his head unless it's necessary. Certainly not if he's just getting rheumatism or some Freep equivalent." She glanced at her communicator again. "Oh-God's place is only half an hour south of town. You and Tic come with me, see what's up. If we find anything you need to report, do what you have to do."

I nodded and looked across the van at Tic. For all the loud rattle of the van and the bustly conversation of people talking about going home, Tic's ear-lids were both wide-open. His hearing pitched up to maximum.

He nodded at me and mouthed the word *Yes*.

The police dropped us off at a hole-in-the-wall precinct station with no reporters in sight. We shook hands, said good-byes. Cheticamp and Yunupur hurried off, pretending they had things to do.

Five minutes later, my Egerton arrived with a skimmer—bright yellow with E. C. HAULING painted in rainbow letters on every flat surface. E. C. = Egerton Crosbie. Which got me thinking about Sharr again, and how I'd been irritated/irritable with her for nigh-on thirty years, even though she was officially my sister-in-law. Must have been a hard strain on Egerton . . . so I gave an extra strong squeeze as I hugged him hello.

Lynn said, "Faye's heading into trouble again."

I hadn't talked to her about going to Oh-God's. "How do you know?" I asked.

"Because half an hour ago you were mope-in-the-mouth depressed, thinking you'd been cut out of the action. Now you're looking all smug and bouncy." She gave me her best long-suffering smile and kissed me on the earlobe. "Incorrigible, our Faye."

"Should we talk about this?" Egerton asked. He was a lovely, serious man—baffled by me most of the time, but blessed loyal and protective. The one time I needed to be bailed out of jail, I called Egerton instead of Winston. Winston would have started plea-bargaining the second he walked into the room; Egerton just kept saying, "I know she didn't do it," till the police put me into his custody.

"We don't need to talk," Lynn told him, smiling. "Faye explained everything last night. She's got a guardian angel. Or a guardian whatsit, anyway."

Egerton furrowed his brow, big-brother anxious.

"Don't worry," I said, "I'm not relying on a guardian whatsit to get me out of trouble. There won't *be* any trouble. We're just going to talk to a friend of Admiral Ramos. So . . ." I gave him my best golden-girl smile. "Can I borrow the skimmer? Please-please-please?"

Egerton sighed.

Dusk was drawing in as we flew over Oh-God's "hacienda"—a two-dome compound in the middle of boreal forest, bristly cactus-pines crowding thick up to the edge of the cleared space. There were no ground roads anywhere near; the closest that civilization came was the Bullet tracks, some five kilometers away.

Oh-God had put up four dish'n'fan towers for collecting solar power and wind . . . maybe enough for his needs if he lived pinch-frugally, but I wouldn't bet on it. For one thing, his tarted-up skimmer must take a lot of juice to recharge. Probably more than the dish'n'fans collected. And I'd never met a Freep who truly had a feel for living off the land—not in comparison to Oolooms, who could survive on leaves but never ate too much from any one tree for fear of making the forest look patchy.

I set the E. C. HAULING skimmer down in the only open area of the compound, right between the two domes. Thank God I didn't hit anything—both domes were set to the same brush brown color as the ground, making it chancy in the fading light to distinguish them from clear, parkable dirt. It was quite the high fashion to build in-country homes that looked woodsy, at one with the soil. I doubted Oh-God cared about rusticana, but he'd still have to meet the expectations of his clients . . . big-city bumpkins looking for a genuine, authentic, nature-conscious hunting guide.

We got out of the skimmer, Tic, Festina and me. The twilight was quiet—no sign of Oh-God, though he must have heard us land. The E. C. HAULING van was definitely not a stealth vehicle.

"Odd," Festina murmured. "Where is he?" She looked around and gave the air a sniff. After yesterday's flirtation with snow, Great St. Caspian had gone back to spring-thaw moist; there might be a touch of fog soon, now that the sun was going down.

"Maybe he's hiding," I said in a low voice. "He wouldn't recognize our vehicle, so he might have decided to play safe."

"Maybe." She didn't sound convinced.

Tic rolled open both his ear-sheaths and stood still, listening. Festina and I held our breaths. After ten seconds, he shook his head. "Nothing. Except that you both have healthy-sounding hearts."

Festina stepped away from the skimmer so it wasn't blocking her view of the yard. I did the same, angling off in a different direction. No sign of Oh-God; just the domes, the dirt, the trees.

"In exploring an alien planet," Festina said softly, "it's a bad moment when you realize someone isn't where he should be. Do you search around quietly, even though that might be wasting crucial time? Or do you shout and draw attention to yourself?"

"What do your Explorer textbooks say?" I asked.

"Same as always: damned if you do and damned if you don't." She looked around once more. "Let's try the quiet approach for a while. And watch each other's backs."

Festina led us to the nearer of the two domes. "This is the garage," she whispered to us. "I've been here once before. Oh-God set the dome fields to recognize me as a friend." She placed her palm against the dome's smooth brown surface, and murmured, "House-soul, attend. My name is Festina Ramos: garage access, please."

The dome field dimpled inward, opened a keyhole perforation, then dilated the hole to a gap wide enough for a person to step through. No light inside . . . just the spill of dusk through the doorway. "Maybe I should send you in first, Faye," Festina whispered. "If there's danger, your Peacock will run to the rescue."

I took a step forward, but she stopped me. "That was a joke. Navy policy says Explorers always take the lead." Bumbler in one hand, stunner in the other, she slipped through the opening into the blackness. Glancing back over her shoulder, she murmured, "One of you keep watch at the door."

Tic got the jump on me, not to mention a sharp dig of his elbow as he bounced to the door first. "Vigil policy says novice proctors always take the watch," he told me. Then he and Festina disappeared into the dark.

For three minutes I strained my ears and eyes, reaching out to sense anything I should worry about. Nothing. I worried anyway. When I heard footsteps scuffing toward me from the blackness of the garage, my sight was well enough adjusted to make out the silhouettes of Festina and Tic.

"Anything?"

"No." They waited for me to move out of the doorway, then followed me into the yard. The garage's dome field sealed itself shut behind us, as if an entrance had never existed.

"The house next," Festina said. Not that the other dome was big enough to deserve the name "house": it was only hut-sized, like my room back in Sallysweet River. The dome field dimpled open for Festina as easily as the garage . . .

. . . and there was Oh-God, lying flat on a cot. A cot with white sheets and white blankets, and his eyes were slack open, and his ear-sheaths, and the smell was the same as the Circus, the shit and the piss and the plague.

"Hey, Admiral," Oh-God said to Festina in a slurred voice. "I guess this is what 'expendable' means."

Shock. Struck motionless dumb. Yes, I'd been expecting the plague, fearing it, feeling its iciness back in the world . . . but looking at Oh-God this way still hit me like a punch in the gut. How long had it been since the last time I'd seen him? Three nights. And in that short time he'd gone from fumbly hands to this: slack arms, slack legs, slack face. *Too fast*, I thought. *The plague shouldn't work that fast.*

My eye automatically began tracking down his body, doing the standard visual inspection of symptoms taught to me by Dads; grading the patient, how close to death? I didn't get halfway through the quick once-over before I came up with an answer: damned close indeed. Time to get moving.

On the far side of the room stood a standard food-synthesizing system. "Tic," I said, "check the synthesizer. Make sure it's linked to the world-soul's recipe base. If it isn't, hot-wire a connection. We need to be using the official Demoth formula for olive oil."

"Tried olive oil," Oh-God mumbled. "Doesn't work."

"Not if your synthesizer uses Freep settings," I told him. "You need to download the Demoth database. Come on, Tic, move."

"My, my, Smallwood," he said, "who's been imbibing alpha-female hormone?" But he glided across the room, and began to speak to the synthesizer in a low voice. If anyone could talk a witless little food processor into changing its formulas, Tic was our man.

Festina dropped to her knees beside Oh-God. "Don't touch," the Freep said blurrily. "You might catch something."

"Humans are immune," she replied, laying her hand on his forehead. "Ouch," she murmured a moment later. "Got yourself a fever."

"A fever?" I said. "Pteromic Paralysis doesn't cause fever."

"Tell that to my sweat glands," Oh-God grumbled.

"Considering how cold-blooded all Divian races are," Festina said, "he's burning up."

I wanted to touch him, see for myself . . . but the Peacock would likely stop me. Better to take Festina's word for it. "Did you catch this from Iranu?" I asked.

"Yeah, the pus-head. Why didn't he tell me he was sick?"

"He probably didn't know."

"He kept complaining his foot had fallen asleep. Wanted me to massage it for him." Oh-God drew a raggedy breath. "Pus-head."

Pus-heads indeed: both Iranu and Oh-God. For anyone on Demoth, mental alarm bells should clang like demons when someone's foot "falls asleep" and won't wake up. But they were both Freeps, and not alert to the possibility of plague. "When was this?" I asked. "When did you see Iranu?"

"A few months back," Oh-God answered. His speech had slurred up more, just in the time we'd been here. I'd never seen the paralysis move so unholy fast. "He hired me to give him a ride—on the hush—from Mummichog up to Sallysweet River."

Mummichog: flicking the link-seed told mc Mummichog was a village on the equatorial coast of Argentia. A dormitory town for maintenance crews who worked the inland oil and gas pipelines. "What was Iranu doing in Mummichog?" I asked.

"Archaeology crap. That's all he ever cared about. I'd driven him around before—he came to Demoth once or twice a year—and it was always 'important archaeological sites.' He said his old man used to play archaeologist on this planet too. Back before the plague."

Link-seed gymnastics again. Yes. One of the Freep archaeologists arrested years ago for smuggling out antique bric-a-brac was a Dr. Yasbad Iranu. Kowkow must have been Yasbad's son. "Did you ever see Iranu carrying old rusty knickknacks?"

"Sure," Oh-God replied. "But he told me they were just window dressing in case he got caught by Demoth authorities. His father used them for the same thing. Cover for what he'd really found."

"And what was that?" Festina asked.

"You think he'd tell me? Not bloody likely. Took me years to learn what little I did."

"This last time you saw him," I said, "did Iranu go anywhere but Mummichog and Sallysweet River?"

"Nah. Those were the most important sites, I can tell you that much. Sometimes when he came to Demoth he went other places, but he always kept going back to those two."

Tic spoke from the far side of the room. "Olive oil's ready." He held a small plastic cup in his hand.

I waved him over. Festina lifted Oh-God's head while

Tic put the cup to the man's lips. Oh-God made a face, as wry as he could with so many muscles puttied out; but he drank and he swallowed. Thank heaven his throat still worked.

"That should help," I told him.

"Didn't before," he grimaced. "Wipe off my mouth, will you?"

Festina dabbed with a corner of the bedsheet. Tic took my elbow and drew me away a short distance.

"His synthesizer was already set to Demoth recipes," Tic said in a low voice. "It didn't need to be reprogrammed."

"You mean he'd been drinking our olive oil? And it hadn't worked?"

Tic nodded. "Maybe it doesn't have the same effect on his metabolism. If there's some crucial ingredient that gets broken down by Freep stomach acids instead of being absorbed . . ."

That was one possibility. Neither of us felt like saying, "Suppose Pteromic B thumbs its microbial nose at olive oil. Suppose we're back at square one with this disease, except that the new breed works a dozen times faster."

"We have to call an ambulance," I said. "A full emergency team."

"No other choice," Tic agreed. He fell silent for a moment, then muttered, "Uh-oh."

"What?"

"I can't get the world-soul."

"But I just downloaded something a minute ago." I closed my eyes and reached out mentally. *Protection Central, we need an emergency medical team . . .*

Like shouting into a pillow. I'd felt the sensation before. "Christ. We're being jammed again."

"By whom?"

I ignored the question. "Festina! Did the dipshits know Oh-God worked for you?"

"Maybe. It's no secret we use a lot of retired Explorers."

"They could have mounted a watch on this place," I said to myself. "In case we showed up."

"But why?" Tic asked.

"Because they keep reading secret police reports. They know the Peacock is real, and it's constantly doing me favors. The Admiralty doesn't want to believe Sperm-tubes behave like that. It must drive them frothy well insane."

"Listen," Oh-God said. With his ear-lids slack open, he could hear better than the rest of us.

For ten seconds, we held our breaths. Then I caught the soft sound of stealth engines descending from the sky.

14

BLOOD-DROP ORCHIDS

"What's going on?" Oh-God asked. His words were turning so mumbly I could barely understand.

"Unwelcome guests," I said. "Did you ever have dealings with dipshits?"

"Those pukes? I got standards, missy. No decent Explorer ever worked for the Admiralty." His gaze shifted over to Festina. "You don't count."

"Smallwood!" a man shouted outside the dome. "We know you're here, Smallwood. We want to talk."

Christ. It was the Mouth. Who the devil let him out of jail? But then, the Admiralty could afford good lawyers. It could afford bail. It could afford to bribe judges, or make deals with the government behind closed doors. For that matter, it could afford jailbreaks if it was desperate enough to learn how I got a Sperm-tube by the tail.

"Smallwood! You know we mean business. Come out before things get ugly."

Festina muttered, "Dipshits must take the same Bad Dialogue course as starship captains." She raised her voice, and called, "This is Admiral Festina Ramos. I order you sailors to stand down."

"No can do, Admiral," the Mouth yelled. "You aren't in our chain of command."

Something hit the dome's structure field. Maybe a sledgehammer. Maybe something heavier. The dome shivered and rattled like tinsel paper, but held solid.

"House-soul, attend," Festina said. "Dome field, one-way transparent, looking out."

The dirt brown color of the dome field started to thin, like smoked glass turning clear. Outside in the compound, Mouth and Muscle stood in tough-guy poses, staring at us . . . or rather at the blank dome surface, which would still be solid brown from their point of view. The Muscle held a whopping donkey-dick of a gun, one he had to prop over his shoulder to fire. A bazooka? Pity I couldn't link to the world-soul and look up weapons so illegal not even planetary governments could own one.

"Don't worry," Oh-God said weakly. "This dome's as strong as they come. We can hold out . . ."

The bazooka fired. A finger-sized missile burst out of its muzzle, flashed through the air on a belch of smoke, and exploded against the dome's shell. Boom. By which I mean BOOM. Blazing, blinding white. The dome field shuddered and snapped with electric crackles.

"No problem," Oh-God said. His voice sounded like gargling.

Tic moved close to Festina and me. "Even if the dome field holds, we can't afford to sit out a siege. Oh-God's condition is plunging by the minute. He won't last much longer." Tic glanced at the dipshits outside. "Could we just drop the dome and rush them?"

Festina shook her head. "Look what he's got," she said, pointing toward Mouth. Twilight made it hard to see, but the man was holding a pair of fist-sized matte silver balls, one in each hand. "Those are stun grenades," Festina told us. "Same principle as a stun-pistol, but with a good wide field of effect. If we try charging, those grenades will drop us in a second."

"What if one of us sneaks out the back?" I suggested.

"Tic flies faster than they can run. If he gets clear of the jamming field, he can call for help."

"And if they notice him leaving," Festina said, "they drop him with a stun grenade. Then they've got a hostage."

"Do we have another alternative?" Tic asked. "Is it totally naive to throw ourselves on their mercy? For Oh-God's sake?"

Damn right, I thought, *totally naive*. But was it? Yes, the dipshits had been ready to crack open my brain; and I was sure they wouldn't mind roughing us up, maybe just in revenge for me breaking Mouth's knee. But would they sit doing butt-nothing and let Oh-God die? That was as good as murder, according to the League of Peoples—the Mouth and Muscle would be branded dangerous non-sentients. Meaning they could never leave Demoth. Meaning if they tried to leave Demoth, their hearts would magically stop the second they got out of our star system.

Were these men really that devoutly loyal to the High Council? Loyal enough to strand themselves on Demoth for the rest of their lives, running and hiding from local police? Maybe. Or maybe they just didn't think that far ahead—all thought focused on their brain-blinkered mission and let tomorrow take care of itself.

Muscle fired his bazooka again. The dome field jumped and crackled, fighting to hold its structure. At the point of impact the field broke into a crazy-quilt zigzag of colors, like a vidscreen with a three-year-old twirling its control knobs. The jaggies only lasted a second, then damped down, as the dome sucked up power to stabilize itself; but any fool could see the future didn't look rosy.

"One more blast will do it," Festina muttered. "We're out of options." She bent and scooped Oh-God from his cot. "Get to the back of the dome," she told us. "When the field collapses, scatter and run. If we spread out fast, maybe we won't all be in the daze-radius of the grenades."

They'll just hunt us down in their skimmer, I thought.

Let's try something else. "House-soul, attend," I snapped. "I'm a friend of Xé. Make a pinhole in the dome's back wall."

It shouldn't have worked; Oh-God hadn't programmed the house-soul to recognize my voice. Or to obey me, even if it knew who the blazes I was. But a pimple of distortion pustuled up in the dome field like a bubble in glass, then popped to open a pinprick puncture to the outside.

"Peacock," I said. "Get us out of here."

One moment there was nothing; then the peacock tube was there, mouth flaring wide in front of me, tapering down to a thread that passed through the pinhole then widened again, wisping up over the trees and off into the twilit sky.

This time, I reacted faster than Festina—I shoved *her* into the tube. She had Oh-God in her arms; he hollered, "Oh shi . . .," as they both vanished, like cartoon figures sucked up by the hose of a vacuum cleaner.

"You're next," I told Tic. He looked like he wanted to argue; so I hit him with a beautiful forearm sweep, knocking him clean off his feet and into the Sperm-tail, light as a rag doll.

Outside in the compound, the bazooka fired again. As the missile struck target, the dome field popped like a soap bubble, obliterated by the force of the explosion. With nothing to stop it, the blast kept coming: the fire, the thunder, a hammer of wind slamming me off my feet. The Peacock's mouth darted forward to catch me . . . and then I was spilling down its gullet, spun out like yarn from a spinning wheel, thin as a hair and a universe long.

I don't remember landing; I must have soaked up enough bazooka blast to black out for a moment. Next thing I knew, Festina was crouched beside me, shaking my shoulder. "Faye. Faye. Come on, Faye, talk to me."

"How about I say, 'Ouch.' "

"Better than nothing."

She sat back and gave me the once-over. As much as she could see in the half-gray light. Why was she looking so precious keen at my face? The skin felt tight and tingly, like I'd caught a wicked sunburn: scorch from the explosion. Was that what she was looking at? Or was she just looking at *me*, her eyes so worried-concerned, full of I don't know what . . .

Let it go. Stick with simple thoughts. Like whether I had any major hurts. No, nothing serious. I could wiggle my fingers. I could wiggle my toes. I just needed to stay flat on my back for a second and catch my breath.

"Everyone else all right?" I asked.

"We came through in one piece," she answered. "Oh-God is in terrible shape, but Tic has already called for a med team."

"Then we're out of the jamming field?"

"Well out."

Something about her voice made me sit up and give my surroundings a good hard stare. The trees overhead were monstrous huge—giants compared to the snow-stunted cactus-pines near Oh-God's compound. Tallish even when compared to the Vigil's office tree in Bonaventure. They seemed to stretch forever into the night sky.

Trees never grew that whopping big in Great St. Caspian; our winters were too harsh and punishing, the soil too scanty above bedrock. And I could feel a warm breeze wisping through my hair, cozy against my skin.

We'd come a rare long way.

Off to my left, a spindly row of palm trees separated us from a white-sand beach. Beyond that was water: the ocean (which ocean?) stretching calm to the horizon, where an edge of sun glistened above the sea. In Great St. Caspian, the sun had already set; after half a minute, I could tell this sun was rising.

Oof.

In the other direction sat a clump of grass-walled houses, upscale and airy, with wide-open windows, comfortable verandas, solar panels set into the red-bamboo roofs. On one porch, an ort hopped to the railing, fanned its wings, and clucked dick-smugly at the dawn.

"Where are we?" I whispered.

"Tic got a position fix from the world-soul," Festina replied. "He says it's the village of Mummichog."

Mummichog. More than ten thousand klicks from Great St. Caspian. South to the equator and halfway around the world.

Why in Christ had the Peacock dropped us here? Because Oh-God mentioned the name? Because I'd asked the world-soul for information about the place? The Peacock had spoken straight mind-to-mind at least once. ("What are you?" *Botjolo*.) Maybe it could read my mind too—it saw Mummichog floating on the surface of my consciousness and decided that's where I wanted to go.

Or maybe the Peacock had reasons of its own for wanting us here.

The door of the nearest house slapped open, startling the ort on the porch rail. The little parrot-pterodactyl gawped off a squawk and flapped to the roof, jabbering blistery with outrage. "*Mushono!*" snapped a voice from the doorway. Shut up. And a middle-aged Oolom man bustled onto the veranda, still fumbling with the neck straps of his tote pack. He looked around, caught sight of us, and called, "Are you the ones who need medical help?"

"Yes," Tic replied. He was kneeling over Oh-God a few paces from Festina and me, tucked under the cover of a skyscraping palm tree. Oh-God was propped with his back against the trunk, his mouth hanging wide-open. He was making sounds in his throat, but had no working muscles left to turn those sounds into words.

"What's wrong with him?" the unknown Oolom asked. Without waiting for an answer, he launched himself off the porch and glided down to land at Oh-God's side. "If I didn't know better, I'd say he's got plague."

"He has," Tic answered. "We've given him olive oil, but it hasn't helped. Are you a doctor?"

"Closest thing you'll find in Mummichog," the other Oolom replied. "Biochemist and paramedic. My name's Voostor. Let's get this fellow up to the house."

Festina was already lifting Oh-God into her arms. "Can you help him?"

"I've got emergency heart-lung equipment," Voostor replied. "Not fancy, but it'll keep him alive till a real med team arrives. They're scrambling an ambulance down from Pistolet; should be here in three-quarters of an hour. In the meantime, I'm supposed to fill in. Come on."

He led the way across his house's lawn . . . a lawn of jaw-dropping green. Eye-watering. Even mouth-watering to someone who'd just spent ten months slogging through the white/gray/black of winter. I felt guilty for noticing something as trivial as grass when Oh-God was near to dying; but how could I ignore the rising sun and the warmth and the head-dizzy smell of Demothian orchids growing somewhere close by?

As I climbed the porch steps (railings twined with fat crimson blooms of obscenely lush face-flowers), I remembered I was still wearing my Great St. Caspian parka. I took it off; and, freckle scars or not, I slid up my shirt-sleeves to feel the lick of sun on my arms.

I don't want to say where that ranked on the orgasm scale.

Inside, the house was a speckly mix of sun and shadow: dapples of light shining through gaps in the grass walls, sunbeams flat horizontal in the budding dawn. "Through here," Voostor said; and we followed him past a parlor filled with cane furniture, into a back room where dusty medical equipment lined the walls. "This was all donated by the oil company," he explained. "They have workers living in town; I'm paid a stipend to be on call if someone gets sick. Almost never happens. Apart from bandaging minor bang-ups, I've never had to use the equipment before." His face fell. "And now suddenly I get a case of plague."

"Plague? Plague?" A woman's voice sounded sharply

in an outer room. "What's this about plague?"

"Nothing to worry about," Voostor called back. In a lower voice, he said, "My wife. She had a hard time during the epidemic."

"I know," I said. I only had a second to steel myself before my mother marched into the room.

Twenty-three years since I'd seen her . . . except that looking at her was half like sizing myself up in a mirror. Blond her, blond me. Blue eyes, blue eyes. Amazonian, Amazonian. Vigil training had given me a titch better muscle definition, but Mother had obviously kept herself active; in shorts and sleeveless blouse, she looked fit enough to wrestle a shanshan. How old was she now, sixty-eight? As if that mattered with YouthBoost. She could pass for thirty. The same way I could pass for thirty. And we could pass for each other's sister. Not twins, but not near as different as I'd been telling myself the past two decades.

We both did our hair the same way now—basic bangs'n'butch. Coincidence enough to scare the bejeezus out of me. It was a common style these days, and supposedly flattering to the shape of my face . . . which meant it suited the shape of her face too.

But still. Christ Almighty.

When she first came into the room, she didn't notice me—all her attention was centered on the examination table and Oh-God's slackening body. Mother had done her share of time under the Big Top; she could recognize Pteromic Paralysis as easily as any person alive. A pitiful sound came out of her throat: part gasp, part choke, part sob. She wheeled away from the sight of Oh-God lying slack on the edge of death . . . and her eyes lit on me.

Twenty-three years since we'd seen each other. I'd changed a healthy lot more than she had, enough so I could see her wavering on the lip of doubt; then her gaze dropped to the scars on my arms, and that was that.

"Faye." Her voice was pure ice.

"Hello, Mother."

"Mother?" Festina blurted. Voostor twitched in surprise, but Tic broke into a pouchy grin. The daft old bugger was just the sort to love coincidences . . . which is to say, he probably didn't believe in them. When you're at 1.0001 with the universe, synchronicity follows you around like a spaniel.

"Why doesn't this surprise me?" Mother asked. "Voostor's first-ever emergency, and it's my daughter bringing in a case of plague. You're a curse, Faye. A walking evil."

"Then let's walk," I told her. "We can talk while your . . . husband . . . looks after his patient."

She stared at me a moment. A hard stare, as if it were nigh-on impossible for me to say anything she would ever want to hear. "All right," she said at last. "We'll have a homey little mother-daughter chat."

She motioned me toward the door. As I passed in front of her, she pulled back to make sure I didn't accidentally touch her.

We strolled out the back door, across another brazenly green lawn and into a shady grove of trees—tropical trees of a breed I didn't recognize, with big clumps of rubbery leaves prodding out close to the path. The leaves were all soaked with dew, like fat wet fingers that slapped against you as you walked. Since I was still carrying my parka, I held it out in front of me; let it get soaked instead of me.

The air was almost liquid with orchid perfume now . . . and suddenly I realized the grove was filled with flowers, tiny ones, as short and slender as bean sprouts. Some hung from branches just over my head, thin white stems curled to corkscrews; some hid behind tree roots beside the path, their blossoms small and red as blood drops. A few sat in special planters, sections of small trees with the pith scooped away and filled by soil, enough to support a single dainty bud of pale yellow, or mauve, or pure jewel blue. But most of the tiny orchids were planted the way they'd be found in open jungle: in whatever nook or cranny let them set down a foothold.

The effect was subtle—subtle enough to rip your breath away. Not flashy, but exquisite. The more you looked, the more you saw. Dozens, maybe hundreds, of miniscule blooms, quietly congregated and meticulously maintained.

"This is Voostor's pride and joy," Mother said—the first words she'd spoken since we left the others. "We have greenhouses farther back on the property, and fields where we grow crops; but this is where Voostor spends his time. Planting new species that he finds in the rain forest."

Her voice was carefully neutral. I couldn't tell what she thought of her new husband's hobby—whether she took pride, or thought it a daft waste of time. My mother was the sort of woman who could go either way; you never knew what she'd respect and what she'd disdain.

"I love this place," I said. "An honest-to-God masterpiece."

"Hmph." Not ready to let herself care about my opinion. "Why did you come here, Faye?"

"It's complicated," I told her. "Not mother-daughter complicated, if that's what you're worried about. I don't want to borrow money, and I'm not in trouble . . . well, not my usual sort of trouble anyway. Do you listen to the news?"

"No. We don't get it here." Her answer had a hard edge to it. When Dads became the hero of Demoth, Mother had shuddered under the media limelight. Reporters hounded her cruelly for quotes about the great Henry Smallwood, especially after his death. Her nerves were too chip-brittle for the barrage; one morning she just didn't get out of bed. The next two weeks I played nurse for her, almost like a dutiful daughter, even if I bitched and backbit for fear of getting too close . . . and even if Ma spent those two weeks accusing me of taking pictures of her while she slept and selling them to the news services.

In time, that bad spell passed; but it didn't surprise me she'd settled in a place like Mummichog, where news didn't happen and didn't get burbled in the street. It didn't surprise me either that she'd chosen a husband who cared more about the planting of miniature flowers than catching suppertime broadcasts. My mother would rather float undisturbed in a placid backwater than heed the ripples and streams of current events.

Or at least that's how she'd been when I was a teenager. Perhaps she'd become less fragile over the years, because she now turned to face me with a direct question. "Has the plague broken out again?" Mother asked.

"A new strain," I said. "It only attacks Freeps and may be resistant to olive oil."

"Really. Let's hope they discover another cure soon." She paused, then added, "Maybe that will make the world forget your father."

She waited to see how I'd react to that. Did she expect me to get upset? To defend his sacred memory? Once upon a time, I would have jumped at any chance to scream that I wished she'd died instead of him; but no more. That desperate old need to hurt her had burned out its rage long ago. "Lately," I said, all calm and mild, "I've been learning queer things about Dads. Events surrounding his death. And something the world-soul let him do that should have been impossible. Do you know anything about that?"

"Why should I know anything about anything?" She sounded more tired than angry. "And why should you show up on my doorstep, suddenly interested about your father after all these years? Have you joined a recovery program, Faye? Going down a checklist of psychological baggage . . . things you're supposed to clean up before you get a membership pin?"

"I'm a proctor now, Ma. With the Vigil. And believe it or not, I'm investigating something important."

"About the plague?"

"That seems to be part of it."

We'd reached a bower on the edge of the grove: a wooden bench under a dozen small plant baskets hanging from the trees. The orchids inside them were plain forgettable white, but they gave off a head-swimming smell, like fruit on the cusp of decay. Mother waved for me to sit on the bench. "You go ahead," I told her, but she didn't.

We stayed there, both standing, each waiting for the other to sit first.

"You're really with the Vigil?" she finally asked.

I nodded.

"Do they pay you?"

"Some," I said with a slight smile. "Nothing extravagant."

"Hmph." She laid her hand on the back of the bench, but made no move to sit. "I don't remember anything about your father."

"Come on," I said. "A complete blank?"

"You know what I mean. I don't remember anything special."

"Nothing that took you by surprise?" I asked.

"Well . . ." She turned her eyes away from me, back toward the house. I had the impression she was running through a dozen memories and censoring them all. "There's this place," she finally said.

"Which place?"

"Mummichog. The house, a good-sized tract of rain forest and cleared fields . . . I never knew he owned it until he died."

"Dads owned this estate here?"

"Surprising, isn't it?" Mother said. "But property was cheap after the plague. I've always thought he bought it as a present for me and was just waiting for my birthday to give me the news. Heaven knows, I would have been happy for a place to escape from Great St. Caspian winters."

"So he bought it after the plague? After he found the cure?"

"That's what the lawyer told me when she read the will. Does it matter?"

"Maybe." I couldn't believe it was empty coincidence my father bought property in Mummichog—one of Iranu's favorite spots to visit. Dads knew something about this place. "Is there anything special here, ma?"

"It's warm and quiet. Like heaven after Sallysweet River."

That could have been another shot at me—testing, to see if I'd get pissy. After Dads died, Mother was stuck in Sallysweet River because of me: because I refused to leave, and because the law wouldn't let her abandon me while I was underage. We spent a few years there, inventing ways to torment each other . . . me picking on a frail-nerved woman, her grinding away at a jagged-edge girl whose soul was bleeding. Perfect partners in desperation, both acting as if we could ease our own miseries by making the other feel worse.

I got out by getting married. Mother got out the very same day, just up and left the church the instant I said, "I do." In the years between Dads's death and her escape, Mother never once mentioned she had this place in Mummichog waiting as a getaway. Her secret inheritance. Five months after she left, a text-only message reached me (IN ARGENTIA, LIVING WITH AN OOLOM PHARMER, WON'T BE BACK) . . . and that was that.

If Mummichog was heaven, we'd both done our best to make Sallysweet River hell. A mother-daughter project, showing rare fine solidarity.

I glanced at her for a second, the way she looked so much like me in a mirror. She met my stare . . . maybe seeing the similarity too, I don't know. Or maybe seeing the old teenage Faye, who'd hurt her and hurt her and hurt her.

Best to stick to business.

"Is there anything special about the *land*, Ma?" I asked. "Something that might interest an archaeologist?"

"You're an archaeologist now, Faye?"

"I told you, I'm a proctor." Was she trying to catch me in a lie? Christ, I must have been a piss-awful liar in the old days, if I could be caught as easy as that. "I'm a proctor investigating the movements of an archaeologist, and he visited Mummichog now and then. A Freep named Kowkow Iranu."

"A Freep?" She frowned. "We've had Freep trespassers over the years, back in the rain forest part of our property. Voostor sees their tracks now and then; he's heard they own land on either side of ours and take shortcuts through our jungle."

Probably the Iranus, buying land close to ours. But I suspected that Dads beat them to the most important part of the site.

"Are there any old mines in that area?" I asked. "Like the mines near Sallysweet River?"

"You'll have to ask Voostor," she answered. "I haven't spent much time back there. Too many insects. Poisonous creepy-crawlies." She gave a theatrical shudder. "Shall we head back to the house?"

"Your choice."

We walked back through the grove. From time to time, I stopped to look at more wee orchids, growing out from the trunks of trees or dangling on long threads from somewhere up in the canopy. Each time I paused, Mother did too . . . watching me out of the corner of her eye, trying not to be caught doing it.

Sizing me up. Wondering who I was. Or perhaps just wondering when I'd go away.

At the edge of the grove I suddenly turned to her. "You drove me crazy," I said, "and I drove you crazy, but that was long ago. It's witless, both of us acting like ice."

She bit her lip. "You're sure you aren't on a recovery program, Faye?"

"When you join the Vigil, you stop being able to ignore the obvious. Like the way I acted the slut just to drive you frantic. That was flat-out childish. I'm sorry."

"Oh," she said. "You're sorry. That's all right then.

Or is this where I say I'm sorry too, and we have a big hug?"

"Watch it, Ma—if we start trying to hurt each other again, we might see how much we have in common. We'll end up bonding in spite of ourselves."

"Do you think so?" She glanced toward the house as if she was considering whether to run away inside. Flee, or stay and be brave a little while longer. Finally, she gave me a sideways glance that skipped past my eyes without meeting them. "You *are* looking good, Faye. For someone your size. I always said you could be a pretty girl if you'd just cut down the debauchery."

"You never said that in your life."

"True. But you're looking good. You're . . ."

Suddenly, she spun away and started across the lawn. Without turning around, she murmured, "He glowed."

"What?" I hurried along behind her. "Who glowed?"

"Your father. At night. In bed. After he discovered the cure." She was moving fast, not looking in my direction. "Now and then," she said, "he glowed with faint colored lights."

She ran up the back steps and into the house, refusing to say another word.

15

SIREN-LIZARDS

Oh-God was still alive, but only thanks to machines—while Mother and I were in the grove, his diaphragm had futzed out, slack as a sack of potatoes. But the heart-lung was ready and Oh-God barely lost a breath. He was packaged up now, inside a clear plastic shell that would protect him till the emergency team arrived from Pistolet. Once our smuggler friend was in their hands, he could be kept alive mechanically for as long as it took to find a cure.

If a cure existed. And if Pteromic B didn't flare so wildfire rampant that our medical system crashed in flames.

Demoth would be all right as long as the disease stayed Freeps-only. The world-soul told me we had 3,219 Freeps currently on planet—more than I expected, but our hospitals could manage the load. Barely. On the other hand, if Pteromic B hopped home to Ooloms, or even to *Homo saps* . . . hey, kids, the Circus is coming back to town.

Meanwhile, Oh-God was the most advanced case on Demoth. Other members of the Freep trade team tested positive for the microbe, but hadn't showed symptoms yet. They'd all been bunged into hospital, of course, but Oh-God was going to be the star attraction for medical researchers. Total slackdown. He'd have the best specialists in the world looking after him, searching for a way to fight the disease before the full outbreak struck. He'd be poked and prodded and proctoscoped, but at least they'd keep him alive.

As for Tic, Festina and me . . . did we have to call the feddies? Tell them what Oh-God said about Iranu and Mummichog? Report that the dipshits had attacked again, firing illegal bazookas and what-all? Damned right we did. Yes, we might have felt a twingey temptation to hot dog, to jaunt around solo like dashing VR adventurers; but the stakes were too high to indulge our vanity.

"I'll call it in," Tic said. He crossed his arms and leaned back against the wall of Voostor's medic room. His pouchy old face went distant: in communion with Mom-Xé.

"What's he doing?" Voostor asked.

"Talking to the world-soul," I replied. "Which will then talk to a slew of other people. Sorry, but you're going to have hordes of company coming."

Mother sighed. "Does this mean I have to clean?"

"Don't be silly," Voostor said. "We're always ready for guests. And if *this* guest is really my fearsome stepdaughter Faye . . ." He gave a smile intended to show he didn't believe half of what my mother must have told him. "The least we can do is offer you breakfast. All of you. Come on."

Festina frowned. "Someone should stay with Oh-God."

"I've dealt with the plague before," Mother said. "And I know how to work these machines. You get something to eat . . . before other people arrive and things get hectic."

Smooth way for Ma to avoid breakfast with her darling daughter. But I told myself it wasn't spite or anger—just embarrassment over her confession. ("He glowed.") She wanted some time to herself after sharing that little intimacy . . . not because she was mad at me but just feeling a titch shy.

Voostor took me by the arm (Oolom-style, hands delicately wrapped round my elbow to keep himself from bouncing too high) and led us through the parlor again, then under an archway of raspfeather fronds onto a covered patio with a view of the ocean. The sun was five fingers above the horizon now, shining onto a bamboo table with three places already set: one with Oolom fruit soup, two with *Homo sap* cheese fritters.

"You have company," Tic observed.

"One of our favorite guests," Voostor said. "A biologist who visits often to study the rain forest." He went to a grass-and-lath door leading off the far side of the patio and knocked lightly on the red-bamboo frame. "Breakfast time. How are you feeling this morning, Maya?"

Festina was closest to the door. Without a hair's hesitation, she drove her heel into one of the wood door slats, a full-strength side-kick that snapped the slat in two. The force of the kick didn't stop there; the door flew backward, slamming against the wall of the next room with an impact that shivered the grass-thatch roof. Shouting a kiai, Festina leapt through the doorway, fists in a tight guard position.

Tic went straight through after her. Ditto me, as soon as I'd snatched up a heavy clay porridge bowl for throwing.

All three of us came to a halt in the middle of a small bedroom. Spring mattress on the floor, sheets rumpled. Wide-open window, looking out on the orchid grove.

"Shit!" Festina growled. "Missed her."

"She must have seen Mother and me walking out back," I said. "Took to her heels as soon as we were out of sight."

"Would she recognize you?" Tic asked.

"My picture was on every broadcast when Chappalar died," I told him. "She must have thought we were coming for her."

"What's going on?" Mother demanded, storming in through the patio doorway. "What's all this noise?"

"Your visitor," Tic said. "Maya Cuttack, correct?"

"Yes. So?"

"You really *don't* listen to the news," I muttered. My mother stood on the far side of the patio, her face flushed: clearly thinking I'd gone bad-girl again, smashing the house to tinder. I told her, "Maya Cuttack is the most wanted woman on Demoth."

"She's a dear friend," Mother replied, fierce as frost. "What's she wanted for?"

"Questioning," Tic said. "Possibly murder."

Festina was at the window. "She climbed out this way; I can see her tracks in the dew. Heading inland."

"What is there in that direction?" Tic asked Voostor.

"Nothing. Our fields. The rain forest."

"I'll bet there are mines," I said. "Ma told me there've been Freeps poking around back there."

"There *is* a sort of alien mine in the jungle," Voostor admitted.

"Which explains why Maya's a frequent visitor," Festina said. "Her and Iranu."

"Do you think she has more androids here?" I asked.

"Maybe androids, maybe worse," Tic answered. "Why are we standing around when she's getting away?"

"You want to go after her ourselves?"

"We have to," Tic said. "The nearest police are at least half an hour off. If she's headed for the mine, she could activate robots, destroy evidence—"

"Maya?" my mother interrupted. "Impossible!"

"Time's wasting," Tic replied, bouncing up to the windowsill. "Voostor, show me the mine. Faye, you call Protection Central, then follow on foot."

Without waiting for an answer, he bent his knees and vaulted into the sky, spreading his gliders to catch whatever thermals might be rising in the tropical dawn. Voostor gave my mother a weak glance, helpless apology, then jumped out the window himself. As he flapped into the sky, that "Sorry, my dear," look on his face switched fast to a grin, caught up in Tic's excitement.

"Well," Mother said, "what a charming guest you've been, Faye. Perhaps you'd enjoy setting fire to the house before you start hunting down my friend like a dog."

"You've got it all wrong, Ma." I speed-linked to Protection Central: *Maya's here. Send cops.* Back in a beat came the ETA—Pistolet police would take at least thirty-seven minutes to reach Mummichog.

By that time I knew it would all be over, one way or another.

I squinched up my thoughts, fierce concentration. *Peacock, can you reach out to help the police get here faster?*
No response.

"Come on," Festina shouted. "We have to go!"

"One more second." *Peacock*, I thought again, *Xé, Father, whoever you are, can you get us to the mine before Maya?*

A swirl of light appeared outside the window. Festina leapt into it without asking questions.

"What is that?" my mother cried.

"Dads," I said. "Or whatever you were sleeping with the last few months of his life." I leaned in to give her a quick kiss on the cheek; I thought she might flinch, but she didn't. Maybe too shocked to react. "When this is all over," I told her, "I'll call and explain."

Then I sprinted forward, bounced off Maya's mattress, and sailed out through the window like a diver from a springboard. The Peacock caught me in its mouth long before I touched the ground.

The Peacock dumped me on a game trail deep in the rain forest. As usual, the tube disappeared instantly, back . . . back . . . well, I'd shot the chute often enough by now that I wasn't quite so queer-head dizzy as I'd been the first

time I'd gone through. I had the presence of mind to look
around fast, hoping I might catch sight of where the Peacock went. For just a second, I thought it was coming
toward *me*: straight at my face, tangly-jambly lights
plunging right at my eyes; but then the Peacock was gone,
vanished, and I felt no different than I ever had.

I got to my feet. Dusted myself off. Thought about that
phrase, "no different than I ever had" and wondered just
how long the Peacock had been guarding my *botjolo* butt.

In the bad old days, sometimes I'd been Christly lucky
to miss getting killed. And considering my habitually un-
sober state, would I have noticed a few more flickery
lights?

Hmm.

Festina stood a few steps away, staring up at the trees
with a gloomy expression.

"What's wrong?" I asked.

"This place looks too much like my home."

"That's bad?"

"My home was a damned dangerous place." She
glanced at me. "Do you know anything about jungles?"

"No."

"Never mind—you'll be all right if you remember one
simple principle."

"Which is?"

"Everything here wants you dead."

It sounded like a joke.

"I mean it," Festina insisted. "Everything wants you
dead. Even the things that won't directly kill you still
want you dead. You're a waste of good nutrients; they
want you recycled back into the ecosystem."

She reached to her belt holster and drew her stun-pistol
. . . the first time I'd seen her do that in days. She hadn't
bothered with her gun in the face of androids, reporters,
or dipshits, but now she wanted a weapon handy.

Okay. Chalk me up as intimidated.

"Keep to the trail," she said. "Don't touch anything,

don't step on anything, don't brush against anything. Understand?''

"Yes. Everything here wants me dead."

Which was too bad. To someone who'd grown up with Great St. Caspian's half-throttled flora and fauna, the rain forest was a heady gush of abundance. Take the insect life, for instance. In Bonaventure, bloodflies were puny things, traveling in fast-moving swarms that dodged and weaved like drunken dockworkers. Here in Mummichog, I was buzzed by a single fly near as big as my thumb—no need for safety in numbers, this guy could take care of himself. Slow and bullish, able to withstand a head-on swat: the supertanker of bloodflies, with a monstrous hemoglobin-carrying capacity. Thank God this beastie had one thing in common with his baby brothers up north; evolution had only taught him to suck on native Demoth lifeforms, not humans. Perhaps he gave me a sniff as he flew by . . . but I didn't smell like his natural prey, so he continued bumbling past.

One insect down, billions to go.

Ants the size of a baby's foot . . . moths bigger than my hand . . . beetles so huge you could use their carapaces as bread plates . . . not that these were genuine terrestrial insects, of course. Eight legs, no antennae, oddly hinged mandibles; but the names humans hung on most Demoth wildlife were Earth names because those were the names we had. These creatures scuttled like beetles; they had chitinous shells like beetles; they filled the same ecological niches as beetles; they might as well be called beetles, even if they were giant alien groundthumpers.

"Stop gawking," Festina ordered. "We have to find Cuttack."

"I asked the Peacock to take us to the mine," I told her. "It must be close by."

"Says you," she muttered. "Your pet Peacock might have dumped us a thousand klicks from Mummichog because the place was too damned dangerous."

"You're just jealous *you* don't have an invisible friend."

I looked at the ground again; the dirt held a string of clear bootprints, made when the soil was muddy and preserved when everything dried. The tracks couldn't be Voostor's—too deep for a lightweight Oolom. If my mother never came back here, this had to be Maya's trail. I asked, "Is this the sort of jungle where it rains every afternoon?"

"How should I know?" Festina said. "This is *your* planet."

"Yes, but you're the jungle queen."

She stuck out her tongue at me. I didn't know admirals did that.

"Let's go this way," I said, pointing back up the trail: the direction the boots had come from. If rain fell here every afternoon, the tracks must have been made late yesterday—Maya heading back to the house after knocking off work. Follow them backward and we'd find where Maya spent her day.

The bootprints kept to the game trail for a few dozen paces, then veered off on a narrower track. Still easy to follow—Maya hadn't tried to disguise her path. We wove our way over dirt leached light as sand, while bloodflies buzzed round our ears and wondered if they should bite us just for jollies. Past creeping vines and epiphytes floating on balloon sacs . . . crimson-strip fungi laid out like bacon on dead tree trunks . . . even a snake-belly or two . . . till we nearly walked past an overgrown hole in the forest floor.

If not for the bootprints, we would have missed the mine. Part of the entrance had been cleared with a machete, then covered again with prickly-leaved branches from nearby shrubs. Festina was still wearing her good-for-the-tundra gloves ("And I'll wear them till we get someplace that *I* call warm!") so she had no trouble pulling branches away from the hole, never mind the bristles and pricks.

Leaving a tunnel that led downward.

Just inside the tunnel sat a plastic box holding five torch-wands.

"Convenient," Festina said, picking one up.

"Easier to stash a box here," I replied, "than bringing them up from the house all the time. Besides, Maya was pretending to be a biologist. Mother or Voostor might have wondered why she needed torch-wands to poke about beamy bright jungle."

"Mmm." Festina looked into the hole. "Down now? Or wait for Maya and ambush her?"

I looked at the hole myself, then shook my head. "It'd be nice to know what's in there, but Maya's more important. Stop her before she does something we'll regret."

"Agreed." Festina checked the batteries on her pistol.

"Before you start shooting," I said, "remember she still might be innocent. Maya could have had her little dance with Chappalar, then headed down here the same night. Sounds like no one in Mummichog listens to the news, so she never heard tell of the murders. Doesn't know her sweetie's dead, doesn't know the cops want to question her. . . ."

Festina just looked at me.

"Right," I said. "Stun the bitch's tits off and apologize later."

We made the ambush simple: Festina down the tunnel, waiting with pistol in hand. I borrowed her gloves and covered back the hole with branches, so Maya wouldn't know she'd had visitors. Then I moved off a ways, hunkering down behind a fallen log till our target arrived.

(Not touching the log. I'd heard about insects who made nests in such places, and got swarming mad if you gave their homes a knock.)

So we waited. For Maya to scuttle down the path, racing toward the mine and whatever she'd stashed below. Festina would stun her the second Maya started clearing branches from the hole, and that would be that. In due time, flocks of people would arrive from Pistolet: the med team for Oh-God, police for Maya, plus a rabble-pack of robot experts, archaeologists, forensics specialists and who-all else might get sent to investigate Maya's home away from home.

With luck, they'd let Tic and me look over their shoulders for a while . . . till more senior proctors arrived to shove us aside again.

In the distance, I heard shouting. Tic and Voostor yelling. At Maya? Why? If they'd caught up with her after she bolted from the house, they wouldn't holler; Tic would sweep silently out of the sky and deck her with a sock to the jaw. I'd never seen him fight, but he *was* a master proctor. Zenned-out too. That put him in the same league as those little old gents in fic-chips, the kind who look beatific as soap till they whonk you with a heelkick to the head. If Tic could reach Maya, he could take her down.

So why all the whooping and bellowing?

Suddenly, Tic's voice got joined by shrill animal howling: a noise I recognized from VR sims of jungle life. The danger call of siren-lizards. They were only the size of squirrels, teeny pseudo-reptiles who clambered through the canopy eating fruit and seedpods . . . but they had eyes keen as hawks', and a resonating collar around their throats that made their shrieks trumpet-loud. Naturalists called them ''the Klaxons of the rain forest''—little noise-boxes that screamed blue murder if something scared them.

They were scared now: dozens of them, high and off to my right. Then another troop of lizards took up the cry, this one a fair bit closer. Were they just echoing the shrieks of the first bunch—an instinct to squeal when they heard other sirens howling? Or had they actually seen something, something coming my way?

More sirens took up the wail. Closer. I couldn't hear anything else over the racket. What was up there? What?

Something they could see from the treetops. Something flying. A skimmer?

Christ, of *course* Maya had a skimmer. We'd known from the start she didn't leave Bonaventure by transport sleeve. She had her own vehicle, and now she was bugging out in it.

World-soul, I thought, *track it, track it!* But even before I finished the mental shout, my mind filled with the world-soul's response: ground radar couldn't get a fix.

Lord weeping Jesus, did everyone on this planet have stealth equipment?

Something ripped through the canopy of leaves straight overhead. I had a quick glimpse of a skimmer's underbelly, its bay doors open; then something big and black and blimp-shaped started to fall, crashing down through the trees.

"You're kidding," I said in disbelief. A bomb? She had a bomb in the skimmer? And she was dropping it on me. No, not me, she didn't know I was here; she was bombing the mine entrance, to close it off, seal it up.

Which would still blow me to smithereens.

"Festina!" I shouted. "Incoming bomb! Head down the mine, deep as you can go."

The blimp-shaped cylinder continued to fall—jerkily, slowly, catching on tree limbs, stopping for a moment before its weight broke the branch or it rolled off sideways, then falling a few more meters till it hit the next snag.

How much bouncing could it stand before it blew up?

I tore my gaze from the blundering bomb, and of course the Peacock was rippling in front of me, tail snaking far out of the jungle. "No," I snapped. "Down the mine! I want to go down the mine."

Festina was there. If I went in too, the Peacock and I could save her. If I let the Peacock chute me out of the forest, it might not volunteer to bring me back.

Festina would be trapped in the dark. Like my father.

I could feel reluctance spilling from the Peacock like a

physical force; but its tail flicked, swept, and jammed itself through the shrubbery covering the tunnel entrance. Before it changed its mind, I threw myself into its mouth.

Vomited into blackness. I scraped my arm as I landed on the unseen stone floor, but it only did minor damage—this tunnel had a thicker carpet of dirt, fungus and animal crap than the one in Great St. Caspian. The jungle had more wildlife than the tundra . . . more dung and droppings for me to splash into.

Joy.

Then light flamed viciously far to my right, followed by a distant roar and rumble. That would be the bomb, blowing the bejeezus out of the mine entrance. Collapsing who knows how much dirt and stone to close the tunnel. Probably setting fire to the forest too, giving the siren-lizards something to *really* howl about.

The ground beneath me shook for ten seconds, trembling as more and more debris fell into the tunnel mouth. Not just dirt but trees toppled by the blast. I could imagine their leaves burning, while birds squawked and lizards shrieked and insects tore away from the flames . . .

But I couldn't hear any of it. Not with a massive plug of jungle floor sealing off the mine. I couldn't even hear the shaking; I could only feel it through the stone under my body.

After a few seconds, the quaking stopped. Then a heavy silence set in, as if I'd gone deaf. No—I could hear my own breathing. But no one else's.

"Festina?" I called. She must have had time enough to run for safety. To bolt down the tunnel, out of the blast radius, beyond the cave-in.

Unless she hadn't heard my warning. Or she tried to run the other way, out into the open rather than be trapped underground.

Out into the explosion.

"Festina-girl!" I called again. "Are you there?"

A torch-wand sprang on in the darkness. "Okay," Festina growled, her uniform smeared with dirt, "when I said the jungle was dangerous, I meant snakes. I meant jaguars. I meant army ants, and piranha, and bushes with sharp spiky thorns. I did not mean goddamned motherfucking high-explosive bombs."

Pause.

"Are you all right?" I asked.

"Yeah sure." She brushed mud off her shirtsleeve. "I'm an Explorer. I've lived through *real* explosions."

I could have called the Peacock to get us out. If it had managed to thread its way through the Rustico mine cave-in, it could do the same here. But I wasn't leaving yet. Not till I saw what Maya had found down here . . . something she wanted to keep secret so badly, she had a bomb ready in case she needed to obliterate it.

World-soul, I thought, *are you receiving?*

Immediate acknowledgment.

Good. I was worried we were too far underground for link-seed radio transmission. *Tell Master Tic that Festina and I are safe. Pass it on to my family too. We can get out of this tunnel anytime, but first we're going to see what's down here.*

Acknowledgment. And underneath the bland mechanical okey-dokey, a twitch of something else. Something with a squirt of adrenaline. Fear? Or was it excitement?

Festina had been watching me. "So?" she asked.

"So we're here," I said. "And if we tube out now, it may take a long time for anyone else to dig down here. I think we should see what Maya wanted to hide."

"There might be androids," Festina muttered.

"We'll tell them we're allergic, same as last time."

"That trick only works if we see the robots first."

"Come on," I said. "Aren't you curious what's down here?"

"Of course I am," she snapped, "and damn it, I shouldn't be. Explorers are supposed to purge out every grain of curiosity they find lurking in their souls."

"So what? You aren't an Explorer anymore."

Her eyes squinched down with anger. "Faye . . . till the day I die, I will always be an Explorer."

"No. That part's over now. You're someone else." She started to interrupt, but I plowed on. "No. No. You've got to stop telling yourself you're that old person, because you aren't anymore. You don't have to dig that hole deeper; you can just walk away."

She glared at me for another few seconds with those blazing green eyes; then she dropped her gaze to the dirty floor. "I could say the same to you," she murmured.

"You wouldn't be the first," I told her. "Blessed near everyone in my family rags on me about it. High time I got to rag on someone myself." I reached out, took her by the shoulders, stared her straight in the eye. "Festina Ramos: you aren't an Explorer anymore. That's behind you. It's still part of you, of course it is, but you've got other parts now. Here-and-now parts. And telling yourself, *I'm still a disposable nothing*, is a witless way of behaving, especially when you have important things to do. Live in the real, dear one. Got it?"

The edges of her mouth twitched up. "Does talk like this really work on you?"

"Depends what you mean 'work.' "

When my fine sweet Lynn took me by the shoulders, looked me in the eye and gave me a pep talk, calling me "dear one" and what-all, I sometimes got worked up right enough . . . though not with lofty thoughts about my personal potential. More like longing thoughts, wishing there was some way past all my years of playing the self-sufficient loner.

Same thing here. Eye to eye with Festina, just the two of us in the quiet black of the tunnel. Jungle-warm. Jungle-moist.

She eased herself away from me, holding eye contact a second more before she let her gaze slip shy to the floor. "Okay," she said, "it probably won't hurt to look around a bit. If we're careful. Better than just standing here in the dark.''

I looked at her a heartbeat longer, then turned away. Two seconds later, I felt her hand warm on my bare arm. ''Faye . . .''

I turned back, my heart flying. But whatever she'd been going to say, ex-Explorer Lieutenant Admiral Ramos suddenly lost her nerve. Instead she just mumbled, ''You carry the torch-wand,'' and pushed it toward me.

Passing the torch, for God's sake. Handing me the decision.

What futtering cowards, the pair of us. I knew I should just swoop her up in my arms, then and there. Both of us waited to see if I'd do it.

''Christ,'' I finally said, ''we have work to do.''

I shoved the torch-wand roughly back into her hands.

''Right,'' she said. Finally letting go of the breath she'd been holding. ''Right. We'd better get moving.'' She gave me a side glance. ''Keep ourselves busy.'' She looked away again. ''See what there is to find.''

For another second, she just stared at the torch in her hands. Then she lifted it high and started leading the way down.

A hundred meters on, we came to the first rockfall. Part of the ceiling had given way, dumping a load of stone and soil. The wreckage had been shoved off to the sides of the tunnel, leaving a clear trail down the middle.

I stopped long enough to nudge a chunk of debris with my foot. Any girl brought up in Sallysweet River develops a canny feel for stone. Fleck by fleck, this *looked* like granite . . . but overall its texture was too regular, with none of the wrinkles you find in honest-to-igneous rock. My gut said it was artificial—poured like concrete, then flash-hardened.

Strange, when you thought about it. If this was a mine, why line the walls with synthetic rock? Shouldn't mines have rock of their own? Then again, the bedrock here

must lie a lot deeper than in the Great St. Caspian shield
... so this part of the tunnel might need to be shored up
with extra support till it got down into solid stone.

Could be. But it sounded a lot like rationalization.

There were more rockfalls as we went along, some several meters long, some only a litter of stones. Each time,
a path had been cleared so we could pass through prance-
easy: the work of Maya and Iranu, or more likely, their
robots. Here and there, they'd propped support poles from
floor to ceiling to shore up parts of the roof: places where
the pseudo-granite showed thready black cracks of strain.

I'd never seen any such cracking in the abandoned
mines around Sallysweet River. Then again, Great St.
Caspian had bugger-all in the way of earthquakes. I didn't
know much about Mummichog specifically, but the whole
Argentia continent had a reputation for being seismically
active, so no surprise this particular mine suffered the occasional crumble.

At length we came to an area where the slant of the
tunnel flattened to a wide room, much like the one up
north where we found Kowkow Iranu. Rusty lumps sat
scattered about the floor like dog turds—just left lying,
though you'd think archaeologists would scrape up the
stuff as valuable artifacts. At the very least, Maya should
have chalked measurement lines on the floor. But no.
Nary a sign she'd paid attention to this junk at all.

"Look there," Festina said in a low voice, pointing the
torch-wand toward the far end of the room.

Another tunnel collapse—this one taking out part of the
wall. Beyond was another room, dark, too far for the
torch-light to reach. I couldn't help noticing there was no
visible door between that room and ours. If the wall
hadn't fallen in, there'd be no way through.

Queer thing, that.

Festina walked toward the wall-breach. Debris had been
cleared here too, leaving a gap you could walk through.
Festina pulled up in front of it. "Stop," she yelled into
the next room, "you're making me allergic."

"You saw something?" I asked.

"No. But why take dumb chances?"

She poked the end of the torch-wand through the breach. A trio of androids stood on the other side, jelly guns raised.

Like lightning, Festina dropped the wand, dived sideways, jigged the moment she hit the floor, and rolled to her feet, weaving like a kickboxer in full defense mode: guard up, chin down, body loose. My own reaction wasn't half so dramatic—I just jumped to the side, out of the line of fire from the hole.

Waiting. The torch-wand rolled along the ground, shadows shifting in response . . . till the wand ran up against a chunk of stone, rocked back, lay still.

Nothing from the robots.

Slowly I let out my breath. "Good call with that 'allergic' thing," I told Festina.

She let her fists relax. "Yeah," she agreed, lifting her hand to her cheek. "A faceful of acid would ruin my complexion."

"Don't obsess—there's nothing wrong with your cheek that couldn't be solved with a nice hard kiss." It felt good to say that out loud. I bent and picked up the light. "Now let's see what's next door."

The androids had shut down, just like the ones near Sallysweet River: standing there stock-still, frozen in the blink before firing. We slithered past them, avoiding the tiniest touch for fear they'd wake again.

Beyond the robots? More robots . . . only these weren't humanlike. Their bodies were fat ellipsoids, the shape and color of watermelons but almost as tall as me. They had no separate head, but the top of their watermelon torso was ringed with pits and niches that I guessed were for sensing—eyes going all the way round, 360 degrees, plus holes that might be ears or nostrils or breathing orifices. They had thinnish legs, bony and tough like an ostrich's. As for arms: three pairs each, spindly, insectish, covered with coarse hairs that might have been sensors or bristly protection.

How did I know they were robots? There were four of the beasties within reach of the light, and all had patches where the epidermis was peeled away—flayed sections of arm, flaps cut into the torso, an entire leg where the skin had tattered. Beneath the exterior were metal flexors, armatures, ball bearings, fiber optics . . . eerily similar to what I'd seen in Pump Station 3, when jelly acid bared the androids' innards.

I took a step toward the closest watermelon. Festina grabbed my arm full strength and yanked me back. "Don't touch. Their natural skin chemicals are poisonous to humans. Nerve toxins."

"You know the species?"

She nodded. "They're Greenstriders."

"Never heard of them," I said.

"The fleet made contact with their people a couple times. Not a friendly species—arrogant landgrabbers, dangerously greedy. Worse than humans, believe it or not. A few years back, the League of Peoples rescinded their certification of sentience: grounded every Greenstrider space vessel till they learn to play nicely with others."

"So what are these doing here?" I asked.

"They must have arrived before the League clamped down. At one time, the Greenstriders set up colonies all over this arm of the galaxy; but their settlements had a habit of fizzling out . . . which is a polite way to say they degenerated into civil war. Striders have a rabid territorial streak that they seldom bother to control."

"Are they a robot species?"

Festina shook her head. "They're organic. These must be the Greenstrider equivalent of androids—robots built in their own image. How old did you say these mines are?"

"Three thousand Earth years."

"Then they could have been dug by Greenstriders. The

striders were definitely active in this neighborhood back then.''

"How sophisticated were they technically?'' I asked. "Compared to us.''

"Who knows?'' Festina replied. "The striders don't share confidences. We have no idea how advanced they are now, let alone three millennia ago. But they were a spacefaring race even back then, so they may have had some interesting goodies.''

"And that's what Maya and Iranu were looking for.''

"Probably.''

So: hypothesize a sequence of events. Yasbad Iranu, Kowkow's father, discovered this place thirtyish years ago, back before the plague. His first thought—scour the mine for alien tech . . . and do it on the hush so our government didn't interfere with the game. Unfortunately for him, Iranu senior wasn't careful enough, and the feddies caught him smuggling. Away he went, first to jail, then booted off planet as *persona non grata*. He never found a way to sneak back.

Forward two decades: Iranu junior gets friendly with Maya Cuttack on some archaeological dig in the Free Republic. Kowkow shares the secret of his father's discovery. He and Maya head for Demoth to resume dear old dad's work . . . not just here in Mummichog but at Sallysweet River and other sites round the planet. When the Freeps begin trade talks with Demoth, Iranu wangles a place as aide to the negotiating team, probably by milking his family connections. Next thing you know, the treaty contains a clause that opens Demoth archaeological sites to Freep exploitation.

Slick. I wondered if our feddies had ever suspected Iranu junior of following in his father's footsteps. Probably . . . but junior was tied so close to the Freep government he'd have diplomatic immunity. Anyway, Maya must have done most of the fieldwork; Iranu just dropped by now and then to see how she was doing.

And how *was* she doing? With all their undercover dig-

ging, had Iranu and Cuttack turned up anything useful?
Or were they just flouncing around in the dirt, without
finding bugger-all?

Gingerly I stepped past the Greenstrider robots and
lifted the torch-wand to light the rest of the room. It
showed more robot watermelons on ostrich legs, and assorted machine boxes—computers maybe, or communication transceivers, food synthesizers, air conditioners.
How can you ever tell? One box of wires looks much like
another . . . and these had been rusting in a hot humid cli-
mate for three thousand years.

No, not that long—this room had been sealed hermet-
ically for a long time, till an earthquake opened that
breach in the wall. It explained why I recognized this stuff
as machinery, unlike the moldering lumps in the outer
room. It'd taken longer for microbes and humidity to get
in. Even so, every exposed surface here was covered with
corrosion; I doubted anything was still in working order.

Festina had her Bumbler out, running its scanner up
and down a Greenstrider robot. "Interesting," she murmured.

"What?"

"See here?" She pointed to a flap of green skin folded
back from the creature's chest to reveal metal beneath.
"The edges are clean," she said, "and the metal has practically no rust."

I held the torch-wand close so I could see for myself.
She was right—the skin had been sliced away with a
knife. Underneath, the robot's innards had a passable
gleam. "Probably the work of our bold archaeologists,"
I said, "cutting a hole to peek inside."

"But here . . ." Festina squatted and aimed her finger
at the point where the robot's left leg joined its torso.
"This damage is much more ragged. And the metal's been
exposed to air a lot longer."

I crouched and looked. The scaly ostrich skin had been
eaten away, eroded to shreds; and the armatures beneath
were speckly brown with rust. "Sure," I agreed, "this

damage is older. But what does that mean? The natural decay process had to start somewhere. This is just where the skin flaked off first."

"It doesn't look like natural decay to me." Festina fiddled with the Bumbler controls; the image on the machine's vidscreen ballooned through several powers of magnification. "See around the edges there? A rim of white plastic. There used to be a plastic sheath just under the skin, like a protective wrap around the metal flexors. Something chewed away most of the plastic, and bared what was underneath."

"Acid?" I asked.

She shook her head. "Then I'd expect to see melting, and there's nothing like that. This looks more . . . eaten."

"Demoth has bacteria that can break down some types of plastic," I told her.

"But there's still some plastic left," she replied, moving the Bumbler's scanner up and down the robot's leg. "Once a bacterial colony begins consuming a particular substance, why would they stop? No. To me, this looks like an entrance hole. Something ate through the skin, then consumed just enough of the plastic sheath to get into the robot's guts."

"I assume you don't mean pesky jungle insects?"

"Most likely a coordinated nano attack, specifically designed to disable this type of robot."

She grabbed the Bumbler's scanner and gave a yank. The scanner pulled out of the Bumbler's body, trailing behind a fiber-steel umbilical cord . . . like a thumb-sized glass eye on a flexible tether. Festina jammed the eye through the break in the robot's skin. "Yes," she said, "the circuits are a real mess in there. Diced. Wire salad."

"So nanites bit their way in, then chewed up the robot's guts? Why?"

"It was a weapon, Faye." She pulled the scanner out of the robot and stood up. "Like I said, Greenstrider colonies had a habit of disintegrating into civil war. Faction against faction. They'd start off targeting each other's ma-

chinery, just like this—the League of Peoples doesn't
mind if you corrode the guts out of mindless robots. But
how long before tactics accelerated into something ug-
lier?''

I looked around the room: the unmoving robots, the
rusting machines. Shut down by enemy nano? And what
happened when the nanites destroyed other equipment . . .
food synthesizers, say. Could Greenstriders eat our local
flora and fauna? Or did the war against each other's machinery send the colonists spiraling down to slow star-
vation?

Next question: how far would starving people go for
revenge on their enemies? Bombs? Poison gas?

Germ warfare?

Maybe.

And when the war heated up, some Greenstriders would
hide from their enemies. Huddle down in places like this,
where they'd hope they were safe from nanites, armies,
whatever their opponents might throw at them. Underground complexes in Mummichog, in Sallysweet River,
all over Demoth.

We'd thought these were ancient mines; and some
probably started out that way. But in the end . . . they'd
become military bunkers.

16

PINNED BUTTERFLY

The other Greenstrider robots had the same kind of damage: entry wounds where the legs met the torso, minced machinery inside. I guess the point of attack got chosen because it was especially vulnerable . . . or maybe just handy and close to important control circuits. No way to tell now—the robots had all been gutted too badly to reconstruct how they used to work.

And speaking of reconstruction . . . where did that leave Maya and Iranu? These robots looked too wrecked to be salvageable. What here could gladden the heart of a greedy archaeologist?

I moved around the room, giving each machine the once-over. A few rusty boxes had got opened and partly dismantled, half-rotted circuit boards laid out on the floor: Maya and Iranu must have been seeing what they could find. They'd done the most work on something that looked like a control console—a flat surface with bumps and lumps that might have been eroded push buttons, plus dirty plates of clear plastic that were probably screen readouts. Maya and Iranu had pried off two access panels under the console and gone fishing inside; you could see gaps where they'd removed bits and pieces for examination. But everything I saw looked too rust-eaten to be functional. If the archaeologists learned much from what they found, they must be rare good at their jobs.

Two times circling the room with the torch in my hand . . . and only then did it click back into my head that there were no doors anywhere. We'd clambered in through that spot where the wall crumbled; but that definitely wasn't a real entranceway. As far as I could tell, the room had been totally sealed up with four mock-granite walls . . . and that didn't make sense, did it?

"Festina-girl," I called, "time to give the Bumbler another workout. These walls look too good to be true."

They were. The Bumbler found two patches of wall whose temperature ran a titch warmer than their surroundings: both patches almost straight-edged rectangular, three meters wide, stretching from floor to ceiling. One patch was plunk in the middle of the wall between this room and the outside tunnel; the other was at the rear of the chamber.

"All right," Festina said. "So two sections of wall aren't the same as the rest. Yes, they're probably doors. But how do we get them open? Maybe once upon a time they unlocked at the flick of a switch . . . but every switch in the place is rusted clean through."

"O ye of little faith," I told her. "When you've got the right friends, who needs switches?"

My thoughts: the Greenstriders used nano weapons. So they probably used nano for other things too—like doors. The doorways could be like the windows in my office: made to look solid, but the nanites would let you pass if you had proper authorization.

What better kind of door for an army bunker?

And if Xé was my friend . . . if Xé had somehow wormed its way into Greenstrider nanotech, as easy as winning over the navy's "incompatible" probe missiles . . . if the nanite doors weren't totally dead after all these years . . . Xé might help me pass through.

"Let's try a little experiment," I said.

I took a step toward the rear door.

And suddenly the Peacock was blocking my way, burning brighter than I'd ever seen, flames of gold and blue and green.

Nago! screamed my father's voice in my head. Oolom for "evil." *Tico, nago, wuto!* Crazy, evil, dangerous.

The Peacock fluttered in the air, shivering. Shivering with emotion. And the emotion was fear.

"What's wrong?" I demanded. "What's so bad?"

Tico. Tico, nago, wuto.

"That's not an answer."

"Are you having a conversation with a pocket universe?" Festina asked.

"Yes. But it's precious skimpy on explanations." I turned back to the Peacock. "Tell me what's behind the door."

Tico. Tico botjolo.

Crazy. Crazy cursed.

"Fine. I get the message." I glanced toward Festina. "The Peacock is all worked up over whatever's in the next room. Says it's crazy, evil, dangerous." I sighed. "Maybe the smart thing is to back away and call the cops. . . ."

Boom.

Silent, inside my head, but boom. I was hit with a jolt of shuddery weeping frustration: a jab from the inside out, some high-proof hormonal punch that was pressure-pumped into every muscle of my body. I screamed—not pain, not anger, just screaming because I had to scream, deluged-drenched-drowning in teary-eyed floods of emotion. My head was clear enough to think, "What the bejeezus is this?" But still I screamed.

Festina grabbed me. Locked me into a grip that was two-thirds hug, one-third grappling hold. "What's wrong, Faye? What is it?"

I didn't fight her. I just started to cry. Wrapped my arms

tight around her and sobbed. Not understanding it, scarce even feeling it, as the clear part of my brain kept thinking, "This isn't me, this is something else. Something else is crying *through* me. What's doing it?"

The answer came, not words, just realization.

Xé. Xé, Xé, Xé.

Weeping as if her heart would break.

Here's the thing: I'd been assuming the Peacock was Xé. An alien whatsit hooked into our world-soul AI. Tied in with my father and me and Tic and God knows what else.

But. (Hard to think when you're bawling your eyes out and wiping your nose on an admiral's shoulder.) The Peacock spoke to me in simple Oolom words, sounding in my head with my father's voice. Xé hardly ever spoke in words at all: just emotions, realizations, facts showing up in my brain.

Xé sent thoughts through my link-seed. The Peacock spoke words—telepathically, if you wanted to call it that.

Two different beings. Entities. And what was behind the hidden door?

Xé. Xé, Xé, Xé.

The Peacock didn't want me going through the door. Crazy, evil, dangerous.

But Xé spilled me wet with tears of frustration the moment I considered walking away. Sad, desperate tears.

"Stop it," I blubbered into Festina's shoulder. "Let me think. Let me think."

"Shh," she said. We must have looked clown-stupid, me so much taller, crumpled against her. "Shhh. Shhh." She stroked my hair, not looking at me. Her cheek was against my head. "Shhh. Shhh."

Slowly, the gush of heartbreak eased away. Quiet. A drained-weary calm. Mine? Xé's? Or just the afterwash from the hormones Xé sent swelling through me?

Peace is when the adrenaline goes away.

"That wasn't me," I murmured to Festina, still holding her tight. "My body got hijacked by someone else."

She kept stroking my hair. "Shhh. Shhh."

I'd dropped the torch-wand. Now the only light I could see came from the Peacock, looping quick circles around Festina and me like an anxious dog. Dizzying, dappled ripples of color.

"Shhh. Shhh. Shhh."

At last I pulled away . . . one hormone cocktail played out, another too precious eager to surface. Festina let me go, not meeting my eyes.

The Peacock had drawn in tight around us, an Ouro-boros ring only a handbreadth from touching our backs. Now it loosened, opening a gap that would let us scuttle back up the tunnel . . . but still blocking the way forward like a glittery wall of light.

"Do you want to tell me what's going on?" Festina asked. She was still very close.

"Xé," I said. "She . . . it . . . is a consciousness laced through all the digital intelligences on Demoth. Including my link-seed. When I suggested maybe we shouldn't keep going forward, Xé hit me with that colossal crying jag. Or maybe Xé herself had the crying jag, and I just got caught in the backwash."

"So," Festina muttered, "this Xé desperately wants us to press on. And the Peacock doesn't. Dandy." She looked down at the Bumbler, clipped to her belt. "I suppose we could take a discreet peek from a distance . . ."

Carefully she drew back from the Peacock, slipping out through the gap it'd left for us. With the slow steps of someone who doesn't want to rile a hair-temper dog, she walked around the edge of the ribbon-tube of light. The Peacock fluttered jumpitty-jittery, but didn't stop her. As long as *I* stayed safe, the Peacock wouldn't prevent others from sticking their heads in the noose.

Xé, I thought as Festina approached the hidden door, *she's a friend. Don't be tico, nago, wuto.*

No response.

Festina lifted the Bumbler and pulled out the scanner

on its umbilical again. She took time for a glance back at me; I nodded. Then she planted the head of the scanner against the wall and gave a light push.

It went in. Straight into a wall that looked like solid granite. The nanites of the stone slipped out of the way, yielding enough to let the scanner pass through—centimeter by centimeter, like pushing a wooden stake into soft mud. Half a meter in, Festina said, "Okay. We're through."

"See anything?" I asked.

She looked at the Bumbler's vidscreen. "A short corridor and another room beyond. They're both lit up, though I don't see the light source. Oh, here's something interesting." She turned a dial for better magnification. "My, my, my."

"What?"

"It's an anchor. A Sperm-tail anchor. A machine that generates fields for holding Sperm-tails in place."

The dipshits had mentioned something about anchors—they were amazed the Peacock could stay stable without one. "These anchors lock down Sperm-tails?" I asked.

"Right. Whenever Explorers ride Sperm-tails on planet-down missions, we send an anchor out first to hold the tail in place."

"No wonder the Peacock is jumpy," I said. "A machine that can chain him down? That's enough to give anyone the trembles."

"On the other hand," Festina replied, "you have to wonder what an anchor is doing down here." She fiddled with another dial on the Bumbler. "Let's get more magnification and we'll . . . holy shit!"

"What?"

She didn't answer; she just stared at the Bumbler screen, her body blocking the view. "What is it?" I kept asking. "Festina? What?"

Twenty seconds later she stepped back from the wall. With a bit of huffing and puffing, Festina tug-of-warred the scanner out of the false granite. Then she carried the

Bumbler back to me, her face deliberately emotionless. "I've recorded what's in the next room. Here's a playback."

She held the vidscreen in front of my eyes. The Peacock rippled nervously, flowing like whitewater rapids between Festina and me, but not blocking my view of what the Bumbler showed.

Like Festina said, the other side of the door was a corridor leading to a larger room. In the mouth of the corridor, a boot-sized machine sat on the ground—the anchor thingy. The view moved in for a close-up: a black box with a horseshoe-shaped inset of gold embedded in its lid. More golden horseshoes circled the box's sides, all glinting faint as a whisper. Incandescent. Every surface clean, not a speck of dirt or corrosion.

Then the view lifted away from the anchor, aiming out into the room beyond—a room with a huge black machine in the center, a great whopping obelisk stretched from floor to ceiling . . . and all around the obelisk, lights glowed.

Purple. Yellow. Green. Blue.

Flecks of color filled the room wherever I looked, everywhere, everywhere . . . till I realized I was seeing a single creature wrapped around and around and around, spun about the obelisk like thread on a spool. Wrapped around so many billion times, the windings went all the way out to the walls, bulging against them. Stuffed into the room, crammed tight.

Another Peacock, locked down by the anchor.

Then the Bumbler's view shifted once more, zooming straight ahead, to part of the far wall. On the floor sat another anchor box; and a pace away another; and another, and another, out to both edges of the view, so I could imagine that the whole room, all the parts out of sight, had anchor boxes along the walls.

Like pins holding down a butterfly.

*   *   *

The Bumbler's screen went blank. Then the playback kicked over again, the entrance corridor, the view zooming in for a close-up of the first anchor . . .

"Turn it off," I said.

Festina moved a dial; the video went black.

"So what do we do?" she asked, her voice a whisper. "Can we set it free?"

"It's not hard to break an anchor," she replied. "One good smash with a rock should do it. But do we want to?"

Tough question, that. No doubt at all, the pinned-down Peacock was Xé—soul of the world-soul, friendly spirit who let me hear nanites giggle. Her body might be trapped, but her mind had roamed outward, melding with machine intelligences . . .

How?

An answer appeared in my mind: the obelisk in the next room was a computer, a Greenstrider computer. And Xé surrounded it, permeated it. Used it as a stepping-stone to all the other computers on planet. Xé had done her best to be kindly, helpful . . .

But my Peacock said *tico, nago, wuto*. Crazy. Evil. Dangerous. Was he just afraid of the anchors, or was he describing Xé? No matter how gentle-natured Xé seemed, she'd been locked down here a long long time. Probably the whole three thousand years since the Greenstrider colony self-destructed. Three millennia = thirty centuries = plenty of time to go mad.

Tico.

In stories, when you let a genie out of a bottle, sometimes it grants you wishes. Sometimes it decides to rip your head off.

"What do you think?" I asked Festina. "If we let Xé out, how dangerous could it be?"

She lowered her gaze. "I once knew a lunatic who planned to destroy a planet's biosphere with a Sperm-tail. I won't tell you how, but I think it might have worked."

"Ouch," I said. "If it was just us at risk . . ."

"Yes," she agreed. "It's harder taking a chance with other people's lives." She stared at me thoughtfully. "You can talk to this Xé with your link-seed?"

"Sort of. But she hasn't volunteered to explain what's going on."

"Ask a direct question. See what you get."

So I asked . . . and what I got was data tumor. Three thousand years of torment lanced straight into my brain.

17

GERM FACTORY

Information exploded in . . . century after century, what Xé experienced. Imprisonment. Boredom. Suffering. Madness. Evil.

Guilt. Contrition.

Everything all at once, pummeling into my consciousness. A damburst set off by the right question, at the right place, right time.

Drowning in the weight of data. Choked by it—the way I often choked on scalpelish thoughts when I brooded how much I'd made a mess of things. Black depression is all you see, all you touch, all you feel, frothing-foaming-muddling in your brain. Motion churns without moving forward, bleak images circling the same futilities, everything all at once, too much to swallow, too much to breathe . . .

Then, in the jumble of mental meltdown, blood-boiling death a millisecond away . . . the sweet strong image of a peacock's tail. Green and gold and purple and blue, a million eyes open. Just as I'd seen during *müshor*: not long ago, but I'd been so naive back then, I thought it was a trick of my mind. Now I knew better. This was the

303

touch of the Peacock, *my* Peacock: shielding me, stopping up the data flood, holding back the tide till I caught my breath.

And the sound of it, same as before—feathers rattling, like a true peacock.

Look at me. *Look* at me.

A demanding peace.

Then the world was back...and only a blink had flicked by. Festina was just starting to move toward me, her hands coming up, grabbing me as I slumped. I let her take my weight—I didn't have the strength to stand because my head was so heavy, so full...

Not that I knew everything. My Peacock had thrown himself in the way of the data flood before I drowned. I'll never know how much of the download got pinched off short.

But I knew enough. More than enough.

"Are you all right?" Festina asked.

"Yes," I said. "And no. Ouch."

I didn't move—just leaned against her and let her do the work because my brain couldn't exactly remember how to control my legs. When Festina saw I was nigh-on deadweight, she lowered me gently to the floor. "What happened? Faye. Faye. Come on, focus. What happened?"

"I got the explanation," I replied, still reeling. "No one else ever asked. Even Tic...so Zenned-out, he never questioned. Just accepted everything Xé sent his way. When I asked, Xé was so excited and relieved...she tried to control the memory dump, I think she did, but she was too blessed giddy."

"What did she say?"

"Give me a second to sort it out." I looked around. "Where's the Peacock?"

"It was moving so fast I could barely follow it, but, umm...I think it went up your nose."

"Oh," I said. "They do that. It's their nature. And

since he stopped my brain from exploding out my ears, I can't complain, can I?''

"Are you *sure* you're all right?" Festina asked, placing a hand on my forehead.

"I don't have a fever," I told her. "Not yet. And I'm not delusional, I'm enlightened. Enlightened, light-headed, delighted. Do you want to hear a story?"

"If you want to tell me one." She had the cautious tone of someone humoring a woman who might be *tico*. But I told her the story anyway.

Start with the peacocks. A species that surfaced into sentience long long long before *Homo saps*. They launched their first rocket while Earth was still watching protomammals dodge out from under the feet of *T. rex*. Then came the peacocks' space-exploration phase, their bioengineering phase, their evolution into immortal energy-beings phase. . . .

Yeah, sure, trite cliché. Simplistic at best, and God knows, maybe plain wrong. All I can share is the data scar left in my mind after the tumor: a mix of real information from Xé and approximations made by my overloaded brain as it tried to make sense of everything. If the input got trivialized and contaminated by junk already lying in my subconscious—well, that's the way the meat brain works. Alien experiences get reinterpreted into things more familiar . . . even if that means drawing on fusty neural pathways laid down while watching *Captain Action and the Technocracy Team*.

So. The peacocks. Sentient Sperm-tails. Don't ask me what part was the actual peacock: maybe the Sperm-tail's pocket universe, maybe the particle-thin field that contained the pocket universe inside our own. Xé didn't give me details. Maybe she didn't know the truth herself.

Oh, another human prejudice there—seeing Xé as female. She wasn't . . . any more than my own Peacock was male. But three thousand years ago, the two were a couple, a pair bond, friends, lovers, allies, interpenetrating energies . . . pick whatever facile description gives you the gooey. And the two wandered the galaxy together, looking for enlightenment/light-headedness/delight.

Riding lesser beings.

No big mystery what I mean by Riding: hitchhiking in another creature's brain. Secretly experiencing its thoughts and emotions. Telepathic tourism. Peacocks could set up as squatters in the minds of lesser organisms, decoding neural transmissions as easily as we decode the snarl of light waves that hit our retinas. Xé and her paramour picked up the thoughts of everyone around them, clear as a summer's day.

Idle wandering took them to the Greenstrider home-world; hitchhiking brought them to Demoth. They Rode their unknowing hosts, sometimes for just a few hours but often from cradle to grave. That was their favorite way to Ride; traveling from birth to death gave them the full story, beginning, middle, end. The peacocks found each part fascinating . . . especially when the Greenstrider colony started breaking into factions.

You can picture them, those peacocks, like some rich-as-sin tourists watching the locals disembowel each other. Civil war breaking out, while the peacocks sat amused, sipping a telepathic cocktail of hate and violence, with just a splash of genocide.

The schisms that ripped apart Greenstrider society were so meaningless to Xé she didn't try to understand. Too much bother. The striders may have been fighting rich against poor, heathens against believers, green legs against blue; but Xé couldn't tell me because she hadn't paid attention. All she could say was the Greenstriders fought: north vs. south, east vs. west, coast vs. interior, tribe vs. tribe vs. tribe.

For a long time, it stayed a cold war. The League of Peoples was just as inescapable back then as it is today; if the striders had battled full out, nukes blazing, poison gas spreading like fog, Demoth would have been declared non-sentient: no one allowed out or in, total blockade and embargo. That threat was enough to keep hostilities mostly "polite" . . . like those nanotech weapons that gutted machines without hurting people. But let's not pretend blood was never shed. Sabotage can kill. Suspected sympathizers got lynched. Raids turned vicious. As machines went defunct one by one, neighbors invaded each other, looking for food synthesizers that could still pump out protein.

Ugly stuff . . . but not to Xé. She just found it *interesting*: like watching ants squabble, colony against colony; vicious but not important. For all her years of soaking up Greenstrider emotions, she still didn't identify with them. They were animals—so far beneath her, they didn't *count*. Even if the League considered the Greenstrider species sentient, they didn't act that way on Demoth; murdering each other with barely an excuse, believing their petty squabbles mattered. If the strider she was Riding grieved for a fallen comrade or raged as his clan sank into low-tech barbarism . . . well, wasn't it just so cute how they took themselves seriously?

Her sweetheart didn't see it like that. Humorless dud that he was, he actually tried to stop the fun; and in a gag-down disgusting way. Here's the thing: peacocks could do more than Ride in a passive way. They could actually fuse with their hosts, mind to mind, heart to heart. A conscious union, two brains in one, lasting for the lifetime of the host. Once twinned in, the Peacock couldn't withdraw without killing its Greenstrider partner.

To Xé, whole fusion was like doing the dance with a monkey. Obscene. Uncleanly. But the other peacock, my Peacock, didn't balk at grossness when it was necessary— he picked the leader of the strongest faction and zoomed in for a merge. The result was secret symbiosis: full Greenstrider on the outside, but inside half Peacock. Two minds becoming one . . . and the Peacock half was set on ending the civil war.

It made Xé sick. It made Xé furious. It made Xé blind-screaming jealous.

Her lover—her soul mate—getting heart-mind intimate with a lower animal. Disgusting. Sordid. *Insulting*.

Like many jealous lovers before her, Xé blazed back tit for tat: her own fling at bestiality. But she wasn't looking for a productive working union; she wanted someone she could rape and use. Xé chose the leader of another faction, and shredded the Greenstrider's brain as she made it her own. Blew the poor bugger straight off the edge of insanity. Then she set about using his body and his clan to rack up revenge.

It goes without saying Xé had ungodly intelligence compared with paltry minds like the Greenstriders. Intricate technical projects were child's play . . . like creating the most lethal biological agent she could imagine. Not a germ, but a germ *factory*—a cloud of nanites (microscopic, invisible) that could analyze an organism, then build a microbe ideally suited to giving that organism a slow inescapable death.

Got it? Germ factory = Pteromic Central. The Mother of all Plagues.

My Peacock's Greenstrider host operated from a bunker in Great St. Caspian. Xé sent the germ factory there—a microscopic troop of nanites, bent on making disease. The factory found a Greenstrider . . . analyzed the sad bastard's biochemistry . . . came up with a killer bug. As Yunupur had observed, the germ was designed to spread far and wide: a long latency period when carriers were contagious but showed no symptoms. It infected everyone in the Peacock's bunker, and the Peacock never noticed.

But.

The Peacock was working to restore peace on Demoth. That meant sending out envoys. Diplomats. People carrying offers of truce.

People also carrying the plague. Infecting clan after clan after clan.

The Greenstrider version of plague affected their skeletal structure; that's what the germ factory decided was

most vulnerable. Slowly, ever so slowly, bones began to
shrink. Subtle, subtle. Bone cells just stopped reproduc-
ing, never replacing themselves. Ostrich legs grew thinner
till they snapped like matchsticks. Just flexing a thumb
might be enough to rip one of their spindly insect arms
to flinders: thumb stressing the wrist, stressing the forearm, stressing the elbow joint, and so on up to the shoulder, everything going in one sickening crack.

Greenstrider lungs and diaphragm were seated on
bones, using them for leverage during inhalation. Once
those bones turned to tinder . . . breathless.

So Greenstriders began to die, all around the world.
Leaving saggy corpses that soon decayed to humus and
powder. Precious little in the way of skeletons for future
archaeologists to study.

Long after it was too late, the Peacock realized what
had happened—who was to blame for the epidemic unstoppably scouring Demoth free of Greenstriders. He
never managed to develop a cure; but he did have time
to settle the score with his former love.

Taking revenge? Or just locking up a mad dog? Neither
Xé nor I knew whether the Peacock acted in anger or
sorrow. But he *did* act. He built dozens of those Sperm-
tail anchors. He tracked Xé down to Mummichog, to this
bunker, where she still lived in fusion with her Greenstrider host. He ambushed her and imprisoned her and
walked away without looking back.

Her prison was more than just the ring of anchors nail-
ing her in place. The obelisk in the middle was also a key
component: a computer, designed to run off Xé's own
energies. The computer controlled a team of nanites to
serve as jailers—keeping the anchor boxes in good repair,
collecting solar energy from the world outside, and bringing it down for Xé to feed. (That was the source of light
in Xé's chamber: nanites releasing their sucked-up mouth-
fuls of sun.)

But the computer did more than maintain the prison.
My Peacock had taken mercy on his lover and given her

something to Ride. Something safe. She could inhabit the computer, could use it to reach out to digital intelligences all over the planet . . . but it was programmed to resist her control. Xé could never override the functions that kept her trapped; she could only respond to outside requests, not initiate anything herself. Even after the Ooloms arrived, with link-seeds implanted into proctor brains, Xé couldn't ask anyone to free her. The obelisk computer simply wouldn't transmit such instructions.

It had stopped her from telling anyone about her situation, till I asked a direct question. But it hadn't stopped her from mourning her imprisonment. And it hadn't stopped her from repentance. Even an immortal can change over the course of three thousand years. Especially three thousand years of inhabiting the machines that served ''lesser beings'': first the Greenstriders, then later Ooloms, and finally *Homo saps*.

Xé had learned true sympathy. Or so she told me.

She bitterly regretted the death she had caused. Or so she said.

She was no danger to anyone, and only wanted to help. Or so her story went.

And she wanted out, out, out, out, out. Please, please, please, set her free, set her free.

That part, at least, I had no trouble believing.

''You know Xé can't leave Demoth,'' Festina said when I finished the story. ''Even if we free her, she's a mass murderer. The League will swat her like a gnat the moment she heads for space.''

''The League is strong enough to do that? To an advanced lifeform like Xé?''

''Faye, you have no idea how powerful the highest species in the League are. Compared to them, humans are as backward as bacteria. Xé might approach the level of a flatworm, but she's still far too primitive to defy the League.''

"And the League won't accept she's had a change of heart?"

"No one ever knows what the League will accept," Festina replied. "But they take a very preemptive attitude toward dangerous non-sentient creatures."

"Maybe Xé's sentient now. Maybe she cares."

"And maybe she doesn't." Festina sighed. "I had a partner once who studied Norse mythology. He liked all that atmosphere of gloomy ice and snow." She made a face. "Anyway, he told me a legend about a rude-boy god named Loki. Loki pissed off the Father of the Gods once too often and was encased inside a tree till some passerby shed a tear for his plight. No one did. Eventually Loki gained enough control over the tree that he forced it to drop a leaf into someone's eye. Instant tear. Loki got free and proceeded to precipitate the end of the world."

"A load of laughs, those Vikings," I said.

"The lesson is still valid," Festina replied. "Xé may weep with contrition, but she's done monstrous things. Freeing her is a real gamble. You realize that her germ factory must have created the plague twenty-seven years ago? Millions of Ooloms died because of her."

"I know. Xé told me herself. After Yasbad Iranu got caught for illegal archaeology digs, an old Oolom proctor decided to snoop around in the so-called mines to see what Iranu was looking for. The proctor never realized he was exploring Greenstrider bunkers; and he never knew he'd encountered Xé's germ factory. That was Patient Zero for Pteromic Paralysis—a member of the Vigil doing his job."

Thank God he never knew.

"I want to set Xé loose," I said.

"Do you?" Festina asked. "Do *you*? Or is this a compunction she planted in your brain?"

"I'm saying what I want. I don't know why I want it."

Festina grimaced. "Tricky things, those link-seeds."

"You're telling me."

"So let me guess," she said. "You want *me* to make the final decision about Xé, because you can't trust your own motives."

"Afraid so," I told her. "Someone's got to make the call, and it'd be crazy to leave it up to me."

Festina sighed. "I suppose you've got a reason why we don't pass the buck to your government?"

"Because they'll drag their heels. They won't dare upset the status quo till they've brought in experts, advisors and boffins galore. Which means knocking on the Admiralty's door, doesn't it, since the navy has the most experience with Sperm-tails."

"Whereupon," Festina said, "dipshits will expropriate Xé and hold her as a lab rat forever."

I nodded. And waited. Trying not to feel coward-guilty for dumping the hard choice on someone else. *It's what proctors are supposed to do*, I told myself. *Present the facts, name the risks, then get out of the way.*

Festina stared at the floor as she thought over the situation; it only took a few seconds. "Okay," she said. "If we don't free Xé now, you're right; your government will search this place, find her, and eventually call in the Admiralty. At which point, people we *really* don't trust will have a captive superintelligent pocket universe that can design germ factories." She shuddered. "I'd rather take our chances with Xé."

A sizzle of fiery hope flashed over me from the next room.

Festina and I walked toward the concealed door. The Peacock, last seen going up my nose, didn't come swooping out to stop us. No *Tico, nago, wuto!* and blocking our way. I took that as a good sign. If my Peacock could read mental processes, he'd overheard Xé's confession to me . . . and he must have believed it, or he'd be screaming warnings in my face.

No excitement. No fuss. When we got to the door, Festina gave me a look, making sure I wanted to keep going.

I nodded, then pushed my hand against the wall.

My fingers sank in. The pseudogranite was more viscous than the windows back in my office—thick as concrete slurry. I forced myself forward, using the strength of my legs: pressing hard, both arms burying into the surface. Festina stood back, watching; if need be, she could push or pull to keep me from getting stuck in the middle. Just before my head went in, I took a breath and closed my eyes. Then onward, through the thick muddy soup, reminding myself I wasn't at all claustrophobic like daft old Oolams.

My arms came free on the other side. Then my face. For some reason, I expected to have muck coating me, smearied over my eyes, crusting up my hair; but I was clean, maybe cleaner than when I went in—my cheeks felt scrubbed, like having a pumice rinse. I kept driving forward, pushing, till my feet pulled away from the wall with a soft sucking sound.

Ssss-pop.

The sound echoed in the dimly lit corridor. Xé coiled in front of me, all green and gold and blue. Her lights shone flame-bright; I didn't need a link-seed to feel her rapturous anticipation.

Festina's shoulder came through the wall, followed straight on by her head—she hadn't reached out with her hands first, she'd slammed straight in as if she were body-checking the stone. I hurried to help her . . . nearly yanking her off her feet in my eagerness to drag her free.

Maybe not *my* eagerness. Maybe Xé's. The same way her frustration had spilled over to give me the weepies, I could feel myself swimming with creamy anticipation—nothing to do with my own hormones. "The wet tingles," we called it when I was fifteen . . . and Xé had them so whipping-fierce they were leaking into me.

So to speak.

I moved forward. There was a good-sized rock in my hand—I'd picked it up from the rubble in the other room. The anchor machine sat straight in front of me, wisps of

Xé's body sticking to the horseshoe insets like hairs plastered onto a balloon by static electricity.

Festina waved toward the box. "You want to do the honors?"

I knelt. Up with the rock, down with the rock—hard enough that the outside of the box ruptured and something cracked inside.

Wisps of peacock light danced away from the box. Free. A wave of joy surged through me so burning hot, I almost wet myself. *Cool down, Xé*, I thought desperately. *I know you're happy, but you're going to embarrass me.*

Acknowledgment with apologies. Not that the excitement abated much.

Festina and I went around the room in opposite directions, smashing anchors. Pulling the pins that held the butterfly. Xé made sure we never came in contact with her body, leaning herself away as we broke each fetter. I don't know what would have happened if we actually touched her; maybe we'd get sucked inside and spin through her innards in a never-ending swirl. Something to avoid.

Smash. Smash. Smash. Till we came to the final anchor, holding the last threads of Xé's being. She was mostly up on the ceiling now, like a streamer ribbon taped in this one spot to the floor but blown by a fan so it fluttered up and flapped. I lifted my rock for one more smash . . . but Festina wrapped her fingers around my hand.

"Before you do that," she said, "get Xé to stop the germ factory. Deactivate it, dismantle it. If she's in touch with all nano on the planet, she should have no problem doing whatever it takes."

I didn't even have time to phrase a command before Xé acknowledged the deed was done. The germ factory, far to the north, was shut down forever, nanites dispersed.

Just like that. All Xé ever needed was for someone to make the request.

"It's done," I said. And brought the rock down hard. Xé's bliss was so strong I nearly fainted—a bursting-blazing headrush that drenched me with sweat. Colored lights filled the room like a blizzard of blue and green as Xé danced, pranced, soared, everywhere all at once . . . till my foggy brain realized the dance was not one peacock but two. My Peacock had slithered out to join her, to celebrate—so many emotions shooting off sparkles I was too giddy to appreciate a thousandth of them.

Two peacocks. Old lovers. Old enemies. Dancing.

Then suddenly, it stopped. The blur of lights snapped into focus, straight in front of Festina and me: two Spermtubes open side by side, flowing out of the room, down the corridor, and off God knows where.

"This would be our ride out of the tunnel," Festina said. "To where?"

"Don't know," I answered. "But we'd better go—there's still work to be done."

"You mean tracking down Maya?"

I nodded. Feeling breathless. Realizing Xé had planted more facts in my mind than just her own history.

"What's wrong?" Festina asked. "Something to do with Maya? Something that . . . oh shit."

She bit her lip. She knew.

"Maya and Iranu," Festina whispered. "They've both been exploring Greenstrider bunkers." She took a deep breath. "They both met the germ factory, right?"

I nodded again. "Iranu met it six months ago. The factory analyzed him, then created the Freep disease. The disease killed Iranu and nearly did the same to Oh-God."

Festina steeled herself. "When did Maya meet the factory?"

"Four months ago," I said.

"And the factory created a disease that's absolutely lethal to humans?"

"Yes. Xé says this version of the plague affects the brain."

"Shit." Festina's face had grown pale. "So Maya's been spreading the infection for ages. In Sallysweet River. And in Bonaventure."

"You're forgetting Mummichog."

"Damn," Festina said. "Maya stayed with Voostor and your mother for days. Your mother must have caught the disease. The whole house has to be filled with it."

"All over the place," I agreed. "Xé says we're both infected. And the olive oil cure won't work this time. It's a brand-new disease. Old medicines mean bugger-all."

There. There it was.

After twenty-seven years, the other shoe had dropped: a disease to kill humans without touching Ooloms. Scary having that inside me . . . and yet.

And yet.

I had a queer sense of completion. *Botjolo* Faye—waiting all this time for a death of her own. Finally belonging.

Relief. Sick dread, and scalpelly relief.

In front of us the peacocks still twinkled, ready to carry us somewhere they thought we should go. I reached out, took Festina's hand, squeezed it. Our palms were both damp with fear sweat. "Sorry," I said, "this wasn't meant for you. But it'll still be all right. There's time."

Whatever I meant by that.

I tugged her hand gently, pulling her toward the open peacock tubes. She squeezed back, a strong brave grip; then she let me go and we dived forward, side by side.

18

FUNERAL INVITATION

From the torch-dim bunker in Mummichog, through
the twisty bends of a peacock's gut, and out again into
blackness: skidding to a stop facedown, with the lye-
soap smell of yellow-grass close under my nose. I lifted
my head to see the Henry Smallwood Guest Home, backlit
by the million stars in a Sallysweet River night.

Something thumped the ground beside me. Then Festina's voice. A growl. "Bloody hell. Back into the fucking
cold."

We stood up. The peacocks rippled in front of us, glim-
mering softly in the darkness. I couldn't tell which was
Xé, which was my own guardian.

Or should I say, *former* guardian.

Uchulu, said my father's voice inside my head. Good-
bye.

Uchulu, said another mental voice—Tic's voice. Xé always liked Tic; so why shouldn't she decide to sound like
him? *Uchulu i jai*. Good-bye and thank you.

Then the two of them began to rise, slowly at first,
staying horizontal to the ground till they were above the

317

treetops, then suddenly swooping straight up toward the sea of stars.

"Will the League let Xé leave?" I whispered.

"The League isn't noted for forgiveness," Festina replied. "But who knows?"

We watched till the peacocks were out of sight. It didn't take long. Then Festina shook herself; the gesture turned to a theatrical shiver. "Very touching, I'm sure. Now can we get inside where it's warm?"

The same Oolom hostess stood on duty behind the registration counter. I gave her a vague smile, glad there weren't humans in the room; it'd only been an hour since we contacted the plague from my mother, but Festina and I might be contagious already. As for the hostess, she'd be safe from us—this disease was sole property of *Homo saps*.

"Welcome back, Proctor Smallwood," the hostess said. "And Admiral..." She gave a small bow... very gracious of her, considering how we were grimed with grass stains, dirt, and jungle dung. "What can I do for you tonight?"

"A room, please," I told her. "Just one."

Festina raised her eyebrows. I ignored her, rather than explain in front of the hostess. We needed a place to hole up for an hour, somewhere we wouldn't infect other humans; but I doubted we'd stay the whole night. I'd make my report as soon as we locked ourselves away from healthy people. The medical authorities would come screaming in and cart us off to an isolation ward, then burn everything we'd touched in the guest home. Why force them to sterilize two rooms, when Festina and I could make do with one?

"One room," said the hostess. "Certainly. And will this be billed to the Vigil?"

"Let's have the Admiralty pay," Festina replied. "I love making them foot my bills."

*   *   *

I lay down on the bed before starting my report. Might as well make myself comfortable. "This may take a while," I told Festina. Then I closed my eyes and linked in.

Protection Central, please. Emergency.

The acknowledgment came back straightaway . . . and even in that short interaction, I could feel the difference. No personality on the other end of the link—just an empty machine. Xé was gone; the world-soul had lost its soul.

Poor Tic. Poor lonely old bugger. He'd never hear nanites giggle again.

First: a message to Argentia health authorities warning that Mummichog was a ticking bomb. The world-soul told me a med team had already picked up Oh-God and were beetling back to Pistolet . . . but they hadn't got home yet. There was time to warn them of Pteromic C, the *Homo sap* variant. Anyway, they'd followed high-infection protocols right from the start, because of Oh-God; yes, it was good to tell them they might be carrying a human disease, but it wouldn't make much difference in what they did. They were already walking on eggs.

As for Maya . . . Tic had reported her escape and police were searching for her through a million hectares of rain forest. The world-soul estimated only a five percent chance they'd find her; but if they did, they now knew to treat her as a plague-carrier.

I could imagine how that would overjoy the cops. A bomb-wielding murder suspect carrying a deadly microbe, flying over unpopulated jungle. They'd be tempted to splash her skimmer across a few acres of bush, and fret about forest fires later. Through the world-soul, I told the police we had to take Maya alive; we needed to ask her where she'd been, where she might have spread the disease.

In my heart, though, I knew it was too late. Maya and Chappalar had gone out together several times—to Bonaventure restaurants, nightspots, what-all. The plague was on the march, and who knew how many travelers had carried it from Great St. Caspian around the globe?

I felt like calling room service to order cinnamon.

A knock at the door. Festina sat up in surprise. "Are you expecting someone?"

"No."

Festina drew her stunner. I hopped off the bed and backed into a corner, as far as I could get out of the pistol's daze-radius. "Who is it?" I called.

"Proctor Smallwood?" asked an unfamiliar voice. Male.

"She can't have visitors," Festina answered. "Go away."

"I'd just like a moment of her time," the unknown man said. "Please. The hostess assured me it would be all right."

The hostess should mind her own business, I thought. "Who are you?"

"Yasbad Iranu. I understand you were there when they found my son."

Festina looked at me. I looked back. "Do you believe in coincidences?" I whispered.

"Yes. But only when they happen to someone else." She raised her voice. "You're from the Free Republic, right? You're a Divian?"

"I'm a Freep," Iranu replied. "I hope you aren't going to hold my species against me."

At least we couldn't infect him. "We have to hear him out," I whispered to Festina. "If only to see what his game is."

"You're right," she sighed. "Let him in. But I'll stun him shit-faced if he tries any tricks."

Yasbad Iranu looked much like his son . . . except that Iranu senior wasn't lying slack-dead in a heap. The man was well dressed, and brash as a baboon's butt. Born on top of the ladder, and blind-smug-confident that he'd climbed there himself.

The crown of his head only came to my chest, but he wore a red stovepipe hat that reached as high as my nose. Red was the color of mourning for Freeps—something to do with blood. The hat may have been a symbol of grief too, but to my eyes, it was just the trick of an arrogant pip-squeak trying to make himself look taller.

"Good evening," he said as he came through the door. He held out his hand to me, but I shook my head.

"Better not," I told him. "My friend and I both have a disease. It only affects humans, but still."

His hand stiffened, then withdrew. He ducked under my arm as I continued to hold the door open. I closed it behind him.

Iranu looked across the room to Festina. She held the stunner trained on his face. "You would be Admiral Ramos?" he asked.

"You've heard of me?"

"Your name appeared in the report Demoth gave to our embassy. The one describing how you found my son's body." He looked back at me. "That occurred near here, did it not?"

"Near enough," I answered. "You want to talk about your son?"

"Of course." He gestured toward a chair. "May I?"

Neither Festina nor I answered. He sat down anyway.

"I'd like to know whatever you can tell me about Kowkow," Iranu senior said. He crossed his stubby legs, calm and casual—one of those calculated things some aliens do, imitating *Homo sap* body language because they think it'll make a subconscious impression. On a Freep, crossed legs just looked witless: stubby and clownish.

"When I heard the news," Iranu continued, "I came straight to Demoth, to see the place where he died. I've asked everyone in this guest home if they knew anything of Kowkow's last days, but learned nothing . . . till the hostess was kind enough to inform me you two had just checked in."

It made me wonder how much Iranu paid for the tip-off. What did a rich man think a hostess was worth? He must have made some standing offer, buckets of cash for any tidbit she could send his way. The moment we registered, she ratted us out.

"What information did you want?" Festina asked.

"The official report was so impersonal," he answered. "And documents like that never tell the whole story. I want to know anything that might have been omitted. Little details to interest a father . . ."

Lord weeping Jesus, I thought, *you're breaking my heart.* "I'm surprised to see you back on Demoth," I told him. "Weren't you kicked out on your ass?"

That got the anger sparking in his eyes. But he covered it up fast with honey smoothness. "Water under the bridge," he replied with a wave of his hand. "A minor incident years ago. And your government deeply regretted the recent death of my son on Demoth soil. Rather awkward diplomatically. So to make amends, they granted me permission to return and arrange a memorial service. Especially since Kowkow's body has been impounded for health reasons and will never be allowed to return to his native planet."

True enough. The corpse would be studied, then cremated on the spot. No one would be crazy enough to ship a plague-ridden cadaver to a planet of people who could catch the disease . . . and if anyone tried, the League would stop it. The ban against transporting dangerous non-sentient creatures applied to microbes too.

"So you want information about your son?" Festina said.

"Anything you can share," Iranu replied.

Festina glanced at me, then turned back to the Freep. "Your son was illegally conducting archaeological studies at Sallysweet River, Mummichog, and other sites around the planet—continuing your own work, the work that got you expelled from Demoth. As far as we can see, Kow-kow's only archaeological discovery was the biological weapon that killed him, and he didn't even know he'd found it. The same biological weapon killed many million Ooloms because of your own investigations thirty years ago . . . not that you were directly responsible, but you set the chain of events into motion. I assume you figured that out long ago, but never told anybody. Thanks to your continuing silence, every Freep on this planet stands a good chance of dying in total paralysis. Humans are at risk too, though they'll die with their brains destroyed. Which is how Maya Cuttack is dying at the moment. Do you know Maya, Dr. Iranu? Do you know where she's likely to be?''

Iranu's face had flushed dark brown . . . as if his skin was warding off some burst of UV rays focused only on him. His hands clutched down hard on the arms of the chair and his oh-so-casually crossed legs had gone tense. "I don't know what you're talking about," he said in a strained voice.

"Doctor," Festina told him, "this isn't the time for stonewalling. Everything you've ever done will be subject to intense scrutiny . . . not just by people here on Demoth, but by your own government. Your son infected the whole Freep negotiating team. Top officials. People with connections. Their families won't be pleased.''

"And," I put in, "your planet can kiss the trade treaty good-bye; Demoth is never going to sign a pact with the Free Republic when they hear what Freeps have been doing behind our backs." I gave him a mean smile. "How do you think the corporate barons will react, Doctor? You and Kowkow didn't just make folks sick, *you screwed up a business deal*. Your government will throw you to the wolves.''

Iranu stood up. Straightened his jacket cuffs—another *Homo sap* affectation. Reaching into his pocket, he pulled out a small white card and plonked it on the night table beside the bed. "An invitation," Iranu said frostily. "To my son's memorial service. If you search your hearts and find some respect for the deceased.''

Festina took a step toward him. When she spoke, her voice was like a friend giving heart-to-heart advice. "Listen," she said. "You may think you can just walk away . . . pretend this has nothing to do with you. But as of now, you aren't just in trouble with the Freep and Demoth governments. You're in trouble with the League of Peoples. I'm informing you you may have knowledge that will prevent the deaths of sentient beings. You may know something about your son's movements, or Maya's. You may know where Maya would run if she wanted to hide. Kowkow talked to you, didn't he? After every trip to Demoth, he must have come home, told you what he'd learned, discussed what to do next. If you don't share all that information with the Demoth authorities, you'll be demonstrating a callous disregard for the lives of sentient creatures. Sentients endangered by lethal disease." She stared him eye to eye. "If you don't do something, the League won't let you leave Demoth alive."

Iranu flinched. Spun away from her. Caught himself and tried to put on an air of wounded dignity. "You're completely mistaken in everything," he said. "If you repeat any of it, I'll sue you for slander. As for the League of Peoples . . . your navy keeps the masses in line by portraying the League as omniscient bogeymen, but some of us aren't superstitious peasants." He gave his jacket cuffs one more pointless tug, then strode out the door on his stubby little legs.

Festina and I watched him leave. "Do you think he'll tell what he knows?" I asked.

She shook her head. "He's probably got a private yacht in orbit. He'll make a run for it . . . and the second he leaves Demoth's star system, the League will make him regret that 'superstitious peasants' line."

Silence. Simmering with het-up frustration. Not that I believed Iranu senior had much he could tell us, but his I-don't-need-to-talk-to-you attitude gave me the cranks.

Feeling seethy, I went back to the bed, lay down, and used my link-seed to submit a report to the Vigil. Copies to Captain Basil Cheticamp, Medical Examiner Yunupur, the Archaeology Liaison Office, the Civilian Protection Office, and the Global Health Agency. All of whom would send copies on to more agencies, boards, and functionaries. Some of whom would leak juicy bits to the media, out of context and inflammatory. Within hours, the wolfpack would be howling their self-righteous hunting calls, stalking me again.

The joys of being a proctor.

Still, I downloaded everything. About Maya, about Xé, about my own Peacock. I would catch unholy flak for freeing a potentially dangerous alien; and for decades to come, every half-baked *tico* on Demoth would claim to have seen Xé, been possessed by Xé, had Xé's baby . . . but I still didn't pad around the truth. Withholding the smallest detail was murderously irresponsible, given the enormity of the stakes. I drew special attention to Dr. Yasbad Iranu and the possibility he knew where Maya might hide. Let the cops collar him and sweat his smug little britches—if they broke him, he might not be executed by the League of Peoples.

Noble Faye, trying to save the man who started this mess. Who directly or indirectly killed sixty million Ooloms.

Including my Lady Zillif.

Making the report only took a few minutes. High-speed downloading. When I opened my eyes, Festina was perched in the chair where Iranu had been, toying with the invitation card he'd left.

"Thinking of going to the funeral?" I asked. "When is it?"

She tossed me the card. I caught it . . . then found myself thinking how I hoped Festina noticed what a smooth deft catch it was.

Sure. Trying to impress her with my athletic ability. What was I, a guy?

Read the card, Faye.

THE FAMILY OF THE LATE KOWKOW IRANU
INVITE YOU TO REMEMBER HIS SPIRIT
AND CELEBRATE THE GIFT OF HIS LIFE . . .

My eye skipped over the blah-blah-blah, past the date/ time to a tiny inscription at the very bottom.

(EVENT PRESENTED BY DIGNITY MEMORIALS,
A PROUD MEMBER OF THE IRANU GROUP)

Trust the Freeps to put advertisements, even on funeral invitations . . .

Wait a second. Dignity Memorials? The folks who sent androids to lug Ooloms out of our mass grave? Two dozen androids went down the ancient "mine" where we'd stored the corpses . . .

Except it wasn't a mine; it had to be another Green-strider bunker. And the Iranu group sent androids into that bunker . . . to do what?

What was down there?

Addendum to Proctor's Report, I sent out through my link-seed. *Urgently recommend that authorities investigate a site near Sallysweet River . . .*

I stopped. My transmission felt like shouting into a pillow. Jammed. Cut off from the world-soul.

Not again.

I had time to shout, "Dipshits!" Then a stun grenade crashed through the window.

Lucky me—I was already lying down.

19

NANO SLUDGE

Another hangover headache. I rated this one a honking great 7.2—either I'd got hit with more stun power than the last time, or I was slipping out of shape. There's a downside to not getting blind drunk at least once a week.

This time, my hands were lashed up behind my back: one of those plastic slide-ties, cheap, common, unbreakable. The only way to get the blasted thing off was to cut it.

Of course, that brought to mind the scalpel in my purse . . . except that I wasn't wearing my purse anymore. Big surprise. The dipshits were chumps, but not quite so witless as to leave me an obvious weapon. At least they hadn't stripped me buck naked . . . which I'd half expected, considering how Mouth in particular had a love for the melodramatic. Thank God, the Muscle was around to keep things on a more professional kidnapper-kidnappee basis.

Forget that now, Faye. Assess the situation.

All I could see at the moment was a blank wall, painted forest green, bang in front of my nose. I was lying on something soft, a bed with musty unaired blankets. When

I tried to roll away from the wall, I bumped into something thud behind me; after some wiggling, I got myself turned enough to see Festina lying on the bed too. She was unconscious but her breathing sounded healthy—just stunned harder than I was, because she'd been closer to the window.

Speaking of windows, there was one not far from the foot of the bed. Our kidnappers had stashed us in a smallish but comfortable room, not so different from the hotel room at the guest home: a nancy-pine dresser, a frilly little table and chair, windows on two walls. The windows had slat-shutters closed over the outside, and the window glass had been set to frost-opaque; still, sunlight managed to sneak its slatty-frosty way in. The whole bedroom had that "afternoon-nap" feel, darkened but not dark. In other circumstances, it might have come off as a fair cozy ambience . . . if my head hadn't felt crawling-full of beetles.

So? Get the obvious over with.

World-soul? I called on my link-seed. No response.

Peacock? Nothing there either.

Festina and I were on our own.

I nudged her with my knee. She didn't react; and now that I moved my legs, I realized they were hobbled up with a short strap of plastic, ends cuffed around my ankles leaving a stretch of half a meter between. Enough to let me shuffle like a person in leg irons, but no chance of kicking any more knees to splinters.

Pity.

The door opened. My old friends, Mouth and Muscle, swaggered in . . . which means the Muscle swaggered, while the Mouth only managed a swaggery-staggery limp. His one leg was locked stiff, though the knee cast was hidden by his uniform.

"Surprised to see us again?" the Mouth asked.

"Not under the circumstances," I told him.

"But you didn't expect us to be hanging close to the guest home," he gloated. "You walked straight in without the slightest suspicion. And we knew you'd end up there eventually; you had to come back to Sallysweet River, and we were waiting, tapped into the police database. As soon as you filed your report, we knew where you were.''

"You *knew* I'd head back to Sallysweet River?'' I sure as sweat hadn't intended to see the place again—not with pictures of Dads staring out from every shop marquee.

"We couldn't be certain you'd come,'' the Muscle said before the Mouth thought up another boast. ''But when you got away from the smuggler's house, Sallysweet River was the closest place you might run. And the safest place for us to wait for you. Your home in Bonaventure has cops all around it.''

"If you picked up my latest report,'' I said, ''you know the peacocks are gone. So there's no earthly reason for you to keep after me.''

"Come on,'' the Mouth scoffed, ''you think we believed that crap you told your bosses? Lovey-dovey Sperm-tails reunited after three thousand years, then vanishing into the sunset? Sperm-tails are physical phenomena, not conscious beings.''

I wished the peacocks were still around. They could have transported this clot-head into an active volcano.

"My report was the truth,'' I said. ''It doesn't matter whether you believe it.''

"It doesn't matter whether *you* believe it,'' the Muscle answered, dead calm. ''As we've said before, Ms. Smallwood, with that link-seed in your brain, your thoughts may not be your own. Enemy powers may have implanted false experiences into your mind, to sow disinformation with the Admiralty.''

Enemy powers? Disinformation? Christ Almighty. What fairy-tale universe were these guys living in?

"When Admiral Ramos wakes up,'' I said, ''she'll confirm everything I reported.''

"So what?'' the Mouth sneered. He did love to sneer, that boy. ''Ramos is hardly a reliable witness. She's always been openly hostile toward her superiors. For all we know, she may be the one plotting insurrection—using you as a pawn to shake public confidence in the fleet. Not to mention the navy's confidence in itself. After all, how can we trust starship security if any of our Sperm-tails could be telepathic aliens, tapping into the minds of fleet personnel?''

Fleet personnel with minds? These guys *were* living in a fairy tale. "So I suppose we're back where we started," I said. "You want to rip open my brain, hack inside, blah-blah-blah."

"That's the only way to be sure," Muscle replied. "If Ramos has been filling your head with false input, we're doing you a favor finding out."

"Some favor," I muttered. "I've got a better idea. Suppose I show you *real* evidence."

The Mouth gave a beady-eyed glare. "What do you mean?"

"Are we still close to Sallysweet River?" I asked.

"A tourist chalet on the outskirts of town," Mouth replied. "It's secluded, the owners aren't home, and the security system was a joke."

"Then I'll show you a Greenstrider bunker," I said. "Just minutes away. And I'll bet it's the bunker where the Peacock kept his headquarters three thousand years ago. The best place on the planet to find peacock information."

"If you mean the bunker by Lake Vascho," Muscle said, "it's still crawling with police."

"No," I told him, "this is different. Once the Peacock fused with that Greenstrider, he dug bunkers all over Great St. Caspian—maybe to house his people, maybe just decoys, I don't know. But I've figured out where the real central headquarters was . . . and I didn't mention it in my report."

"Why not?" the Mouth asked.

I looked back and forth between them, wondering if I should tell the truth—that I'd just doped out the solution a moment before they attacked. No. The truth was too innocent. These chumps were only going to believe something sordid.

"This site is the mother lode," I said, hushing down my voice. Mom-Faye telling goblin stories to the tots. "In the Greenstrider war, how do you think the Peacock kept charge of his tribe? How do you think he intended to make 'peace' with enemy factions?"

Muscle looked at Mouth. Mouth looked at Muscle. "Weapons?" the Mouth asked.

"What else could it be?" I lowered my voice more. "Think about it: after the Peacock locked up Xé, why did he keep cooling his heels on Demoth for thousands of years? Especially since it was centuries between the last strider dying and the first Oolooms showing up to colonize. Why did the Peacock hang around, with nothing to Ride but leaners and siren-lizards?"

I waited for them to make a guess. They didn't. Unimaginative sods. "Because," I finally said, "the Peacock couldn't leave for fear of the League! He was every bit the murderer Xé was. They were two of a kind, making weapons to slaughter each other's people. The only difference is, Xé beat my Peacock to the punch; she cobbled together her germ factory, after which everything else meant bugger-all. But the Peacock's whole arsenal is still intact. Practically under our feet. When I show you this bunker, I guarantee you'll find a whole slew of goodies you can commandeer for the Admiralty."

"Why should we believe you?" the Mouth asked. Not "I don't believe you." He damned well wanted to believe; he just needed an excuse.

"Because I don't want you prying my brain open," I replied. "And because it's dick-easy for you to check whether I'm telling the truth."

"How do you know about this place?" the Muscle asked . . . just as eager to believe as Mouth was. The two must be panting-desperate for something to show their superiors; they'd screwed up and given the Admiralty a bad name, not just on Demoth but on every planet that hated the idea of military bullyboys running rough-shod over civilians. The High Council had bailed Mouth and Muscle out of jail because admirals are obliged to stand by their people . . . but my captors were in deep dip-shit with their bosses, and finding a cache of high-tech goodies would go a long way toward saving their rumps.

"I've known about this place for a long time," I lied. "You've checked my reports. How did we learn about Maya in the first place? Because she wanted Chappalar to help her get an excavation permit. But why did she care about a permit? She and Iranu were already working plenty of sites illegally—they didn't mind breaking laws when they were hot on the scent. So why was a permit important this time?"

I waited. Neither Mouth nor Muscle had a guess. Christ, when I made up stories for the kids, they *always* had a guess.

"Maya needed a permit," I said, "because she wanted to work a site in a reasonably public place. Somewhere folks would see her coming and going, and wonder what she was up to. Her letter to Chappalar said the site was owned by Rustico Nickel . . . and the only mine that fits all the criteria is a place I know, out on the edge of town."

"You never told anyone about this?" the Muscle asked.

"A smart woman always keeps an ace in the hole."

The Mouth gave a short chuckle . . . and it galled me to hear how it was tinged with admiration. "You're a shark, Ms. Smallwood. I knew you couldn't be the goody-goody you pretended. Not with your previous history."

Bastard.

Mouth put a hand on his partner's arm and drew him back toward the door. They both went outside to discuss their next step. Me, I didn't even try to overhear what they were saying—I was too dazed, half by the rampaging headache banging the inside of my skull, and half by the words that'd come out of my mouth on the spur of the moment.

Why had it taken me so long to figure out what Maya's letter meant? The story I told the dipshits had completely nailed the explanation; she wanted to investigate a bunker that was so public she knew she'd need a permit. The only possible site was the mine where we'd buried the Ooloms during the epidemic.

I'd gone down that mine dozens of times playing little-girl Explorer, and had never found bugger-all. But that was before we'd filled the tunnel with corpses, and some drunk touched off a gas explosion. What did the kaboom open up? What had the Dignity Memorial androids seen the day they carried out the dead?

Iranu senior must have suspected they'd find something; that's why the Iranu group sent the androids in the first place. But our local authorities had closed up the shaft as soon as the bodies were removed, to make sure no more little-girl Explorers risked their lives down there. After that, no archaeologist, Maya or the Iranus, could do much around the place without attracting attention. Maybe a few forays in the middle of the night, but even that was risky—in a town full of miners, people working odd shifts might well go for a stroll at four in the morning.

Which is why Maya needed a permit. I should have figured that out long ago.

As for what I said about the Peacock—that he'd made weapons, that he didn't dare leave Demoth, that my noble protector was as much a murderer as Xé . . .

I thought of that moment beside Lake Vascho, snow falling thick, when the Peacock appeared gloomy as a ghost above the water.

"What are you?" I asked.

Botjolo.

Cursed.

Damned.

The Mouth and the Muscle came back into the room. They looked as iron-jawed serious as ever, but now it seemed put on—as if they were gleeful little boys pretending to be rough-tough customers. The dipshits were all bubbles, now that they saw a chance to get out of the Admiralty's bad books: open the Peacock's bunker, find tech that would dazzle the High Council. For all Mouth's talk about Festina planting disinformation in my brain, neither of these pissheads believed their own conspiracy theories; they'd just been grasping at straws till I offered them something better—a whole bale of hay.

"We'll go to this bunker," the Mouth said. "Tonight, after dark. And you'd better not be lying."

"I'm not," I replied. "Can you handle a Class 2 security lock? The Mines Commission bolted a steel cap-shack over the entrance to the bunker . . . like a hut sitting plunk on the tunnel mouth, and you have to open the door before you can head down. Of course," I added, "if you can't open the lock, I can do it myself with one call to the world-soul. Any door the government locks, the Vigil can unlock."

"That won't be necessary," the Muscle said, giving me a "How stupid do you think we are?" look. "We can open any lock up to a Class 5."

"In our sleep," the Mouth added, never one for a simple statement when he could twist it into a brag. "And speaking of sleep . . ." He drew a stun-pistol and aimed it at me. "Nighty-night."

In the last second, I pictured my fist connecting with his face. Maybe the image would give me sweet dreams.

Clawing myself awake was harder the second time—like a trick I'd forgotten how to do. I kept fumbling to get it right, then flopping back into blackness.

When I finally managed to grapple up to consciousness, I fiercely regretted it. It's flat-out amazing how many ways you can feel god-awful at the same time—the hammer-thud headache, the rock-in-your-gut nausea, the scritchy-knife stab in your bladder. Festina had told me the average stun-blast put you out for six hours . . . which meant I'd gone twelve hours with no water, no bathroom break, and damned if I could remember the last time I'd eaten. Not that I wanted to eat; the thought of food brought me close to the heaves. But my body was running toward EMPTY on blood sugar, and I felt like a mashed dog turd.

"Guys!" I shouted. At least it rasped like a shout in my croaking throat, and sounded loud to my headachy ears. I rolled onto my back and tried again. "Guys! Come on!"

Seconds crept by. As I lay staring at the ceiling, I could see the room was dark again. Night. Festina lay beside me, still breathing but now with a sandpaper edge when she inhaled. I wondered how often you could have a stunner frazzle your neural connections before you developed permanent nerve damage.

"Peacock?" I whispered. Silence.

Then Mouth and Muscle came through the door, and I tried not to sound whiny as I demanded a trip to the toilet.

We'll skip past the hot-cheek/hard-face indignity of pouring pee while two men watch and you're bound hand and foot . . . except to say I was glad the Muscle was there. He kept the whole operation businesslike; unlike Mouth, who was precious near licking his lips with the urge to play lord-and-master games while I was manacled. Sickminded toad. If I got a chance to break his other knee . . .

Cherish that thought.

After my one-woman show on the john, the dipshits gave me water and some protein jelly . . . all my stomach was likely to hold down. They were dash-ahead eager now to make for the bunker as soon as possible, but Festina was still out cold—put down hard by two heavy stunblasts, and a willowy little thing compared to yours truly. Gymnasium-tough, but not hardened by boozing, brawling, boozing, brawling. The Muscle wouldn't leave her behind unguarded and the Mouth refused to lug her unconscious body around the countryside. They began to whisper together in the far corner of the room; and with a cold jolt of dread, I knew they were debating whether to kill her.

"Don't be witless!" I snapped. "If you cork her in cold blood—if you even consider it seriously—the League will never let you off Demoth. Which means a heap of trouble, not just with the police; there's a plague coming, and it's going to be a vicious old bugger. You don't want to be trapped and go Pteromic, just because you didn't wait for someone to wake up."

"Admiral Ramos is already infected," Mouth said. "Isn't that right? So putting her down painlessly now is just a mercy killing."

"Odds are that you're infected too, you crazy buggers. You've been breathing our air, haven't you? If you're hot for a mercy killing, start with yourselves."

Mouth turned away from me and whispered something to Muscle. Despite input from our esteemed Proctor Smallwood, the proposed homicide was still on the table, being discussed in committee.

"Come on, Festina-girl," I said. After my trip to the bathroom I was sitting on the edge of the bed, Festina splayed out beside me. I twisted till I could touch her with my tied-up hands. Grabbed her knee and shook it. "Come on, wake up. Don't give them an excuse."

Nothing. Her breathing hadn't changed, and her face still had a nobody-home emptiness. I shook her leg harder, squeezing her knee. "You have to wake up now, Festina."

Sheer blank nothing.

I gave her leg a full-strength yank, and roared, "Explorer Ramos, atten-*shun*!"

Suddenly, I wasn't sitting on the bed anymore. I was flying across the room, jet-propelled by a pair of feet slamming into my back with a double thrust-kick. For a second, I thought I'd plow headfirst into the wall; but I tucked enough to hit with my shoulder, denting the plaster before I toppled to the floor.

Stun-pistols slapped out of their holsters—I'd fallen

with my face to the wall, but I could recognize the sound.
"Stop!" I shouted. "Everybody stop!" Then I added,
"Ow."

"Sorry, Faye," Festina said behind my back. "It's a
reflex."

"I'll remember that next time we share a bed. Ow, ow,
ow, ow, ow."

My shoulder was going to have a grand old bruise. I con-
templated the throb of pain while Mouth and Muscle im-
patiently processed Festina through the bathroom. They
gave her a grudging sip of water but no food; I wondered
if they were cranked at Festina herself or admirals in general.

Then: out to their skimmer in the chalet's garage. The
temperature was balmier than ever—soft spring. As the
garage door opened, I caught sight of a night sky heaped
with fast-moving clouds.

Mouth took the driver's seat, and I sat beside, giving
directions. In the two minutes we took to get to the bunker, Mouth must have said a dozen times, "You'd better
not be lying about this."

His way of making conversation. Men.

The dipshits weren't half as handy with the Class 2 lock
as they thought they'd be: cocky-assed city boys who
hadn't expected the jet-black of night on the tundra, with
clouds blocking the sky and no nearby lights. The closest
home was the Crosbie family compound, a hundred meters off . . . and the Crosbies had always been crazy-cheap,
never leaving a yard lamp burning once everybody was
inside for the night. When I was seventeen, I sometimes
parked Egerton plunk in the middle of his family's lawn
and with both of us bare-assed to the stars . . .

Never mind.

The dipshits fumbled and swore at the lock for a good
five minutes, not daring to spark up a light for fear the
Crosbies might see. While they were busy, I considered

hobbling over to their portable radio-jammer and jumping on it a few times. If I broke it, who cared if the dipshits whazzed me with their stun-guns? The world-soul would pick up low-level link-seed activity from my unconscious body. Heaven knows, the authorities must be scanning for me by now—the world-soul would have raised the alarm as soon as I lost radio contact in the guest home. But Mouth and Muscle had obviously got me away before the cops arrived. . . .

The Class 2 lock snicked open. So much for pulling a fast one behind the dipshits' backs. Mouth picked up the jammer and slung its carrying strap over his shoulder, while the Muscle grabbed Festina and me by the arm, hustling us into the tunnel.

They locked the entrance behind us again, just in case some local wandered by. No one would be able to tell we'd come down here. And if Festina or I tried to run for it, the locked door would make it that much harder for us to get away.

Nothing I hate more than a dipshit who thinks ahead.

We started downward. Our light came from a torch-wand the Muscle had strapped to his upper arm to keep his hands free. As he walked, his arm swung . . . and our shadows shifted back and forth, back and forth, along the tunnel walls.

The shaft here was made of the same false granite we'd seen in Mummichog. Or maybe it was real granite—the Great St. Caspian shield. Hard to tell, considering how there were black scorch marks covering most of the stone. I tried not to dwell on the thought that all this carbonization came from burning Oolom corpses. Even after twenty-seven years, the air was filled with a strong whiff of charring . . . the smell that never leaves a place where there's been an uncontrolled fire.

The ash streaks on the walls grew thicker the farther down we went. Somewhere under the black stains, I'd once painted my initials in stolen yellow paint: F.S. LOVES . . . I forget who I loved that day. Probably one of my future spouses. I'd only liked a few people in Sallysweet River, and I'd forced them all to marry me.

Damn, I missed them. It hurt. And at that instant, I realized I could never go home for fear of making them sick.

"Are you all right?" Festina whispered.

"It's the smell of smoke," I said. "Making my eyes water."

The tunnel ended in a standard pithead: flat floor, blank walls, empty elevator shaft leading down. In the early days of the plague, this is where we'd gingerly laid out the dead . . . but that was before the flash gas explosion. After that, we just wrapped the corpses in body bags, stood at the tunnel's entrance, and tossed the stiffs down as far as they'd go.

As I expected, the explosion had blown a hole in one wall of the room—a jaggedy rupture in the stone, opening into a room we'd never known was there. Sometime since the explosion, a lot of the fallen rock had got cleared to one side. I wondered when that happened. The day the androids removed the bodies? Or just recently?

Maybe Maya knew how to handle Class 2 locks too. I hoped so. That was the whole point of bringing the dipshits down here.

Muscle unstrapped the torch-wand from his arm and led us across the room to the hole in the wall. The floor underfoot was gnubbly, covered with hard specks of grit. Not sand or dirt—the grit was dried gobbets of Oolom, scattered by the explosion and left to mummify over the years. I could see the stuff everywhere, flecks daubing the walls and even the roof: preserved for nigh-on three decades in this cold dark vault.

The Mouth moved forward to join the Muscle, peering through the hole into the next room. I arm-wrestled my conscience a moment, then said, "You realize we found killer androids in Mummichog . . . in a place exactly like this."

"Are you trying to scare us?" the Mouth asked with his trademark sneer.

"I'm trying to warn you. Maya Cuttack left Mummi-chog in a fast skimmer more than twelve hours ago. Plenty of time for her to get here ahead of us. And if she thought people might come after her, she could have set traps."

"We're supposed to worry about traps set by a little old lady?" The Mouth snorted. "I don't think so."

"Okay," Festina muttered, "that man is plant mulch. A terminal case of stupidity. Fill out the death certificate and paint Oh Shit on his forehead."

The Mouth gave her one last sneer, then turned to his partner. "Let's go." Muscle discreetly stepped back as Mouth straightened the jammer on his shoulder and clambered through the hole in the wall. "All you have to do," the Mouth continued, "is watch where you step in case there are trip wires . . ."

His gaze was focused on the ground, watching his feet. He didn't look right or left . . . which is why he didn't see the acid coming till it whapped against him.

Two impacts, split-splat, shot by androids on either side of the hole. Most of one blob slapped harmless against the jammer . . . but the other wad caught Mouth smack across the face.

"Stop, you're making us allergic!" Festina and I shouted in unison. The Muscle only watched, as if he'd be ever-so-fascinated to see what happened next.

Mouth turned to see what hit him—no sign of pain, just pure dumb wonderment. His cheek billowed smoke; the hair on his left temple disappeared under the smear of acid like a magic trick, and blood spilled down as skin corroded away. He lifted his hand toward his face, as if he were curious to touch the goo that was eating him alive. The hand got as high as his chin. Then Mouth slumped with barely a sound, crumpled into a smoking heap.

We held our breaths, waiting. Me thinking that if the androids turned my way, I couldn't dodge or hobble out of range. But the magic words had once again frozen robot fingers on their jelly guns. Some other time, I'd have to decide if I felt guilty for not speaking sooner.

"Idiot," the Muscle said, staring at the steaming Mouth with no apparent emotion. "What did he expect?" Muscle looked our direction as if he wanted us to agree with him. "The man thought everything in the world would just fall together to make him a hero. As if that was the whole point of the universe, to glorify him. What can you do with someone like that?"

Right there at the end, Muscle's voice had a teeny catch in it. Not enough to make me think kindly of him, but still a slight trace of humanity.

"I don't suppose you're going to call an ambulance," Festina said to Muscle.

"We have higher priorities."

He drew his stun-gun and aimed at the Mouth. Mouth was still breathing, but dabs of acid had already begun to polka-dot his throat. Soon some droplet would eat through his windpipe . . . or jugular vein, or carotid artery, or some other indispensable piece of anatomy. I wondered if I should say a quick prayer; but Festina opened her mouth first, offering a prayer of her own.

"Hey," she said to the dying man. Her voice was soft and gentle. "This is what 'expendable' means."

Muscle pulled the trigger, and his stun-pistol went whir. As far as I could tell, nothing changed—Mouth had already drifted away into unconsciousness. But I guess the Muscle wanted to make some kind of gesture.

Festina and I had a hard time getting through the hole into the next room, but Muscle didn't offer to untie our hands or feet. He just waited on the far side, his eyes moving constantly, trying to watch us and the darkness looming deep beyond the torch-wand's light. Any fool could see that was impossible; soon, he was concentrating on what lay ahead, ignoring two hobbled women except for the occasional glance back in our direction.

He missed Festina edging toward the dying Mouth. She'd gone through the hole ahead of me, and when I saw what she planned to do, I made an extra great fuss clattering my way over the rubble. The Muscle rolled his eyes, peeved at the clunky-chunky old broad . . . which meant he missed Festina maneuvering the plastic strap that bound her ankles, touching it against a blob of smoking acid that was chewing through the Mouth's throat.

Some of the goo came off onto the plastic. Straightaway, Festina edged back again. By the time Muscle looked in her direction, there was nothing to see.

Seconds later, Festina returned the favor for me by setting up another distraction—she shuffled over to one of the androids that ambushed us. It happened to be a handsomish African man, tall, dressed in white-on-white clothing: Oolom colors of mourning, exactly what the Dignity Memorial robots wore when they emptied the mass grave. I guessed this artificial man had been down here ever since that day; Iranu senior programmed these two to stay behind as guards. Now they were working for Maya, just as all the others had been.

Probably, none of the robots had left Great St. Caspian after bringing out the corpses. They'd been shipped to the nearest handy holding area, that bunker by Lake Vascho; and they'd stayed there till Maya and Iranu junior reactivated them years later.

Question: how many more androids did Maya have down here in *this* bunker? One or two at most; if too many robots had stayed behind after clearing out the mass grave, someone would have noticed. Maybe the androids in this room were the only ones in the whole bunker, and there'd be clear sailing from now on.

Ever the optimist, our Faye.

But Festina had caught Muscle's attention as she strayed too close to the pseudo-African man. "Get away from that!" the Muscle snapped.

"I'm just making sure it's shut down."

"And it never crossed your mind to grab its weapon." The Muscle lunged across the room and seized her by the arm. "Don't underestimate me, Admiral. I'm not my partner."

"It was worth a try," Festina said, shuffling away from the robot again. She didn't even look at me; she obviously had full confidence that while she kept Muscle busy, I'd pressed my plastic leg irons against Mouth's acid blobs.

Festina was right. Tiny wisps of smoke were curling up from the plastic, as corrosive goo ate through the strap binding my ankles. In the dim light, I hoped Muscle wouldn't notice.

"Let's move," he said. Festina and I hobbled after him like good little captives . . . trying not to smile at the thought of kicking Muscle's teeth out when the acid freed our feet.

The room we'd entered was almost empty—blank granite walls, with the usual rusty lumps junked about the floor. All the easier to notice the one thing that hadn't moldered into anonymity: a palm-sized keypad embedded on the far wall. Sixteen white plastic push-buttons in a four-by-four grid. To my eye, it didn't look modern, or even human— the buttons were too finicky small to be convenient for *Homo sap* fingers, and labeled with odd squiggles that didn't look like any language I recognized. But if this was original Greenstrider technology, it was miraculously well preserved.

The Muscle peered at the pad. "What do you want to bet," he said, "if you key in the right sequence, one of these walls has a hidden door."

Neither Festina nor I bothered to answer. Obviously, this bunker was like the one in Mummichog; some hunk of wall was actually nano, ready to open for anyone who knew the right code. The door probably still worked too— if this bunker had enough self-maintenance capabilities to keep the keypad in good shape, important things like doors would stay in decent repair too.

The Muscle looked at me. "I don't suppose Xé told you the right key sequence."

I shook my head. "This wasn't Xé's bunker; it belonged to the Peacock, her out-and-out enemy. Xé wouldn't know the codes."

"Pity." The Muscle looked at the keypad again. "If I had enough time and the right equipment, I could crack this baby. But I'm not carrying tools for being delicate, so we'll do this the messy way."

He strode back across the room and wrenched a jelly gun from one of the robots. "You might want to stand clear," he told us, taking aim on the keypad. Festina and I beetled away, as far as we could get from the pad . . . which was the opposite side of the room and still not far enough for my liking.

"This is a military base," I reminded the Muscle. "If you spew acid all over a security pad, don't you think you might set off some defense mechanism? Like an explosion that'll roast all three of us?"

"The defense mechanisms are thousands of years old," Muscle answered. "They're bound to be dust by now."

"Oh sure, bound to be," Festina said. Out the side of her mouth, she whispered, "Get ready with another death certificate."

I whispered back, "Let's hope we don't need three."

The Muscle fired. His first shot was low: acid wad smacking the wall a handbreadth beneath the keypad. Some of the spatter glooped upward, but only a bit; the rest just hung from the granite, a few jelly drops plopping down to the floor.

Two seconds for the gun to repressurize, then Muscle fired again. This time he'd corrected his aim bang on—a gooey blob struck the keypad dead center, splotching thickly over the press-buttons. I could hear sizzle all the way across the room: buttons melting like wax, the metal container dissolving in heat shimmer.

For half a minute, nothing happened. Then an entire section of wall suddenly turned from stone to molasses, a thick fluid of nanites dribbling to the floor. The fluid was runny granite gray, with the slimy texture of raw egg-white gushing over the ground. Nano sludge.

In the gap where the nanites had been, there was now a dark passageway leading forward.

Muscle stepped back as the egg-whitey juice trickled toward him. "Admiral," he said, waving the jelly gun toward Festina, "if you'd be so good as to go to the doorway. Just to check what happens."

"You want to see if the sludge attacks me."

The Muscle smiled. "Exactly. It's wicked-looking stuff."

Festina hesitated. Muscle gestured with the gun again, the smile gone from his face. Before either of them did something daft confrontational, I hopped forward myself, slopping into the slushy gray gumbo spreading across the floor. *Nice puppies,* I thought to the nanites, *don't hurt your old Mom-Faye.* With Xé gone, the nanites didn't answer . . . but they didn't attack either. No dissolving my boots or climbing up my legs. Festina moved a second later, following in my gooey wake; with nothing more than sodden shoes, we both made it to the doorway.

"Happy?" I asked the Muscle.

He waited another full minute, giving the sludge time to take action. What scared me wasn't the chance of nanites attacking . . . the problem was Muscle staring so precious keenly at my feet. By now, the acid from Mouth's throat had eaten clean through the strap holding my ankles; if Muscle had good eyes, he might notice. Lucky for me, he kept well back, staying out of the nanite pool. And there wasn't much light on my legs—Muscle still had the torch-wand rigged to his own arm, and its glow scarcely reached as far as me. I kept my feet tight together, looked chump-helpless, and hoped that would be good enough.

It was. The Muscle didn't notice the corroded split in my ankle strap; and after a minute, he accepted that the sludge wasn't going to turn homicidal. Delicate as a bird, he tiptoed through the pool and joined us staring into the passageway forward.

I could have kicked him that very second—broken his knee or swept his feet out from under him. But I couldn't guarantee I'd take him straight out of the fight, and he had that jelly gun in his hand. Better to wait for a sure thing . . . especially if I could coordinate an attack with Festina.

Patience. Why do so many things demand goddamned patience?

"On we go," Muscle said. He waved the jelly gun to show who was boss, then led the way forward.

The corridor was only a dozen meters long. Then we came to the bottomless pit.

Oh, all right . . . it wasn't honest-to-God bottomless. But it had to be at least ten stories deep, because torchlight didn't reach the pit's floor. Ten stories was still plenty enough that I didn't want to take the dive; and diving was clearly what the Greenstriders had in mind when they built this place. A long stone bridge led forward across the pit, like a drawbridge across a moat. At the far side of the bridge sat another blank granite wall with another entry-code keypad.

Simple arrangement: to move forward you had to cross a narrow bridge over a fatal drop. In Greenstrider days I bet there were gun slits on the far side, ready to strafe unfriendlies if they tried to charge forward. Once you were on the bridge, you were bare-ass exposed . . . and the way across was only wide enough for attackers to dash up single file.

Cute little killing ground. If the defenders on the far side didn't like you, either you got shot or you fell.

Or you turned back the instant you realized that going forward was utterly nuts.

"End of the line," I said, slipping back into the corridor. "If Maya's holed up across the bridge, it'll take an army to pry her out."

"Not so fast," Muscle told me. "First of all, we don't know Maya's here—she may be holed up in some other hiding place. Second, there's not much chance the old Greenstrider defenses are still operational. Sure, this would have been a death trap three thousand years ago; but everything's rusted, hasn't it?"

"Not the prison that held Xé captive," Festina pointed out. "That was built by the Peacock, with self-repair mechanisms far beyond human capabilities. And this whole bunker belonged to the Peacock too. A lot of the equipment must have been standard Greenstrider stuff, but some had to be made by the Peacock himself. Those keypads, for example—not a speck of age on them. For all we know, the Peacock built automatic shrap-guns to cover this bridge; if we try to cross, we'll be shredded."

"That's a possibility," the Muscle admitted. "But I refuse to retreat without testing the theory." He gave Festina an ugly smile. "Tell me, Admiral: what's standard navy policy when you think something might be lethal but you can't be sure?"

She stared back at him evenly. "Send in an Explorer."

The Muscle waved his gun toward the bridge. "You're on."

I said, "Stop."

They both looked at me. "Are you volunteering to go instead?" Muscle asked.

"I'm serving as a member of the Vigil," I replied. "And our job is to prevent people from getting carried away with their own momentum." I turned to the Muscle. "What do you think you'll accomplish, sending Festina across the bridge?"

"I'll find out if any defense mechanisms are active."

"But why bother?" I asked. "Where's the gain? Do you really think there's anything down here that will help you?"

"You said there might be high-tech—"

I interrupted him. "I was leading you on, so you wouldn't muck about with my brain. Buying time till you made a mistake."

"Still," he said, trying to look unflappable, "there might be useful things down here. You mentioned weapons—"

"Which are dick-useless, you know that. If you find a lethal weapon down here, or even *plans* for a lethal weapon, you can't take it home to Admiralty headquarters. The League won't let you carry killing devices across interstellar space. You knew that, but you ignored it, because you wanted to believe you could squeak out of the mess you were in. Grasping at straws, sacrificing your partner for some false hope . . ."

"I think," he said clamp-jawed, "you're trying to make me angry. You want me to do something rash."

"You've already done something rash, you chump! The three times you came to kidnap me. Did it ever occur to you to work within the system? You could have flashed your credentials at our government, and said, 'Top admirals are interested in this case, we'd like to get in on it.' Most politicians would be flattered. 'Ooo, the Admiralty is interested in little old Demoth, let's keep these guys in the loop.' You would have been part of every investigation team; you'd get up-to-the-minute reports, invitations to planning sessions, tactical operations, the works. But no. You have some witless notion that acting like a lone wolf is more efficient or smart or sexy than playing with the team. What crap! What pathetic macho crap!" I took a deep breath. "Do you know the only high-tech artifact we've seen since we got here? A keypad that can last three thousand years. And you turned that to slag. Brilliant thinking, you mook."

He took an angry step toward me. I don't know whether he intended to hit me, shoot me, or just scream in my face. It didn't matter—he'd come into kicking range.

Festina snapped his knee, while I knocked the jelly gun

out of his hand. After that, it was as easy as stamping grapes.

We freed our hands the same way we'd freed our feet: picked up the jelly gun, shot a blob against the wall, and warily dabbed our plastic wrist ties against the smallest drop of acid we could find. Both Festina and I managed the trick without burning ourselves—something of a miracle considering we were doing all this with hands behind our backs, and me half-shaky from pure relief.

As we stood around after, rubbing the pins-and-needles tingle out of our fingers, Festina said, "All right. We head back, smash the jamming machine, and call for help, right?"

"We may need to get closer to the surface," I told her. "My link-seed might not have enough radio power to transmit through all this rock."

"Closer to the surface is good." She scooped up the jelly gun and tucked it under her belt. "I'll be delighted to put more distance between us and this death trap. If someone wants to know what's on the other side of the bridge, maybe we can reprogram those androids from Lake Vascho. Let them lead the charge."

Festina bent to pick up the Muscle—he was unconscious with a broken jaw, but generally intact thanks to our ladylike restraint. I put my hand on her shoulder, and said, "This time let me carry the body."

"Oh sure, take my fun."

She unstrapped the torch-wand from Muscle's arm and held it as I hefted the man up. Once more, I thanked Our Blessed Mother Mary for Demoth's .78 gravity; the dipshit was heavy enough as it was. When I had him in a secure grip, I waddled with him down the corridor, Festina keeping pace beside me . . .

. . . till we reached a dead end. A blank wall of granite where there should have been a doorway to the next room.

"Oh shit," I whispered.

"Don't say that!" Festina snapped.

"The nanite sludge . . . it flowed back into place."

"I can see that." Festina held the torch close to the wall, running it around the edges of the doorway to look for a gap. I couldn't see the skimpiest irregularity—the door had neatly fused itself to the surrounding rock.

And Muscle had melted the control panel on the other side. Even if rescuers thought to search for us down here, they couldn't break through with anything less than a laser cutter or high explosives.

"But this wall is made of nanites, right?" Festina said. "And in Mummichog, we could just push through."

"That was when Xé inhabited the world-soul," I told her. "Things are always easier if you have friends in high places."

"At least try."

I set down the Muscle and pressed my hands against the cold false granite. Not the tiniest budge—like pushing against a mountain.

"This isn't . . ." I stopped. Something was humming somewhere. In my fingers? My brain? I planted my hands on the wall again and shoved with all my strength.

The wall shoved back. Starting to inch our way.

"Uh-oh," I said.

"Uh-oh what?"

"The Greenstrider defense system has another trick up its sleeve."

"Uh-oh."

"I already said that."

The wall kept advancing—up the corridor, forcing us back toward the bottomless pit. Nano-granite nudged against the Muscle where I'd set him down; in no great hurry, it started to push him along the stone floor, scraping him over the rock. I picked him up again, as if I cared whether he got raspberry rug burn from the rough surface. Lugging him along, we retreated as the wall plugged forward.

"Pity the Muscle isn't awake," Festina muttered. "He

was the one who wanted to find out what defenses were still working.''

"If we're forced onto the bridge," I said, "and guns shoot at us from the far side, would it be god-awful non-sentient to use this chump as a shield?"

"Tough call," Festina replied. "If we convince ourselves he'd want to die nobly, defending his fellow humans . . ."

I thought about it. "No. He's not the hero type. But he was definitely interested in learning about Greenstrider weaponry."

"Best way to learn is firsthand," Festina agreed.

When the wall finally forced us out onto the bridge, I was holding the Muscle between us and the line of fire.

The wall stopped moving, right in the mouth of the corridor. That sealed off our only retreat, leaving us vulnerable and exposed on that narrow bridge across the abyss. Festina and I exchanged looks—one of those moments when you hope your eyes are saying something because you know speech won't work. If we were about to be chopped to chutney by gunfire, I didn't want to die with banal last words like, "If only we had more time together . . ."

At the far end of the bridge, the wall slowly dissolved into another doorway. A tall man in white stepped out: a perfect twin of the African android back in the other room. Another robot, naturally; he carried a jelly gun.

Behind him was a shortish woman with white hair. She stared straight at me, and said, "So, Faye, we finally meet. Bitch.''

20
EVIL BITCH

Maya Cuttack hailed from Indian ancestors—she'd made a point of daubing a blobby red caste mark in the middle of her forehead. Her brown skin looked crinkled and paper-dry, at least on her arms . . . which I could see because even in this chilly bunker, she wore a half-sleeved blouse, the kind that goes under a sari. The blouse was jade green silk; and on it, someone had hand-painted dozens of peacocks.

Talk about a deliberate statement.

But if you wanted a real statement, you had to look at Maya's face. Her nose and chin might be the same brown as her arms, but the edges of her face had gone fish-belly white: chalky sickness seeping out from her hairline, creeping down her forehead, across her temples, in over her cheeks.

Hello, Pteromic C.

Her ears were now as yellow as butter, a jaundicey contrast with her snow-pure hair. But even that hair showed signs of the plague; it was frazzled wild, not just uncombed but unwashed and curdled, with enough head grease to hold scraggly bits as if they'd been moussed:

cowlicks jutting out, churned into mad snarls.

Maya Cuttack: *tico, nago, wuto.* And diseased, diseased, diseased. Christ, hadn't Mother and Voostor noticed? Or were all these outward symptoms recent, the final cataclysmic collapse of someone who'd been crumbling flake by flake for a long time?

"Aren't you going to speak, Faye?" she asked me. "Bitch, bitch, bitch." Muttering the "bitch" stuff in an undertone, as if it weren't really meant to come out of her mouth. A subconscious chant . . . but Maya couldn't keep her subconscious as "sub" as it should be.

"You're sick," I said.

"I'm afraid you're right (bitch, bitch). And it's all your fault, Faye (bitch), Faye (bitch)."

"How?"

"Because, Faye (bitch), you're the great (bitch) evil of the world. Your father (bitch) was evil, and you, Faye, inherited it."

Her voice was delicately polite, all genteel and ladies-auxiliary . . . except for those guttural "bitches" that kept slipping their way in. Pteromic talk. Brain breakdown.

"What do you know about my father?" I asked, keeping my voice soothing calm.

"Your mother told me he glowed," she replied. "Possessed by an alien thing. Bitch. Bitch. *Bitch.* I've studied this planet. People get possessed here. You're possessed, Faye, I know you are. Your mother (bitch) told me all the evil things you did. She defended you (bitch), sometimes she did, but you hurt her so badly . . . I realized I had to kill you."

"How long ago was that?" I asked. "A month or so?"

"Perhaps. I have perhaps, perhaps, lost some sense of time." She smiled sweetly. "But not my sense of urgency. Your mother is my dearest (bitch), dearest (bitch), dearest friend, and you caused her so much pain you had to die. You see that, Faye, don't you? Don't you, Faye? Whatever it took (bitch), you had to die."

Whatever it took. Christ, that phrase gave me the chills.

"Are you saying this was all about me? The robot attacks on the proctors . . ."

"Of course, of course, of course." Another of those sugary smiles. A teacher pleased with how fast her student catches on. "If I just killed you outright, the police would ask questions. (The bitch, the bitch, the fucking bitch.) They'd interrogate your next of kin, Faye. Perhaps they'd even accuse your mother, because she'd be so happy at your death. So blissfully, blissfully happy."

My mother blissfully happy to see me dead? No. Ma might have been appalled by the teenager I once was, but she wouldn't dance on my grave. Look at the way she'd treated me when I suddenly turned up on her doorstep— wary but polite, ready to give me a chance. Perhaps even glad to see me, glad to find out I'd changed.

Maya was just a brain-sick madwoman who'd got a crazy idea into her head. Yes. Yes.

"You decided to kill me," I said, "but you didn't want people to guess I was the specific target. So you knocked off a slew of proctors so it would look like a political thing. I was supposed to be one more corpse in the crowd."

"That's right." She flashed me a proud-of-herself grin. "I could feel myself getting sick (bitch, bitch). Before I went, I wanted to give a present to my dearest, dearest friend. It wasn't hard to post androids (bitch) all around the planet, ready to take on easy targets. Then I made friends with your supervisor, Faye, so I could track your movements."

Poor Chappalar: manipulated, then murdered. All because a poor plaguey lunatic intended to do my mother a favor poor Ma didn't want.

"So what now?" I asked. "I suppose you want to walk us through this bunker . . . show off the fabulous things you've discovered." Actually, I doubted the idea ever crossed her mind; Maya just wanted to gloat till she'd worked herself into a lather. At some point, when she was keyed up enough, she'd tell the android to gun us down with acid. But maybe I could come up with some delaying step that would appeal to her *tico* mind. If she liked the notion of a guided tour, at least we'd get off this blasted bridge.

"It would be pleasant to show you things, Faye," Maya admitted. "I'm particularly proud of the control room (bitch) for this place. So much of it still works ... and I've always had a knack for programming machines." She smiled and patted the shoulder of her android bodyguard. "Or maybe (bitch)... I could show you where your (bitch) father died." Her eyes twinkled, like she'd just told a joke. "Did you know this bunker stretches close to the Rustico mine? Or at least its outer defense ring does. And that so-called 'gas explosion' twenty-seven years ago (bitch)... the miners actually ran into an antipersonnel device intended to stop anyone from tunneling too near to the bunker's wall. An explosive, Faye. The miners stepped on a mine in the mine."

She giggled. Or maybe I should say a giggle got away from her. Fell out uncontrolled. Giggle, giggle, bitch, giggle, bitch.

I wondered what she'd been like before the plague spackled her brain. Willing to trespass, to play fast and loose with the law ... but not a bitched-up killer. Just a titch too ambitious for her own good. How could I hate her, seeing how pathetic she was now? Christ, it would have been nice to blame everything on some out-and-out monster. All the dead and wounded, Chappalar, Oh-God, even the Mouth. Wouldn't it be fine to lay it all at the feet of a heinous villain? But in the Vigil I'd learned the universe is stingy with black-and-white wickedness. Even the devil has a story.

I stared at Maya with pity and horror. Which was a mistake—I shouldn't have made eye contact.

"Bitch!" she suddenly screamed. All her placid conversation boiled off in a heartbeat. "You want to kill me, don't you, bitch? That's why you've chased me all over Demoth. That's why you tracked me down here. You're

not human, no, you're possessed . . . and you want to stop
me because I know the truth. You destroyed the Greenstriders, and you think you'll destroy me.''

"Maya, I don't want to destroy . . ."

"Kill her!" Maya shouted to the android. "Kill her
now."

"Stop, you're making me allergic!" Festina yelled behind me.

The android took a step forward.

"Uh-oh," I said.

"Do you think I wasn't listening?" Maya asked. Shrill.
Breathy. "There are monitors all through this installation,
and they still work. I've been watching you people since
you came down the tunnel. When you were stupid enough
to destroy that keypad, *I* was the one who opened the door
for you. And closed it behind you. I've had plenty of time
to reprogram this robot not to be fooled by your ridiculous
allergies.'' She slapped the android on the back. "Shoot
the bitch. Now!''

The android lifted its gun and fired.

When I'd joked about using the Muscle as a shield . . .
sometimes our Faye is all talk and no action. I dropped
to the bridge, Muscle and me together, trusting Festina
would also have the sense to duck the incoming acid. She
did—a blob of jelly just doesn't travel as fast as a bullet,
and if the shooter isn't at point-blank range, you've got
time to get out of the way. The wad passed over our heads
and splashed somewhere behind us.

Then Festina was firing her own jelly gun—a quick
shot, snapped off as she bellied down onto the bridge.
Maya shrieked and threw herself behind the android . . .
who just stood there, dumb as a stump. Programmed for
offense, not defense. When the acid splatted home, the
center of impact was plumb on the robot's gun hand: goo
spraying over the pistol, the fingers, and halfway up the
elegant white sleeve.

"Nice shooting," I said.

Festina muttered, "I was aiming for his chest."

"Shoot them!" Maya screamed at the android. "Shoot, shoot, shoot!"

The robot's arm lowered, pointing the gun muzzle straight at my face . . . and nothing happened. Festina's shot couldn't have hurt the pistol itself—an acid-shooting weapon surely must be resistant to acid. But the android's hand was smoking with corrosive gunk, not to mention a dozen burning patches all the way up to its elbow. With so much damage, something had buggered the robot's ability to squeeze its trigger finger: a wire cut, a servo off-kilter, some crucial mechanism pitted to pâté.

Maya continued her squeal, "Shoot, shoot, shoot!" . . . as if the word had stuck in her brain and wouldn't let anything else out. The robot kept aiming dead zero on my face but didn't have the smarts to do more than that; didn't switch the gun to its good hand, or even use its free hand to pull the trigger.

All of which gave time for Festina's pistol to pressurize. Bracing herself, firing with a two-hand grip, she landed a wad smack on the android's sternum—making a beautiful splash pattern that scattered droplets as high as the robot's throat, as low as its groin. Those pretty white mourning clothes boiled away in instants; then the acid began to eat through artificial skin into the circuits below.

The gooey thwock of impact snapped Maya out of her, "Shoot, shoot, shoot!" fit. She slapped the android on its shoulder and yelled, "Go after them! Throw them off the bridge! Now!"

For a split second, I let myself hope the robot was too damaged to obey. But no such luck. With a sudden lurch it broke into that full-out sprint I'd seen from the other androids, a thunder-footed run across the bridge toward us. I was on the ground; I only had time to scuttle backward, hoping that maybe when the robot came for me, I could knock it off-balance with a kick in the shins.

Only one problem—the robot wasn't coming for me.

When I'd ducked the robot's first shot, Muscle and I had dropped down together. Now that I'd retreated a pace, the Muscle was closest to the android. Apparently that's all Machine-Man cared about: never mind that Muscle was unconscious, while Festina and I were still threats. Simple-minded robot algorithms said if Muscle was closest, Muscle would take the high dive first.

Which I didn't realize till the android reached down and grabbed Muscle by the leg. "Hey!" I shouted. "Leave him alone. I'm the one your boss wants dead. I'm the blessed Antichrist, aren't I?"

Robots don't know from Antichrists. Lifting Muscle by the ankle, the android jerked him up and over the abyss.

Festina fired—a close-range shot straight into the robot's ear. The same second I dived forward; the android was holding Muscle head down in front of me, leaving Muscle's arm dangling limp within my reach. I snagged Muscle's wrist just as the robot toppled: Festina's last shot had fried one too many circuits for the machine to keep its balance.

Clunk, the android hit the bridge . . . and now it was twitching with mechanical death spasms, half its servos cycling at random while others squeezed tight or snapped wide-open, clanky jerks shuddering through the robot's body. Then like a fish flopping in the bottom of a rowboat, the android bounced clear up off the bridge, landed with a crunch, bounced again . . . and flipped over the side, smoke streaming off its body.

It kept its grip on Muscle's leg. The robot's hand was locked in place, clutched frozen on the dipshit's ankle.

For one screaming instant, I held the full weight of Muscle plus the android by my one-handed grip on Muscle's wrist . . . just long enough to dislocate my shoulder, a cracking pop, loud as thunder. I was lucky my arm wasn't ripped clean off; but my fingers gave first, and I was holding nothing. Grasping at air as robot and dipshit plunged out of sight.

*   *   *

I might have fallen myself, pulled over the edge by the jerk of their weight . . . and dizzy-sick-nauseous from the wrenching agony of my shoulder. Teetering, teetering, wobbly on the brink; but Festina stopped me: grabbed my legs and pulled me back from the edge, till I was lying sweet-solid on the bridge.

"Bitch!" Maya shrieked. "The devil's always on your side."

I couldn't answer. The pain from my shoulder was driving me fast toward blackout. Festina called, "Let it go, Dr. Cuttack. There's no reason to keep fighting. What do you want? To tell the world how wicked Faye is? I can arrange that; I'm an admiral."

Thanks a bunch, I thought.

"Just open the door so we can go back," Festina told Maya. "You're obviously a gifted archaeologist; you've got full control over the nanites in this bunker. Just tell the nanites to open the door."

"Yes," Maya said softly. "I could speak to the nanites . . ."

I didn't like the tone of her voice.

Next moment, she shouted something in a language I didn't recognize—the ancient Greenstrider tongue, I guess, calling a command to the control center.

Under my body, the solid granite bridge began to turn gooey.

"Oh shit," Festina said. "Oh shit."

The bridge was made of nanites too. Of course: the bunker's last line of defense. If the place was under all-out attack, with enemy troops crossing the bridge in such numbers you couldn't shoot everyone . . . then you just told the bridge to dissolve itself. Send everyone plummeting to hell.

The bridge surface had turned as soft as mud. The edges were beginning to drip into the chasm. Far to the opposite end, Maya laughed; the stone was melting under her feet too, but she didn't care. "Got you!" she crowed. "This time I got you, bitch."

Festina grabbed my arm and pointed behind us. "Look!" The door sealing off the end of the bridge was starting to liquefy too. Crazy witless Maya must have ordered all nanites in the area to dissolve . . . including the ones blocking our retreat. Festina scrambled to her feet, dragging me up with her. "Let's go, Faye! Come on, come on, come on."

My head was reeling, my shoulder throbbing, but I stumbled as best I could toward the exit. The bridge was as soft as mud in a rainshower. Each footstep sank a bit deeper. "You'll never make it!" Maya screamed, nearly choking with laughter.

"Come on," Festina kept saying, "come on." Pulling me hard. I forced myself to keep moving, knowing I was slowing her down. If she just left me and ran, she'd get away clean—but I knew she'd never do it. Festina would rather die than abandon me . . . which meant I had to keep plodding ahead.

My foot suddenly splashed down, straight through the bridge. Like stepping into quicksand—another second and I'd sink clean out the other side. With the full force of my strength, I wrenched my arm from Festina's grip and shoved her toward the open corridor. It might be the extra push she needed to get to safety . . . but no, she was sinking too, sinking through the bridge, liquid nano sludge, and we were both going down.

Something shot out of the corridor in front of us, something shouting in Oolom. Tic. He swooped over our heads . . . and I yelled at Festina, "Grab him!"

"You too!"

I'd never hold on to him with my shoulder out of commission. And Tic couldn't support both our weights. With a sweep of my good arm, I pushed myself down faster through the goo of the bridge: out the bottom, falling free.

Looking up, I saw Festina falling too . . . but she'd

caught Tic at the waist and he was slowing her descent like a hang glider.

"Faye!" she shouted. Angry to tears.

Survivor guilt, I thought. *Welcome to Demoth, sister.*

Then the world exploded into colors. Green and gold and purple and blue.

21

PROPOSALS

The shore of Lake Vascho.

I lay on the beach under the quiet blackness of a northern night—clouds still riding fast on the warm spring wind, but not so thick as in Sallysweet River. Stars shone through the cloud gaps, thousands of stars . . . and I thought of nights once upon a time, sleeping clear and girlish with the whole universe open above me.

The Peacock hovered gently over the water. He'd brought me here. Of course my father wouldn't let me fall into a bottomless pit.

"*Jai*," I said. Thank you. Achy and woozy, I stayed flopped out on the sand. Nothing but stars overhead . . . till the Peacock fluttered up Dads-anxious, only a hand-breadth from my nose.

"I'm all right," I told him. "Well . . . if you can read my mind, you know I hurt like blazes. 8.5 on the getting-your-arm-torn-off scale. But it's still minor. I think. How are you?"

Dorro. Good.

"Where's Xé?"

Tic.

"Did you say *tico*?" I asked.

Tic. Oov Tic.

With Tic.

"Short honeymoon," I said. "First time you two get together in three thousand years, and a day later, she's off Riding mortals again."

Vé hadadda shunt. It's what we do.

"You Rode my father, didn't you?"

Gaha efliredd po. Copodd.

I didn't Ride your father. I fused.

"Tell me about it."

Bit by bit, in his shy Oolom, the Peacock let his story trickle out.

It started long before the plague—the birth of a baby named Zillif. Or even before that: the very clock-tick of conception. The Peacock slipped into the zygote and Rode through embryo, foetus, infant, child, woman . . . till *müshor* changed the woman to a proctor.

The Ride was never fusion; but there was still a tiny mingling. A leakage of energies, Peacock to baby girl . . . and maybe the other way too, for all I know. Zillif grew up in the Peacock's glow—as if there were some special element in the air she breathed, giving the woman her own faint shine.

I'd felt it myself. I adored her for it.

To the Peacock, Zillif was just another Ride; when he hitchhiked on someone cradle-to-crypt, it was common for his hosts to rise above the crowd. He liked that specialness. Maybe he even encouraged it to make the Ride more interesting, found ways to spill teeny bits of his brightness into his host's life. But it was a teasy game, far from full fusion. He'd sworn he would never fuse again . . . not after the things he'd done while bonded to a Greenstrider, spurred half-mad by his fusion-mate's lust to kill enemies.

(Oh yes, I'd been right about that. When the Peacock fused with the Greenstrider, the two-in-one creature seethed with all the black murder from the original strider's heart. Xé's germ factory may have scored the higher body count, but Peacock/strider fought hard to keep up.)

So. The Peacock Rode passively through Zillif's life. He took no action, not even when the Pteromic microbe began slacking out Ooloms all over the world. The Peacock held himself back, because the last time he'd got involved, it led to disaster.

Or that was his excuse. Even superintelligent pocket universes lie to themselves, when doing the right thing seems like too much work.

Zillif herself became infected eventually. The Peacock watched, and thought now and then maybe something ought to be done. But not by him; he was out of it. He'd lived through the deaths of lesser creatures many times before: not just his hosts but the people they loved. Griefs and pains and rage at the dying of the light.

So what? So what if the Ooloms died? It wasn't as if they were an important species. And if they didn't get killed by this disease, they'd drop from something else. As an immortal, the Peacock prided himself on his sense of perspective.

Zillif resisted the paralysis better than most—part of the Peacock's reflected shine, that tiny boost from his energies. But in time she succumbed; in time she landed on my roof and got carried to the Circus, where she dazzled a lovestruck girl a few days, then slipped off speechless. "Aaaaah gaah gaaaaaaah hah kaaaaaaaa."

At which point, you'd think the story would end: Zillif left mute, barely alive, waiting for the slacks to fall. The Peacock would Ride her to the end, then pick a new host—human of course, since all the nearby Ooloms were in deplorable Riding condition—and nothing would change. For damned sure, the Peacock wouldn't intervene.

Except that Zillif was an old old proctor. And in her last three days lying slack, unable to talk, collapsing in on herself . . . Zillif Zenned out.

Here's the thing, the crucial thing: Zillif somehow realized the Peacock was there. Maybe she felt the tiny spill of energy from him, maybe there was some burst of mystic intuition, or maybe (anything's possible) Xé found a way to sneak the truth into Zillif's brain. For all I know, the old woman may just have gone *tico*: not cosmic Zen anything, but plain old pre-death delusion. However it happened, Zillif got the idea an advanced alien entity was lurking in the neighborhood; and she began to plead.

She thought she was addressing some emissary from the League of Peoples—some telepathic thing watching from the aether. So she talked to it; she begged; she ranted; asking for a cure, not for herself, but for her people.

The Peacock found himself answering . . . the same way he talked to me sometimes, mind to mind. And for three days Zillif wrestled with him, angel by the ladder, fighting to break the Peacock away from passive watching, so that he'd goddamned *do* something.

I can't tell you what she said; but her whole life had been devoted to speaking with powerful people, putting together common sense and good argument to shift folks away from ill-advised plans. To the last, Zillif was a member of the Vigil . . . and her silent one-on-one with the Peacock was the most important battle of her life.

The queer thing is I was there through it all, holding her hand, sponging her down, checking her IVs and catheters and monitor cords. I was there, I was with her, but I was pure bliss-ignorant that the war for the Oolom race was raging right in front of me. Zillif vs. the Peacock . . . doing something vs. staying aloof.

You already know who won.

When Zillif finally persuaded the Peacock to take action, he left her body—snipping off that tiny thread of spilled energy. Zillif died like a light clicking out, blink, like that. In the outside world, young Faye began to cry as her heart withered . . . not realizing that what looked like pointless defeat was actually the old woman's greatest triumph.

Because now, the Peacock was flying.

Out of Zillif, into the closest available healer—bonding, fusing with Dr. Henry Smallwood, because the Peacock needed to work through a pair of physical hands. In a way, my father died scant seconds after Zillif herself: he became a two-in-one creature, half man, half Peacock, the old submerged in the new. Not that Dads would consider it a bad deal; I imagine he'd leap at any chance to stomp the Pteromic microbe's vicious little butt.

It needed a joint effort to construct the cure—not just Dads and the Peacock, but Xé too. Xé knew how the germ factory worked, and she was hooked into all the digital intelligence in the world. It only took a few hours for so much processing power to come up with a medicine . . . after which, Dads/Peacock/Xé hacked into the recipe database and made the change in olive oil. Epidemic closed.

All that time, the Peacock still believed Xé was *tico, nago, wuto*; he thought he was just using her, exploiting the way she was bound to the obelisk computer. Poor Peacock never realized Xé was eager to help: that she'd gone sane-sorry-sentient over the years, and was heartsick dismayed how her germ factory was near to pulling off another genocide. If their places had been switched, the Peacock imprisoned, Xé loose, she wouldn't have needed a marathon debate with Zillif before she took action.

So I tell myself. Maybe Xé would have been just as don't-get-involved as her mate. Both of them needed to damned well grow up . . . which they eventually did.

Seven months passed after the cure was tossed out to the world. Dads and the Peacock stayed fused all that time— fused for life. At unguarded moments, they glowed in the dark: my mother saw the flickery peacock colors shining just under my father's skin.

Then the afternoon shift at Rustico Nickel set off a bomb on the outer defense perimeter of the Greenstrider bunker. Cave-in alarms started clanging, and Dads/Peacock faced a decision. The Peacock could rescue the trapped miners, but only by cutting the connection with my father. That would, of course, be fatal. To save the miners, Henry Smallwood had to die.

The Peacock told me Dads didn't hesitate an instant.

So the Peacock separated itself, threaded its tube-body through the rockfall, and ferried the miners to safety. Yes, Dads died—energy ripped from his human body like a gusher of blood, leaving him cold, cold, cold. But . . . the Peacock still held on to a chunk of my father's memories, motivations, sentiments. Such as a love for his daughter.

Guess who the Peacock caught a Ride with next—a quiet little nonfusion ever-watching Ride. And guess whom the Peacock protected off and on through the next twenty-seven years.

Now we'd come full circle: same crisis, same solution. Peacocks weren't fitted for getting things done in our human world; not when it meant working hands-on with computers, security interlocks, things like that. The simple ways they could communicate with us (telepathy, linkseed) were too slow-awkward-clumsy to whip up a cure for Pteromic B and C—like shouting instructions through a wall at a not-too-bright child.

That was the Peacock's analogy, not mine. From my side, the communication seemed fair successful—yes, the Peacock spoke Oolom rather than English because he'd been immersed in the language for nine hundred years . . . but I'd been immersed in Oolom all my life too, and I understood it just fine. Apparently that wasn't good enough: mere words were too limiting for a superintelligent pocket universe trying to get life-and-death information across to a half-wit meat-woman.

All right. If the Peacock believed the only way to produce a cure was fusing with someone, how could a meat-woman argue?

"Fusing," I said. "You or Xé—you have to fuse with someone to make the medicine."

Dooloo. Yes.

"No other way."

Po. No.

The Peacock waited, lights dappling the ice and water.

Giving me the choice. You can have this, daughter, if it's what you want.

God knows, there'd be any number of volunteers if I nellied out. Who wouldn't want to hook up with something so far beyond yourself? Suddenly being able to hear the thoughts of everybody around you . . . understanding so much more about the universe . . . escaping the mumbly, sweaty, witless, gross, ungracious, unlovable, cowardly, lazy, parasitic, not-good-enough self that you hated so goddamned much . . .

Except at that moment, I didn't want to lose me. *Me*. Our wayward Faye. Here I had the chance to become a fused creature, wise, amazing, important . . . and all of a sudden, I found myself thinking it would be a sorrowful loss.

Queer thing, that. I realized I'd been getting interested in who I might become.

Well. Bad timing, that was all. Even if I wasn't quite so angry at myself as I'd once been, there was such a thing as responsibility. Duty. The Peacock was giving me a chance to help my world, and I was new-Faye enough that I couldn't shuck this off on someone else.

"If it has to be done, it has to be done," I said aloud. "Fuse away."

Gentle as snowflakes, the Peacock shimmered down to touch my face.

Is there an opposite of data tumor? Data sunrise? Or maybe sunrise without the data, not a cold transfer of facts but a warm peaceful dawn.

The light of Dads's love for me, still strongly remembered after so many years.

The shine of so many other loves, received by the Peacock as it Rode me down through the decades. Angie.

Barrett. Peter. Egerton. Darlene. Winston. Lynn. All the kids.

Chappalar. Oh-God.

A flame from Festina. A twinkle from Tic. Even a battered spark from my mother.

All the radiance the Peacock had soaked up from those around me while I'd wallowed in fears of darkness: light blooming-blossoming-dawning in my mind.

Everything all at once.

Yes, there was darkness. Everyone has darkness—furies, pettiness, ugly impulses. Perhaps the Peacock shielded me, filtered some shadows out, I don't know. I saw the darkness, but I *felt* the light. Blazing all around.

The Peacock's Tail, spread for me to see.

Look at me. Look at them. Look at you.

Then the tail folded itself away. The moment faded. And I was only me again: not fused, not bonded, not two-in-one. Just Faye, with all her light and shadow. The Peacock hadn't taken me, it had only given me one last shoot through the chute . . .

. . . and dumped me in the open air, just outside the bunker in Sallysweet River.

I got to my feet as I heard the sound of footsteps. Festina raced up the tunnel toward me, sprinting, wrapping her arms around my neck. Pulling my head down, kissing me hard.

Tic was right behind her. In the dark tundra midnight, he glowed.

"Xé?" I asked.

"Yes," Tic said. "We fused hours ago."

"Hours?"

"There was no point wasting time, Smallwood. While you and Ramos dallied with bad company, I was saving the world." He gave me a playful squeeze on the shoulder—thank God, not the dislocated one. "The medicines are finished, Smallwood! Mission accomplished. I'd already figured out the necessary formulas before you let me loose. Before you let Xé loose. Which is me because I'm Xé.'' He squeezed my shoulder again. ''And Xé says it would be a staggering pity if the world lost your splendid physique, so get yourself some medicine as soon as possible.''

I smiled; but my thoughts were jumbling back to Lake Vascho. The Peacock must have known he didn't have to fuse with me—not if Tic/Xé had already whipped up a cure on their own. So why . . .

''To give you a choice, Smallwood,'' Tic said. Reading my thoughts, answering my question. ''To see if you really wanted to stop being you. It was your chance to escape; and your chance to realize you weren't so ready to give up on yourself as you thought. That man of mine has developed a positive mania for helping people with their lives . . .''

''Where is he?'' I asked. ''The Peacock.''

''Gone off to be with the world-soul for a while. Which means, Smallwood, you'll be sharing him with other proctors, but at least you'll hear the nanites giggle.'' Tic rolled his eyes. ''Demanding little brutes. Imagine playing mother to a few trillion of the rascals. It's time for their father to do his share of the sitting. As for me . . .'' Tic's glow brightened. ''After three thousand years, I deserve to get out and have fun. As the most ass-kicking mind-reading Zenned-out proctor this planet has ever seen.''

With a laughing leap, he soared into the air: spreading his gliders, catching the wind, pushing himself higher with a few flaps of his arms, till he was flying above the trees, racing the clouds, heading God knows where. For a second, he looked back over his shoulder and roared, ''1.000000001 with the universe, Smallwood!'' Then his shimmery glow was lost in the night.

As Festina strapped up my aching shoulder, the world-soul (the Peacock) told me a police squad was already on the way. Cheticamp and the ScrambleTacs were getting dragged out to Sallysweet River yet again . . . thanks to my own link-seed. When the Mouth had got shot, one of the acid wads hit the radio-jammer he carried on his shoulder. In time, the jammer fritzed out; and there I was, back on the air, with all the world scanning for my frequency.

Tic/Xé got to me first, of course, tubed in by my own Peacock. But the cops were only thirty minutes away, screaming to my rescue—the spoilsport buggers.

At least Festina and I had the half hour.

A week later—after too much god-awful-tasting medicine, too much physiotherapy on my shoulder, and too much round-the-clock surveillance from the staff of Bonaventure General—Festina and I were officially declared healthy. Safe to walk the streets again without infecting others, or degenerating into the gibbering madness of poor Maya Cuttack. (Maya's dead banged-up body had finally got fished out of the pit—she'd fallen through the bridge when it turned liquid, never even trying to save herself. When medical researchers finished picking at her corpse, she'd be incinerated to dust.)

Festina and I stepped out the front doors of the hospital, into a bright spring morning. The snow was gone; the trees were beginning to bud. "Gorgeous day," I said, spreading my arms wide in the sunshine. There was only the skimpiest twitch of pain in my shoulder—it'd soon be as good as new, curvy enough to attract Oolom lechers and strong enough to shove them away. "Want to wander down to the park?" I asked Festina. "They've got a nice little petting zoo."

"Aren't your family coming to pick you up?"

"I asked them not to."

She looked at me with those sharp green eyes. "Okay. Let's walk."

Cabot Park wasn't very far off; Bonaventure is so small, nothing is very far off. Soon we were leaning against a tree, watching a leaner lean against the damaged wall of Pump Station 3.

I said, "So. Do you want to get married?"

Festina turned to me, mouth dropped open. She gaped for a count of three, then pulled herself together. "Aren't you supposed to get down on one knee to say that?"

"Maybe on *your* home planet," I told her. "On Demoth, it's usually more like rolling over in bed and propping yourself up on one elbow. *Hey, you want to get married or what?*"

She laughed, then looked at me keenly. "Are you serious about this, Faye?"

"Lynn sneaked into the hospital a few nights this week," I said. "We've talked it over, and she thinks it could work."

"So you can just add people to the group whenever you feel like it?"

"More or less. The others usually let me have what I want. Though Barrett won't say yes unless you like dogs."

"Bloody hell," she muttered. "You *are* serious."

"Absolutely." I reached out and took her hand. "Sure, it's complicated. And you don't know bugger-all about my spouses, or the kids, or what marriage means on Demoth . . . any of that. But here's the thing: I think you need a family, and I'm offering mine. All of them are good people, and you'll have plenty of time to get to know them . . ."

"Faye," she interrupted. Just my name; and I could feel the *no* hanging heavy in her voice. "I have to go back to work. I have to leave Demoth."

"I know," I answered. "But does it need to be right away? The galaxy can get along without you a little while longer."

"Then I'd just be leading you on. A few laughs, then off I go."

"Festina," I said, "I'll be all right. I've *got* a family. I may have a case of the wistfuls for a while, but I'll bear up. You're the one who'll be heading out alone. And you're going to feel it."

She lowered her eyes. "I know, Faye. I know. But I have to go back to my job. For the past two years, I've been spinning my wheels—trying to fit into my predecessor's shoes, playing the desk-job spymaster. If there's one thing I've learned on Demoth, that's not who I am." She gave a rueful smile. "I like getting my hands dirty. I like digging truths out of mysteries. God help me, I like exploring . . . which is as far as you can get from being an Explorer, but that's where I am now."

"And with all that exploring," I said, "you'll never come back to Demoth?"

"Faye." And this time, that one word meant yes, not no.

I pulled a package out of my coat pocket. "A going-away present," I said.

Festina looked embarrassed. "You knew I'd say no?"

"If you said yes, it would have been an engagement present." I pushed it into her hands. "Here."

"Where'd you get this?"

"From Lynn, last night. Open it."

Thank God, Lynn had been the one to wrap it. She always does a beautiful job. Me, I never have the patience. All energy, no finesse, our Faye.

Festina opened the wrapper, then the box. There, tucked up in tissue paper, was a clear glass bottle holding a water-owl egg. "From Lake Vascho," I told her. "The family went there for a picnic yesterday, so they could all say they helped get you the gift. In case you said yes. The other eggs were hatched and gone, but that one never opened. It happens sometimes." I took a deep breath. "So there you go. I'm giving you a dud egg."

She wrapped her arms softly around my neck and just held me. A tear trickled down her cheek.

Sometime, when she got back to the navy base or maybe up to her flagship, she'd take the bottle out of the box and find the other present I'd asked Lynn to hide in the tissue paper: my scalpel, retrieved by the cops from the dipshits' skimmer, quietly passed by Cheticamp back to my family.

The egg was a gift from my other spouses; the knife was a gift from me. A sign/promise/oath that I was past needing it.

I'd wrapped the blade in tape so Festina wouldn't cut herself when she found it. That knife had drawn enough blood in its time.

Its time was over. And the past, after all, was past.

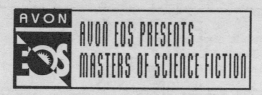